JUMP START

THE GRID SERIES
BOOK 2

KAYLA JAMES

Jump Start

KAYLA JAMES

Cover Illustration by Kayla James

Copy Editing & Proofreading by Kristen Hamilton @ Kristen's Red Pen

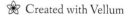 Created with Vellum

For those we've let go but will love forever.
They will come back if and when the time is right.
All you can do is believe.

AUTHOR NOTE

The characters in this story are primarily British, so there are some terms and phrases used throughout that are more popular with those from the UK. I presented these to the best of my abilities and understanding, but forgive me if I or my early readers have missed a few.

Jace and Kinsley's story is one wild ride. It's broken between past and present so you will see them fall twice. Don't worry, though, their happily-ever-after is well worth everything you're about to go through.

This is a slow-burn, open door romance that portrays content meant for readers 18+.

Full list of Trigger Warnings can be found here: https://www.authorkaylajames.com/

I will note that the list does contain some spoilers to Jace and Kinsley's story so proceed with caution if you do decide to take a gander.

PLAYLIST

Close To You by Gracie Abrams

heartbeats by Hanniou

(Kissed You) Good Night by Gloriana

Somewhere Only We Know by Keane

Before You by Benson Boone

Hunger by Ross Copperman

I Think I'm Gonna Love You by Michal Leah, Caleb Hearn

Soul Tied by Ashley Singh

Missing Piece by Vance Joy

There Till The End by JERUB

I Think They Call This Love by Elliot James Reay

BIRDS OF A FEATHER by Billie Eilish

Stargazing - Moonlight Version by Myles Smith

Strange Life by Steelfeather

lose it all by Sam Tompkins

Infinitely Falling (Romantic Redraw) by Fly By Midnight

TERMS AND SLANG

Balaclava: A mandatory head covering made of fire-retardant material. Worn under helmets.

Bevvy: Short for "beverages".

Bloke: American equivalent of "dude".

Cockpit: The section of the chassis in which the driver sits.

Daft: Something a bit stupid.

DRS: Drag Reduction System. Adjustable rear wings that allow the driver to switch between two predetermined settings. Designed to boost overtaking.

Formation Lap: The lap that immediately precedes the start of the race.

Grand: American equivalent of "great".

Halo: A cockpit safety structure that resembles a horseshoe, surrounding the drivers head and is bolted to the chassis at three points.

HANS Device: Head and Neck Support Device. A mandatory safety device that fits over the driver's shoulders and connects to the back of the helmet to prevent excessive head and neck movement in the event of an accident.

Innit: Shortened version of "isn't it?".

Knackered: When someone is extremely tired.

Lad: In the same vein as "bloke".

Mug: Someone who is a fool or a stupid person.

Pit Wall: Where the team owner, managers and engineers monitor the race.

Pole Position: First place on the starting grid.

Qualifying: The knock-out session prior to the race in which drivers compete to determine the starting grid for a race.

Quid: British slang for British pounds.

Reconnaissance Lap: When drivers leave the pits to assemble on the grid for the start.

Retirement: When a car has dropped out of the race.

Race Engineer: The single point of contact between the driver and the team.

Safety Car: The course vehicle that is called from the pits to run in front of the leading car in the event of a problem that requires the cars to be slowed.

Sarnie: Sandwich

Tyre Warmers: An electric blanket that is wrapped around the tyres before they are fitted to the car so that they will start closer to their optimum operating temperature.

Team Principal: The person who is in charge of the team and its personnel.

CONTENTS

Lights Out and Away We Go!

PART ONE

CHAPTER 1

KINSLEY

"You're joking."

I wish I was. Desperately.

But as luck would have it, I'm not.

I guess that's not really considered 'luck' in this instance then is it? Can't say I'm not used to it though. I've never really been a 'lucky' kind of girl.

Not in this lifetime, at least.

Born to a teenage couple who loved getting high more than the daughter they probably shouldn't have had.

Barely survived six years in a run down flat in the darkest corner of London where people came and went all hours of the day *and* night.

Found by the landlord in the closet that was my bedroom after being locked inside for five days. Rent was due, but it wouldn't be paid. She tried to shield me from it, but to this day I remember the sickeningly pale figures slumped on the sofa as she carried me out.

It was foster care after that since neither of the extended families wanted to claim me. They didn't want to care for the living reminder of everything they did wrong with their own kids.

I've bounced from one home to the next. Eleven in twelve years. The one I'm in now will be the last since I've officially aged out of the system.

So yeah, me and luck? We aren't sitting around making friendship bracelets for each other.

"His exact words were 'Listen, Kinney—'"

Lily, my best friend, throws her head back, groaning loudly towards the ceiling. "I absolutely *hate* when he calls you that."

"Can't say it's my favorite either."

"Every time he says it, I roll my eyes so hard. I'm scared that one day they'll be permanently stuck like that."

"Well, your eyeballs are safe from now on."

"Didn't want that at the cost of my best friend's feelings, but okay. Please. Continue."

I clear my throat, lowering my voice to mimic his. "Listen, Kinney. I'm leaving for my apprenticeship soon and was thinking that this would be a great opportunity for us. To take a break, that is. From us—"

"Did he think repeating the 'us' part was in case you didn't know he was referring to you two as a couple when he said to take a break? Who else would he be talking about?"

"Who freaking knows."

"So he wants to break up?"

"He doesn't want to break up, he wants to *take a break.*

From us." I mock his voice for the last part and she huffs a disbelieving laugh. "He said that there's just *so* many things that neither of us have yet to experience and for those few months that he's gone, we should use it as a free pass—"

She gasps and I wince. "Oh, just you wait." I fall back onto the bed, staring at the ceiling as embarrassment claws at my throat. "When he gets back, he said that we could put what each of us has learned to good use. Meanwhile, I'm standing there in nothing but one of his T-shirts."

"The fucking prick," she screams, her chair clattering to the ground as she shoots to her feet.

The prick she's referring to is—sorry, *was*—my boyfriend.

The only one I've ever had.

And he dumped this bomb on me mere minutes after taking my virginity. Barely waited for me to use the bathroom afterwards to clean up.

Who said romance was dead?

The bed dips when Lily lays down next to me and I turn my head, taking in her pinched lips. "I always knew he was a twat waffle, but this is some next level shit. I'm so sorry."

"I should have listened to you one of the first hundred times you told me he was bad news." I sigh, shaking my head. "But he was just so damn convincing."

"You know how much I love being right, but I really didn't want to be this time. I'm sorry your first boyfriend turned out to be a complete knob." She snuggles into my side, whispering, "He doesn't deserve you anyway."

"You can say it."

"Say what?"

"I told you so."

She scrunches her nose. "I don't think you need me to."

I sigh. "Honestly, that's not even the worst part. It sucks, yeah, but it didn't end there."

"I'm suddenly very scared to ask how much worse this can get."

"When he went into the bathroom, I was rushing to get my clothes on so that I could leave before he came out. I was reaching for my phone on the side table when his screen lit up. I don't know why I looked, but I did."

I swallow, blinking rapidly as my eyes begin to sting. "He doesn't have a lock on his phone so at the swipe of my finger, there it was. A group chat with his lads. They were all reacting to a text he sent that said 'that makes six' followed up with a picture of him holding up my underwear. I was in the background, walking out of the bathroom in his T-shirt."

Lily stares at me, a mix of disbelief and fury brewing in her crystal blues. She blinks, shooting up into a sitting position and scoots to the edge of the bed. "That's it, he's dead."

I lurch forward, grabbing her wrist.

"Let me go. I need to have more than words with this piece of shit," she growls, wiggling out of my grasp.

"Lily, stop."

She spins around, throwing her hands up. "Why are you protecting him after what he did?"

"I'm not protecting him. I'm stopping your crazy arse from getting arrested. I don't have nearly enough funds to bail you out," I laugh.

She scoffs, flailing her body around with a groan before stomping her foot and pointing at me. "Fine, but next time I see him—oh, he's going to wish he never even looked in your direction."

I pinch my lips to stifle a laugh when she karate chops the air and moves into a series of aggressive punches. When she swings her leg up, I cringe for any hypothetical man on the receiving end of it.

Halting mid swing, she turns to me and smiles. "I have the best idea."

"You will still go to jail if you get someone else to do it for you."

"No, not about that." Bouncing over, she jumps onto the bed next to me and bumps my shoulder with hers. "Let's go out."

"I'd rather help you find the hitman."

She rolls her eyes. "Come on."

"I don't know, Lils. I'm not really in the mood."

Spoiler alert. I'm never in the mood.

Being social? Not my strong suit.

Big crowds? Anxiety inducing.

I'm too awkward, never knowing what to say or do. It's inevitable that I'd eventually make a complete fool of myself or even worse, someone else.

I've gone my entire life sticking to the sidelines, going unnoticed. It's where I'm comfortable. A wallflower just trying to make it through each day unscathed.

So of course I had to go and get myself a best friend that's one of the most outgoing, vibrant girls in our class. Ever since the day we met last year she's been strong arming me out of that very comfortable zone I try to burrow myself in.

But I'm still thankful every day that I have her.

Even if she makes me do things any normal girl our age would do.

Like, apparently, going out to a club on a Saturday night. *YAY!*

"Oh, come on. There's nothing like a night of dancing, drinks, and hot strangers to chase your worries away."

"I don't want anything to do with hot strangers. The last one utterly sucked."

She smirks. "Making jokes about it already? That's a good sign."

"If I don't laugh, I'll cry, so humor it is."

"You know what? That's fair."

"But I still don't think I want to go out."

"I'm not above begging." She slips to her knees in front of me, binding her hands under her chin. "Please. Please. Please. Pl—"

"You're not going to give up on this are you?"

"I just want to get your mind off of everything, even if it's just for a night."

Sighing, I drop my head back. "Fine."

Her squeal pierces the air and I look over, catching her fist pumping the air in victory. "I have just the thing for you to wear tonight too."

She sprints over and tears through the corner of her room crowded with countless rolls of fabric, sketches, and mannequins draped in half-finished projects.

My fingers itch to capture the beautiful chaos of tulle, sequence, and leather flying in every direction with her kneeling in the center of it, her face scrunched in concentration.

"Aha!" She shoots to her feet and thrusts two fistfuls of fabric into the air. "This is going to look *amazing* on you."

I roll my lips as I take the top and bottoms from her and she nudges me towards the bathroom. "Come. Come. Go change while I figure out what I'm going to wear."

I slip into the bathroom, switching out my leggings and oversized graphic T-shirt for the outfit she chose. Walking over to the floor length mirror, I twist and take in the leather shorts that cut off just above my mid thigh and the fitted cropped long sleeve.

My jaw drops when I turn to get a look at the back. I don't know what kind of magic Lily's working, but this is the best my arse has ever looked and while the top completely covers my chest, the built-in bra lends a helping hand to what I'm usually lacking there.

It's perfect.

I feel sexy yet comfortable and confident.

Maybe she's right.

Maybe what I need is a night where I put on a cute outfit, go out with my best friend, and dance away the pain, the humiliation, the echoing doubts of my worth.

A night to turn off my brain and live in the moment.

I step out of the bathroom and smirk at her scowl when I slip on my favorite trainers.

"You have an unhealthy obsession with those," she

grumbles, buckling the strap of her heels and walking over to my side.

I finish tying the last knot and stand up, smacking a kiss on her cheek. "You love me and my beat up Converse."

"It's because I love you that I put up with them."

I laugh, grabbing my phone to text out a quick text to my foster parents that I'm staying over at Lily's before we walk into the hallway. "Whatever you say."

"Hey." She grabs my hand at the top of the stairs. "Thank you for giving this a go even though I know you'd rather lock yourself away in your dark room. I have a really good feeling about tonight."

"Let me know if that changes. We'll leave immediately."

"Oh, I'm sure you'd love that," she laughs.

"We can even come up with a signal. Like, I'll rub my nose with my thumb or flip my hair over my shoulder or—"

"We don't need a signal. We're going to go, have a couple drinks, dance, maybe even flirt with some cute lads. Then we can come back here and raid the cupboards for some late night snacking."

While I'd love nothing more than to skip to the second half of the evening, I'll concede to the first. It's time to step out of my comfort zone. Who knows? Maybe I'll even have a good time.

What's the worst that could happen?

CHAPTER 2

KINSLEY

This is probably one of the worst things that could have happened.

Top five at least. Maybe third overall, right behind crashing on our way here and someone spiking our drinks.

"Kinney?"

I stumble to a stop when a rough hand grips my arm. Closing my eyes, I internally kick myself for telling Lily that I'd be fine. That I'd be right back and she could keep dancing with the cute guy she'd attracted like a moth to a flame the moment we hit the dance floor.

All I needed was a breather.

But apparently the universe would rather see me suffocate instead.

"What are you doing here?"

"That's none of your business," I mutter under my breath. Wouldn't matter if I said the words louder anyway, he's not even paying attention.

My teeth grind as his glassy eyes roll over my body. "Wow, don't you look well fit tonight." He licks his lips and I suppress a shudder.

"Let go, Drake."

He groans, not in fact letting go, and steps farther into my personal space. Personal space he lost the right to invade. "Oh, come on babes. You're not still angry with me, are ya?"

Is he serious right now?

His gaze doesn't waver as he smirks, biting his lip.

Oh my god, he is *serious.*

My cheeks heat as I twist my arm out of his grip and glare up at him. "You are utterly unbelievable," I seethe, not waiting for his reply as I throw myself into the crowd.

"Kinney, wait!"

He's delusional if he thinks I'll actually do that.

Because I don't.

I keep moving, weaving between groups with quick apologies. Risking a glance over my shoulder, I see him bulldoze his way through a couple, determination in his dark gaze.

"Would you stop?"

"Would you?" I yell back at him.

"Kinsley, you're starting to piss me off. Stop."

"Leave me alone, Drake."

I make it to the edge of the bar when a hand grips the back of my neck, yanking me backwards into a hard chest. His alcohol drenched scent envelops me as he slides an arm around my waist, plastering my back to his front. "Gotcha," he whispers in my ear.

I tense when he dips his head and runs his nose up the side of my neck.

"Let me go," I grit out, wiggling in his arms.

He tightens his hold on me. "What if I don't want to?"

I freeze when he pushes his hips forward, his hard cock rubbing against my arse.

"What if I want one more go at that tight cunt of yours before I leave?"

"S-stop," I croak.

He groans into my hair, his fingers tightening around the back of my neck. "Come on. Just one more time before we call it, yeah? You know you want me."

A breath catches in my throat, fear seizing my heart.

"No!" I scream, using every ounce of strength I have to twist and shove at his chest.

His arm disappears from around my waist and I grit my teeth as his nails scrape against my neck. I trip over my feet and reach out, trying to catch myself as I stumble forward.

I crash into a hard body and glass shatters at my feet, cold liquid soaking my front. Large hands steady me with a firm grip on my waist as I cling to a set of toned arms.

"I'm so sorry," I rush out on a shaky breath, my body and nerves vibrating with a mix of fear, adrenaline, and humiliation.

"Shit. Are you okay?"

My ears perk up at the deep, slightly proper, northern English accent.

I look up and freeze with parted lips when our eyes meet.

That is the most beautiful shade of blue I've ever seen.

13

A stillness wraps around me. Like a warm blanket, comforting and calming me as I watch a winter storm swirl in an icy blue sky.

When his eyes drop, running over my body, I don't feel the repulsion I did when Drake did it. And I don't look away as they settle back on my face.

Someone brushes by us, bumping him into me and I gasp, ripping my hands away as I take a half step back. The world floods in and I blink.

"I'm so sorry about your drink." I look down at his dampened chest and wince. "And your shirt."

He glances down at his chest and shrugs, a small tilt in his lips. "Didn't really fancy this one that much anyway." He freezes, taking in my shaking hands as they hang by my sides. "Are you sure you're alright?"

"I—"

"Everything's grand," Drake slurs, wrapping his hand around my wrist and pulling me forcefully back until my back is pressed against his chest.

I flinch when his fingers brush the side of my neck before he wraps his arm around my shoulders, crossing over my chest.

The stranger catches the movement, taking a small step forward, his eyes solely on me. "Are you okay?"

"Weren't you listening? I said—"

"I'm not asking you." He shoots Drake a hard look. A heartbeat later his eyes soften as they slide back to me. "I'm asking her."

I stare into their cool depths, feeling anything but cold. Instead, I'm flushed with the heat of his simmering dominance, the charge of confidence and the wealth of strength radiating off of him.

Gritting my teeth, I reach up and push Drake's arm off of me as I spring forward. As soon as I'm out of reach, I spin, refusing to ever give him my back again. He takes a step towards me, but before he can get any closer, the man with blue eyes guides me behind him with a gentle hold on my elbow as he positions himself between us.

"I'm pretty sure she doesn't want you to touch her, mate."

He speaks with an easy smile, but there's an edge to it.

Well... obvious to anyone who isn't piss drunk.

Drake takes a swig from his pint before pointing at him with the same unsteady hand. "You should really bugger off, *mate.*" He bites off the last word, his drink sloshing over the rim as he motions to me. "This is between me and my girl."

My girl.

Fury at the right he thinks he has to make such a claim overtakes me as I lean around the man shielding me and point at Drake. My body shakes as aggravation floods my veins and I bite my lip to hide it's quivering. "I am *not* your girl."

Do not cry right now, Kinsley. He will never see you cry. Never again.

He takes a menacing step forward but a hand on his chest halts his advances. "Yeah, I don't think so."

Drake scoffs, tripping over himself as he's pushed back. "You know, you really need a lesson on minding your own fucking business, pretty boy." He looks over his shoulder, nodding to his friends. They step up behind him and I instinctively gravitate closer to the blue-eyed stranger, placing my hand on his back.

The air around us shifts as a tall, dark haired man with tattoo covered arms steps up to the left of us and crosses his arms. Another with black hair and striking emerald green eyes settles at our right. Then a third man with sandy brown hair and hazel eyes fills the space right next to me.

I look around, stunned, as they close in around me, shielding me on all four sides. The panic threatening to unleash inside quickly eases its advances when the man in front of me speaks, his voice low and mocking.

"Go on then." He opens his arms wide. "Class is in session."

Drake stills, taking in the three new faces before his eyes settle on me. They harden with ire and he scoffs. "You know what? You can have the daft cow." The back under my palm goes rigid as Drake moves closer, leaning in so that he has a clear view of me. "She wasn't worth it anyway."

I ignore the stinging hurt at the words, my hand fisting in the soft shirt when the man who's become my lifeline in this moment goes to step forward.

"Don't," I plead. He looks over his shoulder at me and I shake my head. "*He's* not worth it."

He considers me for a heartbeat before nodding and turning to face my ex once more. "You should count your lucky fucking stars right now." He tips his head towards the exit. "Now piss off and hope I don't see your ugly mug again.

Because next time *I'll* be the one giving *you* the lesson on what happens when you mistreat a woman."

Drake downs his drink, sending me a withering glare before he and his goons make their way to the exit.

When he's sure they're gone, he turns to me, ensnaring me in his gaze. "Are you okay?"

My nodding stops abruptly, a hiss escaping my lips when my hair brushes my neck.

His eyebrows furrow, his eyes burning with rage when I shift my hair off my neck. He steps forward and raises his hand like he's reaching for me but fists it instead and drops it to his side.

"I should drag his arse back here—" He shakes his head and walks over to the bar. I watch as he speaks with one of the bartenders who glances my way before nodding. A moment later, he walks back over to me and motions towards the back hallway of the club. "Come on, let's get that cleaned up."

I silently follow him and into the back offices of the employees only area. As he searches the room for whatever he's looking for, I step up to the mirror at one of the sinks.

I twist my head to the side and suck in a breath. Half moon fingernail markings score the left side of my neck. Two of them deep enough to draw blood.

He walks back into the room, meeting my eyes in the reflection and motions towards a small sitting area off to the side. I take a seat on one of the chairs and he perches on the table in front of me.

"May I?" He holds up cleansing wipes and I nod.

17

I hold my hair to the side as he leans forward and gently wipes the cool cloth over the wounds. My breathing slows, shoulders dropping as the weight of what happened comes crashing down.

I wince on the next brush and he stills. "I'm sorry," he whispers, softening his touch around a particularly tender spot. He takes out two small plasters and I close my eyes as he smooths them over my heated skin, his touch lingering slightly.

He starts packing away the supplies and I roll my lips, fingers fidgeting in my lap. "I feel like I owe you more than just a drink and shirt now after all of this."

He smirks. "Don't worry about it. I'm just glad that you're okay."

"Thank you. For what you and your friends did."

"My mum would have my arse if I'd just stood there."

I laugh under my breath as he puts the kit away. "Well she'd be very proud. Standing up for me *and* tending to my wounds? You're a modern day knight in shining armor."

He huffs a laugh and my cheeks heat.

Ladies and gentlemen, awkward babbling Kinsley has now entered the building.

Instead of the usual confusion or uncomfortable silence I'm used to experiencing with people, intrigue lines his handsome face and he slowly holds out his hand between us. "I wish it happened another way, but it's nice to meet you..."

I tuck my lips, slipping my hand into his. "Kinsley. Kinsley Jones."

His hand pulses around mine, his lips tipping up. "Kinsley Jones—"

Why does my name sound so much better when he says it?

"I'm Jace. Jace Collins."

Look at that. Maybe my luck is starting to turn around after all.

CHAPTER 3

JACE

I'M GOING to kiss each of the lads right on their mouths.

Considering I've held back on my urge to strangle them since the second they dragged my grumbling arse out the door, I'd say this is a much better outlook for everyone.

Baku was an utter disaster in more ways than one.

I had to retire from the race early due to braking issues.

My ex was finding every reason under the sun to be in the same vicinity as me, so that was a fun game of hide and seek I absolutely did not sign up for.

And the cherry on top? I found out my sister and mum watched the next three episodes of our re-watchathon of *Grey's Anatomy* without me. Three! Sacrilege!

We got back on Monday and I've effectively locked myself away in my flat to lick my wounds in peace. I was on season three of *New Girl* when the lads apparently decided that enough was enough and came banging down my door.

I'd say I held my own, but let's be real, it was three versus one. Last time I checked, I'm not the leading role in an action film.

So, yes. I lost the battle.

"It's nice to meet you too." Kinsley tucks a strand of dark hair behind her ear and smiles shyly up at me.

But I reckon I've won the war.

"Are you sure you're okay?" I ask, glancing at the bandages on her delicate neck.

My hands curl into fists as I try to calm the fury that's been simmering beneath the surface of my skin, ready to pounce since the moment I saw those marks on her neck.

Here's the thing, I'm not a confrontational guy.

I've got three goons I call my best friends for that.

I'm the easy going one. A kill them with kindness kind of guy.

That is unless a man dares to put his hands on a woman without their consent. In that case, you should know that the only reason I'm smiling is because I'm picturing what my fists will be doing to your face.

Kinsley nods. "Yeah, I'm grand."

I hold the door open for her, the scent of her vanilla coconut shampoo trailing behind her as she ducks under my arm and into the hallway.

She reaches up, ghosting her fingers over her neck. "I just can't believe that happened."

My heart cracks at the crestfallen look in her eyes.

No one this beautiful should look this sad.

I glance down the hallway towards the loos, an idea sparking. Before thinking it through fully, I send up a prayer that hopefully my feeling on her reaction will be right and turn to her. "What if it didn't?"

She watches me curiously. "What do you mean?"

"What if we rewrite what happened?"

Her eyes dance over my face and she drops her hand from her neck. "I *would* like to forget about it..." She nibbles on her lip for a heartbeat before they tip up in a soft smile. "Okay. Yeah. We'll rewrite it. How did we meet then?"

I smirk, holding out my hand. "Come on." She slips her hand in mine and I suck in a quiet breath at the igniting sparks. Shaking my head, I lead her down the hallway and position her in front of the door. "You're there and I come walking down the hall—"

"Uh, pause. Question. Why am I coming out of the men's loo?" She giggles, pointing towards the door's placard.

I dip my head towards the side and cock a brow. "Do you see the state of that line?" She glances at the line of *minimum* twenty ladies leaning against the wall.

She sucks in a breath through her teeth, cringing. "Mmm, alright. Men's loo it is."

"Why is it so long all the time anyway? Is it because of the girl code?"

She barks out a laugh, shaking her head. "And what would you know about girl code?"

"I know that an ex and current crushes are totally off limits. Secrets stay secrets no matter what. You can only post photos where both of you look good. Honesty above all else. And this one is kind of unspoken, but you always go anywhere in pairs, especially the loo." Her jaw drops and I shrug. "Little sister."

"Ah, well then I guess all the women in your life have really taught you well. You've got that as a secret weapon then."

I chuckle. "You could say that."

She laughs before clearing her throat and straightening her shoulders. "Okay. I'm coming out of the men's loo and you're—"

"Making sure you aren't here with anyone."

She laughs, shaking her head. "No, I'm not here *with* anyone."

I nod. "That's good, because then I offered to buy you a drink."

"Which I accepted."

"Gleefully I might add."

"Oh, but of course."

"We were having a smashing time, debating over whether pineapple belongs on pizza—" She grins and I gasp. "Kinsley, say it isn't so."

She laughs, lifting her hands in surrender. "I'm sorry, I'm a sucker for the sweet and savory combination." I gag and she playfully pushes my arm. "Oh come on, it's not that bad."

"You can keep your abomination."

"Fine. I don't like sharing my food anyway."

"Noted. Fingers will stay attached to my body if I leave your food alone."

Her smile lights up the darkened hallway and the last of

my dominating anger from earlier dissipates. "Assuming you forgave me for my choice in pizza toppings..."

"We were sipping on our drinks—"

"Oh, what kind?"

"Sex on the beach, obviously. It's fun and delicious."

Her eyes narrow, but her mock glare wavers as amusement slips through. "Why do I feel like you're not exclusively referring to the drink?"

I reach up, pretending to grasp the strand of pearls I never wear. "Miss Jones, that kind of talk is reserved for at least the second date. Maybe even the third."

"So this is a date now? Tell me. Do you bring your friends on all your first dates?"

"Why not? They have to make sure she isn't some serial killer targeting incredibly handsome men. They're quite fond of me and would be devastated if I suddenly got murdered."

"Isn't there a documentary or show about something like that?"

I shrug. "I'm sure there is, but I wouldn't have seen it. The last time my sister made me watch one of those, I spent the night snuggling a cricket bat. The lights were on the whole time and yet I still jumped at every minor sound."

"So you're saying I shouldn't rely on you to check out the things that go bump in the night?"

"I'll keep the sheets over our heads real tight. They can't get through those, right?"

Her body quakes with laughter and I smile, watching her face light up.

"There you are!" A blonde blur jumps between us,

knocking me back a step. She gasps, brushing Kinsley's hair to the side. "Oh my god, what happened?"

Before she can answer, the tiny woman spins around and pokes my chest. "Did you do this? I hope you're not fond of the tiny prick between your legs, you son of a—"

"What? No!" Kinsley rushes around her and suddenly our roles from earlier are reversed as I cower behind her, hand instinctively covering my dick. "Drake—"

"What? Where? Let me at him!"

Jesus, this one's a bit scary.

"He's gone," Kinsley yells before huffing a breath and lowering her voice. "He's gone. Jace helped me get rid of him when he wouldn't leave me alone."

"And who's Jace?"

I raise my hand. "That'd be me."

The fiery pixie squints at me. "Did you punch him?"

Kinsley groans, "Lily."

"Wanted to."

"Hell yeah." She holds up a fist and I bump it.

"I can't with you two." Kinsley throws her hands in the air.

"Don't think I'm not going to give the prick the swift kick to his nards that's been coming his way the next time I see him." Her friend winks and Kinsley shakes her head, sighing.

"I'm Lily, by the way. Best friend of this one." She nods towards Kinsley.

"Nice to meet you. I'm Jace."

"It's nice to meet you too. Thank you for stepping in for my girl."

I wave her off, my eyes connecting with Kinsley's golden brown ones. "It was my pleasure."

She hums, turning to Kinsley. "I'm hungry."

"Okay? What do you want me to do about that?"

"I know a great snack van around the corner," I blurt out. "And I have a jumper in the car you can change into so you don't get cold."

Jesus man, where's your chill mode?

"You don't have to leave just because of me."

"I honestly already decided that I would have had one more drink before heading out."

"You're not just saying that?"

A few hours ago all I wanted was to be alone. Was going to do just that after this drink too.

But then the universe did its thing.

Sending this timid yet magnetic girl literally crashing into my path. Effectively shifting my want for solitude to a desire to be near her. To do what I could to keep her smiling, laughing.

"I was going to leave either way, but I'd much rather be leaving to hang out with you a little while longer."

I watch the lights of the club dance in her eyes as she considers me. My heart skips as she gives me the slightest nod and I make sure to keep my inner triumph masked with a small grin.

After introducing the girls to Lawson, Ryder, and Nik, we make our way to the small park around the corner. Finding a spot on the grass, we spread out with our food and I try to keep my eyes off the way my jumper swallows Kinsley's slight frame as she settles down next to me.

"So, how do you all know each other?" Lily asks, sipping on her cola.

"We all kind of grew up together." I lean back on my hands after finishing off my smaller portion and glance around at the lads.

Kinsley's eyes light up. "Wait. Really?"

I nod. "What about you? Any sleepover pillow fights you'd like to reminisce on?"

"God, you're such a boy." She giggles, knocking her knee against my thigh. Setting down her now empty tray, she smiles over at Lily. "We met last year when I transferred to her school."

"We actually just graduated," Lily cheers.

"University?"

Please don't say secondary. Please don't say secondary. Please don't—

"University Prep."

Oh thank you baby Jesus.

I bump my shoulder into hers. "Well, congratulations. Do you know what you want to study at university?"

"She *should* go into photography," Lily says, looking pointedly at her friend.

"Photography?" I raise my eyebrows and Kinsley blushes. "I'd love to see some of your photos sometime, but only if you're comfortable with it."

Tentatively, she shuffles closer, her shoulder brushing my

chest when I lean to peer down at the phone screen as she flips through an album.

With each one she shows me I feel like I'm getting even more glimpses at who she is.

A flower blooming from a crack in concrete. *Resilient.*

A woman handing a water bottle to a homeless man. *Caring.*

A sky full of stars. *Dreamer.*

A self portrait of her in a mirror. *Beautiful.*

"Kinsley, these are amazing."

"You really think so?" she whispers, tilting her head to look at me.

"Without a doubt."

I lock my muscles to keep from closing the minimal space between us. Instead, I lean back on my hands, silently smiling to myself when she doesn't move to create distance between us again.

We get lost in stories of our childhoods, the guys taking every chance they get to try and embarrass me or each other. All the while I revel in the vibrations of her laughter from where our arms and legs touch.

When the girls yawn for the hundredth time, I check my watch and grimace. It's already past two in the morning.

The mandatory meeting at seven is going to suck.

I look over as Kinsley burrows farther into my jumper when a cool summer breeze kicks up and my dread about tomorrow morning evaporates.

Because this was totally worth it.

She is totally worth it.

We drive the girls home and as I walk them to their door, I can't help but drag my feet the last couple steps. Not wanting tonight to end. Not wanting my time with her to end.

Lily says goodnight, but I don't miss the wide eyes she shoots Kinsley before disappearing behind the front door.

"So," she draws out as she turns and looks up at me with a soft tilt of her lips. "Tonight was probably the most fun I've had in a long time."

"You deserve to have fun every night," I say quietly.

A blush creeps over her cheeks and she tucks her bottom lip between her teeth.

I clear my throat, shoving my suddenly sweaty hands into my pockets. "Maybe we can do this again sometime?"

"Like a second date or as friends?"

Whatever you want.

My lips tip up as hopefully another grand idea forms. "Can I see your phone?"

She hands it to me and I input my number before giving it back. She glances at the screen and laughs under her breath. "Didn't want to text yourself so you have my number too?"

I walk backwards towards the car and stretch my arms out wide. "You have all the power, Miss Jones. This is whatever you want it to be. You can use it or not, it's up to you."

The wind carries her light laugh as she calls out, "Goodnight, Jace Collins."

The thirty minute drive home is filled with the ghost of

her touch, the echo of her laugh, and the image of her golden-haloed eyes.

My phone pings with a text as I walk through the front door of my flat. I pause, my body tensing in preparation as I pull it out.

I release a breath when it isn't yet another message I'd ignore. A smile breaks across my face as my eyes roll over the screen.

UNKNOWN:

I think I'll use it.

My thumb traces over her words. "Goodnight, Kinsley Jones."

CHAPTER 4
KINSLEY

"WHY DOES your face look like that?"

"That's a weird way to say good morning to someone."

Lily snorts, sliding onto a stool at the island. "Whatcha making?"

"Your favorite."

"Aw, you do love me."

I laugh under my breath as I hold the bowl and whisk together the icing. I've been up for a while, despite the early hour we got back from the club, and when I couldn't wait any longer for the princess to awaken, I came down to her family's kitchen.

I learned how to bake at my eighth foster home placement. The woman was older and already had grandkids of her own. She always made it a point to have some sort of baked goods around, usually homemade.

She taught me a few of her family recipes. I loved those Sunday mornings where it was just the two of us baking.

She ended up passing away only a few months after I came to live with her, but I feel like she's still with me every time I make one of her recipes.

The gooey cinnamon rolls are Lily's favorite.

She leans over, swiping her finger through the mixture, humming as the sweetness hits her tongue. She leans her elbows on the counter, propping her chin on her hand. "So, did you have fun last night?"

I shrug, turning to set the bowl on the counter behind me to hide my heating cheeks. "It was okay." *It was definitely more than okay.*

My phone pings and I turn to glance down at it at the same time Lily pushes up out of her chair, sneaking a peek at the screen. Her eyes meet mine, eyebrows raised. "Want to revise that?"

I duck my head and focus on whisking until the mixture is smooth, my cheeks heating from the memory of last night as her squeal pierces the air.

She shimmies in her seat and I shake my head, setting the bowl off to the side. I look up to see Lily watching me with a grin and roll my eyes. She looks pointedly at my phone, flipping her blonde hair over her shoulder. "So, Jace seems nice."

I hum in agreement and check the timer on the oven. When I turn around, she's watching me with squinted eyes. My cheeks heat and she gasps, straightening in her seat. "Oh my god. You like him!"

I retreat to the sink to wash my hands, pointedly ignoring her laughter at my poor attempt at avoiding her statement.

Of course I like Jace.

How could anyone not like him?

He's sweet and thoughtful. Incredibly funny. A bright spot for anyone to gravitate towards. He listens, *really* listens and makes you feel like you and your words truly matter.

With him, it was all just so... effortless.

With him, I felt like I could really be myself.

"Yeah. I think I do," I whisper.

Her excitement falters, settling with concern. "But you're scared."

"It's just... after everything with Drake—"

"You really think Jace is anything like—"

"No," I cut her off, a defensive tone lacing my voice. Because they aren't comparable. Not in the slightest. "Jace is nothing like Drake. Even the mere hours we'd spent together, I could sense that. I felt like he was... different."

"You were different, too, you know."

"What do you mean?"

She huffs a laugh. "Kinsley, you *never* talk that much. Yeah, you're a complete chatterbox with me. I mean good lord, I can't ever get you to shut up—"

"Hey!"

"But whenever you're around others, especially someone you don't know? I've had people ask me if you were mute before."

"You have not."

"Okay, maybe not, but they've definitely thought it." I roll my eyes and she laughs. "You weren't that quiet girl last night, trying to hide herself away in the shadows. You laughed. You smiled. You looked like you actually *wanted* to be there."

I sigh, running my finger through the dusting of flour on the counter. "It was really fun. Exactly what I needed."

"I'll slip in my 'I told you so' right about now, thank you very much."

I laugh, shaking my head. "You're a dork."

She catches the hand towel I toss at her. "So, if this friendship or whatever you have going on with Romeo—"

"We literally just met less than twenty-four hours ago."

"Semantics." She waves me off. "If it eventually turned into something more, would you truly be opposed to that?"

I bite my lip and shrug. "I don't know."

It's what I say, but it's not what I feel.

Because she's right. I wouldn't be opposed to this friendship eventually turning into more.

But I also can't control the lingering fear and insecurities. Drake wasn't the only one to instill those insecurities. They've been ingrained in my bones since my first breath.

I wasn't wanted by my parents. Neglected by the countless stand-ins. I couldn't keep friends since I changed schools so often. I kept to myself, accepted the solitude and eventually found comfort in the quiet.

I didn't know how much I truly craved being wanted until I met Drake. He was the older, more experienced lad I met last year when we went out to celebrate Lily's eighteenth birthday.

I thought I'd finally found someone I could let in. Someone I could let see me, unbridled.

I thought it was real.

What a fool I was.

Because the moment I met Jace, everything was different. There was something about him that made me feel safe. Valued. It was different enough for my excitement at the possibilities to far outweigh my fears.

I slowly look up at her, my heart racing as the single word slips through my lips. "Maybe."

She studies me before leaning over the counter, whispering, "That's not a no."

Before I can react, her hand shoots out, snatching up my phone and she scrambles off the stool. I'm frozen in shock, but the click of my phone unlocking jump starts my senses.

"Lillian Madison Campbell, you give that back this instant."

She gasps. "You did not just full name me."

"Bet your arse I did. Give it back Lily," I growl, rounding the island.

She barks out a laugh. "You look about as ferocious as a kitten."

"Oh yeah? Then why are you still backing away?"

"Last time I checked, kittens still have claws." She squeals and sprints around the island as I chase her. The oven beeps and she grins. "Don't want those to burn, do you?"

My head darts between her and the oven. With a groan, I run over and shut off the timer, pulling the cinnamon rolls out.

Multiple pings come from my phone as Lily types away

and I hurry to set down the hot dish before picking up the bowl of icing.

"Don't forget to add the sauce while they're hot!"

I mock her as I pour the vanilla cream icing over the hot rolls. She bounds over just as I set down the spatula, snatching it up to lick off the remnants.

I pluck my phone from her hand and scroll as I walk over and slip onto one of the stools. "Oh my god, you changed his contact name?" I laugh, glancing up at her.

She shrugs, setting two small plates on the counter. "This one's more fitting."

KINSLEY:

Hey! This is Lily, I'm going to make it quick because we don't have much time.

ROMEO:

Well, good morning to you too.

What universe are you trying to save today?

KINSLEY:

The universe where my best friend is happiest.

ROMEO:

You've got my attention.

KINSLEY:

What are you doing today?

ROMEO:

I'm about to head into a meeting, but after that... I was hoping your beautiful, talented friend would allow me to occupy some of her time.

KINSLEY:

Now THAT is a great answer!

One might think you have a little crush.

ROMEO:

I 100% have a crush. Love notes in her locker and cheesy serenades level.

KINSLEY:

You do know she will be reading this right?

ROMEO:

Oh I know.

KINSLEY:

Don't want to keep that a mystery for her?

ROMEO:

Not at all. I've been told that I wear my heart on my sleeve, so I wouldn't be able to hide it even if I tried.

Any tips on how to win her over?

KINSLEY:

Something tells me you won't need the help.

ROMEO:

Wait. Did she say something?

Does she like me too?

[SENT WITH FIREWORKS EFFECT]

KINSLEY:

That wasn't at all embarrassing...

ROMEO:

You know what? I'm sticking by it.

KINSLEY:

I respect that.

Do you remember where you dropped us off last night?

ROMEO:

I do.

KINSLEY:

Well I know that if you took her out today, she'd be really happy.

ROMEO:

And that's always the goal.

KINSLEY:

It is.

And I GUESS if I were to give a certain someone a little tip on how they could possibly win her over... I would tell them that she's huge on honesty and being open. So, be yourself and don't hold back.

ROMEO:

I can be there by 10.

Lily settles onto the stool next to me and bumps my

shoulder with hers. "Well? Are you going to just sit there and leave the poor sap hanging?"

I bite my lip and suck in a steadying breath.

KINSLEY:

I'll be waiting.

This is Kinsley BTW.

Lily snorts. "And you say *I'm* the dork."

"What? I wanted him to know it was actually me for that last bit."

"Come on, you beautiful soul. We've got delicious cinnamon rolls to eat and then you have to get ready. Specifically in that order because these smell amazing."

"But of course," I laugh as butterflies take flight in my stomach.

CHAPTER 5
KINSLEY

My HEART SKIPS when there's a knock on the door and I pause, taking a steadying breath. Glancing over my shoulder at Lily, I laugh when she grins and gives me two thumbs up.

Swinging the door open, my nerves immediately dissipate when his blue eyes lock on me.

"Kinsley."

He breathes out my name like he's been waiting to say it forever and my cheeks heat.

"Jace," I whisper.

"Lily," she sings.

"Lily. Nice to see you again."

"Same, Romeo, same. Now, you take care of my girl or you're next on my shit list, okay?"

"Understood." Jace nods and I roll my eyes at her.

"We're going now."

I rush through the doorway and gently grab his forearm. Butterflies take flight when he slips out of my

40

grip, sliding his hand down my arm and interlocking our fingers.

He leads me down the steps and to the passenger side of his car. I slide into the seat, smiling up at him when he winks and gently shuts the door. Rounding the hood, he waves at my best friend who leans against the doorway smirking.

I laugh at her, sticking my tongue out. "You crazy kids have fun," Lily calls out as Jace slips behind the wheel.

He glances over at me as the pur of the engine fills the quiet air and I smile, but it quickly drops with a gasp as he leans over the center console. His face is mere inches away, his eyes never leaving mine as he reaches around me.

"Safety first," he whispers, pulling my seatbelt across my chest and clicking it in place. He lingers, his focus dropping to my lips a second before he settles back in his seat and effectively taking all the air in my chest as he goes.

Is it hot in here? Am I blushing?

I turn towards the window and place my palm on my heated cheek. My eyes catch on Lily as she stands by the still open front door, her jaw practically on the ground.

"Oh my lord," she mouths, fanning herself.

I laugh under my breath and turn to look at Jace only to find he's already watching me with a small tilt in his lips. He nods towards the road ahead. "Ready?"

"Absolutely."

His smirk breaks into a blindingly handsome smile as he shifts the car in gear. I squeal when he accelerates down the street, the car's power pressing me back into my seat.

He glances over at me. "You okay?"

"Huh? Oh, yeah. Of course. Why do you ask?"

His lips twitch. "I don't think sitting ramrod straight with your hands pinned to your thighs means you're comfortable. Am I going too fast? I can slow—"

"No. No, you aren't driving too fast."

He pauses, eyes dancing between me and the road. "You're sure?"

I nod. "I'm sure. I've just never been in anything this nice before, unless you count Lily's family's town cars. I'm scared to touch anything in here. Like I'll leave fingerprints or something."

"Planning on stealing my car to commit a crime, are we?"

I bark out a laugh. "Even if I wanted to, there's no way I'd be able to drive this thing."

"What? Can't drive manual?"

"Can't drive, period."

He slows to a stop at an intersection and shifts in his seat to face me. "You don't know how to drive?"

I shrug. "No one's ever wanted to teach me. Well, Lily tried, but we don't talk about how horribly that went."

"What about your parents?"

I swallow, dipping my eyes down.

I'm not ready to share that part of me. Not ready to see the inevitable pity in his eyes.

I'm not ready for things between us to change that way. Because this part of me has only ever brought sadness and with him all I want are the good parts.

So instead of flooding our time together with the sorrows of the past, I simply reply, "No."

My eyes move up to his and I hold my breath as he watches me. He sighs, turning his head to glance around the empty roadway before nodding. "Okay."

My eyebrows furrow. "Okay? Okay what?"

He throws the car into park and shuts off the engine. "Okay, I'm going to teach you how to drive." My eyes widen and he chuckles. "Don't look so panicked. I'm a professional, trust me."

Without another word, he opens the door and steps out of the car. I watch as he rounds the hood to my side.

"Jace, you don't have to do this," I quickly say when he opens my door.

He simply holds out his hand and my body moves on its own accord, unbuckling my seatbelt, sliding my hand into his, and letting him pull me to my feet on the side of the road.

He reaches up, tucking a wayward strand of hair behind my ear. "You can do this. I'll be right here the entire time."

My eyes dart to his polished sports car. "What if I crash?"

"You won't."

"What if I scratch the paint?"

"It'll buff out."

"What if—"

"Kinsley," he whispers, chuckling under his breath as he frames my face with his hands. "You. Can. Do. This."

His eyes hold me hostage and with every heartbeat, I feel my mind calming. I nod, taking a deep breath. He lets me go and I walk around to the driver's side on slightly shaky legs before sliding behind the wheel.

After adjusting the seat so that I can reach the pedals, I

secure my seat belt and place my hands on the steering wheel. "What now?"

"Now, you turn on the car. This is a semi-automatic with a PDK transmission so—" He reaches over and gently guides my fingers over what feels like a metal wing. "Feel that? It's the paddle shifters. These let you switch between gears quicker than a regular gear shift."

"That's cool, but I won't be going fast enough to do that."

He barks out a laugh and my lips twitch in amusement as he settles back in his seat. "This is a push start, so what you'll do is press down on the brake. Good. Now push this button here and the car will start."

My hand flies back to the wheel when the car rumbles to life. "You okay?" He asks, failing to smother his amusement.

I fidget in my seat. "Mhm. What's next?"

"I don't want you to freak out, okay? The great thing about this being semi-automatic is that this transmission won't let you harm the engine. You don't have to use the paddle shifters if you don't want to and the car will switch to automatic for you."

"Oh thank god," I breathe.

He nods towards the road. "Now, all you need to do is put her in drive and press on the gas."

I fumble with the shifter but get it in drive before settling my hands on the wheel at ten and two. It's ten and two, right? Or has that changed? He was driving with one hand, but he's much more comfortable behind the wheel than me.

"Hey." His whispered words draw my gaze to him and he tilts his head. "We don't have to do this if you don't want to."

I shake my head. "I want to do this. I've come this far already, right?"

He looks at me with a soft expression filled with assurance. "Yeah."

I glance back at the road and take a grounding breath. Easing onto the gas, the car rolls forward down the quiet street.

"Oh my god, I'm doing it!"

"Yeah, you are," he cheers, laughing.

I giggle and press down on the gas more, picking up a little more speed. He coaches me every now and then when I start to drift out of our lane.

All the while, my smile never falters.

"Want to try turning?"

My eyes dart between him and the road. "You think I'm ready for that?"

"Absolutely." He points towards a small turn-off up ahead.

Approaching the turn, I slow, practically stopping, before turning the wheel. He reaches over and helps me move the wheel a little more to the right to avoid going off onto the shoulder.

When I've successfully turned onto the next road, I slow to a stop and move the car into park. "Okay. I think I'm done. I don't want to push my luck."

"You did amazing, Kinsley."

I look over at him and blush at the pride in his eyes as he watches me. Emotions burn up my throat and without thinking, I unlock my seat belt and throw myself across the center console.

He freezes a heartbeat before wrapping his arms around me as I bury my face in his neck, hugging him with all I have.

"Thank you," I whisper.

"Thank you," he says quietly back and I pull away.

"For what?"

"For trusting me."

I smile, pulling him in for another hug only to spring apart with a shriek when my foot slips and the car roars. Jace bursts out laughing and reaches over to press the ignition button, shutting the car off.

"Whoops," I cringe and he laughs, shaking his head.

"Come on, speed racer."

He climbs out of the car and I follow. When we're back in our rightful seats, he pulls back onto the road and I lounge back in my seat, tracing my fingers over the gear shift.

"What is it?"

"What?"

"The car. What is it?"

"You really want to know?"

I shrug. "Why not? I know nothing about cars, but apparently I'm up for learning new things lately. So, yeah." I look over at him. "Teach me."

His hand flexes on the wheel and clears his throat. "It's a Porsche 911 Carrera."

"I like the color. It reminds me of your eyes. It's pretty."

He glances over, eyes dancing over my face. "Yeah, she really is."

My cheeks heat at his soft words. I don't look away when he focuses back on the road, too captivated by the way his arm flexes when he reaches up, running his fingers through his dirty blond hair. The tapping of his long fingers on the wheel. The bob of his Adam's apple as he talks.

"Oh! I forgot. How was your meeting this morning?"

"A bit brutal to be honest."

"I'm sorry. We don't have to talk about it if you don't want to."

"It's okay. I just need to make some changes. Had the feeling going into it and what was decided only confirmed that."

"Are these hard changes?"

"Nothing I can't handle."

Before I know it, he's pulling into a parking spot in front of a small building.

"What is this place?"

"A guilty pleasure of mine. Top secret, though."

I mime zipping my lips and tossing away the key. He huffs a laugh and holds the door open for me as I walk into what I'm realizing is an art studio.

"You're here!" An older woman with red hair thrown into a messy bun comes speeding around the corner. "Everything is set up for you in the back. Why don't you get settled and I'll be right back."

She disappears as quickly as she appeared and I look over my shoulder at Jace with wide eyes. "Did you bring me to join a cult?"

He barks out a laugh. "Maybe."

We walk back towards the back and enter a small private space that's adorned with two easels facing one another with a third set up against the wall.

I suck in an excited breath when it dawns on me. "Is this one of those painting places where you paint and drink wine? I've always wanted to do one of those."

I shuffle over to my stool, taking a seat as he settles on his across from me. "It's kind of like that, yeah. Beth, the red-headed tornado you saw earlier, is the owner. She's been friends with my mum for years. I used to come here with her every week when I was young. I try to come as often as I can."

"That's so sweet. I love this." I look around, taking in the clusters of paintings covering almost every inch of wall space.

"This is where I come to just *be*. My mind always settles the second I walk in."

I bump his knee with mine. "Thank you for sharing this with me."

Beth tears into the room and we make quick introductions before jumping into what we'll be painting today.

It's an hour full of laughter, soft music, trying and failing to get peeks at each other's pieces, paint getting all over my hands, and Beth sneaking stories about a young Jace when he's too concentrated on his painting to stop her.

We finish the lesson and Beth leaves us when the phone rings.

Jace glances over at me. "Flip them on three?" he asks when we've set aside all our supplies.

"On three."

"One..."

"Two..."

"Three," we say in unison.

My jaw drops. "Okay, what the heck? Are you a professional at this or something?"

"Must be all those years of coming here with my mum?"

"Don't play humble. Jace, that's amazing!" The bouquet he painted is beautiful, surely something an ordinary person wouldn't be able to produce in just sixty minutes.

That's me. The ordinary person. Because no, mine looks nothing like his.

"Yours looks—"

"Like the previous view when you're getting your eyes checked at the eye doctor before they show you the correct prescription?"

He chokes on a laugh. "I thought you were an artist?"

"Photographer. Big difference. I can't draw to save my life."

"Well, I love it."

"You're just saying that again so I'll agree to see you again."

He watches me with a hopeful hesitance. "Would you? Want to see me again, that is."

"Say you hate my painting."

"No."

"Say it looks like a five year old did it."

"It does, but I still don't hate it."

"Why?"

"Because you did it."

I pause at the conviction in his voice, his eyes claiming all my attention. Something drops out in the larger room, startling me and my hand whips up to smother my squeak in surprise.

Laughing, I drop my hand and stand to untie my smock. A low chuckle draws my attention up to a grinning Jace. "What?"

"Hold on."

He stands, moving to wet a cloth before coming back and standing close. Slowly he reaches up and wipes my cheek, pulling the cloth back to show green paint. My breath seizes in my chest and I instinctively tilt my head up so he has a better view.

His eyes dance between mine as he continues to gently caress my skin, his other hand coming up to hold the other side of my face.

"You never answered my question," he whispers.

I can barely remember my own name right now thank you very much.

"What question?"

"Would you want to see me again? Maybe tomorrow?"

My lips twitch, my head tilting into his hold. "I could be persuaded."

He smiles, his fingers flexing on the side of my face before dropping to his side. "Challenge accepted, Miss Jones."

CHAPTER 6
JACE

"One hundred," I grit out, pushing the bar up off my chest and racking it.

Lawson shakes his head above me and steps away as I sit up.

"Who are you trying to impress over there?" Ryder asks, grunting when he pushes out another rep on the leg curl machine.

"You, always." I wink, blowing him a kiss and he barks out a laugh.

Lawson taps my shoulder and I take the bottle he holds out for me. Guzzling down water, I stand up and switch positions with the brooding man.

I toss the bottle to the side and run to the side of the rack. "Wait wait wait. Let me take some of this off for you princess."

"Oh fuck off," he grunts, pressing the bar up.

I hop back to my spot above his head and place my hands on my hips. "You're extra grouchy this morning."

He rolls his eyes, bringing the bar down to his chest before pushing it up. "I'm fine."

I glance up at Ryder and he shrugs. Nik walks over, wiping his face with a towel before draping it over his glistening shoulders. He looks around at the group, eyebrows furrowing. "What did I miss?"

"Lawson's cranky."

"I'm not cranky."

"He says crankily."

"Would you knock it off," he yells, throwing the bar onto the rack and sitting up on the bench. "I wasn't grumpy or cranky before you started saying I was. I'm fine. I've been fine. But I won't continue to be fine if you don't shut up about thinking that I'm not fine."

"Bruv, that was a lot of 'fines' you just word vomited there," Ryder says cautiously, getting up and wiping down the machine.

"I've learned that when someone says that they are fine, there's a good chance they're not," I point out, leaning against the bar.

"And where did you learn that?" Lawson grunts, squirting water into his mouth.

"Mum and Sydney."

He scoffs. "Pretty sure that logic only really pertains to women, J. Anyway, can we cast this interrogation light on someone else? Like you." He looks up at me pointedly. "How are things going with the girl from the club?"

I scowl. "First, her name is Kinsley, not *the girl from the club*. And second, great. Things are going very well if I do say so myself."

I head towards the water fountain and refill my bottle before turning and leaning on the counter. "She's sweet. Talented. Funny—"

"Thinks you're funny," Ryder muses.

I shoot him a glare without any real heat behind it. "She's amazing. I feel like I can really be myself around her, you know? And that feeling is hard to come by."

There's a beat of silence and I look up from where I was focused on a dent in my water bottle when the words started pouring out. Each of them watches me with wide eyes and I curl in on myself. "What?"

"You sound like you may like this girl, Collins." Nik smirks, leaning his shoulder against the weight rack next to him.

My lips twitch and I shrug. "What if I do?"

"What happened to women are snakes?" Lawson asks, his eyebrow lifting as he leans his elbows on his knees.

My jaw ticks. "Not all women are like *her*. Kinsley is *nothing* like that."

"And you're sure about that? It's been what, two days? You've been around the girl once, not counting the night you met. You really think that's enough time to know who a person is?"

"I—I don't know what to tell you mate. It's just different with her," I snap, suddenly defensive about her.

"Does she know what you do for a living?"

"No, she doesn't." I swallow. "I was going to tell her soon."

"How do you know she isn't playing you?" He squints. "Not like that shit hasn't happened in the past."

"She isn't like that." Okay, he's starting to piss me off. "What are you doing? Are you trying to get me to walk away? To make me think the worst of her when the first time I felt like I could breathe easy in weeks was when she's around?"

"I'm trying—"

"Because it isn't going to work. Yes, I may have only met her two days ago, but we have been talking non-stop since. With her, I don't have to put on a show. I can just be me. Not the world's best driver—"

"Whoa, hold on there. Best? You wish," Ryder cuts in.

The four of us laugh and I sigh. "I planned on telling her soon. Tomorrow in fact."

If only my nerves could get on board with the idea that it'll all be fine.

"You're bringing her to the event with the kids?" Lawson stands, throwing his towel over his shoulder.

"Hoping their cuteness will distract her enough from you being a famous driver?" Nik asks, and the guys break out into another round of laughter.

"No," I pout. "But it doesn't hurt to have cute kids on your side."

Lawson huffs, shaking his head.

I quirk a brow. "Are you done with the fifth degree on my love life now?"

"Oh, it's a 'love life' now? I thought you two were *just friends*."

"We are." I shrug, a smile tugging at the corner of my mouth. *For now.*

I look up at Lawson and see the fierceness that's always lingered in his gaze. Even when I met him at the ripe age of eleven that hardness was there.

He hasn't always had it easy, still doesn't at times. Only a few have ever seen under the blank mask he wears. But no one's ever gotten close enough to know what's really whirring behind those dark eyes of his.

Except for one person.

And it isn't any of us standing here now.

A rare smirk tilts the corner of his mouth and I grimace. "What are you doing? Stop that."

"I'm not doing anything."

"You're smiling. It's creepy."

He rolls his eyes. "You're insufferable."

"You love me anyway, you big lug."

"Unfortunately, I do. Enough to make sure you aren't rushing into anything like you usually do. Head first, repercussions later."

I sober and push off the counter. Stopping in front of him, I clap my hand on his shoulder. "I have a really good feeling about her, Law."

He sighs. "I'm not against this, you know. I just needed to see you fight for it. That you had actually sound reasons to want to let another girl into your life after—" His words cut off as he looks over my shoulder, his face tightening.

"What are you looking at?" I turn my head and a chill runs over my body.

"Oh shit," Ryder whispers, nudging Nik.

My head whips back to them with wide eyes. "Has she seen me?"

"Looks like you're the only one she sees, mate," Nik cringes.

"No doubt the entire reason she came in here in the first place," Lawson grumbles.

I glance over my shoulder again and stupidly make eye contact. A strangled squeak slips out and I frantically look at the boys. "What do I do?" They collectively start to back away and my eyebrows raise in realization. "Don't you dare—"

"I, uh, need to go call my mum to see what she wants me to pick up for dinner," Ryder throws a thumb over his shoulder.

"It's ten in the morning," I point out and he shrugs, raising his hands.

"I need to go get my after workout massage," Nik nods, almost tripping over a bench.

"I hope it's deep tissue," I sneer.

"I just don't want to be anywhere near what's about to happen," Lawson deadpans.

"Some best mates you are. You're all dead to me," I hiss as they scurry away.

I look around the weight area, hoping for some grand excuse as to why I can immediately vacate the premises.

"Jace." I freeze, my body tensing and my eyes closing at

her voice. With a locked jaw and stiff movements, I turn to face her. Glaring down, I meet her gaze and she purses her lips in a pout. "I've been calling."

"I know," I grunt.

She pops a hand on her hip, her perfectly shaped eyebrow rising. "You know? Then why haven't you been answering them, or my texts for that matter?"

"Don't really think there's much for us to talk about, Angie."

She sighs, stepping into my personal bubble and places her palms on my chest. "When are you going to forgive me? I said I was sorry and it wouldn't happen again."

My jaw ticks. "You cheated on me with your photographer. Twice."

"I—"

"You used my name and my money to land those contracts. In your defense, I let it happen. Because while I was working my arse off to try and make you happy, you were showing a whole lot more than your arse to someone who sure as hell wasn't me."

She has the decency to look embarrassed, but my simmering hurt and anger from what she did doesn't show any sign of cooling down.

"And when you got caught, you tried to turn it around on me. Say it was my fault. That I wasn't giving you enough of my attention."

"Jace—"

"But it really wasn't just my attention you wanted, was it? You wanted the worlds."

"No, that's not what I wanted."

"What did you want then?"

"You. I wanted you."

"You had me, Angie. You had me. You used me." I lean in and lower my voice. "You betrayed me. And now you've lost me."

Her eyes widen and I see the frantic look in her eyes before she steps closer, fisting my shirt. "Jace, baby. We've overcome this before, please. We can work this out."

"The thing is, I don't want to. Not anymore." I uncurl her fingers and turn to start walking away but she grabs my wrist and throws herself in front of me. "Ang—"

She cuts me off, pushing up to her toes. I instinctively turn my face to the side and her glossed lips slam against my jaw.

I'm momentarily stunned, but within seconds, disgust rolls through me. Taking her by her arms, I shift back a step. She stares up at me with wide pleading eyes, her bottom lip trembling.

"Jace, please. We're so good together. I'll do better. I'll be better. Just, please—"

"I'm seeing someone."

Her eyes flicker between mine and I watch as the hurt quickly vanishes, anger blanketing her features. "What? Who is she?"

My jaw ticks. How did I not see it before? How did I not see how easy it is for her to switch her attitude to make things go her way?

Well you know what? I'm done being a pawn in her game.

"That's none of your business." I move around her but she follows behind me as I make my way to the mens' locker room.

"You think she's going to be any different? That she won't get swept up in the lights and the fame and—"

"The money?" I stop walking and turn to her. "Is that what happened to you? All of this was just too much to ignore? That it's my world that made you do all these things?"

"I didn't need your money," she sneers.

"Yet you took it anyway."

I know she didn't need my money. She came from a wealthy family. Hell, her grandfather was one of the investors of my racing team. It's why I thought this would have never been an issue between us.

Yet, it was only one of many.

As Ariana Grande once said, I've got ninety-nine problems.

And Angie is every single one of them.

"You took everything Angie. That's what you do. You take and take, all for yourself. Giving nothing in return."

She takes a step forward and I move, not letting her make contact.

"Jace," she whines like the spoiled princess she is.

"Go home, Angie. We're done. We've been done."

I leave her in the hallway, entering the mens' locker room and freeze. The lads stand just inside the room, watching me.

"How much did you hear?"

"The walls are apparently very thin," Nik grunts.

I nod, ducking my head and walking over to my locker. Lawson steps up next to me and I glance over at him.

"Are you still sure about tomorrow?"

"Yes," I say automatically.

Lily said to be honest and open.

So even though I'm riddled with nerves about tomorrow, I know I need to show Kinsley every part of me.

And pray that she proves everyone wrong.

CHAPTER 7

JACE

IF THESE NERVES could fuck off, that would be grand.

I never get this nervous.

Not when I slipped into my first kart.

Not when I asked out the cutest girl on our street.

Not when I first had sex.

Not my rookie season in Formula 1.

I don't even get this nervous before a race.

I'm the perpetually over confident, outgoing, golden retriever—as my sister calls me—guy.

So why now?

Oh, that's easy.

Because I'm about to lay it all out there for a girl.

But not just any girl.

Kinsley Jones.

The girl that has ruled all of my thoughts since the moment she crashed into me. It's only been three days, yet I can't ignore the fluttering in my chest when I think about her, the smile that blooms whenever I'm reading her texts, or the way everything else fades when she's near.

I leave tomorrow for this weekend's upcoming race, but before I'm gone for days on end, there's something important I need to do. Something I need to tell the girl that's had my insides all twisted up in the best of ways.

I knock on the door, swiping my clammy hands on my jeans as my eyes take in the small terraced house with vines overgrowing the stone walls. There's a crack in one of the second story windows and I watch as a light pink fabric blows in the soft breeze.

Please tell me that isn't her room.

I pull out my phone and am scrolling through a list of window repair men when the door swings open. My head shoots up and my nerves dissipate in the glow of her smile.

"Kinsley," I breathe.

"Jace," she whispers.

"Ready?"

She glances behind her quickly before slipping on her bag and stepping outside. "Ready."

We walk side by side down the short walkway and I rush around her, opening her door. When she's settled, I close the door and round the hood, slipping behind the wheel.

I fumble with my seat belt three times before I successfully secure it. Breathing out a steadying breath, I look at her sheepishly and turn the car on. She peers over at me as I pull onto the street and I shift in my seat.

"Are you okay? We don't have to hang out today if you don't—"

"What? No. No." I glance over at her and sigh. "I'm sorry. I'm just nervous."

"About what?"

"I—I have to tell you something. Well, it's more showing than telling."

"Okay," she hums. "Is this a good something or a bad something?"

"Good?"

She giggles and the worry in my heart lightens its hold. "You don't sound very confident."

"That trait seems to be on the fritz today," I grumble.

"If you're planning on taking me to the woods to murder me, all I ask is that you make sure Lily doesn't use my camera for nefarious activities."

"Last I checked, you were supposed to be the murderer."

She shrugs. "That was Saturday. Wednesdays are my day off."

I huff a laugh, shaking my head. "Well, you don't have to worry. I don't plan on murdering you and your camera will keep its innocence."

She blows out a breath and wipes at her brow. "Dodged a bullet on that one." She leans her head against the headrest. "I'm sure I'll love whatever it is you have to show and tell me. Unless I'm supposed to hate it, then bleh, off with their heads!"

Chuckling, I weave through traffic, sneaking quick looks at her. "You don't even know what I want to show you. It may not even be a person who can lose their head."

"Well is it *something* that can lose its head?"

"You aren't getting a hint, but nice try though. Also, are you sure you're not a murderer?"

"Dang, so close. And yes, I'm sure. Me and Lily have just been binging a lot of documentaries lately. It's our background sound for when she's sewing and I'm editing photos."

I hum, nodding. Blowing out a breath, my hand flexes on the wheel. "I'm nervous. I just don't want this to change how you see me."

She reaches over, placing her hand on my forearm resting on the center console. "It won't."

"You sound so sure about that."

She shrugs. "I'll be sure enough for the both of us."

My eyes flash to hers and she smiles, her thumb brushing my arm before she settles back in her seat. We leave the city behind, trading the busy streets for quiet tree lined roads.

Kinsley sits forward in her seat as I pull through the compound's front gate decorated with a metal script reading Miller Racing. I park in front of the main building and help Kinsley out of the car.

She looks up at the sleek building with wide eyes. "It's, uh—"

"A bit intimidating, innit?"

"A bit," she says through a breathy laugh.

Looking up at me with a raised eyebrow she bumps her shoulder into my arm. "Evil lair?"

I smirk. "Some would say." She giggles and I nod towards the entrance. "Want to go inside?"

She nods and I look down, slipping my hand into hers. Smiling, she follows me through the massive front glass doors.

Memorabilia decorates the entry leading into a large atrium. Groups of people are scattered around and I reflexively tug Kinsley closer to me when a gaggle of kids comes running by.

She laughs as they trip over each other to get a closer look at the replica of our team's first race car. "Is it always like this?"

"Not usually. There's a kids camp thing going on today. They get to tour the garages, see how everything is built— well, to an extent—and later on, they get to ride a couple laps on our practice track out back."

"So cool," she whispers in awe, her eyes dancing over the room.

"Collins! Back already?" I look over as a man with graying hair calls out from across the room. He strolls over, breaking away from what I assume is a group of parents and his eyes slide to Kinsley. "And you brought a friend."

"Kinsley, this is Mitch. He's the team principal."

"I have no idea what that is, but cool?" She laughs, shaking his hand.

He raises a single brow at me and I wink. "She'll get there."

Nodding, he claps me on the shoulder. "Okay then. Kinsley, it was lovely to meet you. I'd love to stay and chat, but I've got lord knows how many kids are snooping around this place. Jace, let me know if you need anything—"

"Actually. Think we could slip in on the practice track later?"

"Of course. I'll let the boys know." He turns and winks at Kinsley. "Have fun out there."

"Thank you," she calls out to his retreating back before smiling up at me. "He seems nice."

"He's great until he's yelling at you through a headset."

She looks up at me with confusion and I smirk, holding out my hand. "Come on, all will be answered soon."

We head through the doors out back and pass by garages filled with more groups of energized kids. Parents stand around them as team members walk them through the basics of one of our cars.

I chuckle when Kinsley steps towards the open bay door and pushes to her tiptoes, twisting this way and that to get a look. She stumbles into me with a laugh when I gently tug on her hand and glances back towards the garage as we walk away when the kids cheer.

We stop in front of a closed bay a few doors down with the number 24 above it. I tap in my code and hold open the side door for her.

She peeks inside before tentatively stepping over the threshold. I follow her in and flip the lights on as the door softly clicks closed behind us.

"Wow," she whispers. Spinning in a slow circle, she scans the room with wide eyes. Pausing, she looks over at me and points towards the car. I huff a laugh and smile, nodding once.

Excitement ripples over her features as she practically

skips over to the car. I lean against the wall, watching as she runs her hand over the glossy blue paint, fingers tracing my name by the driver's cockpit.

She glances around the room again, her eyes snagging on the wall across from her. Walking around the car, she steps up to the wall of photos.

I move to stand next to her as she reaches up, brushing her fingers over a picture of me in my race suit, sitting on the wheel of my car.

She looks over at me, her eyes sparkling. "You're a race car driver."

I nod, my eyes never straying from hers. "I am."

She scans the endless pictures and article clippings. "You love it."

"With everything I am. How can you tell?"

"Your eyes." She looks at me, smiling. "I saw it the moment we pulled through the gate," she waves a hand over the wall of pictures, "and I see it in every one of these."

I take in the 'Wall of Jace' as my sister calls it and take a deep breath, letting the scent of metal and rubber calm my nerves like it always does.

"Why were you so nervous to show me this?" Her voice is barely above a whisper and I look down into her cautious eyes.

"Because in the past, this is all I've been for people. I didn't want that with you. I didn't want you to see me as only Jace, the Formula 1 driver." I swallow, tucking my slightly shaky hands into my pockets. "I wanted you to like me as Jace, the man."

I sigh, shaking my head. "Then I got that talking to from Lily about honesty, and this," I motion around the garage, "Is a pretty big part of who I am. So, I wanted to share it with you, but I'd be lying if I said I wasn't nervous about how you would react."

She studies me for a moment with something akin to wonder. "This is all amazing. Truly. What you've accomplished and are still achieving is incredible. *You're* incredible."

I suck in a breath when she steps closer and slips her hand in mine. "But I like Jace, *the man*. With or without racing. He's a pretty great guy off the track as well."

I take the first full breath since coming up with this idea and dip my head to hide the relief I know is flashing across my face. "So this doesn't change anything for you?" I look up, our eyes meeting. "For this?" I squeeze her hand and she smiles, shaking her head.

"Not in the way I feel like was driving your worries earlier. I'm not here because you're this big fancy race car driver—and please don't feel offended by the fact I didn't recognize you, I'm just not a big sports girl." She laughs and I breathe out a sigh of relief.

"I think my ego can take it."

"Good. Good," she hums and takes a deep breath. "The racer isn't the man I've been excited to see every day. Although it is a nice bonus knowing I don't have to ever drive again as long as you are around."

The quiet garage fills with our laughter. "You're not getting out of those lessons."

"Dang it." Her pout disappears with a sigh. "There is one change I'm worried about though."

My body tenses and her eyes spark with mischief. "My sleeping schedule. Now I'm going to have to get up at ungodly hours to watch you kick some serious butt."

The floodgates holding back my relief open and I sag against the tool box. Shaking my head, I pull her in for a hug and bury my face in her hair. "Thank you," I murmur.

"Thank you," she whispers, my chest warming with her words. "Thank you for sharing this with me." Her arms tighten around my waist and I hold her against me for a moment longer.

An engine roars to life outside and she pulls away, bright eyes flashing to the door before looking up at me. I tuck a piece of her hair and smirk. "You want to go have some fun?"

Her eyes light as she bounces on her toes. "Absolutely."

I spend the next few hours showing her my world and the entire time I'm left wondering why I ever doubted the two colliding.

Because it already feels so much better now that she's a part of it.

CHAPTER 8

KINSLEY

"Who would have thought a dark room is actually dark."

I laugh, shaking my head. "Hang on, let me turn on the light."

He hisses, throwing up a cross when the bright light comes on and I snort. Stepping into the room, I spin around with my arms spread wide. "So. This is it."

"I like it." He walks over to where I'm standing as he looks around. "It's peaceful."

I glance over the space, feeling exactly that. At peace.

Counters line up against two of the walls, creating an L intersection on one side of the room. Along the other is built in shelving where all the chemicals are organized with wash basins nestled beside it. Three long tables float in the open space, clothes lines strung up over them.

"It may not be much, but this is mine. Well, not mine, but

it is my safe space." I lean my hip against the counter. "This is where I come to escape."

He's quiet as he takes in the room again as if he's seeing it from my perspective. "This is your race track."

I smile softly up at him. "You showed me your world. I wanted to show you mine."

"Well, I'm honored."

I huff a laugh and slide my bag off my shoulder. Pulling out five cassettes, I set them in a row on the counter. "I don't have too much to do today. These will have to hang up to dry at least overnight."

He perches on one of the stools and leans back against the counter. "Take all the time you need, angel."

"Be careful what you ask for, I could spend all day in here." I laugh and he watches as I walk over to the shelves to grab my supplies.

"Question."

"Answer." His soft chuckle caresses my senses and I bite my lip as I return with the chemicals I need.

"How do you do this in the dark if you can't see?"

I point at the lights bar above us. "Red safety light. It gives off enough light so we can see but it doesn't damage the film in the process."

He nods, pulling out the bag of Sour Patch Kids he brought. Feeding me one every so often, he continues to ask questions as I work through processing the first three cassettes. I explain every step as I do them and he listens, his eyes tracking every movement.

I can't remember the last time I brought anyone here.

Oh, wait. I can.

Drake.

He spent the entire *five minutes* he was here telling me how pointless all of this was if I wasn't ever going to put them in a show. And how film is too tedious with too many chances to 'fuck up' and lose everything, whereas you don't have those issues with digital.

"Digital is just far superior, Kinney. Quicker too," he said.

"Yeah, Drake," I whispered, pulling him out of my safe space before he tainted it. "You're right. You're always right."

I never brought him back with me here again.

I stopped talking about photography altogether after one of his friend's newest girls asked me about it and he cut in, replying, "It's her silly little hobby. You won't see any of her stuff hanging in galleries anytime soon. Or ever."

The girl stared at me with pity as he laughed it off and I shoved that special part of me farther into the darkness of my mind, refusing to let him diminish my love for it. Refusing to let him break that part of me like he did everything else before and after that night.

So, yeah, I was nervous to bring Jace here today. Worried that he would see how solitary, quiet, and uninteresting my world is compared to his loud, enthralling, and exciting one.

But then he told me he was nervous to show me that part of himself. That he thought it would change how I saw or felt about him. And if he could take that step to be his true self with me, then I could borrow enough of his strength to do the same.

Even if it was terrifying.

"Do you want to do one?" I hold up the last two cassettes. "We can do it together so you can follow me through the steps, but if you don't want—"

My words cut off, my heart pounding when he stands up and steps in close enough that I have to tilt my head back. His hand slides over mine holding one of the cassettes.

"You wanted to learn about my interests. I want to do the same. So, yeah, I'd love to." His lips tip up. "Teach me."

I huff out a laugh and my breathing hollows as I slowly nod. "Okay," I whisper.

We work side by side and he follows every move I make, asking every so often if he's doing it right. I glance over as we measure out the developer mix and giggle.

His tongue is sticking out of the side of his mouth as he squats eye level with the beaker. When he's poured equal parts of the mixture, he glances up at me. "Are you laughing at me?"

"Do you always make that face when you're concentrating?"

He huffs breathlessly, standing to take the mixture's temperature. He caps the film tank and gently turns it around to agitate the mixture. "Mum says I've been doing it since I was a toddler. She was always scared that I'd one day bite it off."

I scrunch my nose. "Ouch. I didn't think about that."

We walk over to the sink and drain the liquid before pouring in the stop bath. He chuckles, shaking his head. "I've actually almost done that."

I stare up at him with shock. "Wait. Really?"

"Not the whole thing but I took a good chunk out of it. We were trying out those hoverboard things. I tipped too far one way and fell. Honestly didn't realize it until I got up and turned to ask my sister if she got it on video."

"I feel like almost biting off your tongue is something you wouldn't be able to miss." I hand him the fixer solution.

"You would if you'd just come from a dentist for a cavity and they numbed you."

"Oh my god," I laugh, covering my mouth with my hand.

He takes the film out and sets it in the bin I place in front of him. I clean up the containers around us as he rinses the chemicals.

"I needed four stitches." He sticks out his tongue, leaning in for me to inspect.

Because of the dim lighting, I step in closer and squint at the faint scarring across the center of his tongue. My hand moves of its own accord and his breath fans across my fingers, knocking me into reality and I yank my hand back before making contact.

WITH HIS TONGUE.

It's the chemicals. Must be going to my head, right? Right.

My eyes shoot up to his as he slowly closes his mouth. I clear my throat and shift to the side, pulling the film from the bath and unraveling it. "Did she get it on video?"

He barks out a laugh. "Oh yeah. Haven't brought myself to watch it though."

"That's fair. Although, if you did, maybe you'd learn your lesson on not biting your tongue?"

He shakes his head with a smile and we cut the film into five even strips, before hanging them on the clothesline.

"That was fun. I felt like a mad scientist mixing up all the potions," he says as he wipes down the counter.

I laugh and shake my head. "I think a lot of people would argue that what you do is way more fun than doing this."

"Fun doesn't always have to mean adrenaline pumping. Some of the most fun I've ever had is in the quiet moments. Sitting by a fire with the lads. Taking a walk. Watching a beautiful girl geek out over developing film."

I pause at his words and thank my recently lucky stars that he can't see the blush creep across my cheeks thanks to the red light.

"What got you into photography?"

"One of my teachers back in primary school. She was the best. I started on her polaroid camera and quickly became obsessed."

"Were your photos just as good back then?"

I laugh, shaking my head. "Absolutely not. There were a lot of blurry shapes. Eventually figured it out though."

"I loved the stuff you showed me the other night."

"Thank you," I whisper. "I like capturing parts of the world that most people would see as ugly and show them the beauty in it."

"Well, you're exceptional at it. I think I like the way the world looks through your lens a lot better, Miss Jones."

I giggle and we finish cleaning up. His phone goes off with endless notifications as I lock up the room. "Okay, Mr. Popular," I laugh.

"Nah, it's catching up since I turned my phone off before we went in."

I stop walking. "Why would you do that?"

He turns to me and tucks his phone in his pocket. "Because you were showing me something important and I didn't want anything to get in the way of that."

My heart skips and my treacherous eyes water at his sincerity. I duck my head and tuck a rogue strand of hair behind my ear. "You have no idea how much that means to me."

I feel the heat of him before his finger tucks under my chin and tilts my head up. "And you have no idea how much what you've done means to me."

"I haven't done anything," I whisper.

His lips twitch. "You've done more than you know just by being you."

His eyes drop to my lips when they part before quickly lifting back up and I inhale a shaky breath at the inferno melting through their icy depths. He leans down and I gravitate towards him, rising on my toes.

The ringing of his phone breaks through our haze and I startle with a laugh. He clears his throat, pulling out his phone and holding it up to his ear.

"Yes, your majesty?"

"Where are you?" I hear the low voice bark over the line.

"Exactly where I want to be." His eyes don't stray from mine and I take a grounding breath as my heart threatens to beat out of my chest at the conviction in his gaze.

"How about where you're supposed to be?"

My eyebrows furrow and Jace shakes his head. "I'd already told Law that I was taking a later flight out."

"Well that would have been nice to know. Oi, Moore! Where's your teammate?"

"Said he'd meet us." I hear the faint baritone of Lawson.

"Where? Where would he be meeting us because it sure as fuck isn't on this plane!"

I giggle as Jace rolls his eyes. "Ryder, mate, I think it's time for your nap."

"Fuck off," the man—I'm assuming is Ryder—grumbles.

"Love you too," Jace coos.

"Yeah, yeah. You too." He hangs up and Jace tucks away his phone.

"Am I keeping you from something?" I ask as we walk to his car.

"The lads are heading out for the upcoming race this weekend. We're always out there a few days early for any media stuff before practice on Thursday."

He opens the passenger door but I don't move to get in as my mind races. "I'm sorry if that took too long. I didn't know you were supposed to head out with them."

He chuckles, crossing his arm over the door to lean on. "You do know there are flights going out all the time right? It's not just the one. The lads will be fine without me. I booked a commercial flight for later tonight."

"Why?"

"Because I wanted to spend the day with you."

"But don't you have other things you wanted to do before

you needed to leave? Like pack or get a sitter for your plants or I don't know, hang out with your family?"

He shrugs. "This *is* what I wanted to do."

"Jace."

"Like I told Ryder, I'm exactly where I want to be, angel."

It's with those words that I realize just how easy it would be for me to fall for this man.

CHAPTER 9

JACE

"Not great. Not horrible either."

"You always say the sweetest things to me."

Mitch stares with an unimpressed expression and shakes his head. "I'm serious, Jace. You've got the speed, but you're all over the track. Right now you're sitting at a solid P4, but that's without you having to defend against anyone. It's not going to mean shit come race day."

I sit up straighter, nodding. "I understand. I'll tighten it up."

"Good. They'll get on some of the mods we discussed, but if you're able to hold it all together, lord help the rest of the guys out there. Now go get some rest." He looks out the window and grimaces. "And maybe save that poor girl by taking Moore with you."

I look over my shoulder and chuckle. Lawson glares down at a five foot nothing reporter as she asks him questions. He's probably giving her next to nothing that's actually usable—if anything at all—like he does for every interview he's ever done.

That's where I come in.

The light to his dark.

The shining personality to his 'get the fuck away from me' glower.

The golden boy of Miller Racing and the perpetually moody teenager that they yell at for playing his devil music too loud.

I'm used to it though. It's been this way since we were kids. It's just how he is.

But to other people, like this poor—probably new because all the seasoned ones know not to even try to interview the lug—reporter, he's a bit intimidating.

I walk out of the meeting room and creep up behind Law. The reporter's eyes meet mine and immediately fill with relief when I wink. She interviewed me earlier. Nice girl.

Jumping on his back, I wrap my arm around his neck and bring him down to my level in a headlock. "Oi, I thought I raised you to play nice with the lovely reporters?"

Lawson pushes me off and straightens back to his full six foot one height. The lads all like to have a giggle about my five foot eleven, but there's nothing better than seeing them shove their giant frames into the seat of their cars every weekend.

"I am being nice," he says in a not-so-nice tone.

I ignore his grumbling and smile at the girl. "Apologies for the interruption, but I need to steal this one away." I clap Law on the shoulder.

"No problem at all. I got all that I needed. Thank you guys and good luck in the race Sunday." She quickly gathers her bag before beelining for the exit.

"Well, Law. I've gotta hand it to you, you really have a way with the ladies."

"She's not a lady—" I glare at him and he rolls his eyes. "You know what I mean. She's basically a co-worker and you above anyone else should know to never cross that line."

My mood takes a nosedive at that particular reminder. "Yeah. Ten out of ten, absolutely do not fucking recommend."

I shake off the reminder of my latest bad choice.

The one that doesn't seem to be very accepting of the fact that what we had is long gone. As if the endless texts and calls I leave unanswered aren't enough of a hint. Or the fact that I told her we were over countless times.

Lessons learned and all that, am I right?

Since our team had a later practice session today, the sun is setting by the time we make it to the hotel. We walk into our suite to the sounds of Ryder in a yelling match, clutching the mic of his headset as he points towards the video game on the TV. Nikolai sits next to him, shaking his head.

"Is he losing to that ten year old again?" I ask him, leaning against the back of the sofa.

Ryder shoots to his feet before he can answer. "You little shit, my mum is hot and you'd be so lucky!"

Nik chokes on his spit. "Mate, I don't think that came out how you meant it to."

I hear the faint cackling of multiple high voices through

their headphones and nudge Law. "Tenner says he rage throws the controller."

"You're daft if you think I'm taking that bet." He walks over to the other sofa, catching the controller as Ryder launches it across the room.

Nik chuckles. "Alright, go torture some other poor soul." He signs off, setting his headphones on the table.

"Getting bullied by little kids again, King?" I ask, sprawling out on the lounge chair.

"How old were they this time?" Lawson smirks.

"Fuck right off the both of you."

I lean my head back and raise a finger in the air. "Anyone else starving?"

The lads all mumble their agreements and Nik gets up to place a call to room service. He passes each of us a water as he comes back into the sitting area before collapsing back onto the sofa. "How are we feeling?"

I smirk. "Like you better watch your back on Sunday."

It's been a rule since we were kids that we'd never discuss anything revolving around our race teams that wasn't already in the media. But that doesn't mean we won't smack talk.

"Cocky as always, Collins," Nik chuckles.

When the food arrives, we all settle in to eat, the telly playing some reruns from today. I'm slicing into my *beautifully* cooked steak when my phone rings.

I pick it up and smile at the name flashing across the screen. Dropping my fork, I stand and head towards my room.

"Oi, I thought you were starving," Ryder calls out to my retreating back.

I slam the door closed, letting that be answer enough as I answer the FaceTime call.

"Kinsley."

"Hi. I hope I'm not interrupting anything. I waited a couple hours after the practice sessions would end, but I couldn't remember if you had something else tonight."

"You watched the practice?"

"I didn't know exactly what it was I was watching, but yeah."

I walk over to the bed, falling back into the plush pillows. "Well since you saw how my day went, tell me about yours."

"It was okay. I helped Lily fill out her application for this fashion competition in the States."

"Shit, really? That sounds awesome."

"It's an incredible opportunity for sure. She'd be gone for three months and completely immersed with little to no connection to the real world. I don't really understand it but apparently some of the best and hottest designers have come out of it."

"Sounds kind of like fashion boot camp," I chuckle and she giggles.

"That's what I said."

"Did you do anything else?"

"I went to the studio to process some pictures. Ran some errands. Then I came home and watched your practice. Nothing really exciting."

"So what you're saying is that you miss me?" I smirk, tucking an arm behind my head.

Her eyes follow the movement before she blinks, that adorable blush flooding her cheeks.

"I do. Miss you, that is." She groans, falling to the side and burying her face into her pillow. "I don't know why I said that."

She peeks at me with one eye when I chuckle. I take in her make-up free face, messy bun, and bright eyes, smiling. "I miss you too, angel. My days haven't been as exciting either."

If I'm being honest, I've missed this girl since the moment I dropped her off at home on Tuesday. We've been texting non-stop over the past three days, but that hasn't been enough.

I just didn't realize how much until I answered this call and saw her.

She reveals more of her beautiful face. "How about you? I know I saw the practice session, but I want to know how *you* are doing."

My heart skips at her words. The fact that she's always wanting to know more than what's shown on the surface. That she wants to know *me*.

"It was a tough day, but it's infinitely better now that I'm talking to you."

I take a breath as I watch her through the screen. Ever since she—quite literally—crashed into my life a week ago, I've felt this comfort in her. This kind of safe space where I don't have to put on an act all the time. Where I don't have to pretend everything is sunshine and rainbows.

With Kinsley, I can just be.

And she has no idea how much that means to me.

How much she's beginning to mean to me.

"I'm just ready to get this race over so that I can come home."

"The next one is here right?"

"It is."

"When's the next one after that?"

"On the thirtieth and just like this one, I'll have to fly out that Tuesday before."

"So you get to be home for two weeks?"

I nod. "I get to be home for two weeks."

She nibbles on her lip. "You must be looking forward to that."

I hum. "I am. I've got some things I'm excited for."

My phone notifies me of an incoming call and my face drops.

And some things I wish would go away.

I push the decline button a little too harshly and lose my grip on my phone. It connects with my face and I groan.

"Jace? Are you okay?"

Yeah, just my unhinged ex—who apparently isn't winning any awards for world's best listener—won't leave me alone.

Oh, and she kissed me the other day. Don't worry though, I told her we were seeing each other to get her to back off even though we haven't said whatever this is between us.

For all I know, you only want to be friends!

I'm grand.

I pick the phone back up and smirk. "Yeah, you'd think

my reflexes would have come in handy there, but apparently they are as tired as I am from today."

She laughs under her breath when there's a knock on my door and Lawson pokes his head in. "Sorry to interrupt. The guys just left and I'm turning in for the night. I tucked your food away in the fridge."

"Thanks, mate."

"No problem." He closes the door yelling out, "Goodnight Kinsley," before it clicks shut.

"Do you need to go to sleep?"

I shake my head. "While I probably should, I don't want to."

"Jace, go to bed. You need your rest if you're going to go kick some arse tomorrow."

"Oh, bossy, Kinsley. I like it."

She rolls her eyes, smiling. "Well if I don't get to talk to you before qualifying," her eyebrows crease, "Break a leg? Knock them dead? Godspeed? I don't know what you're supposed to say to someone who's a race car driver." She laughs and I smile.

"I think good luck will do."

She shakes her head. "You don't need luck though. The other drivers do."

I snort. "Yeah. Sure."

But when I secure my starting pole position the next day, I start to believe her words a little more than before.

CHAPTER 10

KINSLEY

I WIPE my clammy hands on my thighs for the fifth time in three minutes. The commentators on the screen drone on as the reporters walk down the starting grid and I wait for the tiniest glimpse of Jace when they make it to the front.

"Where's this one again?" Lily asks, munching on her popcorn.

"Austria. It's roughly 4.3 km long with ten turns, elevation changes, and seventy-one laps."

She snorts. "Okay, Wikipedia."

"What?" My cheeks heat and I take a sip of my drink.

"You really did your homework, didn't you?"

I shrug. "I didn't want to be clueless going into this."

"And what is *this*?"

I raise a single brow and glance at her. "Uh, a race?"

She rolls her eyes. "I'm talking about you and the man who's a Disney prince come to life."

My mouth falls open in an 'o.' "I, uh, I'm taking it one day at a time."

She hums. "Well, there's nothing wrong with that."

I duck my head, fiddling with the sleeves of Jace's jumper.

When I woke up this morning, I saw it hanging off the back of my closet door and nothing else felt right to wear today while I watched his race.

It's the one he gave me to wear that first night we met a week ago. I meant to give it back, but there's a possibility that I may keep forgetting to.

It definitely isn't on purpose, though.

Maybe just a little?

"Don't get your hopes up though, okay?"

"Who? Me? I'd never." I stare at her with a 'let's be real' expression and she scrunches her face. "Excuse me for wanting a lifetime of happiness for my best friend."

The anthem finishes on the TV and I watch as the drivers disperse. The camera sticks with Jace as he walks over to his car, confidence radiating off of him.

My stomach flips when he looks directly in the camera and winks before turning to the team member next to him. He puts on the gear handed to him and hops into—what I recently learned is called—the cockpit.

His entire focus shifts to the track in front of him as he slips on his gloves and grips the wheel. My fingers flex in time with his and a shiver runs down my spine at the look of pure determination glinting in his blue eyes.

"I am happy." I meet her stare and shrug. "I don't know

what's going to happen and there's a good chance it won't end well, but right now I'm happy."

"One day at a time," she smiles.

"One day at a time."

———

My phone pings with a notification and I look down to see I have a new follower on Instagram. I've gained a lot of those lately, starting with Jace. His friends joined those numbers a few days later.

It settled after that. Well, until he shared one of my posts on his story and the floodgates burst open. In the past two days alone, I've gained around five thousand followers.

Clicking on the profile, her feed is plastered with professional pictures mixed with selfies and videos of her partying with friends. I don't recognize the blonde with blue eyes, but then again, I don't know who the rest of these new followers are.

"I am immensely impressed with how quick they can do that. Like how is that humanly possible, I don't understand."

"Huh?" I look up and Lily laughs, pointing to the screen as someone drives into the pit lane.

We're halfway through the race and Jace is back on the track after a seamless pitstop. The cameras catch the pit crew cheering as he races off, closing in on Ryder in second place.

"I saw them practice when he took me to the teams headquarters and it was nuts. It's like they're training for an Olympic level sport."

"Did you get to try? Please tell me you tried lifting those tyres." She cackles. "God I would have loved to see that."

I scowl. "For your information, I did get to try something. I did the gun thingy that puts the tyre on the car. And I was fantastic."

She snorts. "So you could go out there and do that real time?"

"Absolutely not, but I liked the *'vrip vrip'* noise it made when I pulled the trigger."

Our laughter cuts off when the commentator's voice ramps up. I shoot off the couch as I watch his car propel down the straight, its twin rounding the corner just ahead.

"Come on," I yell.

"How can you tell who is who?"

"Oh! I know this one." When the screen changes to a shot where you get a glimpse of both cars, I point. "See that yellow T shape?"

She nods.

"Those are the T-Cams. They transmit all of the car's information to the engineering team. But they're also used to distinguish between the drivers on a team. One driver gets the yellow while the other gets the black."

"The more you know." She raises her hands and slowly drops them down like a rainbow as she laughs. "I don't think you studied this hard for our exams, and that's saying something."

I fall back onto the sofa. "I didn't study."

"You're telling me you didn't make a single flashcard?"

"Nope."

She squints at me before glancing at my bag on the chair. We jump for it at the same time and she takes me to the ground. We roll and she pins me down with a cry of victory.

She springs off of me and grabs my bag, sticking her hand in the opening. "Aha!" She pulls out my box of notecards and smirks. "I knew it, you little love sick nerd."

I jump to my feet and snatch my stuff out of her hands. "Shut up," I grumble, shoving the flash cards back in my bag and tossing it on the chair. "I don't want to be the girl that just smiles and nods when he talks about this stuff."

"That's fair. No one wants to date a bobblehead."

"What?" I laugh.

My head jerks back, eyes wide as she puts on a wide grin and nods her head repeatedly. "Stop that. It's creepy." I sit on the couch and glance at the TV, smiling when I see Jace is now in front of Lawson, taking second. "And we aren't dating."

She plops down next to me. "Yet."

I shake my head, my eyes not straining from the screen. She peppers me with questions as we watch and by the time there are five laps left, her eyes are as glued to the screen as my own.

The room is silent as we watch the lap counter tick up until they pass under the solid white flag, signaling the last lap. We huddle together as Jace's car creeps closer to Nik, who leads the race. I clutch her hand, my body vibrating with nerves.

"You got this," I murmur.

"Come on, Collins. Get your shit in gear," Lily yells.

A laugh bursts out of me and we jump to our feet when he gets within inches of the car's back wing. We cheer him on as if he can hear us when they pull out of a turn side by side.

I squeal, eyes going wide as he pulls ahead. We wrap our arms around each other, screaming at the TV as he takes the last corner. He passes the finish line, the checkered flag waving high above him and my voice breaks with a cry of pure joy.

"That's your man," Lily screeches, pointing at the screen.

I ignore her, watching as the camera switches to the dash, showcasing his captivating eyes when he flips the visor of his helmet up. They light with pride and he lifts a hand fist pumping the air.

"Woohoo, hell yes!" His voice cracks through the loud speakers of the TV.

"Good job, Jace. Incredible race, mate." A man's voice comes over the radio.

"Thank you, thank you, great job, lads. Couldn't have done this without you." He sticks his hand out, waving to the crowd as he drives by, heading for the pit lanes.

He pulls into the first place spot and hops out, ripping his helmet off. Lily whistles and I glance at her. "Explain to me how someone can still look like *that* after hours of sweating their arses off."

I look up to see him talking with a reporter. He takes his hat off and runs a hand over his hair, his eyes twinkling in the light. His sweat slicked hair falls forward as he laughs, brushing the impression lines of his helmet.

I press my legs together as I track a bead of sweat rolling down his temple and over his jaw.

Whoa, what the hell?

I look over at an oddly quiet Lily and she points at me. "Oh, you *so* have the hots for him."

"Shut up," I grumble, snuggling into the couch as I watch Jace walk out onto the stage.

He steps up to the tallest podium moments before the British anthem plays. His shoulders are back, chest puffed with pride, and eyes alight with triumph as he looks over the crowd.

My lips tip up as he lifts his trophy in victory while holding up the number one on his other hand. It breaks into a full smile when Ryder and Nikolai soak him with champagne.

He whips his hair back and forth, spraying everyone before flipping it out of his face. Running a hand over his soaked hair, he locks eyes with the camera and winks.

Lily swoons—literally, falls onto my lap with her hand over her forehead—and I laugh, shoving her off. She sits up next to me and we turn so the celebrations are behind us.

Lifting my phone, I snap a quick picture and send it with a text telling him that his two newest fans are very proud of the first place win.

A few hours later, we are lounging on the sofa, watching a rerun of *Project Runway* when my phone rings. I pick it up and smile at the name flashing across the screen. Putting it up to my ear, I slide off the couch and walk into the kitchen.

"Kinsley." His smooth voice sends shivers down my spine.

"Don't tell me you're done celebrating already."

He chuckles. "I had an important call to make."

"Oh yeah? How did it go?"

"It's going pretty well so far. What do you think?"

I laugh. "Good. Really good."

I just hope it isn't too good to be true.

CHAPTER 11

KINSLEY

"Shoot shoot shoot," I whisper as I sprint across the hall in my bath towel.

Slipping on the floor I collapse on my small bed face first, sucking in a breath when my ankle twinges. Pressing up to my elbows, I reach over and snag my phone, not bothering to see who it is.

"Hello?" I huff, trying to catch my breath.

"Is this a bad time?" A shiver runs down my spine at his chuckle.

"Jace." I smile.

"Kinsley."

"Hi." I roll onto my back, my hair soaking the bedding.

"I was wondering if you were busy?"

"Uh—" I look down at my towel covered body, water still beading on my skin. "Nope. I'm just at home, laying in bed."

"I was hoping you'd say that."

"Why?"

"Look out your window."

I hesitantly slide off the bed and creep over to the window. Carefully, I peek my head around the sill, lifting the curtain just enough so the side of my face would be visible from outside.

Jace waves as he leans against his car, phone to his ear. "Hi, angel."

I laugh but my eyes widen when my fist tightens on the towel. Throwing myself up against the wall and out of sight, I clear my throat. "Um, give me five minutes?"

After breaking the world record for any girl to get ready, I run down the stairs and quickly write a note for my foster parents that I'll be home later. Locking the front door behind me, I skip down the steps, my satchel bouncing off my leg with every step I take.

Jace pushes off his car and bends when I get within arms reach. I squeal as he wraps his arms around me and lifts me off my feet.

"God, I missed you," he sighs into my neck.

I giggle as he set me back down. "We talked every day you were gone."

"I guess texting and FaceTime wasn't enough." He shakes his head and tucks a strand of my hair behind my ear. "Hi. Ready?"

"What should I be ready for?"

"It's a surprise."

I spend the twenty minute drive trying to get him to crack, but the man is a sealed vault.

He finds a prime parking spot and my brows furrow at

the crowded park. Jace helps me out of the car and I look around at the stands stocked with colorful kites decorating the pathways.

"What's going on?"

"It's a kite festival with floating lanterns tonight." He looks at me with a small tilt in his lips. "I thought it would make for some cool pictures."

My smile grows and I blink several times as emotions clog my throat. I pop up to my toes, kissing his cheek. "Best surprise ever."

Smiling, he leans into the car and grabs my bag. I pull out my camera, fixing it around my neck with the fraying strap and we weave through the crowd.

We find a spot in the middle of the grass and Jace lays out the blanket he brought. He drops down onto it and I join him, snapping pictures as people move around us.

My eyes catch on a family of three. A mum, dad, and a little girl. I watch as the dad helps her set up the kite, the mum fixing some snacks off to the side. Lifting my camera, I capture the moment the little girl gets her kite in the air, all three of them cheering.

Dropping my camera, I look over to see Jace watching me. "You okay?"

I nod, my eyes sliding back to the family. "Did you ever do this kind of stuff with your family growing up?"

"When I wasn't karting. We always went to at least one every season." He shifts back, leaning on his palms. "Did you?"

I shake my head. "I bounced around too much." His

eyebrows furrow and I dip my head, wishing I didn't have to put a damper on the day, but knowing I'd have to tell him at some point.

"I've been in foster care since I was six."

He sits up. "Kinsley, I'm so sorry."

I shrug. "It's okay. I'm okay."

"Do you—"

"Remember anything about my parents? No. Nothing that would make me miss them." I wince. "Sorry, that sounded really bad."

He shakes his head. "Don't apologize if that's how you feel. It's your story, you're the only one who knows how it feels to live it. Who am I to judge?"

My lips tip up. "Thank you. For listening. For not judging me or treating me differently."

"I'm more sorry for everyone else. They're missing out on having you in their lives. Then again, that means I get more of you, so I'm not *that* sorry."

I laugh, shaking my head and he nudges his leg into mine. "They didn't deserve you, Kinsley. And I'm selfishly thankful if it meant you ended up here with me."

I bite my lip. "Lily always says things happen for a reason. Maybe all that's happened was because I was supposed to be right here."

"My Kismet Kinsley," he whispers.

A group of kids run by squealing and I watch as they run through a cluster of bubbles. I glance at Jace and he watches me with a soft smile.

"Do you want kids?" My eyes widen and he sits up

straighter, raising his hands in front of him. "I don't mean right now. Obviously. I mean in the future. The way *way* future. I'm going to shut up now."

I laugh under my breath and shrug. "Yeah. Someday." I look out over the park. "I want to give my kids what I never had. A childhood filled with this kind of stuff. With movie nights in the backyard, pillow forts in the living room, Sunday pancakes, and stories every night before bed. And love. I'd give them so much love."

"I have no doubt you'll be an amazing mum some day."

I watch him for a moment before ducking my head and clearing my throat. "Anyway. I—uh—have some news."

"Oh yeah?"

"I got an email this morning that my photos are going to be in a local photography show."

"What? Kinsley, that's amazing." He tackles me in a bear hug and I laugh, wrapping my arms around him. "I'm so proud of you," he whispers.

"Thank you."

He pulls back. "For what?"

"For giving me the courage to do this. You made me feel like my pictures could really be something and that feeling was enough. So thank you. This wouldn't be happening without you."

He opens his mouth, but a little girl and boy run up to us before he can say anything. "Are you the guy?"

He shifts so he's kneeling in front of them. "Depends. Who is this guy?"

The boy's cheeks redden. "Jace Collins? The Formula 1 driver."

"Then you've got the right guy, lad. What's your name?"

"Zach Millroy. You're my favorite driver."

Jace chuckles. "I'm lucky to have a fan as cool as you, Zach. Ever been to a race?" When the boy shakes his head, Jace pulls out his wallet and hands him a card. "Call that number. The secret password is 'Lawson sucks.' He'll hook you up for whatever race you'd like."

The kids giggle when he says the words 'sucks' and I tuck my lips to hide my own laugh.

"I'm sorry I don't have anything to sign—actually, you know what?" He pulls his hat off and takes out a Sharpie, scrawling his name over the bill. "Here you go, little man."

Zach looks at him, beaming so bright that he showcases his two missing front teeth. "Oh my gosh, I'm never taking this off. Thank you."

Jace looks at the little girl before standing. "Hold on one second." He jogs over to one of the vendors. After paying, he comes back over and kneels in front of the girl.

"What's your name sweetheart?"

"Anna," she whispers.

"That's a beautiful name." He pulls the pink flower from behind his back, holding it out to her. "A pretty flower for a pretty girl."

Okay. Wow. My heart can't take this much longer. The preciousness is too much.

She blushes and takes the flower, glancing at me. "She's pretty too. Where's her flower?"

Jace looks at me and I laugh. Someone calls the kids' names and they run off, yelling their goodbyes. He falls back onto the blanket, sitting next to me with his arms draped over his bent knees.

We spend the rest of the day at the park, talking, eating, taking pictures, and when the lanterns take to the sky, I lay back on the blanket and watch them dance in the wind.

"Beautiful," I whisper and Jace hums in agreement. I glance at him and his eyes move from my face to the sky.

When the last lights fade into the distance, we pack up and load back into the car. The drive home is filled with a symphony from the wind as we ride with the windows down. He pulls up outside my house and I take his hand when he helps me out of the car.

"Thank you for today. It was perfect."

I turn to him when we stop in front of my door. His eyes bounce between mine. "I'm glad I could do that for you. It was a great day."

"It really was," I whisper.

He shuffles on his feet and pulls his arm out from behind him. I suck in a breath as he holds up a single pink camellia flower. "Beautiful flower for the stunning girl."

I laugh under my breath and reach out, sparks shooting up my arm from where our fingertips brush. His phone rings, but he ignores it as we stand there just watching one another. Like neither of us want to move or break the spell. Not wanting to let go of the moment.

It stops ringing only to start right back up again. "You should probably answer that."

"They can leave a message."

I smile and reach behind my back, pushing open the front door. "Text me when you get home so I know you're okay?"

His eyes dance between mine as he nods.

"Good night, Jace," I whisper.

"Good night, Kinsley."

I close the door and watch through the peephole as he stands there before shaking his head and walking to his car. He gets in and the quiet night air fills with the purr of his engine. My brows furrow when he doesn't drive off right away.

"What are you doing?" I whisper, but I'm not sure if the question is more for him or for me.

The driver door opens as he quickly gets out and jogs around the hood. I open the door and step out as he reaches the bottom of the stairs.

"Did you forget some—"

"Yes." He jumps up the steps and his hands frame my face.

He steals my breath, all my thoughts, and the strength to keep standing when his lips crash down on mine. My hands clutch the front of his shirt as he presses in.

My back meets the wall and his hand slips into my hair, cradling my head so it doesn't hit the stone. I wrap my arms around his shoulders and lift onto my toes as one of his hands slips down my side, gripping my hip hard enough to leave marks.

And I want him to. I don't ever want to forget this kiss.

A kiss that devours every one of my thoughts as all my senses fill with him.

The rough yet tender way he cups my jaw as he tilts my head.

The taste of him when his tongue traces the seam of my lips and I willingly open for him.

The smell of his cologne as I rip at his shirt, trying to pull him impossibly closer.

The sound of his throaty growl when my teeth graze his bottom lip.

It's a damning kind of kiss.

One that erases any that came before it.

A kiss so consuming that it leaves a mark on your soul.

A car door slams in the distance and Jace pulls away, leaning his forehead against mine. My eyes slowly open, meeting his molten ones. His drop when my tongue swipes across my bottom lip. His jaw ticks, his fingers tightening slightly in my hair and on my hip.

He takes a deep breath and his lips tip up. Leaning in, he presses his lips to mine softer than before. Once. Twice.

I watch as he takes a step back and kneels, picking up the flower I dropped before standing and slipping it between my fingers. He steps back, nodding towards the front door and I take a breath before following the silent command.

I fall back against the door after I close it, lifting the fingers of my hand not clutching the flower stem up to trace my swollen lips. His footsteps retreat and I listen as he climbs into his car before he drives away.

I drop my head back against the wood, one thought breaking through the fog of him.

I'm in so much trouble.

CHAPTER 12

JACE

"Did you seriously just growl at me?"

I stare wide eyed at my little sister and smack her hand when she reaches for the tray.

She stomps her foot. "Would you quit that?"

Arms band around me, pinning mine to my sides.

"Oi! What the fuck?"

Lawson's chuckle vibrates through my back. "Hurry up, sunshine."

Sydney snatches two biscuits and sprints away. He releases me and I jump away, pointing at him. "Traitor!"

He rolls his eyes, snagging a treat for himself. "I just saved you from being mauled by your hangry sister. I think the words you're looking for are 'thank you.'"

"I could take her."

He pats my chest. "Sure you could, mate."

Mum walks over and I pout. "Mum, Lawson's bullying me."

She stifles a laugh. "Boys, behave."

Sydney pops out of nowhere and steals his biscuit as he lifts it to his mouth. She high tails it over to where our dad mans the grill and uses him as a shield when Law prowls closer.

Dad throws his hands up and steps aside. "You're on your own, baby girl."

She gasps and looks at Lawson with wide eyes, shoving the entire biscuit in her mouth. He lunges for her and she squeals.

"Good luck ever getting me to help you with anything again, sunshine," Lawson calls out as he snatches her around the waist, throwing her over his shoulder.

"Don't you dare, Law—" her protests break on a scream when he launches her into the pool.

"So." Mum's soft voice draws my attention. "This girl—"

"Kinsley."

"Do we *like* like her?"

"I'm definitely starting to."

"Does she feel the same?"

"God, I hope so. She's a little shy at first, but once she opens up—she's incredible. Too sweet for her own good. Caring to a fault." I smile thinking about our afternoon in the park and how her eyes lit up with every shutter of her camera. "Unbelievably talented."

Mum reaches up, cupping my jaw. "She makes you happy?"

Images of her bright face and the sound of her laugh flash in my mind. My lips tingle with the phantom feel of hers from when I kissed her the other night and my heart skips at the memory of her clutching on to me like she never wanted me to let go.

"More than I thought possible."

My phone vibrates and I pull it out, grinning at the screen. "Be right back."

I head through the house and open the front door. Kinsley whips around, beaming. "Jace," she whispers.

"Kinsley."

I open the door wider and she steps into the foyer. Slowly, she spins to face me and holds up a cling wrapped plate. "I made some banana bars. They're basically mini breads with vanilla frosting. No nuts, though, since you said your sister is allergic."

"You remember that?"

She shrugs. "It's kind of an important thing to remember."

I huff a laugh and shake my head. It was an offhand comment I made when we were talking about our favorite snacks.

I told her I loved trail mix, but never really got it growing up since Sydney liked to steal my snacks when she was younger. She still does it, but now she knows better.

Of course Kinsley remembers. That's who she is. Someone who pays attention, from the biggest moments to the quietest whispers.

Without thought, I step forward and cup her face. She sucks in a breath as I tuck a strand of her hair. "I really want to kiss you, again."

Her lips twitch and she nods. "Okay."

With a smile, I lean in and gently press my lips to hers. She shuffles closer, placing her hand on my chest and I swipe my tongue over her bottom lip.

I pull back before I'm ready, leaning my forehead against here. "Thank you."

For caring to remember.

For seeing me as more.

For staying.

For being you.

"Do you want the tour now or introductions?"

"Tour, please."

I set her plate down on the hallway table before leading her around the first floor. We pass the family trophy case and she whistles, glancing up at me with a raised eyebrow. "Trying to impress me or something?"

I scoff. "Always."

She giggles as we walk up the stairs. I fail to keep her distracted as we pass a picture of me with a mouth full of braces and a face covered in the lovely gift of puberty acne. She covers her mouth with her fingers, lips twitching.

I pout and she reaches over, brushing her fingers through my hair. "It's nice to know that even someone like you couldn't escape the dreaded awkward phase."

We walk into my childhood bedroom and I sit on the bed, watching her slowly spin with a soft smile. She sits down next to me and her eyes slide to the nightstand.

I lean in when she picks up the frame, and look down at

the four younger versions of me and the lads. "That's the first race we all competed in together."

She turns her head, our noses nearly brushing. Her eyes drop to my lips and I lean in, but a voice calls out a second after I hear the front door slam shut. "We're here!"

I drop my head to her shoulder as she sighs. "We should—"

"Just give me a moment," I grumble as her shoulders shake with silent laughter.

"Is there anything I can do to help?" she whispers.

"I'm okay," I chuckle and stand. "But know that the next time you ask me that, I'll have a *very* different answer."

She tucks her lips, cheeks flaming, and slips her hand in mine. Ryder's mum sees us first as we walk down the stairs. "Jace!" Her eyes slide to Kinsley. "Oh, you're a pretty little thing. Why can't you bring home a sweet looking girl like that?" She backhands Ryder's chest.

"I need a drink," he grumbles, scrubbing his face and nodding at Kinsley. "It's good to see you again. This is my mum, Alice. I apologize in advance for the nonsense bound to come out of her mouth."

Alice gasps. "Just for that, I'll be standing with the Collins in their garage this weekend."

"Wait, I didn't mean it." Ryder jogs after her.

We follow them down the hallway and I clear my throat. "Speaking of this weekend. How do you feel about standing around a packed garage, watching twenty grown men play with their fast cars, and later on maybe celebrating a win?"

She smiles. "I feel really good about that. Especially the last part." We step out into the back garden and she sighs. "Guess I need to get my hands on some Miller Racing swag then."

I wink. "I think I know a guy."

Mum pops out of nowhere and pulls Kinsley into a hug. "You must be Kinsley. I'm Eleanor, Jace's mum, and the handsome fella on the grill over there is his dad, Julian."

"It's nice to meet you. Thank you for letting me join today."

They separate as Sydney shoves her way between me and Kinsley. "Oh my god, you're here and you're real. Hi, I'm the much better Collins sibling, Sydney."

"Hi." Kinsley laughs, then glances to our left. "Lawson."

He dips his chin. "I see this one hasn't sent you running for the hills yet."

She winks at me. "Not yet."

He nods. "Give it some time."

I elbow him as we take our seats. Kinsley sits next to me and our legs brush. She glances at me and I slip my hand over her thigh, squeezing.

"Sydney, there's a plate full right there." Lawson scowls as she steals a chip from him.

"But they taste so much better off your plate."

Kinsley giggles and I lean over. "Don't worry, yours are safe."

"Then so are your fingers," she whispers back.

After everyone is done eating, she's stolen away by the ladies while the gentlemen clean up before changing into our swimsuits. The lads sneak up behind Sydney and snatch her, swinging her into the pool before jumping in after her.

"Please don't do that to me," Kinsley pleads.

I scoff. "I'd never."

She takes a step away. "Jace. Don't you—"

I wrap my arms around her and throw us over the edge. Her squeal is cut off as we hit the water and when we come up, she splashes me.

"What? I tripped."

Two bodies shove me from behind and Sydney jumps on Lawson's back with a battle cry as I dunk Ryder. I catch Kinsley out of the corner of my eye, stifling her laugh behind her hand.

I swim over and perch myself on the side of the pool beside her. "Enjoying the show?"

"Immensely. I especially liked when you used Ryder as a shield."

"Syd was after my nipples," I pout and yank her onto my lap when my sister swims over.

Sydney rolls her eyes. "Big baby."

"Am not."

"Okay then, I challenge you and Kinsley to a chicken fight."

"Absolutely not."

"Aw, you scared? Like a baby?"

"No. You two are just a couple of cheats."

"How can you cheat at a chicken fight?" Kinsley asks.

"I don't know, but they do."

She shrugs. "Well, I've never played."

My sister perks up. "I'll go easy."

"She's a dirty liar," I whisper into her ear.

"Come on." She looks at me over her shoulder.

Damnit. Try and find me someone who can say no to that face. Oh wait, you can't.

Sydney swims over to Lawson as I move in front of Kinsley.

"This okay?"

I grunt, trying to tamp down the growing, well, everything as she slides her legs over my shoulders. I band my hands over her thighs when she shifts and clench my jaw.

Good lord, that isn't helping.

"Who's ready to rumble?" Sydney calls out.

Kinsley leans over my head. "I think I fucked up."

"Too late now, angel. Time to put your game face on, we're in it to win it."

Ryder stands off to the side and counts us down, barely getting out the last number before they pounce. Kinsley squeaks, arms intertwining with Sydney's as she tries to shove her off.

My sister curls a hand around the back of her head as Lawson takes a step back. Kinsley dips down, curling over me, and Sydney's hand slips off.

She sits up and we circle them. This time I take the step forward and Kinsley grabs both of Sydney's hands, yanking them off balance for a second. Lawson steps into me and tries to slip a hand under Kinsley's calf.

I growl and yank us away. My mind rationalizes that it's

because I don't want to lose and not because I don't want my best mate to touch her. But it may be a little bit of both.

Lawson slips behind us and Sydney grabs onto Kinsley's arms, but I spin and Sydney wobbles. Kinsley uses the opportunity to shove her shoulders.

Sydney hits the water with a shriek before popping back up with a look of disbelief.

"Yes," I cheer and clap my hands on Kinsley's thighs.

She laughs when I flip her over my shoulder, catching her in a hug.

"Oh my god, that was so much fun. Can we go again?" She laughs, bouncing on her toes.

We play three more rounds, winning all of them before the sky darkens and we gather around the firepit. I watch her across the flames as she laughs at something Sydney says.

As if she senses me, she glances up and I get lost in the golden glow as flames dance in her eyes. She smiles and my heart beats faster.

We haven't talked about what this thing between us is and I know we will eventually. And as I watch her across the fire, I hope that when the time comes, she feels the same.

CHAPTER 13
JACE

"Jace, how are you feeling going into today's race?"

"I'm feeling good. We're in a prime position with a P2 start, the car feels great, our strategy is solid, and it's a beautiful day to go racing."

The reporter laughs. "That it is. You really left it all out there last weekend in Austria. Any chance we'll see a repeat performance from you today?"

"That's the goal."

"Let's hope that trend continues for the second half of this season then, yeah? Any word on a new contract for next year?"

I put my hand in my pocket to hide my fist and force a lighthearted chuckle. "Not yet." I glance over at my press advisor, Nate, and nod.

He steps over, clapping a hand on my shoulder. "Sorry to cut this short, but they need him back at the clubhouse."

The reporter stops his recording and nods. "Of course, good luck out there today."

With a nod, we turn for the paddock lane.

"You good?" Nate asks as we weave through the crowded walkways.

"I thought we told the press there wouldn't be any more questions about contracts."

"We both know that the press is going to do what the press wants to do. You can always hit them with the 'no comment' card."

"That's what I've been doing for the last three weeks."

"Just hang in there, mate."

My souring mood lifts as the clubhouse comes into view. Sydney's the first to spot me and waves, gaining everyone's attention.

My heart skips when a pair of golden brown eyes land on me. Kinsley's face lights up and she waves before slowly twirling around, showcasing my racing number on the back of her shirt.

When she faces me again, I place a hand over my heart, mouthing 'wow' and watch her shoulders shake with a laugh. I glance at Nate and grin. "Did they actually need me or—"

"Oh you're good to go. Just make sure you're ready for pre-race."

With a salute, I pick up my strides only to jerk to a stop when the bane of my existence slides in front of me. My face drops when she places her hand on my chest.

"Nuh-uh. Not today." I remove her hand and she pouts up at me.

"Jace—"

"Lucifer's Mistress."

She stomps her foot. "Come on. You have to talk to me at some point."

"I did. Last week. And yet, you still aren't listening to me, so why even bother now?" I go to step around her but she blocks me. I huff a strained laugh and nod as people pass by. "Angie, let's not make a scene."

"I will if that's what it takes to get you to talk to me."

My head snaps down to her and she quirks a brow, daring me to test her.

"Fine. Say what you want to say," I grit out.

"When are you going to forgive me?"

"Oh, that's easy. Never. Bye now."

She calls out my name as I maneuver around her, but I don't stop. Shaking out my hands as tension builds with every step I take towards my family, I block everything else out until there's only them.

Until there's only her.

Sydney scowls over my shoulder as I walk up the three small steps. Dad looks at her with furrowed brows while Mum watches me with concern.

And Kinsley...

Her head is downcast as she fiddles with the strap of her camera. Her lips pinched tight with no trace of the smile that belongs there instead.

I head straight for her and tuck my finger under her chin, guiding her head up until she looks at me. "Hey there, angel."

Her shoulders relax. "Hi, Jace."

With those two words, I feel completely at ease.

It's the Kinsley effect.

I pull her into a hug and her arms band around my waist. Turning my head, I breathe in her toasted vanilla scent, and place a kiss on her temple. Her hold tightens, fingers twisting in my shirt at my back as she presses her forehead against my chest.

Reluctantly, I pull away and tap her camera. "Get any cool shots?"

She beams. "So many." I lean over her shoulder as she flips through a couple. She quickly flips over one but I place my hand over hers.

"Wait." I click the back arrow and the screen switches to a shot from this morning's track walk we took with the family and Lawson.

Except none of them are in this one.

It's a close up of me squatting right over the finish line, hand pressed to the ground, my head down and eyes closed. It's something I do before every race, taking a quiet moment between me and the track.

"Sorry," she whispers.

"What are you sorry for?"

"I shouldn't have taken that. It was a private moment for you and—"

"Amazing." Her head shoots up and I lower my voice. "It's absolutely amazing, Kinsley."

"Well I'm *absolutely* ready to go see all the cute drivers, can we go now?" Sydney whines.

Kinsley giggles as I scowl and my parents shake their

heads. For the next hour we walk around the paddocks before I get them situated in the garage.

When it's time for me to gear up, my parents send me off with hugs and Sydney with a punch to my arm. I turn to Kinsley and freeze when she pops up on her toes, brushing her lips against the corner of my mouth. "You got this."

"Not going to wish me good luck?"

She scrunches her nose, shaking her head. "You don't need it, remember? They do." She juts her chin out towards the opening of the garage bay.

I huff a laugh and lean down, stealing a quick kiss as I move around her and down the hallway before she or anyone can say anything more.

The phantom touch of her lips dances over my skin as I stand for the starting ceremonies.

It ignites an inferno as I slip on my helmet and buckle into my car.

It calms my racing mind during the formation lap.

And as I look up at the five illuminated red lights, her whispered words sing along with the steady beat of my heart.

Every race is important, but this one? This track? It's special.

It's me and the lad's home race.

The Silverstone Circuit is just under six kilometers long with eighteen turns throughout, totaling fifty-two laps for a full two hours of racing. It's one of the tracks with fewer laps, but that just means you have to make each one of them count.

Which is exactly what I do.

With fresh tyres, I fly back out on the track after my pit

stop as my race engineer, Oscar, comes over the radio. "Great first half. You're now only four seconds behind the race leader."

"Who is it?"

"King. Morozov is five seconds behind you, Moore right behind him. But don't worry about them. Just keep pushing, only twenty-four more laps to go."

"Understood."

Lap after lap, I push my body and car to its limits. But it all pays off when I catch a glimpse of Ryder's back wing as we weave through turns ten, eleven, and twelve.

By the time we come out of the straight and into lap forty-eight, I'm breathing down his neck. He shifts to defend and I curse.

Ryder King is one of the best defenders I've ever seen. It takes nothing short of a miracle to get past him on a good day.

And I guess today is a great one.

For me.

Not him.

I ease back, avoiding a collision as we pull through turn four and take advantage of DRS, sliding up next to him. He gets me on the inside of turn seven and we battle it out until one of his wheels locks up.

I don't hesitate.

I slam on the accelerator and fly down the straight.

"Morozov closing in on you and King."

"Fuck."

Where Ryder dominates at defending, Nik's the last person you want on the attack. The man is fearless, taking turns tighter and at higher speeds than any driver would ever dare. I have yet to see any amount of space this man has failed to close between him and his next target.

Today, that target is me.

"Let him and King fight it out. Keep pushing and hold on for these last few laps."

"Understood."

When we pass under the waving white flag, signaling the start of the last lap, I'm holding on by a two second lead. One that's quickly dwindling.

"One point two behind."

"Respectfully, Oscar. Shut up and let me drive."

The wheel creaks under my grip as I take turn eight for the last time. Ryder and Nik swing out behind me in their own battle. I chance a glance in the mirror coming out of turn nine and grit my teeth when I see Nik nipping at my rear wing.

Oscar calls out a warning as we enter the last DRS zone. Nik comes up on my left and I hold off long enough to cut him off on the inside of turn fifteen. My heart beat drills through my head as we come into the final three turns neck and neck.

There's a moment of stillness as we pass over the finish line and I go through the motions of downshifting into a cool down lap. The quiet seconds tick by, the sound of my heavy breathing echoing in my helmet.

"You just won the British Grand Prix!"

A disbelieving laugh burst out of me. "Yes. Hell yes!" I

stick my hand out and wave to the crowd as I drive by. "Thank you, I couldn't do it without any of you."

"Excellent driving, mate. Really good job," Mitch's voice breaks through the radio.

I pull into the first place spot and climb out of my car to the cheering crowd, lifting my fists in the air. I twist and hop down, jogging over to my garage team lining the fence and launching myself into their arms.

I pull back, yanking off my helmet and balaclava as I lean in to hug my mum. Tears stream down her face and she kisses my cheek before Dad pulls me in for a crushing hug.

"Not bad, big brother, not bad at all," Sydney cries.

Kinsley stands slightly behind her and I reach out, pulling her forward.

I hold onto her tight, ignoring the tapping on my shoulder as a guide tries to get me over for my after race interview. Pulling back slightly, I cup her face.

Her shining eyes bounce between mine and she smiles. "You were amazing!"

"Buckle up, angel, because I think you might just be my good luck charm."

She shakes her head, attention shifting to the side. "I think they need you over there."

"I'm good right here."

Laughing, she shoves my chest and I relent, walking over to set my things down and placing the first place hat on my head before stepping up for my interview.

"Jace, congratulations. What an incredible race. How are you feeling right now?"

"I'm on top of the world, mate."

"Those last couple laps were a bit rough. What was going through your mind?"

"Get the heck away from me," I laugh. "They definitely made me work for it."

"I see your family over there. What does it mean to you to have them here for this moment?"

I glance at them and smile. "It means everything to me. I couldn't imagine celebrating this win with anyone else."

"Ah, big plans?"

My eyes slide to Kinsley as she winks over the edge of her camera. "Big hopes."

CHAPTER 14
KINSLEY

I KNEW this day was coming.

Everything was going too well.

My luck had just started to turn around.

But I guess it's already run out.

"I'm sorry, Kennedy."

"Kinsley! My name is Kinsley!" I want to scream but instead, drop my eyes.

"You have to understand, we didn't think—"

"It's okay. I understand." I don't, but then again it's not like they promised. "I, um, have to finish processing these photos for Friday." Without waiting for a response, I flee the house and run out into the pouring rain.

Within minutes my clothes are soaked and by the time I make it to the bus stop, my teeth are chattering and limbs are shaking. Lightning strikes across the sky before a big clap of thunder and I stare up at the angry sky.

Fitting.

The conversation plays on a loop in my mind the entire bus ride. It isn't until I unlock the door of the dark room that I can take a full breath without fear of breaking down.

I set my things on the counter and wring out my jacket in the sink before draping it over a stool. Taking out my phone, I open up Spotify and my lips twitch at the two new playlists.

After the race, Jace surprised me by bringing Lily out to meet us at the club. He told me that he thought having my best friend there would make me a little more comfortable since I'm still not big on crowds.

If I hadn't already been crushing on the man *before* seeing him in his full race suit, sweat soaked hair, and those—seriously, why are they attractive—indents left from his helmet pads, *this* would have done it.

The moment I introduced Lily to his sister, it was like they'd been best friends since nappies. The three of us danced the night away and made plans to hang out at the pool the next day while the guys were in a team meeting.

It was the perfect day with the best people. Especially when the guys joined us later.

I laugh under my breath, thinking of Jace pouting when he found the girls' day playlist. Who was I to say no when he asked if we could make one for just the two of us?

We laid on that lounger for hours, my back against his chest, adding songs to both of our phones. "Now I'll have something to listen to when I'm missing you," he whispered, his lips brushing against my shoulder.

My stomach still hasn't returned from where it dropped

at the reminder that he'll be gone soon for the second half of the season.

I click on our playlist—One Song at a Time—and let the opening chords of "Yellow" by Coldplay fill my ears. I close my eyes and take a deep breath, letting the music tuck away my worried thoughts.

I lose myself in the process of developing the strips of film as song after song plays. I don't know how much time passes, lost in the comfort of the one thing that's always been here for me.

I tip over the container of the developer, but nothing comes out. Setting the empty jug in the trash, I turn for the shelf and slip on water left over from my shoes.

My arms flail and I stiffen in preparation for the ground, but hands grab my sides, holding me steady. The air rushes out of me and I squeeze my eyes shut in relief.

But then the strange hands still on my waist register and my eyes spring open. I throw myself out of reach with a scream and whip around, ripping my earbuds out.

Clutching my heaving chest, I bow my head and sigh. "Jesus christ, Jace."

"I'm so sorry, I didn't mean to scare you. But I didn't know how to approach without doing it either, so I just kind of stood there—"

"Watching me?"

"Yeah. But then you slipped and—"

"You caught me."

He steps closer, his fingers ghosting over mine on the table. "I'll always catch you."

I breathe out a sigh. "How long have you been here?"

"Longer than I care to admit." He chuckles, shuffling from foot to foot. "I stopped at your house to see if you wanted to grab something to eat, but your foster mum said you'd run out."

He looks around the room before settling on me again with concern blanketing his features. "I figured something was wrong since Lily also hadn't heard from you so this was the first place I looked. And here you are."

"Here I am," I murmur, perching onto a stool and fiddling with the sleeves of my jumper.

His jumper.

His finger tucks under my chin, lifting my face up. "What's wrong, sweetheart?"

"What makes you think something's wrong?"

"I may not be able to see you that well right now, but I can hear you. Your voice is giving you away."

"There's nothing wrong with my voice," I whisper.

"There. That. The last time I heard you sound like that was when that prick had his hands on you." His thumb traces over my bottom lip. "Your voice is small. Like there's so much going on around you that you don't know what to do, like you're seconds away from breaking."

He cups my face. "So let me help because I swore to myself I'd never hear you sound like this again."

The first tear rolls down my cheek and he pulls me into his chest. "I'm here. I've got you," he whispers as his fingers thread into my hair.

I feel the brush of his lips on my temple and squeeze my

eyes shut as a sob racks through me. His leg slips between mine on the stool and when I spread them, he steps closer until every part of us lines up.

"I don't know what to do," I cry.

He leans back, wiping away my tears. "What happened?"

"They're kicking me out."

His eyebrows dip. "Your foster parents? How can they do that?"

"I've technically aged out of the system. I'm eighteen so they don't have to let me stay there. But we'd worked out an agreement before—ugh, I knew I should have gotten it in writing. They're already approved for another placement and I have two weeks until he or she will be here." I huff, wiping my cheeks. "They said they expected me to go off to university. With what money would I have been able to do that?"

I hiccup and lean my forehead on his chest. "I'd started looking at jobs and Lily played around with the idea of getting a place together, but that was before she was leaving for this program. Now I have nowhere to go."

He squeezes me. "We'll figure it out, okay?"

"How?"

He pulls back, swiping his thumbs under my eyes. "I'm not quite sure yet, but I promise you we will." Placing a soft kiss on my nose, he lays his forehead against mine. "You're not alone, Kinsley. You've got Lily, who I know for a fact would commit some major crimes if something bad were to ever happen to you. We're talking John Wick level."

A water logged giggle slips out as he continues. "You also

have the lads and Sydney. They adore you and I have no doubt that she wouldn't hesitate to release the hounds if she needed to."

"I won't tell the boys you referred to them as dogs," I whisper and he chuckles.

"Much appreciated." He shifts, drawing his thumb over my bottom lip, pulling it from between my teeth. "And you have me."

I reach up, grabbing his wrist as I close my eyes.

"You've become one of my best friends, Kinsley. There's very few people in this world that I get to be myself with and you're one of them. I don't think you understand how much that means to me or how important you've become."

He brushes my hair behind my ears, bending down so we're eye to eye. "We'll figure this out. Together. Because you're not alone and if I have it my way, you won't ever be again."

Taking a steadying breath, I nod and lean in. Wrapping my arms around his shoulders I hold onto him with everything that I am. Hoping he can feel just how much his words mean to me.

His hands fist the back of my jumper and I tighten my arms, not wanting to let go yet. Needing to stay in this feeling for a little bit longer. Needing to stay in his arms longer.

"Thank you for finding me," I murmur.

He leans back and cups my face. "I'd do anything for you, Kinsley."

My eyes bounce between his as my body relaxes with his touch. With his words.

I've never felt this before. A sense of belonging. Of being wanted.

But with Jace, I don't have to wonder because he's shown me every day since we met that I'm right where I need to be. With him. Safe. Cared for. Maybe one day even loved.

And as I lean forward, pulling him into a kiss, I hope he can feel just how important he is to me too.

It starts off soft. The light brush of his lips, the teasing of his tongue. His fingers flex along my jaw and I run my hand up his back.

A growl vibrates through his chest when I slide my tongue over his bottom lip. His other hand shoots up gripping my hip as my arms slide around his neck.

I fall into his chest when he tugs me closer, our kiss deepening with every passing second. A whimper slips out when his teeth graze my bottom lip and my knees threaten to give out when the sexiest deep chuckle rumbles in his throat.

His hand runs up my side, over my shoulder, and brushes my neck before he's holding my face in both of his hands. Like he's holding on to make sure I'm right there with him.

If our first kiss was explosive, this one is grounding.

This is the kind of kiss you read about in romance books. Ones you cry to in movies. It's the type of kiss that stays with you long after it ends. Rewriting your hopes and dreams because nothing will ever measure up with anyone else.

We break apart when a door slams closed in the distance and the room fills with our heavy breathing, his hungry eyes holding mine.

"You've become my best friend too," I whisper and his

jaw flexes. "I don't know what this is, but I know it feels right. After everything with my ex, I didn't think I'd be able to put myself out there like that again. At least not so soon."

He shakes his head. "Kins—"

"I never saw this coming. Never saw you coming." My eyes dance between his and I reach up brushing my fingertips across his lips. "But someone once told me that the best things in life happen when we least expect it. And you're one of the best things that's happened for me in a *really* long time, Jace."

A breath rushes out of him and he cups my face. "We don't have to define it. We can just be us and take this one day at a time. Together."

I nod and he leans in, kissing me softly. "Tell me to stop and I stop. Tell me you've changed your mind and we can go right back to being friends. It might take me a while, but I'll do it if it means I still get to have a piece of you. Whatever you're willing to give me, Kinsley."

I lean back cupping his jaw. "One day at a time."

He smiles. "One day at a time."

CHAPTER 15

KINSLEY

"I THINK I'm going to throw up."

"Don't be so dramatic."

"It's not dramatics. It's a fair warning."

This feeling has only grown as today has gotten closer.

Lily and Jace tried their best to keep my mind occupied and it worked for a while. But then I'd lay in bed at night, staring up at my blank ceiling and obsessing over every little thing.

Tonight my photos will hang in a real life gallery. They'll be available for purchase by the attendees. Some of which will be curators for the most prestigious galleries around the world.

This is a big step up from the albums on my phone practically collecting dust.

"Okay. Okay. Look at me." Lily turns me to face her, hands on my shoulders. "Let's take a deep breath shall we?"

She leads me through four cycles until I can feel the tips of my fingers again and my heart isn't threatening to beat out of my chest. "Thank you."

She shrugs. "I sent out one email. You and your work did the rest."

I lean my hip against the counter. "I couldn't have gotten this far without you and you know it. So I'll say it again. Thank you."

Her lips tip up and she shakes her head. "You're welcome. Now will you stop freaking out about tonight? Everything will be fine. *More* than fine. Your date is smoking hot—"

"Wait, Jace is here already?" I ask, glancing at the bathroom door with wide eyes.

"Uh, excuse me. I wasn't talking about him, I was referring to myself."

I laugh. "Oh, how silly of me. Of course."

She waves a hand through the air. "There's no doubt Jace will draw many, many eyes tonight." She smiles, wiggling her eyebrows and I hold back a laugh since only one of them has been filled in. "But so will you. Tonight's your night to shine, Kins. We're all here for you."

"You do know that I'm not the only artist being showcased tonight, right?"

"Pft, details."

Our laughter is broken by a knock on the door. "Twenty minutes until final checks," one of the gallery assistants calls out.

My best friend claps, finger twirling around me. "Let's get you dressed."

My eyes dart to the black garment bag hanging off the back of the door. It's another Lily Campbell original, made just for tonight.

She pulls out the floor length, black dress decorated with glittering jewels, almost as if the stars themselves are falling down the skirt. It has a low back—one I'm positive she lowered even more than the last time I saw it—and a slit so far up my left leg that I'm a little scared to take a decent step.

I carefully slip the delicate fabric over my hips and slide my arms through the sheer sleeves. Lily zips up the side and secures the clasp before adjusting the neckline to lay perfectly across my collarbone.

I stand in the full length mirror and twist.

It's absolutely beautiful.

And I feel beautiful in it.

My thick chocolate hair runs down to the middle of my back in soft waves. Soft eyeshadow accentuates my golden brown eyes, and my lips are painted a muted pink to compliment the heels Lily surprised me with.

After finishing her makeup and changing into her own gown, we gather our bags. She slips them over her shoulder and picks up her keys. "I'm going to take our stuff to the car. Be right back." The door closes with a soft click as she leaves.

I face the mirror and take a steadying breath. "You got this."

I run shaky fingers through my hair. "You got this."

I smooth out the front of my dress. "You got this."

I place my palms on the counter and drop my head, closing my eyes. "You got this."

"You do."

I suck in a quick breath and my head shoots up, my eyes connecting with my favorite shade of blue in the mirror.

"You're here," I whisper.

"Passed Lily outside. She told me I should come in here and make sure you don't try to make a break for it." He smirks, stepping into the bathroom. "Little does she know, I'd be your getaway driver if that's really what you wanted."

I laugh, turning as he walks over. He cages me in with an arm on either side of me and leans down, brushing his lips against mine softly.

Pulling back, he lifts his hand and cups the side of my face, running his thumb over my cheek. "You look absolutely breathtaking, angel."

I reach up and smooth my hands over his chest. He's dressed in a deep blue—almost black—suit with the top three buttons of his crisp white shirt undone. His jaw is freshly shaved and his dirty blond hair is styled back with a few stubborn strands falling over his forehead.

"So do you."

His lips tick up on the side, his eyes dancing over my face. "You doing okay?"

I nod. "Just a little nervous."

About tonight.

About the looming deadline set by my foster parents and not knowing what I'm going to do or where I'm going to go.

About him and whatever is going on between us.

About basically everything.

His other hand comes up and he holds my face in both of his hands. "What can I do?"

I lean into his touch, feeling the steady beat of his heart under my palm. "You're doing it."

I press my forehead against his, breathing in his cologne. With every passing moment I feel the nerves and worries fade away. Because in his arms I feel safe. I feel wanted. Like nothing will ever harm me as long as I'm with him.

He shifts closer and I tilt my head, pressing my lips to his. Once. Twice.

His tongue teases the seam of my lips on the third kiss and I open willingly. His hand trails my neck, over my shoulder, and down my side. I shiver when his warm palm slides across the bare skin of my back and he moans.

"This dress," he growls, using his hand on my back to press me against him as he kisses me with unabashed hunger.

My head tips back as he drags his lips down, nipping and licking where my neck and shoulder meet. I suck in a breath at the sharp bite of his teeth, whimpering when he chases the sting away with his tongue.

I turn my head, catching his lips with mine and we both groan. I throw my arms over his shoulders as his hand trails down my side, his fingers finding the top of the dress's slit.

We pause and he pulls back, our eyes meeting as our chests rise and fall on heavy breaths. His eyes dance between mine and I drop my hand over his on my thigh.

Without looking away, I slowly guide him farther down until the fabric covers his hand before moving it back up. I pull away and clutch his arm as he takes over, slowly skating his fingers up my leg.

My hips instinctively press forward when he traces the lace of my thong at my hip, following its path towards my center. I close my eyes, dropping my head back when his fingers ghost over me and bite my lip to contain my moan.

His ragged breath fans over my heated skin. "Kins—"

A bang on the door cuts him off and we freeze. "You better not be in there ruining all my hard work."

He removes his hand from my thigh, a smirk playing on his lips. "Still nervous?"

I laugh and he leans in to steal one last kiss before walking over to the door. I bite my lip when he adjusts himself before cracking it open.

"Lily."

"Romeo." She squints up at him in amusement. "Don't think that's quite your color."

He looks at his reflection in the mirror next to the door and smirks. "I don't know. I kind of like it."

She snorts and glances at me. "You ready?"

I nod, grabbing my clutch and walking over to them. Reaching up, I brush my thumb over his bottom lip, wiping away the smeared lipstick. He turns his head, kissing my palm as his other hand slides across my lower back.

The three of us walk down the hallway and I rush over to join the other artists in our pre-opening meeting. Five minutes before the doors open, I find Jace standing in front of one of my photos.

I took it the night we watched the floating lanterns in the

park. He's sitting on the ground, leaning back on his hands with his head tilted to the sky. The soft light casted by the lanterns highlight the soft smile on his face.

I titled it 'More Than Just a Man' because that's what he is. He's more than the driver the world sees. More than the son his parents raised. More than a friend. He's just... more.

"Do you like it?"

He twists, watching me as I slowly step up next to him. "It's incredible, angel. Truly."

"He is." I lean my head on his shoulder.

He chuckles. "I'm serious, Kinsley. You're so talented." He shakes his head. "If I knew it wouldn't mortify you, I'd scream it from all the rooftops in London."

I lift my head and we turn to face each other. A single tear runs down my cheek as my chest constricts. His thumb catches it and his eyebrows furrow.

I reach up, placing my hand on his chest. "Thank you."

"For what?"

"For wanting to shout it from the rooftops."

For making me feel like I'm enough.

He throws a thumb over his shoulder. "I can go right now? I'll start on this one. Think I saw the stairs around here somewhere."

I giggle, grabbing his arm when he takes a step away. "No. No. This is definitely one of those 'it's the thought that counts' moments."

"Doors are opening," someone calls from the front of the gallery.

My smile drops and he steps closer, cupping the side of

my face. "You got this. I'll be right here all night if you need me."

That's the thing though.

I'm beginning to feel like I'll always need you.

I nod and he kisses my forehead before linking our fingers. I follow him over to where Lily stands by the open bar and we watch as people filter through the open doors.

A familiar head of blonde hair and deep blue eyes catches my attention seconds before Sydney pops up on her toes and waves.

"Is that—"

"I may have shouted from one rooftop."

I laugh as his entire family emerges from the growing crowd. His mum walks over hand in hand with his dad as Sydney drags a grouchy Lawson behind her, Ryder and Nikolai talking behind them.

I blink rapidly to keep the tears at bay as his mum pulls me in for a hug. "There she is. Congratulations, Kinsley."

We pull back and I glance at everyone. "Thank you all for coming."

Eleanor smiles. "We wouldn't have missed this for the world."

Is this what it's like? To have people in your corner, cheering you on. To have unconditional support? Is this what I've been missing out on all my life?

Hours pass as we float around the gallery. I hold onto Jace, onto his mum's words, onto this night. And as the last of the guests leave, instead of packing up and going home alone, he and his family are there to celebrate the purchase of all my photos with me.

With his jacket draped over my shoulders, a tray of ice cream between us, and his parents bickering over where to hang their new prized possession, I know this is a night I don't ever want to forget.

Don't think I'd be able to even if I tried.

CHAPTER 16
JACE

I THINK it's fair to say that I'm the luckiest man on earth.

Fuck that. I'm the luckiest bloke in the universe.

Why do I think this? Oh, well, because I'm on a date with an angel.

I smile up at her as she skips down the steps of her house. She jumps into my arms when she's within reach and I catch her, holding her tight.

"Hi," she whispers.

"Hi," I echo before taking her lips in a soft kiss.

She hums and I set her back on her feet. I tuck her into the car before striding over to the driver's side and sliding behind the wheel.

"Are you going to tell me where we're going this time, or..." Her words drift off as she raises her eyebrows, looking at me expectantly.

I chuckle, turning on the car. "It's a surprise."

"How did I know you were going to say that?" she grumbles.

Leaning on the center console, I pull her head to the side with a gentle touch on her chin. The light of the street lamps dance over her face and I can't help but brush my thumb over her cheek.

"Trust me?"

Her eyes don't waver as she shifts closer. "Of course."

My lips twitch and I close the distance between us. She sighs into the kiss and grabs onto the front of my shirt.

A car drives by and I pull back, our shallow breaths playing a symphony with the purr of the engine. She giggles and lifts her hand, her thumb wiping my bottom lip. Her eyes heat as she stares at my mouth.

"You should stop looking at me like that, angel."

"Why?"

"Because I'm two seconds away from throwing all the plans I made for tonight out the window and taking you home."

She tsks. "That's not very gentlemanly of you, Mr. Collins."

I huff a laugh, shaking my head. "The way you're looking at me makes me think you want anything but gentle right now, sweetheart. And I'll always do whatever you want. Whatever makes you happy."

She studies me a moment before leaning over and placing a soft kiss on the corner of my mouth. "I'm always happy when I'm with you, but I have been looking forward to tonight. So, let's go before I drag you home."

She flops back into her seat, securing her seatbelt with a devious smirk and I shift in my seat, spreading my legs to give my hardening cock some much needed breathing room.

She smothers a laugh when I stiffly shift the car into drive and speed down the street, my knuckles white from my grip on the wheel.

"Evil," I whisper.

"Thought I was an angel?"

I glance at her. "You are. You're my angel."

Her cheeks flush pink and she reaches out, placing her hand on my thigh and resting her head against my bicep. We drive down the darkened streets listening to our playlist, Kinsley softly humming along to each song.

When we reach the park, I find an available spot and pull in, turning the car off. Climbing out, I look over the decent sized crowd as people walk around, settling in their spots on the grass.

"Another festival?" Kinsley asks as I help her out of the car and we grab the small bag and blanket I brought along with us.

"Something like that." My lips tilt and she threads our fingers as I lead her through the park to a less populated area on a small hill with a tree.

She looks around at the people situating themselves over the lawn. I watch as it clicks into place when she spots the big screen at the front.

"Oh my gosh. This is that movie in the park thing, isn't it? I've always wanted to come to one of these."

She spins to me and I shuffle on my feet. "I remember

you saying something about how you and Lily were coming to the last one but it got canceled because of rain."

She steps in close, wrapping her arms around my waist. "Thank you."

I cup her face, brushing her hair behind her ear. "Did I do good?"

She presses up on her toes for a kiss, speaking against my lips. "It's perfect. You're perfect."

With one last kiss, we set up our little area. Kinsley unpacks our snacks as I situate myself with my back against the tree.

We have a perfect view of the screen with couples scattered across the lawn all around us. When I saw the announcement a couple days ago, I bought tickets without a second thought.

Hoping that even though she was going to come here with her best friend, she'd still be just as happy if it was with me instead. And as she looks over at me with a smile, I breathe a little easier knowing that I'm the one who put it there.

She sits down next to me and I scoff, reaching for her. She squeals when I pick her up, settling her between my legs and holding her against my chest.

"You could have just asked," she laughs and I nuzzle my face into her neck.

Giggling, she shuffles until she's comfortable and completely relaxes in my arms. Her fingers trace my forearm and I hum, brushing my lips over her shoulder.

"Uh, Jace?"

"Yeah?" I grunt, dotting her neck with kisses.

"Isn't that your sister?"

My head shoots up and I look in the direction she's pointing. "What the—"

Sydney runs over with wide eyes. "I'm so sorry. Apparently they already had tickets to the film and I may have let it slip that you were bringing Kinsley here."

I look around her, and find my mum and dad strutting up the small hill with a blanket and picnic basket under each arm. Mum waves and I raise a hand before glowering up at my little sister.

"You didn't think to keep them on the opposite side of the park from us?"

"They saw you. What was I supposed to do?"

"I don't know. Tell them they're old and seeing things?"

Kinsley's shoulders shake with a laugh and I squeeze her hip, pouting. "Think this is funny, angel? My family crashing our first date?"

She twists to look at me, eyes filled with amusement. "If I remember correctly, this isn't our first date. Your friends tagged along for that one, remember?"

I bark out a laugh as my parents reach us.

"Fancy seeing you here," Mum sing-songs. "Mind if we join?"

I drop my head back against the tree. "If you must."

Kinsley nudges my ribs with her elbow and I lean forward, nipping at her shoulder. "Be nice," she whispers.

Mum glances over at us as her and Dad set up on our

right. I catch her gaze and match her smile, pulling Kinsley closer.

We all settle in for the film and I fail at hiding my jealousy when the girls talk about their mutual love for Hugh Grant. Sydney pokes fun and Kinsley tames the beast with soft touches and short kisses.

The lights around the pathways shut off and we're plunged into darkness, the only visibility coming from the projector screen as the opening airport scene of *Love Actually* plays.

I glance over at my parents, my heart humming when Dad presses his lips to Mum's head as she cuddles into his side. He looks over at me and winks. A chuckle vibrates through my chest and Kinsley burrows deeper into my hold, pulling my arms tighter around her.

For two hours I breathe her in and cuddle into her warmth, stowing away every sigh, giggle, and sniffle that comes from her. And when the end credits roll, I'm nowhere near ready to let go.

"Look," Sydney whispers and we all watch as various couples stand, swaying to the end credits soundtrack.

Mum sighs and Dad gets to his feet. Dusting his pants off, he makes a grand display of holding out his hand for her. "My love."

Mum places her hand over her heart before slipping her hand into his and we watch them walk over to an open area. Her light laugh flits through the air as he twirls her before pulling her into his chest and a small smile tilts my lips as they sway to the music.

"I want a love like that one day." My sister sighs and I glance over at her, a Twizzler hanging from her mouth as she watches our parents.

Kinsley hums. "Doesn't everyone?"

"I think some more than others," she mumbles, looking down at her lap and spinning her worn bracelet around her wrist.

"I do too," I say, my arms instinctively tightening around Kinsley.

For the longest time, I never thought I'd experience love like my parents.

It doesn't help that they set the bar in the stratosphere.

But lord help me, I want it.

I want the love that comes out of nowhere and knocks you on your arse. That doesn't fit societal norms because what you feel is extraordinarily not. Where the timeline doesn't matter because you have forever.

I want the kind of love that feels right without even trying. Where you can be exactly who you are and it'll always be enough. Where the bad days don't stand a chance because they're waiting for you at the end of them. And the good days are made that much better.

I want a love where you fall all over again, every single day.

And as Kinsley lays her head back against my chest, the same girl who's had a chokehold on my every thought from the moment she stumbled into my life, I feel like maybe what I once thought was unreachable, could be mere inches away.

After the screen has gone dark and the music has faded,

we pack up and say goodnight to my family. I turn on the car and Kinsley snuggles into the seat, humming. "Is there anywhere that's open for food? I'm kind of hungry."

"What are you feeling?"

"Spaghetti." My head whips in her direction and she bursts out laughing. "Don't judge me."

"I'm not judging. I'm just—spaghetti?"

She bites her lip and shrugs. "What can I say? I'm a carbs kind of girl."

I chuckle and pull out of the parking spot. "Okay, then. My girl wants spaghetti, we're going to get spaghetti."

CHAPTER 17

JACE

W<small>E END</small> up stopping at the shop, gathering ingredients to make it back at my flat since most places near us were closed.

It's the first time she's been here, but it doesn't feel like it. The moment she walked through the door was the first time there had been any warmth to this large empty space.

She sits at the island, buttering the bread as I stir together the sauce. I glance over my shoulder, eyes roaming over her in my jumper.

Glancing up, she smiles and I tilt my head towards the pot. "Want to come try the sauce?"

She nods, hopping off the stool. "It smells so good."

I hold up the spoon and she leans in. Her head falls back on a moan as she licks her lips. "Oh my god, that's the best thing I've ever put in my mouth."

And now I'm hard. How delightful.

"You should try it," she whispers.

The space between us has dwindled and I swallow when

she shifts on her feet, her chest brushing mine. Her eye's bounce between mine as her tongue slips out, wetting her lips.

And the last of my restraint snaps.

The spoon clatters to the floor and I reach my hands up, threading my fingers through her hair. She lifts onto her toes, throwing her arms over my shoulders as our lips crash.

Her fingers drift to the back of my head and into my hair. I moan into her mouth when she pulls at the thick strands, my tongue diving past her lips. I slip my hand up to her jaw, using the hold to tilt her head.

"You're right. The best thing I've ever tasted," I growl, backing her against the island.

She sucks in a breath when I bend, grabbing her behind her thighs and lifting her onto the cool counter. I straighten, my lips dotting her neck as she throws her head back on a moan.

Her hands come to either side of my face and she dips her head as she pulls me up, capturing my lips. I use my hold on her thighs to pull her to the edge as I step forward. The height of the counter lines us up perfectly and a growl rumbles in my chest when she rolls her hips.

I pull back. "You better stop doing that if you don't want this to go any farther."

She looks at me, breathing heavily. "Who says I don't want it to?"

Dropping my forehead to hers, I try to gain control of the need pulsing through me. "Kinsley," I sigh.

Her fingers trace my lips. "Jace."

I pull back and my eyes dance between hers as I try to calm my racing heart. "Are you sure?"

She tucks her bottom lip between her teeth and nods.

"I need your words if this is going to happen, angel."

"Yes," she whispers, leaning forward and brushing her lips across mine. "I want you." She pulls back slightly, her hands drifting across my chest and over my shoulders. "All of you." She rolls her hips, her warmth rubbing against me and I groan.

Her squeal pierces the air when I throw her over my shoulder and lightly slap her arse. She laughs, pulling at my shirt as I round the island. "Wait, the food!"

I pivot, using one hand to hold her and the other to pull the pots off the stove and shut everything down before I all but run to the bedroom. I kick my door closed and walk over to the bed, dipping my shoulder.

She falls onto her back with a giggle, her chocolate hair spilling over my sheets.

"What do you want, sweetheart?"

"You."

I drop over her, bracing myself up with a hand on either side of her head. Leaning in, I whisper against her ear, "You want me to fuck you?"

Her choppy breath fans over my neck and I feel her nod as she grips my sides.

Pulling back, I make sure I have her attention. "Words, remember? Don't get shy on me now, angel. Tell me what you want."

She licks her lips. "I want you to make me feel good."

I lean back slightly and rip my shirt over my head, reveling in the way her eyes heat. "How do you want me to make you feel good, sweetheart? With my cock?" I lean back over her, pressing my hips against her center and she moans.

"Or with my fingers?" I trail my fingers up her thigh.

"Or with my mouth?" I capture her mouth, my tongue diving between lips.

She presses up, seeking the friction and I pull away. "What will it be?"

"All the above?" she rushes out through a gasp and I chuckle.

"What my girl wants, she gets." I lean down, taking her mouth.

Her fingers dig into my back and I pull away. Slipping my hands under the hem of the jumper she's wearing. Pausing, I look at her and she nods. Sitting up, she helps me pull it over her head and I groan.

"You weren't wearing anything under that this whole time?"

"You told me to make myself comfortable."

I shake my head and dip down, taking her perfectly rose colored peak into my mouth. She sucks in a breath, her fingers diving into my hair as I move to the other one.

She shivers as I brush my fingers down her stomach, our eyes meeting when I reach the button of her shorts.

"May I?"

"Yes," she whispers and I smile against her skin.

She lifts her hips as I pull down the denim and her

panties in one go. My mouth instantly waters at the sight of her and I trail my lips up her leg.

"This okay?"

"No one's ever..." she trails off, her legs twitching over my shoulders.

"I don't have to—"

"Please," she rushes out, her hips pushing up with her plea.

I chuckle darkly, pressing my lips to just above her center. "You'll never have to beg with me, sweetheart, but it sounds damn good on your lips."

She throws her head back on a moan at the first swipe of my tongue. Her fingers twist in my hair and I wrap my arms under her legs, draping them over my shoulders.

Her quick breaths and quiet moans fill the room as I flick my tongue over her clit before teasing her entrance. I press forward and her legs tighten around my head as she looks down, eyebrows furrowed and lips parted.

I hold her stare as I fuck her with my tongue, my fingers leaving indents on her thighs from the force of holding her against me.

"Oh fuck. I think I'm going to—" She throws her head back and I drink in her release.

I ease her through the aftershocks and kiss my way up her body, sealing my mouth over hers. She wraps her arms around my shoulders, her tongue tangling with mine as I swallow her moans.

Pressing at my chest, she follows as I push off the bed and stand, slipping to her knees in front of me.

"Kinsley, you don't have to—"

"I want to," she cuts me off, her finger teasing the hem of my jeans as her eyes hold mine. "Teach me how?" She slips the button out and pulls down my zipper. "Please?"

I growl and she smiles, pulling my jeans and briefs down. I step out of them and her lips part as I wrap my fist around my hard cock, pumping once.

"Open." I step closer, brushing the head against her lips and she obeys.

Her tongue sticks out, sliding against the underside as I slowly press forward. I swear I stop breathing all together as her lips wrap around me. My fingers slip into her hair and I guide her head up and down with each of my shallow thrusts.

Gaining confidence, she takes me farther and gags, eyes watering. I go to pull back but she hums, reaching up and wrapping a hand around me while the other digs her nails into my arse.

"Fuck, that's it," I manage to say as she works me over. "Just like that."

Her fist works in tandem with her mouth until I'm at the brink and I pull out of her mouth completely. She sucks in quick breaths, looking up at me with confusion. "Why—"

"I'm not going to last much longer if you keep doing that."

I pull her up, cupping her face and capturing her mouth. She hums against my lips and slides her hand between us, pumping my aching cock.

I growl, walking her backwards and we tumble onto the bed. I slip my hand under her back and shift her up farther as I climb between her legs.

She wraps her leg over my hip, pressing up with the other as she pulls me down. We hiss when the head of my cock rubs against her soaking center.

"Did sucking my cock make you this wet?"

"No, it's just you. All of you."

My eyes dance between hers and I reach into the night table, grabbing a condom. She watches as I roll it on and fit myself between her legs.

I lean down, resting my forehead against hers. "Are you sure?"

"I'm sure," she whispers against my lips before pulling me into a deep kiss.

I press my hips forward and my whole world—everything —shatters.

Fuck. Me. Nothing will ever compare to this. To her.

She gasps into my mouth when I bottom out and I clench my jaw at how tight she's wrapped around me. I pull back and look down to see her face scrunched. *Fuck.* "Are you okay?"

"Big," she says and I huff a laugh.

"Careful, sweetheart. You'll give a guy a complex."

She laughs, opening her eyes and her hands trace over my back. Licking her lips, she leans up, kissing me softly. I lean into her touch, soaking up every second of this moment. Every part of her that she allows me to have.

I pull back my hips slightly before pressing in and she mewls into my mouth. The kiss deepens as I move faster, her legs coming up to wrap over my hips and nails scoring my back.

My hand slips between us and she whimpers, hands dropping to fist the sheets.

"I'm going to—"

"Me too," I grit out, slamming into her.

The room fills with the sounds of our moans and bodies coming together. She screams out my name as she comes and I groan, giving myself completely to her.

I pump into her once, twice, coming with her name on my lips.

Dropping my head to her shoulder I suck in greedy breaths as her fingers tickle my back. Pulling out, I roll, taking her with me.

I tighten my arm around her as she kisses my chest, my heart threatening to beat out of my chest. She snuggles into my side, resting her hand over my chest, her leg slung over my hips.

Our breathing evens out and she tilts her head to look up at me. I reach over and tuck a strand of hair, brushing my thumb over her cheek.

"Are you okay, sweetheart?"

She hums. "Better than okay." She turns her head, kissing my palm. "I'm perfect."

Yeah. You are.

CHAPTER 18

KINSLEY

Soft light streams through the bedroom's curtains.

Jace's bedroom.

Oh my god. I'm in Jace's bedroom. In his bed.

I snuggle into my pillow, my face heating at the memory of last night.

It was perfect.

He was perfect.

The arm around my middle tightens and I smile as his lips brush the back of my neck. He cuddles into me and I giggle, rolling in his arms until we're face to face.

"Hi," I whisper.

He blinks at me sleepily. "Hi."

Dear lord, can I get a recording of his 'I just woke up' gravelly voice?

He leans in, softly brushing his lips against mine. Humming, he settles his forehead against mine. "How are you feeling?"

I nuzzle into his warmth. "I'm perfect. How about you?"

"Stunning." He kisses my forehead, speaking against my skin. "Absolutely stunning."

I slip my hand between us and trace patterns over his chest. "When do you leave?"

He sighs, his arms tightening around me. "Tomorrow morning. They want us there a day early for a mini media day since we've been off this past week."

I hum, nodding and we settle into a comfortable silence. I go to lean back to see if he's fallen back asleep, but he speaks quietly as his hand pulses on my hip, "So, I was thinking."

My fingers pause, my heart stopping.

What did you expect, Kinsley? Did you really think someone like him would actually want anything more with someone like you?

He got what he wanted.

And you gave it willingly. Happily even.

Foolish girl.

I shrink away but he tightens his arms around me, pulling me back against him and cupping my face. "Hey, hey. Sweetheart, what's wrong?"

I shake my head, tears threatening to spill. "It's okay, I understand."

His eyebrows dip. "Understand what?"

"You're this big time race car driver and I'm no one—"

"Wait. Kinsley. No. That's not—"

"It's okay. Really. I—"

"Kinsley, look at me."

My eyes shoot up at the pleading in his voice and I pause

157

at the softness in his gaze. He's looking at me as if he's afraid I'll disappear. Like his whole world would come crumbling down if I turned away.

But maybe that's just me who feels this way.

He tucks my wild hair behind my ear, his thumb brushing my cheek as he speaks softly. "I want you to come with me."

My eyebrows furrow in confusion. "What?"

Leaning in, he places a delicate kiss on my lips before speaking against them. "I want you to come with me."

My mind reels as my mouth pops open and closed multiple times before I get a single word out. "W-why?"

"Because the idea of leaving you tomorrow makes me ill."

"You're not serious."

"I am." His voice doesn't waver and his eyes don't stray from mine as he says it. "I told you we'd figure out what to do and we will, together. So come with me. *Be* with me." He leans down and kisses my shoulder. "It'll be an adventure."

"Jace. I—" Emotion overwhelms me and my mind scrambles.

He wants me.

"You don't have to decide right now. I know it's a lot to think about and I know it's crazy, but I believe in this. I believe in us." His thumb swipes over my cheek. "I'll respect whatever you decide."

I nod, tears threatening to spill as he pulls me tight against his chest.

And as his fingers trace along my back, I let myself fall.

―――――

"Did you hear anything I just said?"

I look up. "Hm?"

Lily laughs. "I'll take that as a no."

Sighing, I set down my fork. "I'm sorry. My mind is kind of a mess right now."

She pinches her lips. "Jace leaves tomorrow?"

I nod. "But it's not just that." I take a steadying breath. "I haven't told you this because you were so excited about the program in the States—"

"Kins, what's going on?"

"Fred and Rebecca are kicking me out. I have one more week to figure something out before their new placement gets here."

Her jaw drops in shock. "You've got to be joking."

"I'm not." I shake my head. "I knew this day was coming but I thought I had a little more time to think of where to go, what to do."

She pauses, a sly smile blooming on her lips. "What if you came with me?"

Come with me.

Jace's voice echoes in my mind and my cheeks heat. Then her words register. "Wait. Go where with you?"

She grins. "America."

I gasp. "You got in?"

"I got in," she squeals.

I jump up and pull her into a hug, cheering her on. She

pushes me back gently and waves a hand through the air. "I don't want to make this about me."

"Lily, we're absolutely going to make this about you. Congratulations." I pull her into another bone crushing hug.

"You're not mad?"

"Why would I be mad?"

"Because first Jace is leaving and now I am too."

We sit back down and I shake my head. "I'm nowhere near mad. I'm so incredibly happy for you. You earned this."

"So then what if you came with me? And then when we got back, we could get a little flat just like we always talked about."

I sigh. "You know I can't do that. Your program is pretty strict, remember?"

She deflates into her chair. "Maybe they'd make an exception?"

"I don't want you risking your spot for me. I'd never forgive myself if I cost you this."

"Then what are you going to do?"

I duck my head, mumbling, "Jace asked me to go with him."

She shoots forward in her chair. "I'm sorry. Rewind and repeat that. Who said what?"

My lips twitch. "Jace asked me to go with him. To *be* with him."

Her mouth drops open. "Oh my god. How did I not see this until now? You slept with him."

My face drops in disbelief. "How on earth did you figure that?"

"Look at you, you've totally got that post sex glow going on. Was it good? Oh, please tell me he's got a filthy mou—"

"Lily," I hiss, glancing at the tables around us. "Can you not?"

"I'm sorry. I'm just surprised, is all. I mean, not surprised per say. I'm more proud." She nods. "Yeah, I'm proud of you for getting that D."

I sink into my chair, covering my face. "I can't with you sometimes."

She laughs. "Well, I'm guessing it was good if he's asking you to travel the world with him?"

I roll my lips, but a smile slips through. "It was amazing."

She squeals, hopping around in her chair. "So what did you say?"

"I didn't know what to say."

"So you just said nothing?"

"He laid it all out. Said that I'd be with him and he would take care of everything, but that he understood if I couldn't let myself rely on him completely like that. So, he made some calls and said the team would gladly take me on as a photographer. Apparently he showed them some of the shots I got from Silverstone and they really liked them."

"Kinsley, that sounds amazing."

"I know it does." I sigh. "But it's also a lot."

"Yeah, it is. What would you do if you stayed here?"

"I've got a good amount in the bank from Friday's showing. I could probably find a small place to stay while I looked for a job."

"That's a lot to take on by yourself."

I shrug. "People do it all the time."

"But you don't have to." She reaches across the table, taking my hand. "He makes you happy, doesn't he?" I nod. "Then come on."

She pulls me out of my chair, drops some money on the table, and drags me to her car. Before I know it, we're pulling up outside my house and I'm stumbling after her up the stairs to my room.

We spend the rest of the evening going through everything I own, deciding what I should take, have her keep for me, or things I should try and sell.

By the time the clock on the night table reads just past midnight, I have two fully packed bags and a box of other small things that Lily is taking home with her to keep safe while I'm away.

We yawn for what feels like the hundredth time and she stands, brushing off her hands. "I think that's it."

I zip the bag closed and roll it over to the door. Turning, I face her and she smiles. We meet in the middle, wrapping our arms around each other in a crushing hug.

She sniffles. "You better message me every single day."

"I promise."

We separate and she runs her hand over my hair. "Just go and be happy. You deserve it."

"You too. I know you're going to crush it."

"I'm going to make that program my bitch."

"I have no doubt." I wipe away a tear as we laugh.

"I love you, Kinsley."

"I love you, Lily."

With one last hug, the girl I've long considered my sister walks out the door. I watch her drive away from my bedroom window, rear lights fading into the dark night.

Turning, I look over the small room I've called mine for the past year. I walk over and sit on the bed, tucking my hands into the sleeves of Jace's jumper. Pulling out my phone, my thumb hovers over his name.

I roll my lips and glance at my bags.

Would it be too much to just show up at his flat at one in the morning?

My phone pings in my hand with a text.

ROMEO:

You have all the power, Miss Jones.

Fuck it.

I bound off the bed, snatch up my backpack, and extend the handle on my suitcase. I write a note thanking the Munsters' for everything, wishing them luck with their next placement and hoping that it's everything they didn't find with me.

I close the door, locking the handle before I do since I left my key on the counter, and with my bag rolling behind me, I walk the couple blocks to the bus stop.

The next one should be here in ten minutes, so I pull out my small digital camera and scroll through some of the images I took yesterday.

"This seat taken?" I jump clutching my chest and the girl winces. "I'm so sorry, I didn't mean to scare you."

I laugh. "It's okay, I just didn't think anyone would be up right now."

She takes a seat next to me and nods to my suitcase. "Going on a trip?"

I nod. "Something like that."

Her eyes glance down to my hands, freezing on the screen. "Cute guy. Boyfriend?"

I hum, shutting off the camera before tucking it back into my bag. A feeling of protectiveness over him pulses through me.

"I'm sorry. My boyfriend says I'm too nosy for my own good sometimes."

I shift in my seat. "I have a friend like that too. It's okay."

Her eyes move over my shoulder and I turn, seeing headlights.

I guess the bus is running early.

I stand up and slip on my bag, grabbing the handle of my suitcase. Stepping up to the edge of the curb I catch a glimpse of the bus sign, sighing when I realize it's not mine.

"Kinsley."

I whip around with wide eyes to see the girl standing close. The sound of the oncoming bus gets louder and I open my mouth to ask her how she knows my name.

But I never get the chance.

CHAPTER 19
FOUR MONTHS LATER

SYDNEY

Dust coats my fingertips as I run them over the fireplace mantel.

"It's been ages since we've been here." I look over as Jace walks through the front door, carrying collapsed boxes under his arms with Mum and Dad behind him.

He looks around the room silently as he comes to stand by me. I bump my shoulder into his. "Remember when you and Lawson used to slide down the stairs on our sleds? The one time you let me join, we crashed so hard at the bottom and I broke my arm."

"I was grounded for months." I revel in that small smile while it lasts before he slides back on the stoic mask he's been wearing for months. "I'm going to start upstairs."

Without another word, he disappears. Mum comes over and rubs my shoulder before heading into the kitchen. I sigh and look around the family room one last time before I grab a bag and start to clean up.

The day passes with boxes packed, surfaces wiped down, and silent passings from my brother. By the time the sun starts to set, we're finishing up the last room.

I eye a package in the back of one of the closets and pull it out.

"What's this?" I ask as I rip the paper off.

"Wait. Darling, don't," Mum calls out from the other side of the room but it's too late. The paper falls, revealing a black and white image of Jace looking up at the sky, floating lanterns surrounding him.

Kinsley.

My eyes shoot to where my brother stands, staring at the portrait. Mum rushes over and covers it. "I'm so sorry. I forgot I was going to hang it here."

His jaw ticks and he looks away. "It's okay." I scoff and his head whips up. "Do you have something you want to say?"

I move to clear off a shelf. "Nope."

"Are you sure? Because it seems like you have something to get off your chest?"

Mum shakes her head, but I glance down at the photo. The paper slips and a sliver of Jace's face peeks through.

"Don't you ever wonder?"

"Wonder what, Syd?" he asks.

My eyes meet his. "Why she didn't show up?"

"I don't want to talk about this."

"No. You haven't for four months, Jace. But we all see it!"

"See what?"

"You're heartbroken," I huff, my chest rising and falling on quick breaths. "You've always worn your heart on your sleeve and right now it's in pieces."

His jaw ticks and I throw my arms out.

"I miss my brother! I miss the guy who would spell out inappropriate things with the peas on his dinner plate. I miss our twice a week FaceTime calls where we see who can make Lawson freak out the fastest. I miss your smile and laugh because no matter what's going on, it makes me feel better. I miss you."

Tears fall down my cheeks and I watch his eyes glisten. "You haven't been the same in months. Ever since..." I trail off and his head drops. "I know a lot happened that day and we've given you time to work through it, but you don't have to go through all of this alone. We are here. I am here." My chest heaves. "I'm ready to have my best friend back."

He looks back up at me and my heart shatters as a tear rolls down his cheek. "I don't know what to do," he whispers.

"Talk to us," I plead.

He collapses onto the small leather loveseat, his head in his hands. I rush over and sit next to him, wrapping my arms around his shaking shoulders.

"It wasn't supposed to be this way."

I press my cheek against his shoulder. "I'm so sorry, J."

"I thought she felt the same."

"Why haven't you reached out to her?" I ask.

"I've wanted to—"

"What's stopping you?"

"Because I told her I'd respect whatever it is she decided." His eyes are overflowing with tears when they meet mine. "Too many people have gone back on their word with her. I wasn't going to be one of them."

"Jace—"

"Does it really matter now anyway?"

"You don't think she would've stayed?" Mum asks, sitting down in the chair across from us.

"I don't think I would have made her. This would be too much for anyone." He huffs a tired laugh. "Hell, I'm barely holding my head above water as it is."

"You're not alone though. Let us in, Jace."

He smiles sadly at me. "Sydney, you're just a kid yourself—"

"Which makes me practically an expert on what they like right?"

Chuckling, he leans back and wraps an arm around my shoulders. "Remember what you needed as a babe, then?"

"Pfft." I wave him off. "That's what home videos are for."

"Great idea. I'll watch and then do the opposite so I have a chance at them not turning out like you."

"Hey! You'd be lucky for her to turn out like me."

"Could be a boy," he smirks and I groan.

"Lord help us if there's a mini Jace Collins running around." I point at him. "As long as they don't turn out like their mum, you'll be golden."

Mum tsks. "Sydney, be nice. Angie's carrying your nephew."

"That was me being nice." *To the universe.*

Jace huffs a laugh, shaking his head and I bump my knee into his. "Seriously, though. You're going to be an amazing dad."

"Had a pretty good role model for the job." He looks up at our old man in the doorway.

Dad's jaw ticks and he sniffles. Mum smiles at him and he walks over, placing his hand on her shoulder. "Whatever you need, my boy. We're here."

"Thank you." He glances at me. "All of you."

My lips tip up. "No more closing in on yourself okay? They say it takes a village."

His chuckle dies off as his eyes move to the picture and Mum stands. "I can just get rid—"

"Wait." Jace cuts her off. "Just put it in the closet for now."

"Are you sure?"

He nods, eyes frozen on the covered picture. "I'm not ready to fully let go yet."

"Okay," she whispers, moving the frame into the closet.

He watches her the entire time and I see the longing in his eyes even when the door closes.

That image plays over in my head as Mum, Dad, and I head home. Jace opted to stay up at the country house—wait, I guess it's *his* house now.

After he came home from his race in Hungary, he sat us down, telling us two things. Things with Kinsley had ended. And he was going to be a father.

Apparently his—pardon my French—bitch of an ex had been trying to talk to him for weeks. In his defense, I also wouldn't give the person I walked in cheating on me any of my time either.

At first, he didn't believe it.

None of us did.

So, he asked for a DNA test which she surprisingly agreed to.

Two weeks later, we had the results... and a new Collins to go with it.

The revelation rocked his world for the second time in less than three weeks.

But this one had a bitter sweetness to it.

The first one came with heartbreak.

I saw him with Kinsley. I saw what was blooming between them. It was something that comes around once in a lifetime. Which is why I couldn't understand why she would just disappear on him.

I can't shake the feeling that if she could, she would be here, right by his side because that's just who she is. She's always there for the ones she cares about and damnit, I know she cared for him like no one before.

My heart races as I pick up my phone later that night, everything he said and everything I know playing through my mind. I navigate to my contacts and click on the name I hope will lead to answers.

The phone rings, and I twist my bracelet as nerves flood my body.

"Hello?" She picks up on the fifth ring.

"Lily? It's Sydney. Can we talk?"

GROUP MESSAGE

P.I. DUDE:

Good afternoon, Miss Collins and Miss Campbell.

LILY:

You better have something good for us Reggie or I swear to god the next missing person someone goes looking for will be YOU.

SYDNEY:

And she'll do it too.

P.I. DUDE:

Well then I'm very happy to report that I've found your girl.

LILY:

You better not be messing with us.

P.I. DUDE:

I'm not really a 'messing' kind of guy.

SYDNEY:

Give us the damn information then! Where is she?!

P.I. DUDE:

There are some things you need to know first.

PART TWO

EIGHT YEARS LATER

CHAPTER 20

KINSLEY

WHY DO I feel like there's something I'm forgetting?

It's something important—I know it is.

But what is it?

I watch the sun rise as my mind wanders, the rays glittering across the shop's green checkered floor and pastel pink walls.

I love this place.

It's been my home for the last eight years.

It's been my saving grace.

So is the woman who owns it.

When I met Rose all those years ago, I was lost, confused, and in desperate need of a purpose. She was coming from her yearly checkup when she saw me sitting at the bus stop, the rain soaking through the meager clothes I had on.

I still remember her standing over me, an umbrella blocking out the downpour. Her wrinkled face as she asked me where I was headed. I told her that I didn't know and she watched me for a moment before telling me to grab my things.

Wordlessly I followed her to her car and we drove an hour outside of London. Not once did she ask me about my story or pepper me with questions about what I was doing there.

When we got to the small town of Stratford-upon-Avon, she pulled up to a coffee shop and climbed out of the car. I followed her as she unlocked the front door and strode into the kitchen.

She made us each a warm cup of hot chocolate and brought out ingredients for what she called her world famous moose track scones. For hours she showed me recipe after recipe, until the countertops were littered with baked goods.

I spent the rest of the day helping her in her coffee shop and when the open sign was flipped to closed and all the lights were shut off, she led me to the back staircase that went up to a small two bedroom flat.

Tears sprang to my eyes the moment she placed the keys in my hand.

"Why are you doing this?" I sniffled.

"Because I too was once a young lass with nowhere to go." She smiled and patted my hand.

I don't know where I'd be if it wasn't for her. If I hadn't been sitting at that stop, or she hadn't come out of her appointment in time, or if it hadn't been raining.

I don't necessarily believe in fate, but every time I wake up and come down to this coffee shop, I believe in it a little bit more.

I take a deep breath and turn, my eyes roaming over the small tables sprinkled throughout, the shelves filled with donated books, and the pastry display case I'll need to fill up.

I still feel like I'm forgetting something and the thought follows me as I walk into the kitchen and begin prepping all the pastries we'll feature today.

When the last batch of cookies is put in the oven, I grab the flowers I picked up yesterday from the market and walk out to the dining area. After each table gets a refresh, I go to the front door and unlock it, flipping the sign to open.

This has been my routine every morning since I started working at Rosebuds, making sure to open promptly at six so those who commute to the city still have enough time to stop in for their fix before tackling the drive in.

The quiet streets are painted in the morning glow and I take a deep breath, reveling in the peace of it all.

There's nothing like the stillness of a calm morning.

I've just walked into the kitchen when the bell above the front door rings, soft footfalls echoing soon after.

"Welcome to the Rosebud, I'll be out in just a second," I call out as I hurry to put the batch of scones in the oven. Swiping a cloth from the counter, I wipe my hands as I push through the swinging doors. "Sorry about that, I just had to— oh, hi. You came back."

The petite blonde with blue eyes smiles. "I did. It's the scones. I swear they were all I could think about for days."

"You're in luck. I just put a fresh batch in the oven."

"You say the sweetest things to me."

The quiet shop fills with our laughter. "What can I get you?"

"I'll take a caramel macchiato with extra whipped cream and caramel drizzle and..."

"One of the moose track scones?"

She laughs. "Make that two. I'll take one with me for later."

After I ring her up, I get to work on her drink. I glance over at her as she walks around, taking in the photos on the walls and grazing the book selections, before settling in at the table in the corner.

"This place is so cute," she says as I set down her drink. "I love the pictures over there." She nods to the photos hanging behind the pastry display.

My lips tip up. "Those are actually mine."

"Really? They're amazing."

There's three of them. All black and white. One is of Rose as she rolls out dough, flour coating her apron. The second is of the sunrise through the shop's windows, the individual rays visible over the empty space. And the last is of the shop's storefront.

I hum. "It's just a hobby, but Rose surprised me with hanging some of them up one day saying it was a right shame for them to collect dust on a computer."

"Well, I have to agree with the wise woman. They're amazing."

I smile. "Thank you. I can't take credit for the rest, though. That's all Rose." I wave a hand around the shop.

"Is she the owner?"

I nod. "Yeah. She's a sweet old bat with a heart of gold—"

"And the mind of a thirteen year old boy," a weathered voice calls out as the front door opens with a chime and a small blur of brown hair rushes in.

"Mummy!"

I bend, scooping him up and peppering his face with kisses. "Hi, my sweet baby."

"I'm not a baby," he declares, scowling.

"Oh, is that right?"

He nods. "I can go potty all by myself now. Babies can't do that."

I giggle. "When you're right, you're right." I look at Rose. "I thought you wouldn't be here until later."

She stares at me with a not-very-surprised expression. "You forgot."

"No. No, I didn't." *I totally did.* "But maybe you can just confirm what I'm thinking?"

She chuckles, shaking her head. "I have that doctor's—"

"Appointment this morning, of course. See, I didn't forget."

She hums. "It shouldn't take long. I'll come get this little rascal right after."

"Granny says she's going to make spaghetti and mega meatballs tonight for dinner."

I laugh, tickling his sides. He giggles, his eyes sliding to the side. "Do you like spaghetti and mega meatballs too?"

I turn to the girl, her wide eyes bouncing between us. She blinks, shaking her head slightly before smiling. "I do love spaghetti, but I don't think I've ever had *mega* meatballs."

179

"Mega balls are my mummy's favorite."

My eyes widen as the girl coughs and Rose bursts out laughing.

"Okay, on that note. Run upstairs and get your coloring book. Looks like you're hanging out here until Gran gets back."

"Can I have a cookie?"

"Dude, it's like six thirty in the morning."

"But it's got oats in it and that's a breakfast food."

"He's got you there," Rose snickers.

"We'll see. Now go."

He takes off for the back stairs and I shake my head. The timer goes off on the oven and I excuse myself, heading into the kitchen.

I take a deep breath of the delicious chocolate and toasted marshmallow smell of the scones and package three up. When I walk back out, Rose is helping my son set up at the table just off to the side of the stairs.

I drop a cookie in front of him and he cheers, thanking me as I kiss his head.

"Here you are, I threw in an extra scone for you."

I set the bag of sweets on the table. The girl thanks me quietly, her blue eyes casted to the side where they sit. "You have a beautiful son."

I glance over my shoulder and smile. "Best thing to ever happen to me."

"How old is he? I have a nephew that looks about the same age."

"Cooper's six."

"Cooper?"

"Yeah." I laugh remembering the day he was born. "He actually didn't have a name when I first gave birth. It took me two days to figure it out. But one night I had a dream and when I woke up, 'Cooper' was all I could think about." She watches me, her mouth parted and I sigh. "I'm sorry, I don't know why I just said all of that."

"No. No. It's okay. My brother kind of did the same thing. He tried out all these different names, literally yelling around the house 'Jameson, you get your arse in that bath right now' or 'Freddie, you better not be drinking from the dogs bowl again.'"

I burst out laughing. "That's definitely one way to do it."

"None of them ever sounded right. He was also very paranoid about nicknames."

"I didn't even think about that."

"Oh trust me, my brother thought of it all. Drove our parents up the wall."

"Sounds like you two are close."

Her smile dims and she nods. "Yeah, he's the best big brother in the world and is one of my best friends, even if he can be annoying at times."

"That's what siblings are for though, right? Built in best friends?"

"Yeah, I guess so."

Her phone rings and she quickly puts it away. Standing up, she grabs her stuff and looks up at the pictures behind the pastry box one last time. "If you ever want to make that more than a hobby, I know someone who is looking for a photographer. It isn't scenery stuff like that, but I have a feeling you'd really enjoy it."

"She's interested," Rose calls out. She quirks a brow, patting Cooper's head and walking over to us, taking the offered card. "I've alway told her that she needed to do something with photography—"

"But you need me here."

"I can hire people to be here and you know it."

I open my mouth but she cuts me off. "You are meant for more than just this shop, Kinsley. Just promise me you'll think about it?"

I sigh, glancing up at the pictures before focusing back on her. "Fine."

She smiles. "Good. Whatever happens, we'll get through it. As long as my babies are happy, I'm happy." She pinches my cheek and I laugh.

"Now, I've got to go. You get all the information from this beautiful young lady and tonight, we'll put together whatever we need for the application. Okay?"

"Have I ever told you how bossy you are?"

"You love me."

"I do."

She hugs me and gives Cooper a kiss on his head before heading out the door. I do what I'm told and get all the information for the job, writing down the web address and what the general idea of my duties would be.

I'm hesitant when she says there will be a lot of travel, but Rose's words echo through my mind. If this is meant to be, we'll figure something out and just take it one day at a time.

Twenty minutes, and two interruptions from Cooper to give his new friend a drawing, later, we finish up and she checks her watch.

"I have to go or I'll really be late for a meeting at work, but here's my personal phone number if you have any more questions."

I take the pink napkin with her number. "Thank you."

"It's like Rose said, Kinsley." She shoulders her bag. "You were always meant for something more than just this."

I hum, glancing around the shop.

"It was nice meeting you, Cooper." He waves at her and she walks to the door.

I blink, stepping forward. "I'm sorry, I don't think I ever caught your name."

Turning back, she smiles. "Sydney. My name's Sydney."

CHAPTER 21

JACE

"Beckham! Come on, my man, I have to go," I yell, sighing when he comes running to the top of the stairs in only his shorts and socks.

"I can't find my shoe."

"Why wasn't it with your other one?"

"I don't know."

"Okay. Okay. Just finished getting dressed, mate, and I'll help look for your shoe."

"Knock, knock," Sydney calls out as she walks through the front door. "I brought goodies!"

I groan at the sight of a large pink bag and a tray of coffees in her hands. "You're my favorite sister ever."

She snorts. "I'm your only sister."

I take the bag and coffees from her, moving into the kitchen. The lingering sleep drains from my system the moment the sweetness of the scone hits my tongue.

"Good god, I needed this," I moan.

"Please refrain from making your sex noises in front of innocent ears."

"Who's innocent here? Because I know you aren't talking about yourself."

She scowls. "See if I ever bring you another scone from there again."

"Wait." I jump over and wrap my arm around her shoulders. "You know I'm just kidding. I'll keep my noises in my head from now on, deal?"

"Thank you." She claps her hands together and tilts her head back, yelling, "Where is my favorite little man in the whole universe?"

Little feet thunder above us and down the stairs as Beckham screeches, "Auntie Sydney."

She swoops down and flips him over, holding him upside down by his legs. "Dude, why do you only have one shoe on?"

I chuckle, grabbing the largest coffee and my car keys. "Okay, I should be back by dinner at the latest. Should I assume you'll be joining us?"

She nods, putting Becks back on his feet. "Yep. If you're going to be late, just text me and I'll cook so you don't have to worry about it when you get back." I grimace and she scowls. "You burn dinner one—"

"It was Easter dinner, Syd."

"Lawson was supposed to set the timer!"

I pat her head. "Now, now. It's not fair to place blame on the man when he's not here to defend himself."

She scoffs and I ruffle Beckham's hair. "So what are you doing today anyway? Not that I'll ever complain about having to hang out with my main man." She wraps her arms around Beckham's shoulders, shaking them.

"Mitch called in a team meeting to introduce some of the new members before everything for the season gets underway."

She stands up straight, face paling. "Wait, t-that's today?"

My eyebrows furrow. "Yeah, it's today. That's why you're here."

She laughs nervously. "Obviously."

"You okay there, kid?"

She scoffs, fiddling with her bracelet. "I'm peachy. Grand, even."

I chuckle. "Okay, you weirdo. I'm out of here. Call if you need anything, okay?"

She hums and I head for the door.

"Jace," Sydney calls out as I'm one foot over the threshold.

"Syd, I'm already running late—"

"I know I just..." she trails off, staring.

When she doesn't say anything more, I shake my head and point at Beckham. "Be good for your aunt, and find that shoe."

He sends me off with a salute and I close the door as my sister grumbles to herself.

The forty-five minute drive to headquarters flies by and I barely have the car parked before I'm springing out of it.

Fumbling with my keys, I throw open the door and jog down the hallway. I wave to some of the crew members as I pass and round the last corner that leads to the larger meeting rooms.

My head is down as I check my phone so I'm not watching where I'm going and the next thing I know a small body collides with my chest.

I hiss when the hot liquid of my coffee spills over my hand and a muffled squeak leaves the person as they bounce off my chest, sprawling out on the floor.

"Shit, are you okay?"

"I'm so sorry!"

Everything slows at the sound of her voice and I pinch my eyes closed as awareness skitters down my spine. It could be five hundred years and I'd still know the sound of her voice by heart.

But this isn't her.

This can't be her.

Slowly, I open my eyes and my heart stops when she tilts her head back, golden-brown eyes meeting mine with a mix of embarrassment and worry.

"Kinsley," I whisper under my breath.

I don't think she hears my broken word, her attention drawing to the belongings scattered around her as confirmation. She glances back up at me, her gaze freezing on my chest.

A sense of déjà vu rolls over me as she grimaces. "Oh god. Your shirt. I'm so sorry."

"What?" I ask in a daze and look down. Sure enough, what little was left of my coffee is splattered across the front of my shirt. "Oh. It's, uh, it's okay."

The words come out numb as my mind races.

She climbs to her feet and my eyes drop to the floor. Squatting, I swipe up the employee pass and trace my thumb over her picture.

What? How? This—this can't be happening.

I stand up and hand her the pass. She sucks in a breath and my fingers tingle when hers brush over them as she takes the plastic.

"Oh my god. Thank you. Last thing I need to do is lose that on my first day." She laughs, slipping the lanyard around her neck before looking up at me with a smile.

I've thought about this moment more times than I can count over the past eight years. Ever since she didn't show up to the airport.

I thought about what I would say.

What she would say.

What we would do.

I pictured our eyes meeting across a crowded room and the seas parting until she was in my arms. My hands would frame her face as I told her I loved her and have been waiting for her.

She would kiss me softly like she always did when words got to be too much and we would defy the odds of finding our way back to each other.

I'd tell her that I kept my promise to respect her decision, even though it killed me little by little every day since. And that eventually the hole she left in my heart—in my life— dwindled, but never truly disappeared.

I don't think my love for her ever did either.

Because as I stand here with her mere inches in front of me, my heart races, my hands twitch with the need to reach out for her, and my mind screams at me to say something. Anything.

Angel.

Her eyebrows furrow. "What?"

Wait.

I shake my head, her hesitant tone splintering my daze. I take her in, all of her. She looks the same, if not even more beautiful than the last time I saw her. Her dark brown hair flows down her back in waves, her delicate features perfect in every way.

But it's the lack of recognition in her eyes that has my knees threatening to buckle.

My heart twists painfully when she shuffles on her feet.

"N-nothing," I whisper brokenly.

She opens her mouth to say something but someone shouts down the hallway, pulling her attention. I reluctantly look past her as Lawson jogs down the hall.

"Jace," he calls out, his steps slowing when Kinsley fully turns towards him. He stumbles to a stop, his eyes flicking between the two of us.

She waves shyly at him and he nods, his face frozen in a state of bewilderment.

I clear my throat and he looks away from her, his dark eyes locking with mine. I shake my head subtly and his jaw ticks before he jerks his head down the hall. "Everyone's in the big room already. Mitch sent me to find you."

"Yeah. I'll be right there."

His eyes linger before he nods and heads back down the hall.

Kinsley turns back to me, her fingers fiddling with the hem of her team branded polo. "Sorry, I just realized I didn't introduce myself. I'm Kinsley. Kinsley Jones."

My entire being ignites when I wrap my hand around her offered one. "Jace. Jace Collins."

My throat tightens and she laughs nervously. "Yeah, I—uh—I'm friends with your sister. Well I guess friends is kind of a stretch, but—"

I blink. "Wait, you know Sydney?"

"She's come into the coffee shop I work at a couple times over the past few weeks. She saw some of my photos there and said that she thought I'd be perfect for this job."

"She did?"

She nods, smiling.

My jaw ticks and I let go of her hand, fisting my own behind my back to work out the sparks prickling my skin at her warmth.

She throws her thumb over her shoulder, slightly turning in that direction. "I guess we should head in there. Don't want to make a bad first impression." Her eyes drop to my chest. "More than I already have."

"Yeah, I'm right behind you. I just—I think I need a second."

"Okay," she whispers, her eyes dancing between mine before she walks off.

I watch her disappear and it's only when she's over the

threshold of the meeting room do I take a full breath for the first time since I heard her voice.

I collapse against the wall, propping myself up on my forearms as I drop my head against the cool surface. Taking in slow breaths, I try to calm my racing heart as my head pounds, my mind scrambling to make sense of the last few minutes.

My hands shake as I pull the wet shirt from my chest and I jump when a hand claps me on the shoulder. I push off the wall and face my team principal. "You okay, lad?" Mitch asks.

I nod, fearing if I try to say anything that my voice will give away my inner spiral.

"Alright then, let's get this over with shall we?"

He strides down the hall and I follow silently behind him. As soon as I enter the room, I beeline for the open seat next to Lawson, consciously forcing myself not to look in the direction of the media team.

My best friend and teammate watches me wearily as I plop down in my seat. He glances around the room before leaning over, speaking quietly. "What the hell is going on?"

I give up on my restraint and my eyes lock on Kinsley as she sits with the other photographers. She laughs at something the girl next to her says and I swallow as the melody reaches my ears.

"I have no idea." As if sensing me, she looks up and her eyes meet mine across the room. Smiling, she ducks her head and tucks her hair behind her ear. "But I'm going to find out."

CHAPTER 22
JACE

I PULL into my driveway and shut off the car, my breathing filling the sudden quiet air. Tilting my head back, I close my eyes and let the weight of the past few hours fully sag against my shoulders.

Kinsley's here.

She's here and she's the newest photographer for the team.

She's finally here with me... but she isn't.

Because she doesn't remember me.

Whether that's on purpose or by chance, I don't know, but there wasn't an ounce of recognition in her eyes and I looked for it like the desperate man I seem to become when it comes to her.

It was painful sitting there with her just out of reach when my entire being screamed for me to pull her into my arms.

But I did it. And I watched her leave, taking more than my heart with her.

I didn't speak to anyone as I left, drove home in silence with the echo of her voice playing on a loop in my mind.

Lawson asked me what was going on and I wasn't lying when I told him that I didn't know. I also wasn't lying when I told him I'd find the answers. And something Kinsley said tells me there's a certain sibling of mine who might be the one to give them.

My ears perk at a high pitched squeal and I open my eyes to see Sydney through the living room window spinning around with Beckham in her arms.

"She's come into the coffee shop I work at a couple times over the past few weeks."

"Saw some of my photos there and said that she thought I'd be perfect for this job."

The words spark a dull annoyance beneath my ribs and my knuckles turn white from the punishing grip I have on the steering wheel. I watch as Sydney runs around cheering in victory as Beckham plays dead before she disappears in the direction of the kitchen.

My jaw ticks and I twist my head, cracking my neck to release the tension building there.

Time to get my answers.

I unfold myself from the driver's seat and walk up the pathway to my front door. Laughter and music flood my ears as I enter the foyer and the door slams shut behind me.

Seconds later Beckham comes running, slipping slightly on his socked feet. "Dad!"

A smile breaks through my stiffened features and I stoop down, swinging him over my shoulder with a playful battle cry.

I carry him through the short hallway and into the living room, throwing him down carefully on the sofa's ottoman before tickling his sides. He breaks out into a fit of giggles and I jostle him with a growl. "Were you good today?"

He nods, speaking through his contagious laughter, "Do I get to have one of the cookies Auntie Sydney brought?"

I chuckle, straightening. "After we eat dinner, and only half."

He cheers and I head into the kitchen as he loads up another round of his video game. Sydney stands at the stove, stirring something in a pot. The ingredients for Mum's chicken noodle soup prepped out on the counter.

She turns and freezes when she sees me standing there, pasting on a meek smile. "Hi, big brother. Didn't know you were home already."

I grunt, crossing my arms. She drops her head, setting the spoon she was holding down. She runs her fingers over her bracelet before fidgeting with the bowls full of vegetables. "How was the meeting? Did you—"

"Don't."

She winces, her eyes slowly rising to meet mine. "Jace—"

"You had no right."

"Jace, just let me—"

"No," I bellow, chest heaving. "How could you?" My voice cracks and she sighs, settling her hands on the counter.

"You don't understand—"

"You said you'd drop it."

"Well guess what? I lied," she screams, throwing her arms out. "Lily and I have been looking for her for years, ever since the night we cleaned this place up."

"Why did you do that? You had no right, Sydney. I told her—"

"Yes, I know. You may have told her you'd respect her decision, but I made no such promises." Her shoulders straighten and she stares me down. "I was so angry for you and I needed to know how she could walk away."

"It was none of your business though, Sydney. Don't you see that? What happened or didn't happen is between me and Kinsley."

"You are my brother, Jace. And you were in so much pain. You really thought I'd just let it go? Because if the roles were reversed, I'd bet everything I own that you wouldn't have either." Her chin wobbles. "But never in a million years would I have expected to find out what I did."

Before I can say anything, she shuffles around the counter and reaches into her bag. Pulling out her laptop, she settles into one of the stools and places it in front of her.

She looks over at me still standing in the threshold of the kitchen and pats the seat next to her. Dropping my arms, I plop down next to her and watch as she types in the search bar.

Before she hits enter, she looks over at me. "Did you notice something different about her?"

My jaw clenches. "She acted like she didn't know who I was."

She slowly shakes her head, a look of sorrow flashing across her face. "It wasn't an act, Jace," she whispers.

I open my mouth to ask what she means when she clicks the button and I watch as articles pull up, all about an accident involving an eighteen-year-old girl. She clicks on the first link and an image of Kinsley pops up.

I pull the laptop from her and click open another site. I scan the text, and with every word I read, my world turns on its axis. Collapsing against the back of the stool, my hands fist and my breathing labors.

"Look at the dates," Sydney whispers.

I scroll and freeze when I see the date of the accident. "Oh my god."

"She had a packed bag with her, Jace." I look over at my sister and she places her hand on top of my clenched one. "She was coming to you."

"You don't know that," I say tightly.

"Yes, I do."

I shoot off the stool and glare down at her. "How could you possibly—"

"Because that evening, Lily helped her pack her bags. She told me that when she left her, Kinsley was so excited about going on this adventure with you."

A breath rushes out of me and I drop my head, mind racing over everything.

She was going to come with me.

She chose me.

But she never made it.

And then she disappeared.

What happened to you, angel?

Sydney slides off the stool and comes to stand in front of me. "I called Lily the night after we cleaned this place. When she answered, she asked how everything was since she hadn't heard from Kinsley. I asked her what she was talking about and she told me that Kinsley had chosen to go with you. She was supposed to send all the updates, but she never heard from her."

"And she never thought that something might be wrong?"

"She didn't think anything worse than just losing contact with her friend until I called, raging about how Kinsley could just completely shut you out."

I sigh. "Syd—"

"We hired a private investigator to find her since any report we'd seen didn't go farther than the accident. It took him almost three years to find a lead since her trail ended at the hospital."

She hops back onto the stool and I slink back onto mine. She takes my hand and squeezes. "But he caught a break with admission papers from a small hospital just outside of London."

My body tenses. "Was she okay?"

She nods. "She—uh—she had a baby."

"What?" I rush out, my head spinning.

I sway in my seat and Sydney's eyes widen as she frantically shakes her head. "He isn't yours, he's only six."

"Jesus, Syd. Maybe lead with that," I grit out as I try to ignore the disappointment flooding my chest as she continues.

"The investigator was able to track her down to Stratford-upon-Avon. The reason he couldn't sooner was because she wasn't renting the place she was in. She was living in a small flat above the coffee shop she works at, owned by the woman who took her in after the accident. Everything had been in this woman's name, so there was no way of knowing she was there."

My eyebrows furrow. "You said he found her years ago?"

Sydney ducks her head, nodding. "When he told us he found her, he also told us that there were lingering complications from her accident."

Her eyes dance between mine and her sigh weighs heavily with sorrow. "She'd lost her memories, Jace. The past year before her accident? All of it was gone."

I heave out a breath and look back at the laptop screen. The still image of her accident looking back at me. "That's why she looked at me like she didn't know who I was," I whisper.

I look back at my sister, tears threatening to spill. "Because she doesn't. She can't."

Shaking my head, I run my fingers through my hair, pulling at the roots. "Why did you bring her back? She has a life, Syd. What gave you the right—"

"Her son's name is Cooper."

I freeze, staring at her. "What?"

Sydney sniffles. "Her conscious mind may not remember, but somewhere deep down there's still something lingering."

"And you thought seeing me would bring it all back? Well guess what, it didn't. And I had to watch the girl I love stare at me like I was a complete stranger. Like I was nothing more than another bloke on the street."

My heart twists at the memory of her walking away, of the realization that I may have lost her forever for the second time.

"Jace—"

"No." I shove away from the counter and stand. "You went too far this time, Syd."

I walk back into the family room, relieved when I see Beckham has his headphones on as he twists his controller like it's the wheel of the car he's driving on the screen.

I bend over the back of the couch, kissing the top of his dirty blond hair. Sydney calls out my name as I jog up the stairs, but I ignore her.

There's only one person I want to talk to right now.

And she has no idea who I am.

CHAPTER 23
JACE

ALL I SEE IS her smile.

All I hear is her laugh.

All I smell is that damn toasted vanilla shampoo she still uses.

And all I feel is the racing of my heart when she's near.

It's been three weeks since Kinsley stumbled back into my life and much like the first time, she's consumed every single one of my thoughts.

Do I linger a little longer at practice, hoping to catch a glimpse of her?

Do I have to hide my keys when I get home so I don't drive to the coffee shop she works at?

Do I lay awake at night wondering what she could be doing, only to fall asleep and have the memories of us together play like a movie?

Do I have multiple tabs open on my search bar with

articles written about her accident and read over them for any hint as to what could have happened?

Do I wish I could go back in time so that I could hold her in my arms and never let her leave my flat that morning?

Yes. To all of it.

But there's nothing I can do.

After Sydney told me everything, I gave myself a few days to be upset, not at her, not at Kinsley, but at the universe for thinking it was okay to play with someone like this. To play with her like this.

Then I got myself together, opened my laptop, and researched everything I could about amnesia caused by traumatic accidents. I talked with multiple doctors, seeing if there was any way I could help get her to remember, but they all said the same thing.

If she hasn't regained her memories by now, there's a chance she never will and I couldn't tell her about our past.

If I did, she could lose whatever there is left of them forever, replaced by false memories.

And I'd never chance that.

I'd never chance her.

So I watch her from a distance. From here, I won't slip up and cost her everything. From here, I know she'll be okay. From here, I can protect her heart... and mine.

Shoes scuff on the pavement and Lawson stops next to where I stand. He leans against the open garage bay, arms crossed and signature scowl on his face. "Ready for this?"

"Not at all."

"Not even going to ask what I mean by 'this'?"

"Nope. Because I'm not ready for any of it."

"Seriously, J, are you okay?"

I shrug. "None of this is okay. What happened to her isn't okay. What Sydney did isn't—"

"You know she didn't mean to hurt you."

"Don't." I glare at him.

He squares up on me. "Don't what?"

"Don't take her side like you always do."

He sighs. "There aren't any sides, stop acting like you're five and not almost thirty years old." He twists his head in the direction of where the girls stand. "Do I think the *way* she went about this was wrong? Yes, she should have told you the moment she found out. But do I think *what* she did was wrong? No. You would have never done it for yourself."

He meets my eyes. "And you need this. Don't act like you didn't. Do you really think after all the years we've known you, none of us would pick up on the fact that you have never once hit on someone with brown hair or brown eyes?"

My jaw ticks and he chuckles. "Yeah, you're not that discreet. I once saw you scream 'stranger danger' while you lifted your hands over your ears when a girl tried to hit on you."

"She had crazy vibes."

"Whatever you have to tell yourself, bruv." He claps my shoulder, walking towards the girls backwards as he continues. "You can say you're upset with all of this as much as you want, but I know there's a part of you that is thankful for this second chance."

Is it a second chance if she doesn't even remember the first one?

Sydney beams as he walks over and she wraps her arms around one of his. Kinsley nods and holds out her hand, my own fisting when Lawson shakes it.

"Collins, you're up next," Mitch calls from inside the garage and I nod.

With one last look at Kinsley, I stalk off to my drivers room and change into my gear. I'm slipping my earphones in as I walk back into the garage when I nearly take someone out.

"Oh shoot. We've really got to stop meeting like this," Kinsley laughs.

If you only knew.

I swallow and she glances down to my helmet. "Are you heading out there?"

I nod, my throat suddenly dry at her proximity.

Jesus man, get it together.

Her eyes dance over my face. "You know, everyone's warned me that you're a bit of a talker, but maybe they have you confused with a different Jace Collins?"

I open my mouth but nothing comes out and her lips tip up as she sighs.

"Good luck out there. I'll make sure to get your good side." She steps around me and I watch her walk down the hallway.

"Left," I yell out after her, suddenly finding my voice.

Smooth as ever, mate.

"What?" She turns back and the sunlight coming from the doorway creates a halo around her.

"My good side. It's the left."

She smiles and my heart skips. "Noted." With that she disappears into the sunrays.

I watch the space she stood for a moment, memories knocking on the back of my mind. Locking that mental door, I slip my helmet on and hop over the halo, sliding into the cockpit.

Pre-season testing is underway and four of the ten teams have already used up their twenty-four hours on the track. Lawson and I have each been out there twice already, and each time the crew or us found something that needed tweaking.

Here's hoping the third time's the charm.

Overall, my hopes for the season are high. We have a killer car ready to be let loose. And after winning a championship two seasons ago, I'm hungry for another.

My race engineer gives me the thumbs up and I hit the ignition, the car rumbling to life around me. I pull out of the garage and exit the pit lane as his voice comes over the radio.

"Okay, mate. Let's give her a rip and see what she's got."

"Understood."

When I'm given the all clear, I let the roar of the engine chase away all of the outside worries as I make my way around the track. On my fourth lap, I'm called into the garage after a cool down turn.

Hopping out of the car, I shuck off my help as Mitch walks over with hiked eyebrows.

I guzzle down water, speaking through labored breaths. "What?"

"Do you have any idea how fast you were going out there?"

"Uh, fast?"

He chuckles. "Incredibly. You beat the record by two seconds."

"What?"

He nods, eyes glancing at the car. "How'd she feel?"

I turn and look over the car with him. "Amazing. She ran perfectly. No braking issues. Handling is exactly how I like it. Your crew built me a perfect car."

He claps a hand on my shoulder. "This seasons going to be it. I can feel it."

I smirk. "Let's hope so."

I head off to shower and change after he gives me the thumbs up that I'm done for the day. A laugh I'll never forget catches my attention the moment I step out of the clubhouse.

I glance to my left to see Sydney, Lawson, Blake, Ryder, and Kinsley. Walking over, I instinctively throw an arm over her shoulder and everyone quiets. Reality slaps me in the face like a jilted lover and I pull my arm back, shoving my hands in my pockets.

Clearing my throat, I smirk down at her. "Consorting with the competition already?"

"Hardly competition if you keep up what you just did. What kind of fire lit under your ass and where can I get some?" Blake laughs, leaning into Ryder's side.

Sydney bumps her elbow into my arm. "Seriously. Good job out there today, big brother."

I glance at her and hum a quick thanks.

Her face dims and she drops her eyes, scuffing her shoe against the pavement. I look over to see Lawson scowling at me and I glare back.

Ryder and Blake glance at each other, having one of those silent conversations only a husband and wife can have, before she smiles over at Kinsley. "So. Kinsley. Have you always wanted to be a photographer?"

"Kind of? I don't know. I've always liked photography but I never really thought I'd be able to make it a full time job. Even now I still have to pinch myself to make sure this is all real."

Blake laughs. "I was the exact same when I started racing last year."

"I may have done it for her a couple times." Ryder smirks and she backhands his chest.

Kinsley sighs. "It's definitely a great opportunity and I'm very thankful for it. But it's also hard to leave my son like this."

"You have a son?"

Kinsley nods, pulling out her phone.

I hold my breath as she pulls up a picture of the two of them. He's her spitting image. Dark brown hair and glowing eyes.

She turns her screen and Blake coos.

"He's my everything, so leaving him for this was extremely hard."

"Is he with his father while you're gone?"

Leave it to Blake to ask *all* of the questions. She's really come out of her shell this past year. Long gone is the nervous, bumbling rookie. Now we have to wrangle her to leave people alone.

She's my best friend, I can say she talks too much if I want to.

Especially since that's usually me.

But ever since I bumped into Kinsley in that hallway, I haven't had the words.

Her being here has quite literally stunned me into silence.

"His dad isn't in the picture."

My eyes shoot to Sydney in surprise.

She never told me that.

Then again, I never gave her the chance to. I couldn't even bring myself to open the files she sent me. I tell myself it's because I was mad, but the reality is I didn't want to find out about her life that way. I wanted to learn who she was now from her, not some words on paper.

"My gran is watching him. She's helped out ever since he was born. Pretty sure he prefers her house over ours since she lives to spoil him."

Blake nods. "At least there's a lot of good breaks where you can go see him. Maybe we can even get him out to a race or too when he isn't in school?"

"Can we do that?"

Blake shrugs. "You have a hookup with four drivers, they can't say no to us."

Kinsley glances up at me and my lips tip up. "I'll see what I can do."

Her smile knocks me right in the chest and I lock my muscles so I don't do something stupid like pull her into my arms.

I glance at the group, each of them watching me. Clearing my throat again, I clap my hands. "Okay, I don't know about you all, but I'm starving."

"I could eat. What about you, pip?" Ryder glances down at Blake who rubs her stomach.

"I need a burger in me like five minutes ago."

He leans in, whispering in her ear and she blushes.

"Hey, stop that before I lose my appetite instead." I point at them and grimace.

Blake laughs and glances at Sydney. "What do you say, Syd?"

My sister looks at me with hesitant eyes before she turns back to her and pastes on a smile. "Maybe next time, I have some more things to wrap up here. I'll just grab something from the food court."

"Are you sure?" Lawson asks, watching her fidget with her bracelet.

"Yeah, you all go, I'll be fine." She waves before walking off towards the Nightingale Race Teams clubhouse just on the other side of ours.

Lawson glares at me, but I ignore him as Blake asks Kinsley if she wants to come.

"Sure. Is it okay that I tag along?"

"Of course it is." Blake links their arms together and they start walking in front of us.

Ryder and Lawson flank me as we follow them down the paddock lane.

"Have you told her?" I ask Ryder.

"I tell her everything, so yes. But she has a lot of questions —hell, so do I."

"You're not the only one," I mumble.

"It's all a bit fucked, innit," he chuckles.

"You're telling me," I sigh, running a hand over my face. "The girl of my dreams is right there and there's nothing I can do about it."

"Why do you think you can't do anything about it?"

"Because I can't tell her about our past, the doctors say it isn't smart and can distort her memories, making it hard for her to differentiate between what is real and not."

"Then don't tell her," Lawson says. "She's not the same Kinsley you met eight years ago. And you're sure as hell not the same either."

We stop at the curb, the girls a few feet away as Blake calls for a car.

"Lads, I don't think I'd survive losing her again," I confess.

"So what's your plan then?" Ryder asks.

Kinsley throws her head back and laughs. Blake notices us staring and winks at her husband, causing her attention to follow. Her golden eyes sparkle in the fading sun as she looks at me, a smile on her face and pink tinging her cheeks.

"I guess I'm going to have to get her to fall for me all over again."

INSTAGRAM POST

@KINSLEYTHROUGHTHELENS

Carousel of images:

1. Clouds outside an airplane window
2. Open suitcase spilling out on a hotel bed
3. Neon sign reflection in a water puddle
4. Framed picture of a little boy sitting on the nightstand

Caption: First ever flight in first class? Check. Dump out my entire suitcase to see that all my toiletries aren't there? Yep. Finding a framed photo of my son with a note saying he had to take out the pink bag so this would fit and that he was sorry? Completely worth the midnight trip to the drug store.

Comments:

@shessosydney: Ah! I'm so excited that we get to work together!

@smileforthecamera: Congratulations on the new job!

@thelawsonmoore: Welcome to the team

@lilybellfashion: Who could ever stay mad at that face?

@thejacecollins: Remember it's the left side

@kinsleythroughthelens replied to @thejacecollins: I remember

CHAPTER 24

KINSLEY

I ROLL over and blindly reach for my blaring phone. My hand slaps down on the screen until sweet, sweet silence cuts through the air. I sigh and snuggle deeper into the fluffy comforter.

Just a few more min—

"Mummy?"

My eyes spring open and I flail, trying to free myself from under the covers. Snatching up my phone, I smile sleepily at my little boy. "Hi, baby. I didn't know you were calling, I'm sorry."

He giggles and points at the camera. "Your hair is all funny."

I glance over at the mirror across the room and grimace. My hair sticks up in every direction, looking like I got in a tussle with a nesting mama bird and lost.

Flopping back on the bed, I sigh and scrunch my nose at the phone screen. "It does look funny, doesn't it?"

Cooper giggles, nodding and holding up pieces of his hair to match mine.

I laugh under my breath, grinning from ear to ear. "I love you, my little goofball."

"I love you, too, Mummy. When are you coming home?"

My heart twists painfully and I swallow back tears. "What does your countdown say?"

He perks up and I have to close my eyes as he takes off running, the scenery on the screen blurring as he waves the phone around wildly.

"Dinner is almost ready, darling," I hear Rose call out to him when he skids to a halt in the living room. "Whatcha doing over there?"

"Talking to Mummy."

"Oh?" I hear her shuffling feet before her face pops up on the screen, her face breaking with a smile. "You look like you had a night of fun," she says, wiggling her eyebrows.

I snort. "If you think that battling jet lag after traveling for almost twenty-four hours is fun, then yes. I had the time of my life last night."

"Ah, sleep is a fickle one," she hums.

"Can we count how many days until Mummy's back now?" Cooper asks, hopping up and down his toes.

We count the chocolate kisses in his jar that he gets to eat over the next ten days and I giggle at his happy feet dance when I tell him that I'll be home for a whole week and a half before having to leave again.

"Okay, let's say bye to Mummy so she can try and get a

few more nips of sleep. We need to get ready for dinner anyway."

"Bye, Mummy. Love you." Cooper leans in and kisses the camera.

"I love you, too, sweetheart. Maybe if you eat all your food, Granny Rose will give you an extra chocolate kiss for me."

I wink and he looks up at her with hopeful eyes. She smiles, pinching his cheek before pulling the phone away so only her face fills the screen.

"Sorry that he woke you. The little bugger is slippery and hid my phone. Now I know why." She chuckles, but I wave her off.

"Nothing is better than seeing my little boy. I miss him. I miss both of you."

"We miss you, too, and we're so proud of you. You should have heard him this morning. He told every customer that came into the shop that his mum is taking pictures of the fast cars."

I bite my lip and hold back the stubborn tears that don't seem to want to give me a break as she speaks softly.

"You've raised a good boy, my girl."

"Thank you, Rose. For taking me in and giving me a second chance at life. For pushing me to do this and watching Cooper. Thank you for everything, really."

"I'd do it all again in a heartbeat, sweetheart. Now try and get some more rest. We'll talk to you tomorrow."

The room fills with the quiet hum of the air conditioner after we say our goodbyes. I stare up at the ceiling and will my mind to shut off so I can get a couple more hours of precious sleep after having such little the past two days.

I tilt my head to the side and my eyes land on the image of me and Cooper. It's from his fifth birthday where one of Rose's friends' granddaughter came and painted all the kids' faces.

Sighing, I roll out of bed and pad over to my suitcase. If I stay in this room alone any longer, I'll start to cry and I'm so exhausted that I don't think I'll have the energy to stop.

After getting ready for the day, I take the short elevator ride down to the lobby and blink at the brightness of the morning sun shining through the massive windows.

Shuffling over towards the dining area, my stomach grumbles, needing more nutrients than a pack of homemade trail mix has to offer.

I look over the buffet offerings as they start to set things out, my lips twisting as I contemplate what I want.

"I'd recommend avoiding the eggs," a voice whispers right next to my ear.

My shriek echoes off the walls of the quiet dining room, garnering weird glances from other early risers. I whip around and close my eyes with a sigh.

"Jace."

His deep chuckle caresses my suddenly alert nerves and I look up to see him grinning down at me. "Sorry. I didn't mean to scare you."

"Didn't anyone ever tell you not to sneak up on an unsuspecting woman?"

"Yeah, I think my mum and sister said something about that once."

I hum. "Smart ladies, giving you all the secrets."

He pauses, almost as if he's lost in thought, before shaking his head. "Yeah. They're my secret weapon."

I smile, turning back to the line of food. "So, why should I avoid the eggs?"

He shrugs. "No particular reason. I just don't trust hotel eggs. Last time I ate them, I was one lap away from shitting my pants. I think that was possibly the fastest I'd ever driven."

I smother my laugh with my hand and he bumps my shoulder with his chest. "It's not funny. I had to cut the interview short so that I could sprint to the bathroom. I almost shit my pants on world wide telly."

"I'm sorry," I rush out through my giggling. "You're right, it's not funny. I'm so sorry that happened to you."

"Well, I won't let that happen to you." He gently grabs my hand and leads me away from the food. "Come on, I know just the place."

"But—"

"Poopy pants on live telly, Kinsley!"

I jog after him as he quickens his steps, my laugh echoing through the lobby. The heat engulfs us as soon as we step outside and Jace steps up to the curb, tracking down a taxi.

When one pulls up, he holds open the door for me with a flourish and I thank him as I slide in, holding back my school girl smile when he settles down next to me.

He gives the driver the name of the place and I look out

the window as we pull out onto the already busy streets of Melbourne, Australia.

"So, what's got you up so early?"

I lean my head back against the seat and turn it so I'm looking at him. "I got an unexpected wake up call from my little man."

He nods. "Same here. No matter how many times I tell him, or show him, Beckham always seems to forget the time differences."

"Yeah, I didn't even try with Cooper. And I'm not all that mad about him waking me up. I miss the little monster already."

"First time being away from him?" There's no judgment in his voice, more understanding than anything and I nod.

"It is. I was honestly supposed to be out here two days ago with the other photographers, but I was able to stay home at least until yesterday."

"What was yesterday?"

"His birthday."

"Really? Well happy birthday to him. How old is he now?"

I blow out a breath. "Six."

"That's a good age. God, I loved Beck's at that age. I mean, I love him at every age, but six?" He shakes his head, smiling at me. "Six is the best."

I huff a laugh. "How old is Beckham again?"

"He just turned seven, actually."

"Oh yeah? How's this age treating you?"

He chuckles. "Let's just say, I hope you soak up those six

year old moments. Apparently they turn into daredevils when they hit seven. I swear the kid thinks he's indestructible."

"Lord help me. I want him to stay this small, cute, sweet, cautious little boy."

"Don't worry." He nudges my elbow with his. "I'll be here if you need any pointers."

My eyes dance over his face and my lips twitch. "I think I'd like that. Thank you."

He smirks, his attention shifting over my shoulder as the taxi stops. "We're here."

Hopping out of the car after paying, he runs around and swings open my door. I slip my hand into his offered one with a laugh and he helps me out onto the curb next to him.

"Sun Up Sun Down," I read the sign and look over at him.

"Best meal any time of day. Me and Law met the brothers who own it a couple years back. Real cool lads, even better food."

I bounce on my toes and grab his hand, pulling him towards the entrance. "Well let's go. I'm starving and someone told me this was *the* place to get the best food."

He follows behind me, beaming. I startle when two loud voices call out as we walk through the front door, instinctively stepping closer to him.

"Aye, there he is. We were wondering when you'd pop in." Two tall men with shoulder length wavy blond hair walk around the bar and over to greet us.

Jace does the whole man hug thing with each of them

before stepping back to my side. "Mates, this is Kinsley. Kinsley, this is Jack and Jacob. They own the place."

My stomach growls at that exact moment and I cover it with a hand as my cheeks heat. The brothers look at me and chuckle identically.

"Let's not keep the pretty lady waiting. You can take the booth in the back."

Jace thanks them and we weave through the already bustling restaurant towards the back, sliding into a cozy corner booth.

I take in the vibrant colors on the walls, pictures of people from all over hanging, mementos decorating every square inch. Laughter breaks out on the other side of the room and I see the two brothers talking with a rowdy group.

"I can see why you like it here." I lean my arm on the table, propping my head on my palm as I look over at him.

He leans confidently back in his seat, spreading his arms over the cushion. "What makes you say that?"

"It's warm here. Inviting. Like you can come here no matter what's going on and immediately feel better."

He nods, leaning his arms on the table. "When me and Law came here the first time, it was the first season without Nik or Ryder driving right alongside us. It felt like a part of me was missing without them out there."

He shakes his head. "I won the first race of the season but I didn't feel like I actually won. I feel like that entire season shouldn't count."

"Didn't you win the championship?"

He raises an eyebrow. "Has someone been studying my stats?"

"No," I draw out the word, fidgeting with the napkin on my lap. "Maybe," I whisper.

Looking at him, I want to equally wipe that knowing smirk off his face or kiss him.

Wait. What?

I drop my gaze to my hands trying to figure out where that thought came from when a plate suddenly lands on the table in front of me.

"Oh, I—" My words cut off as soon as I take in the most delicious looking French toast I've ever seen.

Jace chuckles, reaching over and wiping the corner of my mouth. "You got a little drool."

I knock his hand away with a laugh and look up at the twins. "How did you know this was exactly what I wanted?"

They both shrug, smirks plastering their faces. "It's a gift," Jack says before pointing at us. "Enjoy, it's on the house."

"Thanks mate," Jace says as they walk away.

I pick up my fork and cut off a piece of the fluffy yet perfectly crusted toast and load the bite up with whipped cream and berries.

"Oh my god, this is the best thing I've ever put in my mouth," I moan around the mouthful.

Jace coughs into his cup, wiping his face as some of his orange juice runs over his chin. I smile sheepishly at him and mumble an apology.

He shakes his head with a smile and reaches over. I

instinctively pull my plate back and he laughs as he picks up the hot sauce at my side.

"I know. I know. If I want my fingers to stay where they are, I'll keep my fork far away from your plate," he says, digging into his breakfast burrito.

I watch him for a moment, something flaring in the back of my mind at his words.

Shaking it off, I take another bite of the best French toast I've ever had, soaking in the unexpected yet completely needed morning to kick off my first official weekend on the team.

CHAPTER 25

JACE

I've been on cloud nine for three days since having breakfast with Kinsley and I swear nothing could bring me down.

There's been this smile I can't seem to wipe off my face. One that Lawson's already made multiple comments on during testing and qualifying about how my good mood seems a bit more 'extra' lately.

But I don't care. I got to have alone time with my girl for once and I didn't make a fool of myself. *Mental fist bump.*

Now it's race day and I'm itching to catch a glimpse of her like I have the past couple days.

There's a knock on my hotel room door and I finish pulling on my T-shirt as I go over to open it. My sister stands, shifting foot to foot, on the other side.

"I'm sorry," Sydney rushes out before I even open my mouth. "I should have told you instead of going behind your back. But I'm not sorry that she's here now."

I raise a single brow and she straightens her shoulders. "I

knew from the moment I saw you two together that you were meant to be. Because I saw what I see every day with Mum and Dad. Just because you lost those years with her doesn't mean you also lost your chance at a happily ever after."

"I know."

"Just lis—" She freezes, looking at me like I've grown two extra heads. "What?"

"I know this is my second chance and I don't plan on wasting it."

"Really?" Her eyes light with hope and I wince when she squeals at my nod. "Does this mean you're not angry with me anymore?"

I sigh, pulling her in for a crushing hug. "I was angry at first, but I don't think it was ever with you, specifically. I think I was angry with myself because I wouldn't have been strong enough to do it myself."

Her arms band around my waist tight. "I only want to see you happy, big brother."

I pull back and look at her. "You swear you didn't pull any strings to get her this job?"

"I only got her the contact information, she did the rest herself."

"I just don't want to feel like we manipulated her into being here."

"I only opened the door. She's the one who decided to walk through it."

The door across the hall opens and Lawson leans against the door jam, arms crossed. Sydney turns around and matches his stance. "Eavesdrop much?"

"Just making sure I didn't have to break up another Collins sibling scuffle. This is a nice hotel and I'd like to be able to stay in it again."

She rolls her eyes and turns back to face me. "So, what's the plan?"

"Plan?"

"The win Kinsley's heart plan. You need one because I don't have any clue how you pulled it off the first time."

I squint. "I *just* forgave you—"

"This is serious. You've been given a second shot at the love of your life! Are you really going to just wing it and hope for the best?"

"No, I'm not going to just wing it. I have a plan."

"Oh, really? What is it?"

"I'm not going to tell you. My life. This is my girl. Ergo my plan."

Sydney sticks out her bottom lip. "Aw, you just called her *your* girl. Lawson catch me while I swoon at the cuteness."

I frown at her. "Stop that."

"Please let me be a part of the plan."

"Okay. You're the annoying sister who keeps her mouth shut about the past and doesn't try to play matchmaker anymore, got it?"

She pouts. "I don't like that role, can I put in a request for a different one?"

"Request denied."

"Ugh, fine. But I'm adding on a tiny detail. I also get to be the new best friend."

"What?"

"I want to be Kinsley's new best friend."

"Sorry. You can't."

"Uh, and why not?"

"Because that's going to be me."

Her smile drops. "Oh god, please tell me you aren't going to try and be her friend and then make your move. That never works out."

I smirk. "It did eight years ago."

———

"Let's go out there and have a great race." Mitch claps his hands and I catch sight of Kinsley with the other photographers when everyone stands.

Lawson bumps me with his arm. "You're really going to do this?"

"Do what?"

"Be yourself?"

"What's wrong with being myself?"

"I'm just saying. It may not have chased her off before but do you really want to press your luck for a second time?"

I scowl. "Sometimes I wonder why I stay friends with you."

"My shining personality, obviously."

I snort. "Obviously."

We make our way through the garage and I catch Kinsley's attention as we walk by. Someone bumps into her, making her stumble forward and I stop in my tracks to steady her.

She smiles through a breathy laugh and looks up at me. "Hi."

"How are you feeling today?"

"Still a little nervous."

My hand flexes on her arm before I let it drop to my side. "You got this, Kinsley."

"Shouldn't I be the one telling you that?"

I shrug. "Someone once told me that I didn't need luck. It was the other drivers who did."

She hums. "Sounds like that person's pretty smart."

"Yeah," I whisper. "She really is."

"Oh, I didn't see you yesterday, but congrats on starting P2 today."

"Thanks. I think it's going to be an exciting season opener that's for sure."

"I'll make sure to have my camera ready." She holds it up for emphasis.

Someone calls her name and she throws a thumb over her shoulder. "I should—"

"I got—"

We both laugh and she motions to me. "You first."

I clear my throat, pulling the small bag out of my back pocket and holding it out to her. "I, uh, got you something. In honor of your first day."

Her eyes drop to my hand. "You didn't have to do that."

"I wanted to."

She takes the package and unwraps it, revealing the brown leather camera strap. Her thumb traces over her initials branded into the side.

"Oh my god, Jace. I love it, thank you so much."

I watch as she pulls her camera off and unlatches the plain black strap, switching them out. I take the old one from her and stuff it along with my hands into my pockets to hide their shaking.

After I got home from preseason testing, I thought long and hard about what I was going to do. And it all came down to one thing.

If I couldn't make her remember why she fell for me, then I'd have to do it all over again. But I didn't want to recreate our story. I love it just the way it happened.

So I'll start from where we left off.

And this camera strap is the same one I held tightly in my fist that day on the airfield. I don't know why I held onto it like I did, but something kept me from throwing it out.

Now I know why.

Because it was always going to be hers.

We're just a few years behind schedule, is all.

"Beautiful," I whisper and she looks up at me, a small smile on her lips.

Someone calls my name this time and she glances to the side before meeting my eyes. "I'll see you out there, speed racer."

Her words echo in my mind as I get ready for the race. When we've gone through the opening ceremonies, I make my way to my car and catch a flash of yellow.

Looking up I watch as Kinsley jogs up the steps of the grandstands, snapping pictures of the crowd. She turns around once she gets to the top of a section littered with Miller Racing fans.

She must catch me watching through the lens because I see her lower it slightly before waving to the left. I chuckle and turn, smiling when she gives me a thumbs up.

Slipping on my balaclava and helmet, I look up at her one last time before hopping over the halo. I give my thumbs up and the rest of the track guys run over to the sidewall.

We pull out of the starting line up for the formation lap and my race engineer checks in. Everything looks and feels good with both me and the car.

I tune everything out as each red light goes up, until there's only the purring of my engine and the sound of my steady breathing. It's like everything freezes for those few seconds with everyone on the edge of their seats, afraid if they blink that they'll miss it.

Then it all comes rushing back in as the lights go out and I fly down the track, side by side with Ryder.

It's make or break with a first tight right turn that immediately rounds out to the left. Picking up speed for the short straight, I hang back to avoid Ryder as he breaks for turn three before immediately swinging out.

It's a dance between us as we work our way through the next series and we're neck and neck when we hit the outside curve of turn seven, swinging side by side through eight's longer stretch to the right.

It opens up to a long straight, really the perfect opportunity to overtake.

And I don't waste it.

We approach turn nine at higher speeds than we've hit so far on the track and he pulls ahead by a fraction, but I'm right there, eating up the inside of turn ten.

I punch it, pulling out in front the short straight into the tight right turn of eleven and hold strong in P1 through the next series before we cross the starting line.

I breathe out a harsh breath as Oscar comes over the radio. "Great first lap. Only fifty-seven more to go."

"Let's get to work then."

Lap after lap, I push myself and the car to its limits, working to grow that lead time so when I stop for a tyre change, I won't drop too far in the rankings.

The thing about this track is, aside from the long stretch between turns eight and nine, everything else is so tight. It's one of the more compacted tracks with tight turn after tight turn.

I always say that these types of tracks are a dance with the devil. Tempting fate. They're more prone to accidents, whether that's between two drivers or someone in a losing battle with the side walls.

Which is why, aside from being in the leading position, your main goal is to get as far away from other drivers as possible. There's nothing like being taken out of a race at the hands of someone else's mistake.

"Box, box. Box, box."

"Understood."

"Moore is stacking in right behind you so let's be cognizant of that."

"Got it."

We pull into the pit lanes, Lawson a few seconds behind me. I stop at the garage and before you can say 'Peter Piper picked a peck of pickled peppers,' I'm swerving back out onto the track with fresh tyres and renewed energy to clench my first win of the season.

"Okay. You've got both of the Nightingales in front of you. Stone is one point two away."

"And King?"

"Three point four."

I nod, calculating the moves I'll have to make over the next twenty-four laps to catch that speedy fucker.

He's one of my best friends, I can call him a fucker if I want to.

I'm gaining on Blake when I see her rear brake lock up seconds before it slips out from under her in turn twelve. The accident is a blur as I fly by, but I check my mirrors, seeing a plume of dust from the gravel lined runoff.

"Is she okay?"

"Let me check."

I move through the next set of turns as yellow flags wave behind me.

"She's good. Out safe and unharmed."

I blow out a breath and focus back on the race. The weight of worry off my chest.

Last year, Blake got in a life threatening accident at one of our races. Ryder's ex-teammate had it out for her since the announcement of her signing.

But he took it too far.

Cutting her off in a turn, she had no option but to brake.

Except I was right behind her. We collided and at the speeds we were going, it lifted her car up and over Jean's car. She flipped multiple times until the fence of the paddock lane caught her.

Hanging upside down, the engine caught fire.

To this day I can still hear Ryder's screams that were so loud, they transferred over the open radio line I had with my race engineer.

This job isn't for the faint of heart.

It can cost our friends and family their lives. Ryder lost his father to an accident when we were kids. And just three years ago, he was in an accident that took him out for an entire season. To this day, I see him battle his migraines every once in a while.

And Nik? It almost cost him his life that same year.

We can cover up our scars and mask our emotions all we want, but every time one of us straps into this car, we do so with the understanding that we might not come out.

It's why Blake and Ryder trade off their wedding rings before every race.

It's why Nik—even as a team principal now—Ryder, Lawson, and I stand in a circle and look each other in the eyes for a silent minute. Sharing claps on the backs before we go our separate ways for the race.

It's why I stare at the image of Beckham that I tape to the backside of every steering wheel before I clip it in.

It's why, if I get this second chance with Kinsley, I'm going to show her every day how much she means to me. How much I've missed her. How much she's loved.

"Green flags out. Go get him."

Now that I know Blake is safe and there's no doubt they've relayed it to Ryder, I don't feel as bad when I do this...

I close in on him and open DRS down the straight. Swinging around him, I take the lead. It's a battle to the finish line, but I'm able to hold him off as we pass under the waving checkered flag.

Cheers greet us as we pull into the first and second place spots, Lawson taking third. We walk over to where our teams stand, Nik right in front.

After we celebrate with our respective teams, we circle around, Nik on one side of the gate, us on the other. Ryder pulls him in for a quick strong hug and I lean in bumping our foreheads together with a tight grip on the back of his neck.

"You should be out there with us."

"There are only three podiums, Jace." He pulls back. "I'm where I need to be."

"Bossing around this one is that much fun then?" I throw a thumb to Ryder.

A rare smirk tips up at the corner of his mouth as he looks at the three of us. We're pulled away for our interviews before given a moment to cool down.

"How's Blake?" I ask as we make our way to the stage.

Ryder chuckles. "Pissed. She thinks she would have had me if her brakes didn't lock up."

We all laugh and I clap a hand on his shoulder. "And you?"

He shakes his head. "I never want to see the woman I love hurt ever again."

"None of us do."

And I'm not just talking about her.

Hours later, after I've washed off the sticky champagne residue, I step out of the clubhouse with my bag thrown over my shoulder. Looking down the paddock lane, I spot a familiar head of chocolate waves and break into a jog.

"Well, hey there." I slow to a walk next to her.

She laughs. "This is new."

"What is?"

"Not bumping into each other."

"I guess you're right." I smirk, bumping my shoulder into hers. "Better?"

She giggles. "Immensely."

Yeah, it is. Everything is immensely better when she's here.

CHAPTER 26
KINSLEY

"This seat taken?"

My head jerks up. "Jace?"

He smirks. "One in the same."

"Excuse me," the lady behind him says, sending me a look.

"Oh, sorry. Let me just..." I quickly unfasten my seatbelt and shoot up, slamming my head into the ceiling.

A couple people in line cringe and Jace's arms twitch as if he was about to reach out to me. I lift a hand and place it on the top of my head with an embarrassment filled laugh.

"Are you okay?" he asks, his eyes shining with worry before sliding to the ceiling with fire like the inanimate object offended him.

"All good." I move to shuffle out of the row, but the universe must be having too good of a laugh with me because my foot catches on the strap of my backpack and I stumble with a squeak.

"Jesus, I'm going to have to wrap you in bubble wrap."
He curses under his breath as he catches me before I can face
plant into the seat across the aisle.

I clutch onto his strong arms as he helps me stand,
sucking in a breath when my chest brushes his. A sense of
déjà vu hits as I lose myself in the calming depths of his blue
eyes.

A throat clears and I shake my head, taking a step back
from his gravitational pull. I wave a hand to the row and dip.

*Did I just freaking curtsy? Where's the emergency exit? I
need to throw myself out of it immediately.*

He watches me with an amused tilt in his lips and slides
into the window seat. I throw myself into my seat with an oof
and reach up to rub my head.

"Are you okay?"

My vision blurs slightly and I shake my head to clear it.
Reaching into my bag I whimper when I see my stash of
granola bars is completely depleted.

"Kinsley."

I look over at Jace. Both of them.

His eyes drop to my wrist and I shiver when his thumb
runs over the silver medical bracelet. He glances up, concern
blanketing his features. "Have you eaten today?"

"Of course I have. I ate this morning and then..." I trail
off, trying to remember everything else I did today.

"And then?"

"Oh my god, I forgot." I cover my face with my hands.
"I'm never this spaced but I think I was so focused on getting
here after the race that everything else didn't matter."

"Your health matters, Kinsley." His tone is serious and slightly pleading. "Here." He leans forward, pulling out a protein bar before unwrapping the top and handing it to me.

I'd give more than a fleeting thought to the sparks that shoot up my arm when our fingers brush, but I only have enough energy to get this chocolate covered cardboard into my mouth.

He watches me as I finish the entire thing and raises his hand for an attendant, asking for a juice. When she scurries off, he turns to me. "Do you have your kit?"

"What?"

"Blood sugar kit."

"Oh, yeah. It's in my bag."

He leans forward, grabbing my bag off the ground and placing it on his thigh. I reach over and open the pocket, pulling out the small case. The flight attendant walks by, handing him the juice before disappearing down the aisle.

Watching my every move, he releases a breath when the screen shows that my blood sugar is within normal range. He helps me put everything away before handing me my juice.

The juice I almost spill all over when he reaches over and buckles my seatbelt.

"How did you know to do all that?"

"Your bracelet." His voice holds a sort of sad curiosity as his eyes slowly meet mine. "I didn't know you were diabetic."

I shrug. "I don't really advertise it so there's no way for you to have known."

"How long ago were you diagnosed, if you don't mind me asking?"

"I was initially diagnosed with gestational diabetes when I was pregnant. It stuck around after that. So I guess I've been living with it for just over six years now."

His eyebrows furrow, eyes growing distant. "Is that common? For someone to have diabetes develop that way."

"There's about a fifty percent chance, yeah. Why?"

"Someone I know had that happen. I guess I just didn't really know how common it was."

"Is that how you know what to do for low blood sugar?"

"My son, Beckham. He was diagnosed when he'd just turned four."

"Four? That's incredibly young."

"Yeah." His jaw ticks. "It was hard. I almost thought of quitting racing so that I could be home for him more than I was. But my mum stepped up and said she'd take care of things. It helped a lot in the first year, but I got so distracted while I was away that it was easier to bring him with me."

Something niggles in the back of my mind and I shift in my seat.

"Sorry if this is overstepping, but what about his mum?"

"Wasn't an option. Hasn't been for a while."

"Oh, I'm sorry."

He shrugs. "Is what it is."

"Who's he with while you're away this season?"

"My parents."

I smile. "I bet he's having the best time."

"Oh, no doubt. They spoil him rotten."

I laugh. "Gran does that for Cooper. I'm afraid that when

I get back, he won't want to come home because she has all the *cool stuff* and I have broccoli."

He chuckles. "Trust me. There's no way he'd want to be anywhere else than at home with you."

My eyes begin to sting at his sincerity and I smile. "If it makes you feel better, I know someone in a similar situation and he's honestly one of the best fathers I know. It's always hard at first, but with a support system like you have and a little boy as brave as Beckham sounds, everything's going to end up okay. Great, even."

His eyes dance between mine. "All we can do is take it one day at a time." I laugh and he smiles. "What?"

I shake my head. "I've been saying that for years."

He chuckles, his eyes growing distant like he's lost in a memory. Someone stumbles catching themselves on my chair and Jace shakes himself out of his thoughts.

Sighing, he shakes his head. "I just want Becks to live the best childhood he can."

I smile. "Well it doesn't sound like this has slowed him down at all though. At least not from what Sydney's told me about their adventures."

Jace chuckle is drowned out as the plane taxis out of the gate. "The friend I was telling you about taught me a trick early on. I told him that the insulin is like his super power. So now whenever it's time to find a new site for the pod he's like 'Dad, hurry! The bad guys won't wait to try to take over the world.'"

I freeze and he looks over, eyebrows furrowing. "What's wrong?"

I shake my head. "I once said the same thing to my friend when he was concerned about how his little boy would handle the medicine."

He pauses, eyes flicking between mine. "Where did you say you met this friend?"

"A support group for family members who are either living with or know someone living with diabetes. I joined it a year or so after having Cooper. My doctor thought it would be a good way to connect to others in the community."

He quickly brings out his phone and opens a chat, typing something. My phone dings a moment later, but I don't move to pick it up. We both know what we'll see.

He looks up at me, disbelief and something else swirling across his face. "It's you."

"Oh my god."

He huffs out a laugh and falls back in his seat, murmuring something under his breath that I can't hear over the roaring of the plane as we soar into the night sky.

He looks over at me. "I can't believe this. Who would have thought that out of all the support groups recommended to me by Beckham's doctor, the one I joined would bring me to you without even realizing it."

"Some might say it's serendipitous," I muse.

"Kismet."

I smile. "That's me. Kismet Kinsley."

He tenses, his eyes trained on my face. "Yeah. Kismet Kinsley," he whispers.

Shifting in my seat, I dip my head to hide my burning cheeks.

"Thank you." His soft words garner my attention and I look up. "Thank you for helping me all these years. With Beckham. Really, with everything."

I smile. "He seems like a really great kid, Jace."

"He's the best. A miniature version of me."

"Did you just inadvertently give yourself a compliment?"

His cheeks blush and he clears his throat. "Definitely didn't mean to."

I bump his shoulder with mine. "Well I'm thinking it's deserved. You're a really great guy, Jace. Clearly an amazing and caring father. I learned as much just from talking to you through the group. Plus, Sydney has sung your praises from day one."

His eyebrows furrow. "What, uh, has she said?"

I shrug. "Just that you're her best friend. I can always count on you whether it's for a laugh, a shoulder to cry on, or a getaway driver."

He hums, leaning his head back. "I was only the getaway driver once."

"For what?" I laugh.

"It had to be when she was still in secondary school, maybe eleventh year? I don't know, but she'd just broken up with this tool for cheating and she had all this pent up rage in her. So the boys and I decided to give her some advice."

"Oh no."

He chuckles. "We were all well into our careers at that point, so it couldn't be anything too serious. Then Mum walked into the room, threw out the idea of egging the little prick's prized possession, and walked out like it was nothing."

I giggle. "Your mum sounds awesome."

"She is."

"So you went and egged this guy's house?"

He chuckles. "No. We egged his brand new sports car. The prick had just picked it up from the detailer too."

I smother my laugh behind my hand. "That's so bad."

He shrugs. "He deserved it."

He closes his eyes, smiling.

"What are you smiling about over there?"

He peeks over at me. "I just can't believe it's been you all along."

I tuck my lips and look down at my hands, afraid if I look at him any longer something embarrassing like 'it's like it was meant to be' will come bursting out of my mouth.

I'm saved from my own awkwardness when the flight attendant stops by asking if there's anything we need. We both ask for bottled water and she hands them over before making her way down the aisle.

I watch as she goes, noticing she isn't stopping at any of the other patrons in economy. Twisting my lips I glance at Jace beside me. "Question."

He hums and I immediately feel guilty. He has to be exhausted. I mean he was just driving in a race no less than a few hours ago. And here I am keeping him awake when all he probably wants to do is sleep. "Never mind."

"Kinsley."

"Hm?"

"Ask me."

I chew on my lip, fingers picking at the paper on my bottle. "Why are you here?"

"What do you mean?"

"Why are you here? On this plane?"

"I'm going home."

I blow out a breath. "Yes, I gathered that. But why are you here, on this particular flight, in this particular seat when I know everyone else is flying home tomorrow."

"How do you know that?"

"Sydney asked if I wanted to join you all on the private jet you share."

"Ah." He shifts in his seat until he's facing me. "I'm here because this was the first flight out to England tonight. I didn't want to wait until tomorrow because I couldn't wait to get home to see my son. This is the first season I'm traveling without him and I seem to be struggling with the separation more than I thought I would."

His eyes dance between mine as a nervousness overtakes his features. "My original ticket was for first class, but then I saw you at the loading area and the next thing I knew, I was at the desk asking them to switch whoever was in this seat to mine so that I could move back here."

"Why would you do that?" It comes out as a whisper as I try to calm my racing heart from his complete honesty.

"I told them that me and my wife had been separated due to a mix-up."

"You totally used your fame, didn't you?"

His lips tip up. "I'm not saying I didn't try, but the ladies at the desk had no idea what I was talking about."

I giggle, tucking my lips. "You wanted to sit by me."

He smiles, his eyes dancing over my face. "I did."

Why do I feel like I'm back in secondary school where you get the butterflies because the cool jock decided to sit next to you on the bus for the school field trip?

Oh, because this is just like that.

The air around us fills with the soft snores of other passengers and we both yawn. Jace checks his watch, rubbing the back of his head.

"We should probably get some shut eye if we don't want to be dog tired when we land at six in the morning our time."

I nod, another massive yawn taking over. We settle into our seats, turning off the overhead lighting. I tuck into my sorry excuse for a blanket provided by the flight and shift until I find a comfy spot.

————

It feels like I've just closed my eyes when a soft hand lands on my shoulder. I look up and the flight attendant smiles sheepishly. "I'm sorry, I just wanted to let you know that we will be landing in a few minutes if you and your husband could return your seats upright."

I nod in a sleepy haze and lift my head. A massive jumper slips down from where I was clutching it to my chest and I look over to a T-shirt clad Jace, his head laid back, arms crossed, eyes closed.

My lips tip up, chest warming at the thought that he laid

his jumper over me. I take in his sleeping form as something sparks in my chest.

He is quite handsome.

Probably—no, definitely. He's definitely the best looking guy I've ever seen.

Dirty blond hair is styled in haphazard waves, the longer bits on top falling into his eyes. His strong jaw is peppered with a trimmed stubble that looks like he has a permanent five o'clock shadow.

My eyes drop to his strong shoulders and the veins in his crossed arms. He shifts in his seat, a low sigh coming from his throat.

Gently I place my hand on his shoulder and nudge him.

"Jace," I whisper.

He hums, lifting his hand to cover mine. I giggle, shaking him a little more.

"Just one more minute, angel," he murmurs, his voice deep and gravel ridden.

I suck in a breath when he lifts my hand, brushing his lips over my knuckles before laying our joined hands against his chest.

I'm frozen as I feel his steady heart beat under my palm, his words echoing in my mind in a voice I've only ever heard in my dreams.

Angel.

CHAPTER 27

JACE

She's been here all along.

Without me knowing it. Without her knowing it.

She's never truly been gone.

I think I went into shock when her phone pinged with the notification of my chat message. And even though neither of us confirmed that's what it was, we knew.

Because she has been and always will be my kismet Kinsley.

The revelation clouds my mind as I pull into my driveway and hop out of the car. I practically skip up the steps but come to an abrupt halt as soon as I open the front door and see the slim figure sitting on my sofa.

"Honey, you're home," she purrs.

I grit my teeth and hold myself back from slamming the door closed. "What are you doing here, Angie?"

"Just dropping our son off."

"I wasn't even scheduled to be home until tomorrow.

How did you know I would be here today? What were you planning to do, leave him here by himself overnight?"

She sighs, standing and walking around the coffee table. "Of course I wouldn't leave him alone like that. I took a peek at the Life360 app you had downloaded on his phone and saw you were on your way home. I thought we could surprise you."

"Consider me surprised. You can leave now." I hold the door open for emphasis.

She steps into my space, pouting. "What, I can't stay to have breakfast with my boys? Come on, we can make pancakes like we used to."

I move back just in time before her hand can make contact with my chest and she sighs.

"This is ridiculous, Jace."

"No, you continuing to think you have a right to enter my home and invite yourself into my life more than I've already established is my limit is ridiculous."

She sucks in a breath, her face twisting in anger before she checks herself. "You always love to put up a fight, but you and I both know how this little dance of ours always ends."

With that, she walks out the door, swaying her hips a little more than usual and I slam the door behind her with a growl.

Not anymore.

Those dark moments where I'd find myself grieving for the life I wished so hard for but couldn't have and drowned myself with bad choices vanished the moment Kinsley came back into my life.

My phone dings and I look down at a text from Sydney, saying she hopes everything is going okay. My gut twists and I quickly shove my phone away as I go in search of my son, finding him playing a video game in his room.

I'm a dirty, dirty little liar.

I told my sister and the lads that I had to rush home for an emergency, which in hindsight wasn't brilliant since they are all overly involved in my life.

Using Beckham as an excuse was a non-starter because they'd have left with me.

Mum and Dad were also a no go. I couldn't scare Syd like that.

So I told them that a plumber was coming out to the house because it was flooded and since Beckham was with his mum, no one was there to meet the workers.

It was a solid excuse since they know I'd never let the viper be in my house by herself.

Damn the need to make sure my son has access to his own house at all times.

They didn't need to know the real reason was because I'd overheard Kinsley tell my sister that she couldn't go out with us because she'd booked an earlier flight back home.

They didn't need to know what I did to get on that plane, in that seat, with eleven plus uninterrupted hours with my girl.

I'd actually had time to talk to her. I saw her relax and slowly open up to me. Hell, I even opened up and shared about my struggles without realizing it. Because with her, it's always been that way. Easy.

And just like she did all those years ago, she didn't judge me. She lifted me up. Told me she thought that I was an amazing dad. She showed me that even though years have separated us, we're still those kids deep down stumbling their way through life.

When I woke up to her cuddled into my side, it took everything in me to not pull her tighter against me. Then she shivered and before I could tell myself no, I was gently propping her up so I could strip out of my jumper and lay it over her.

They always did look better on her, anyway.

Then I had to push it, just once. I reached out and ran a finger over her temple, tucking a strand that had fallen from her messy bun behind her ear. I froze when she hummed, breathing out a broken sigh of relief as she turned into my hold before laying her head on my shoulder.

For hours I sat there afraid to move even an inch if it meant the moment would be broken. Because right then we were Jace and Kinsley, together. But the moment she'd wake up, I'd turn into just Jace. The pretty boy race car driver and brother of her new friend.

But that moment was worth it all.

And no one would know.

Everything was going according to plan too.

Until the lads and ladies showed up at my house a day later with boxes of towels to help me clean up the mess I'd told them would be here.

"Looks awfully dry for something that was supposed to

be 'devastatingly disgusting' doesn't it?" Blake deadpans, lifting a single dark brow and crossing her arms.

Sydney leans to look around me. "Not a single turd in sight. Tell me brother." She lifts onto her toes, poking me in the chest with each word. "Where. Are. The. Turds."

I was momentarily saved when Beckham came screeching out of the house, running straight for Blake.

Lawson scoffs, "Dude. That hurt." He places a hand over his chest.

Ryder chuckles, pushing past me and calling over his shoulder, "It's only because she's new. It'll wear off."

Sydney pats Lawson's shoulder as Blake sticks out her tongue, waltzing through the doorway with my son clinging to her.

"It's okay, Law. If it makes you feel better, you're my favorite."

"Favorite person to annoy, maybe." He scowls and walks into the house.

Sydney's eyes linger on his back before shifting to meet my stare. She slides on her picture perfect smile and I shake my head. "Are you ever going to tell him?"

Her face slips into a scowl much like my best friends. "I have no idea to what you're referring to." With that, she shoves her way past me and into the house.

I take a deep breath and square my shoulders for the interrogation I'm about to endure before turning and closing the door.

Walking into the living room, everyone's scattered over the sectional couch and chairs as Beckham stands on the ottoman, telling them all about his adventures over the past few weeks.

Maybe if I could keep him talking...

"So why do you have all these towels? Oh! Are we going swimming?"

Would someone shut this kid up?

"Yeah, Jace. Why *do* we have *all the towels*?" Ryder leans back, stretching his arms over the back of the couch. His eyebrows raise expectantly and a nervous laugh bubbles out of me.

"You were doing some spring cleaning?"

Everyone's faces remain blank.

"Donation?"

Sydney rolls her eyes.

"We're all doing spa treatments?"

Blake closes her eyes, pitching the bridge of her nose.

"Practicing for a towel whipping contest?"

Lawson growls.

"So we aren't going to the pool?" Beckham asks, glancing around the room at everyone.

I swallow when Sydney squints. Putting my hands on Beckhams shoulders, I steer him towards the stairs. "Of course we're going swimming. Go get your suit on and we'll head over to Granny and Grandad's soon."

He cheers, his feet thundering up the stairs. The second his door slams shut, Lawson leans his forearms on his thighs. "Speak."

"It's really not that big of a deal—"

"You lied. To our faces." Ryder stares me down and Blake

places her hand on his thigh. "Why did you fly home right after the race, Jace? What possibly couldn't have waited another day? What would make you lie to us for the first time in over twenty years of friendship?"

Sydney's silent, but she watches me closely. I make the mistake of meeting her stare and a smile slowly spreads over her face.

"Oh my god. It's Kinsley."

I drop my gaze to the ground and she shoots up off the couch.

"You heard her tell me she was flying home that night."

"And what? He found out which flight she was on, got a ticket, told us this elaborate lie about his house being flooded, and—oh my god, that's exactly what you did." Blake's jaw drops.

I look up to see shock, amusement, and disbelief on my friends' faces.

"You're as fucked for her now as you were back then, aren't you?" Ryder chuckles.

"I'd say even more so now." Lawson snickers. "Dude, you haven't sat in economy on a plane since we got pulled up. I remember you saying once that you could never possibly go back now that you've had a taste of the private jet life."

"Are you all really surprised that he would do this for her? Because I'm not." Sydney looks around at them, shaking her head before meeting my eyes with a smile. "It's Kinsley."

"It's Kinsley," I echo.

"You're really going to try and get her to fall for you again aren't you." It isn't a question and I look over at Blake.

"I am. And if she forgets this time, I'll do it again. I'd do it over and over because if she's still Kinsley, then I'm still the boy who swore she'd never be alone ever again."

"Oh my goodness, it's like that movie 50 *First Dates*," Sydney squeals, clapping.

"The one with Adam Sandler?" Lawson asks and I look at him with raised eyebrows. He shrugs. "She wouldn't give me the remote to change it."

"You cried."

Lawson growls. "I didn't cry, I had dust in my eye from when you threw popcorn at me."

"What are we talking about?" Ryder looks at Blake with furrowed brows and she pats his chest.

"We'll watch it on the next flight."

Ryder glances at Lawson who shakes his head. Clearing his throat he throws an arm around his wife. "Uh, sure, love. Whatever you want."

Sydney snaps her fingers. "Focus, people. Small ears are about to be with us." She steps around the coffee table. "How did it go? Did you end up getting the same flight as her?"

A smile slowly spreads and they all cheer. Sydney shushes them and motions for me to spill the beans. And I do.

By the time I'm done telling them, the girls have melted into a combined puddle of heart eyes and the lads are watching them with concerned looks.

"When do you see her next?" Sydney asks.

"We have a team meeting tomorrow for some promotional thing. I'm sure the team photographers will be there too."

"What are you going to do?"

"Don't you remember your role? The annoying little sister who *doesn't try to play matchmaker*." She scrunches her face and I nod. "Yeah, quit trying to talk me up."

"Would you rather I tell her the embarrassing things?"

"I'd rather you not talk about me at all."

"Fine, I'll keep the boasting to a minimum."

"Zero."

"That's what I said."

"Sydney," I growl.

"Jace," she mocks.

"Children, please." Blake laughs.

"I've got it handled, Syd. Let me get my girl my way, okay?"

She sighs. "Fine. Just don't screw it up."

Ryder scoffs. "Well now that's inevitable. As long as he knows the proper way to grovel afterwards, he'll be golden."

Blake turns to face her husband with a raised brow. "And what is the proper way to grovel?"

Ryder smirks. "With my mou—"

"Ready!" Little feet slap the floor as Beckham comes down the stairs in his new race car swimming trunks.

I rush over and throw him over my shoulder with a pointed look at Ryder. He mouths his apologies and I put my giggling son back on his feet.

"You're not in your trunks?"

I ruffle his hair. "They're at Grans. We'll all change when we get there."

"Then why did I have to change? I've got swimming trunks there too."

I nudge him in the direction of our shoe cupboard. "So many questions, so little time for swimming. Hurry, and get your shoes on."

There's a knock on the door and Beckham takes off running. "I'll get it!" A moment later, we hear the door open and his excited screaming. "Uncle Nik is coming swimming too?"

I drop my head back and sigh.

And this is why you never lie, kids.

CHAPTER 28

JACE

"What did you think?" I climb out of the car, whipping off my helmet.

The ten-year-old boy beams up at me. "That. Was. Awesome!"

His mom laughs off to the side and I take his helmet. "If you're lucky, we'll see if we can't get you another go at it later, cool?" I wink at him and he cheers.

"So cool." The guide steps up and takes them over to the area where they can see pictures from when we were driving.

Today we've partnered with the Great Ormond Street Hospital to give children with all kinds of diagnoses the Formula 1 driving experience. They get to come to headquarters, see how our garages work, how testing works, get to build their own mini car out of legos, and even get to participate in a ride around the practice track.

We do this multiple times a year with many different

programs, but this one is special. These kids are hospital bound and don't get to live, well, like a regular kid.

But while they're here, they get to immerse themselves in a totally different world, leaving the harshness of reality behind for even just a little while.

I can relate to that on some level.

I hand off my helmet to one of the crew members and head over towards my garage. Lawson's on duty for the next few laps, and so I'm taking the moment for a small break.

Kids stop me as I walk by and I bend, making sure to give each of them the attention they deserve. The parents quietly thank me as I do and I wave them off, thanking them and letting them know that if they need anything, we are here for them.

Mitch waves to me as I pass by one of the open garage bays and I nod, chuckling when a kid pulls on his shorts to show him their hand is covered in grease.

Stepping up to the closed garage, I'm about to punch in my door's code when I hear a sniffle. My eyebrows furrow and I look around, a familiar camera strap catching my eye to the left.

On quiet feet, I walk over and peek around the corner. Kinsley sits with her back to the wall, knees to her chest, and her hands covering her face as her shoulders shake.

"Hey," I say softly.

Her head whips up, waterlogged eyes meeting mine. "Oh my god, Jace." She wipes at her face furiously as I squat. "Sorry, I just. I needed a second. I'll be back out there in a moment."

"Kinsley, I'm not here to drag you back out there." Shifting to sit at her side, I lean my back against the wall next to her. "Do you want to talk about it?"

She shakes her head, her fingers twisting with the hem of her shirt. "It's Rose."

My heart stops. "Is she okay?"

She sniffles. "She took a fall yesterday and hurt her hip. She had hip replacement surgery years ago. The doctor put her on bed rest for the next week, but even after that, she's limited to no stairs or excessive walking."

Realization hits. "Cooper," I whisper.

She nods, dropping her head back against the wall. "I don't know what I'm going to do. I love this job, but I can't just leave Cooper with her when she's recovering. She says it's fine and he's already said he'd be her little helper, but I just can't do that to her. She's already done so much for me over the years."

She covers her face, shoulders shaking. Instinctively I reach over and gently pull her hands away. Memories invade my mind as her glistening golden eyes meet mine.

Instead of sitting against the side of a building, we're in a dark room.

Instead of the team polo, she's wearing my jumper.

Instead of crying into her hands, she's pressing her face into my chest.

"We'll figure this out, okay?"

"How?"

Without thinking, I reach up, thumbing away her tears.

My heart skips when she leans into the touch instead of pulling away.

"I have an idea, but let's talk to some people and see what we can do, yeah?"

Her eyes dance between mine before she slowly nods.

My lips tip up and I swipe my thumb across her cheek. "Now no more crying, it breaks my heart to such a beautiful face wet with tears."

A watery laugh bursts out of her and she shakes her head with a smile.

"There she is."

There's my angel.

"Thank you," she whispers.

"You aren't alone in this anymore, Kinsley. You have the team, the lads, Blake and Sydney." I bump my knee into hers. "You have me. You can lean on us—lean on me to help when you need it. We're a family here. No one gets left behind."

She sniffles, wiping her cheeks. "Yeah, I'm starting to see that."

"Well believe it. Your pain is my pain. Your struggles are my struggles—"

"Your successes are my successes?" She raises an eyebrow and I chuckle.

"Exactly."

"So when do I get my turn at holding the trophies you've —sorry, the trophies *we've* won?"

A laugh bursts out of me and I wink at her. "We can draw up an agreement on joint custody."

"I'll start clearing my mantel," she says through a chuckle.

Sighing, she leans back against the wall, rolling her head to look at me. "Seriously, though. Thank you."

"For what? I haven't done anything yet."

"You've done a lot more than I think you realize. You just always seem to always know exactly what I need."

I look off towards the clearing, my mind warring with the need to tell her the truth. That I always know what she needs because I know her. I've known her.

Those few weeks all those years ago, this girl became such an important part of my life that I swear my heart beat in time with hers.

I was only happy if she was happy.

I laughed when she laughed.

I wanted to fight whatever battle she was going through that made her cry.

Everything I was, everything I wanted to be fell in line the moment she smiled at me.

And now as I turn to take in her calmed features as she leans back, soaking in the rare rays of sunlight, I know those feelings are stronger than ever.

"I'll always be here for you, Kinsley." She looks over at me and I lean my arm against hers. "Always."

———

"There he is. How was the event today?"

I lean down, kissing Mum on the cheek and ruffling Beckham's hair.

"It was grand. Nothing better than seeing those kids' faces light up after a turn around the track."

I snag a biscuit and throw my arm around Sydney's shoulder.

"And how's project halo going?"

My eyebrows furrow and I look down at her in confusion. "What the hell is project halo?"

She rolls her eyes, lowering her voice. "How is it going with getting Kinsley back?"

I scowl at her. "None of your business."

"Oh, come on," she cries as I head out back to join Dad at the grill.

"Smells good, Pops." I clap him on the shoulder.

"Thanks, Son. How was your day?"

"Can't complain. I got to make dreams come true, they served curry chips in the cafeteria, and I'm working on something super special for a friend."

He nods, taking a sip of his beer. "This a special project for a special friend?"

I peer at him and he glances at me out of the corner of his eye. It clicks and I set my beer down. "Excuse me. I seem to need to remind my sister what happens when you snitch on your brother."

"No throwing this time. Your mother just got the last hole you two put in the wall fixed," he calls out to my back as I stalk across the yard.

"No promises," I yell over my shoulder.

I enter the kitchen as Sydney tips back laughing while

Lawson stands next to her with an unimpressed look on his face. She glances at me as she works to catch her breath.

"Oh, Jace. You just missed it. Here, I'll recreate it for you. So—" Her words cut off when Dad walks in behind me and her eyes move between us before settling on me.

"Uh-oh," she whispers.

"Uh-oh," I echo.

With lightning speed, she grabs a roll and throws it across the room at me. It bounces off my chest and I growl, taking steady steps towards her.

She squeals, throwing herself off the stool and shoving my best friend out of the way.

"Hey man," I nod as I pass him.

His chuckle follows behind me as I prowl down the hall after my sister.

"Why's Dad chasing Aunt Sydney?" I hear Beckham ask.

"Because your Aunt Sydney didn't eat all her vegetables," Mum replies.

Their voices fade as I round into the living room, finding Sydney on the other side with a sofa between us.

"I can explain," she says breathlessly.

"What happened to the part of the plan where you keep your mouth shut?"

"That only pertained to Kinsley," she defends, yelping when I hurdle the sofa and she sprints back to where I was just standing.

"I'm sorry," she yells. "Mum and Dad were asking how you were doing and I let it slip."

"Oh, you just let it slip," I mock.

She throws a pillow at me and sprints towards the hallway. I bat the cushion away and take off after her.

"This is why I didn't make you part of the plan," I grit out when I chase her into the dining room. "How can I trust that you won't 'let it slip' to Kinsley about our past when you couldn't pass the parent questions?"

"Hey," she yells. "You know Mum could medal in interrogation. Everyone eventually cracks. It's the whole 'kill them with kindness' thing she's mastered."

"That is so not the point, Sydney."

When I lunge for her, she slips on the rug and tumbles to the floor. I pounce on top of her and pin her hands over her head.

"What did you tell them?"

"Nothing," she shrieks, wiggling underneath me. I grunt when her shin connects with my dick and she freezes, eyes wide. "I'm so sorry."

"I don't think you are."

I make a show of pooling as much saliva in my mouth as I can and she starts to try and buck me off ferociously. I let the strand of spit slip out and she screams, tilting her head away.

"Okay, I swear I'll eat my veggies," a small voice yells and we both look up to see Beckham watching us in the doorway.

He runs off towards the kitchen and I look down at Sydney. She flashes me a smile and I glower, rolling my eyes. Shoving off of her, I collapse against the wall and wipe my mouth with my shirt.

"I can't believe you were about to do that. We're grown adults."

"You're still my annoying little sister."

She props herself up on her elbows and looks at me. "I'm sorry I told Mum and Dad about Kinsley being back. If it means anything, they're cheering you on just as much as we all are."

I huff a laugh, letting my head fall back against the wall.

"I'd ask how it's going, but I've officially run out of energy to run away from you."

I chuckle, looking over at her as she sits down next to me. "It's—" I'm cut off when my phone rings and I pull it out, Mitch's name flashing across the screen.

Smiling, I stand up and look down at her. "It's about to get a lot better hopefully."

CHAPTER 29
KINSLEY

"Are we there yet?"

"Not yet."

"What about now?"

"Cooper."

He looks up at me and whispers, "Now?"

I laugh under my breath and run a hand over his brown waves. "We'll be there soon."

He leans into my side with a dramatic sigh and I shake my head, looking out the window. The grass of the rolling hills dances in the breeze, a storming brewing in the distance.

Please don't let that be a sign.

The past forty eight hours have been... interesting.

I don't think I could have made it through everything if it weren't for Jace.

Jace.

The man who caught me crying and instead of turning the other direction, sat down and listened to my blubbering words. Who took my hand, wiped my tears, and told me that everything would be okay. That we would figure this out.

The man who spent the last two days making calls, coming up with a plan and who called this morning, asking to meet him at the team's headquarters... with Cooper.

I don't know what to expect when we get there, but they wouldn't fire me in front of my kid right? *Right?*

The thought may have crossed my mind when I fussed over Cooper's clothes and hair more than normal before we left. You know, just in case. Because who can do something like that in front of a cute kid?

My knee bounces as I check my watch, Cooper giggling that I'm making him all wobbly. The bus ride to the Miller Racing Headquarters isn't terribly long. I would have preferred to drive, but Rose had a doctor's appointment this afternoon.

She told me she'd be fine taking the bus to which I crossed my arms, giving her my best 'not going to happen, lady' look. Still the old bat tried sneaking the keys into my purse every chance she got.

But I had the world's cutest little trojan horse on my side.

Is using my kid to do my bidding a little out there? No, that's what they're there for.

Was he all too excited to pull a fast one on his Gran? Absolutely.

He took the wrapped scone I'd given him over to her in the coffee shop with a beaming smile, handed it over before high tailing it back behind the counter, and snickered behind his hand as she opened the bag.

His wide eyes met mine when she yelled out his full name and I snatched him up, making a break for it as he giggled with every step.

Kinsley and Cooper: 1

Granny Rose: 0

I smile at the memory of his cheers and take a deep breath, running my hand over the back of his head as he snuggles farther into my side. I let the motion of the bus and the feel of his soft curls under my fingers calm my racing heart.

Jace told me to meet him there at one, and we would have made it if it weren't for the bus running behind on top of getting stuck behind a farmer herding his sheep across the road. I glance at the clock above the door and I internally groan when it shows that it's now fifteen minutes past one.

Another ten minutes later, the bus slows and I lean down. "We're here."

Cooper's head pops up with renewed energy and he shoots out of the chair, calling for me to 'hurry up already.'

He has no idea where we're going, but to a six year old, anywhere new is exciting. We could be going to the mail center and he'd be vibrating with the need to get as many postage stickers as possible.

Ah, to see the world through kids' eyes.

I laugh as I follow him down the stairs, grabbing his hand when we hit the sidewalk. We walk down past the back of the bus and I freeze when I see the man standing on the other side of the street.

Jace leans against a golf cart, arms crossed as he watches a little boy with blond hair twist the wheel as if he's driving a race car. The boy looks up at him with a beaming smile and bright blue eyes before focusing back on the imaginary track in front of him.

Beckham.

Since finding out that we've been pen pals all these years through the Facebook group for families living with diabetes, there's this simmering connection between us. Like how I know things about him and he knows things about me someone usually wouldn't after only meeting in person just over a month ago.

I'm not scared to admit that I might have had a crush on his secret identity all this time. And now I have a face, a whole man, to put to the words I read countless times.

And what a man he is. Both versions of him.

A startled squeak leaves me when the bus hisses before pulling away from the curb. Cooper giggles and I look down at him. "What are you laughing at?"

"Mummy got scared by the bus." He breaks into another fit of laughter.

I scrunch my face and bend down, wrapping my arms around him and acting like I'm going to eat him. He squeals through his laughing, trying to push me away with his hands on my face.

"Who's the scaredy cat now?"

He koala's himself to my chest and I laugh, stumbling back onto my butt with him on my lap. His wide eyes meet mine and we laugh.

"Sorry, Mummy."

"It's okay, my little monster." I tuck a wayward strand of hair off his forehead.

He leans forward, raising his hands like he has claws. I press my forehead against his, scrunching my face and match his growl.

Pulling back, we stand and I dust off both of our clothes. Straightening, I glance across the street and my cheeks heat.

Jace stands with his hands on his son's shoulders. Beckham's head is twisted up so he's looking at his father, but Jace's attention is glued on us.

I raise my hand and wave, watching his shoulders shake with a chuckle. Tucking my lips, I look left and right before leading Cooper across the street.

"Hi," I whisper.

He smiles. "Hi." His eyes drop to the boy clutching my arms that are wrapped around his shoulders. "You must be Cooper."

"Yes, sir."

He squats down in front of him. "Your mum's told me a lot about you. I'm Jace and this is my son, Beckham." He turns his head to his son. "Beckham, this is Cooper and his mum, Kinsley."

"Hi." Beckham waves, glancing up at me.

I smile. "It's nice to meet you, Beckham."

Cooper glances up at me and I nod. He steps out of my arms. "Hi. I'm Cooper, but Mummy and Gran like to call me Coop."

"My dad calls me Becks. So I guess you can too if you'd like."

"Cool."

"How old are you?"

"I just turned six."

"Really? When's your birthday?"

"March the twelfth. You?"

"February the fourteenth. My Aunt Sydney calls me her little love baby."

Both of the boys' faces twist in disgust with a chorus of 'ews.' I catch Jace's gaze as he stands and he smothers a laugh by rubbing his hand over his scruff.

"Okay, who's ready to head inside?" He claps his hands and the boys jump up and down in excitement. He points at Cooper. "Have you ever driven a golf cart before?"

Cooper looks up at him in shock before shaking his head.

Jace chuckles. "Well, if it's okay with your mum, would you want to be the one to take us to where we need to go?"

"I got to drive out here and it was awesome," Beckham says.

Everyone's attention slides to me and I blush. "Oh, um—"

"He'd be sitting on my lap and I'd have my hands on the wheel the entire time," Jace says reassuringly.

I tuck my lips, and look down at my little boy. He folds his hands under his chin, sticking out his bottom lip. Beckham joins him and before I know it, they're both putting all other puppy dog eyes to shame.

I laugh under my breath and sigh. "Okay." The boys cheer and run over to the golf cart, Jace and I following at a much more appropriate pace. "You swear it's safe?"

"Promise. With the pressure I put on the gas, you'd

probably get there a lot faster at a jog than on this thing. But to them it's like we're whipping around corners at the speed of light."

We load into the cart with Cooper on Jace's lap and Beckham between us. He shows my boy where to place his hands before grabbing onto the bottom of the wheel like he promised.

The sound of excited giggles pierce the air as he eases onto the accelerator pedal.

"Mummy, look, I'm doing it!"

Smiling, I pull out my phone, open the camera, and press record. Cooper shifts on Jace's lap as Beckham makes racing sounds from their side. When we veer a little off the road, Jace gives him directions on how to correct it.

"Good job, Coop," he cheers.

Beckham makes a radio sound and covers his ear as if he's holding headphones. "Alright, mate. You're holding strong in first place, let's clench that win with one last push."

Cooper makes a static sound before talking out of the side of his mouth. "Copy that."

Jace chuckles as the two boys continue to talk with their radio voices until we reach the main building. Beckham makes a screeching sound when we stop and throws his hands in the air. "And that's P1!"

Cooper starts to join in the celebration but stops abruptly. "Wait, what's P1?"

"It means 'Position 1' which is really just first place. Right, Dad?"

"Right." He chuckles. "That was some great driving there, Coop. We'll make a race car driver out of you yet."

A laugh slips out of me as I end the video and Cooper looks over. "Can I do that, Mummy?"

"What? Be a race car driver?" He nods frantically and I tilt my head. "You can be anything you want to be, love."

He throws his head back—nearly colliding with Jace's chin—and throws his hands in the air as he screams 'yes.' Beckham hops up on the seat and taps his arm. "We can be on the same team just like my dad and Uncle Lawson!"

"That would be so cool. Can we?" Cooper twists, looking up at Jace.

"I don't see why not. Now let's hurry inside, I've got some important people I want you and your mum to meet."

He helps Cooper down and I slide out of the seat with Beckham hopping to the ground behind me. We walk into the main building, the boys running ahead to look at all the memorabilia. Their drawn out 'woahs' and 'cools' echo around the empty atrium.

I watch them a little longer before turning to look at Jace. His eyes are still on them as they run to a replica of one of the older race cars. There's a glimmer of something in his eyes as he watches them, but my attention is brought to the side when Mitch calls out.

"There they are."

A woman that looks to be in her mid forties walks beside him, a smile on her face. Stopping next to us, Mitch claps a hand on Jace's shoulder. "Have you told her the good news?"

Jace scowls. "No, thank you for stealing my thunder."

"Tell me what?"

He motions to the woman. "Kinsley, this is Anne. She's Beckham's home school teacher."

"Nice to meet you," she greets.

I return her smile as Jace continues. "Last season she traveled with us, doubling as his nanny of sorts. She's agreed to do it again this season. Even add on a new student."

I pause, my mind racing. "What are you saying?"

"I'm saying, you can bring Cooper with us. Anne will be his teacher so that he doesn't fall behind and when you're working, she'll watch the boys."

"What?" It comes out as a whisper and he takes my hand.

Stepping closer, he lowers his voice. "I told you we'd figure it out, but if this isn't something you're okay with I completely understand. I just thought—"

His words end on a grunt when I throw myself at him, my arms around his neck.

"Thank you," I whisper.

His arms slide around me, his hands pressing against my back and pulling me tighter against him. "I'm taking this as a sign that you like the idea?"

I pull back, relieved tears threatening to spill. "I love it."

He breathes out a sigh of relief and I laugh.

"Mummy?" We break apart at the sound of Cooper's small voice and I turn to him, kneeling so we're eye to eye. "Why are you sad?"

I wipe my eyes. "I'm not sad, love."

"But you're crying." His little face scrunches in worry.

"These are happy tears." I glance at Jace as he squats

down next to me, Beckham at his side. "Really happy." Facing Cooper, I take his hands. "You know how Granny Rose got hurt the other day?"

He nods. "I didn't like it."

I scrunch my nose and shake my head. "Me neither."

"Is Granny Rose going to be okay? Is that why you're crying happy tears?"

"Granny Rose is going to be okay, yes, but remember how we said she wouldn't be able to watch you while I was away for work now that she's recovering?"

"Mhm." He nods. "You said that you might be home all the time again, but how would you be able to still take Mr. Jace's pictures if you're home?"

Jace chuckles and I blush. "Well, Mr. Jace was able to save the day."

"Like a superhero?" he whispers.

I nod, glancing at Jace. "He was able to call on some of his other superhero friends, like Miss Anne here—" I motion towards her.

She smiles. "Hi, Cooper."

"So that you could come with me."

He gasps, jaw dropping. "You promise?"

My heart constricts when I see that the question he's asking isn't for me. Cooper turns to Jace, eye's full of wonder. Jace glances at me and I nod. He looks back at my son. "I promise."

Cooper throws his tiny arms around his neck, the momentum knocking them over. Jace grunts when his back hits the floor, but it's quickly followed by a low chuckle. "I can guess where you get this from."

"Pile on," Beckham yells, jumping on top of them.

The boys wrestle with Jace who pretends to be helpless against their combined strengths. I glance off to the side and mouth 'thank you' to Mitch and Anne who nod back.

"Okay, you little maniacs." Jace stands up with each boy hanging from one of his arms. "Are you ready?"

They both giggle when he sets them back on their feet and Beckham tilts his head. "Ready for what, Dad?"

Our eyes meet and he winks. "For an adventure."

INSTAGRAM POST

@THEJACECOLLINS

Carousel of images:

1. Cooper and Beckham sitting on a wheel of Jace's race car

2. Cooper and Beckham sharing a seat on the plane with an iPad between them

3. Cooper and Beckham with a bowl of ramen the size of both of their heads

4. Cooper and Beckham in ninja costumes posing with Jace playing dead under them

5. Beckham with a portrait that Cooper drew of him

6. Cooper with a portrait that Beckham drew of him

7. Cooper and Beckham running down the paddock lane

Caption: BFF Goals.

Comments:

@kinsleythroughthelens: Thank god you didn't include the picture I did of you

@thejacecollins replied to @kinsleythroughthelens: That beauty deserves it's own post

@jcollinsfanpage: It's giving daddy AND step-daddy energy

@sassycassie: I'm having flashbacks to me and Blake

@ladyblakeking replied to @sassycassie: When had we EVER eaten that much ramen

@ryderking replied to @ladyblakeking: Last winter when we went to visit

@sassycassie replied to @ryderking: Okay, but did the world need to know this???

@fortheloveoff1: Haven't shipped anything this hard since Blake and Ryder

CHAPTER 30

KINSLEY

"Hi-yah!"

"Ow," I mumble into my pillow.

There's a shuffle of fabric before a quiet voice whispers next to my ear. "Mummy? Are you awake?"

"Mummy isn't here right now, please leave a message."

His sweet giggle brings a sleepy smile to my face and I turn my head, peeking at my mini ninja. He hasn't taken the outfit off since we got the boys matching ones two days ago. Well. Except for the mandatory cleaning I gave it yesterday after Soy-Sauceagedon.

"It's race day, Mummy."

"That it is, my little genius."

He giggles, hopping on his knees. "Get up. Get up. Get up."

I pounce, his shriek echoing off the walls as I drag him under the blankets with me. "Sleeper hold initiated," I whisper.

His laughter is muffled against my arm but he breaks free when his elbow accidentally digs into my very full bladder and I let go of him with a groan.

"Cheap shot, kid."

"Sorry. Are you okay?"

"I'm okay, baby." I roll out of bed and stretch. "I guess it's time to get up. Let me get ready and we'll head out for some breakfast, okay?"

Today's the first race since Jace pulled everything together so the boys could come with us. To say I'm a little nervous is quite the understatement.

What if all the noise is too much for him?

What if he needs me and I'm not there?

What if he gets lost?

What if this was a mistake?

Every scenario of what could happen runs through my mind as I get ready for the long day ahead and pack a bag with anything I think Cooper might need for the day.

There's a knock on the door and I check in to make sure the little man is brushing his teeth before going to open it.

"Oh."

"Well good morning to you too," Jace chuckles and I snap out of my shock at seeing him standing outside my door.

"Sorry. Hi. Good morning. Would you like to come in?"

"Uh—"

"Is Cooper inside?" Beckham hops up on his toes, cutting off his dad.

I smile down at him and nod. "He's finishing up brushing his teeth."

"I started using grown up toothpaste."

"Really? That's so cool."

"I don't really like it."

"Oh," I laugh. "Then that is so not cool."

"I'm still going to use it though because my dad uses it and I want to be just like him." He looks up at Jace who's smirking down at him.

"Alright. Alright. You can go in if you want, you don't have to keep trying to butter me up."

"Sweet," Beckham cheers, speeding into the room when I hold the door open wider for him.

"So what brings the Collins boys to my door this morning?" I ask, leaning against the door.

"I was actually coming to see if you and Cooper wanted to join us on a track walk."

"Track walk?"

"Yeah. We walk the entirety of the track, kind of plan out what our game plan is going to be. It's a great opportunity to see the conditions of the roads on race day. We do it at every race and when Becks traveled with us last season, he came along on them too."

"Oh, that's actually really cool."

He nods. "He loves it. He's always making up his own plan for how he'd take on the race."

"Does he make race car noises?"

"Of course. It's required."

"It's required to make race car noises when you're walking the track?" I laugh.

"Yep, we'll be cursed if you don't."

"Well good thing I've been studying up on my racing noises lately."

"Is that what that was last night?"

"No, that was just my snoring," I shrug.

"But you don't—" he cuts off abruptly, clearing his throat and ducking his head.

His phone goes off and he pulls it out of his pocket, shutting off an alarm. He looks up at me and smiles. "So what do you say? Do you and Cooper want to join us on a turn around the track?"

I pause, shocked for the second time this morning. First by his presence at my door and now by the hopeful sincerity in his... everything.

It's in the way he stands, watching my every move for any hint at what I'll say. In the way he drops his voice into a whiskey smooth timbre that would probably hypnotize even the most guarded mind.

I smile, tossing a thumb over my shoulder. "Let me grab my bag."

———

"Vroom," the boys race by us for the fifth time, crossing the finish line at the same time so both of them win.

That was the main part of the plan they concocted when we first set out on our walk. When Jace tried to tell them that the likelihood of them ending in a tie was unlikely, they blocked their ears and ran off singing that they couldn't hear him.

No one, not even the realities of the world, will get between these two and their hopes and dreams.

I lift my camera, snapping a picture of the two of them cheering and I smile. A hand lands on my arm, bringing me to a stop and I look over at Jace.

"I think there is a requirement of this walk that you have yet to do, Miss Jones."

"What?"

The noise starts low, slowly increasing in sound until he's speeding around me before taking off towards the finish line.

I watch him with a disbelieving smile on my face, laughter caught in my throat. When he crosses the white line, he spins, cupping his hands around his mouth.

"Your turn," he yells. I shake my head and he lifts an eyebrow. "I guess you want me to be cursed for today's race then."

My face drops and I quickly throw my camera strap over my head before holding up my hands like I'm gripping a steering wheel.

I lied when I said I'd been practicing my race car sounds. Why would I ever need to do that? But now as I'm standing here with my hands hanging in the air, I make a mental note to add it to my to-do list.

With the most embarrassing noise I've possibly ever made, I take off at a jog towards the boys at the finish line. I weave left and right like I'm battling it out with someone before zooming across the line and circling them.

I come to a stop in front of Jace and he watches me with a stricken expression.

"What?" I ask, slightly out of breath.

Adding more cardio to the to-do list as well.

"That was your race car noise?"

"Yes," I draw out the word cautiously, yet I know exactly what he is going to say next.

"It... it could use some work."

"Oh, I know."

"I thought you said you'd been practicing it?"

A laugh bursts out of me. "Why would I ever need to practice that?"

He pauses, thinking of a retort. "You know what? That's fair, but starting today we're going to work on it. I can't have you walking around making that noise."

"Is it really that bad?"

"It sounds like you are pinning the accelerator and your engine is two seconds from exploding. No shifting, nothing. Just straight full throttle."

"Yikes. Please, teach me the way of a proper race car noise."

"Don't worry, we will have you fake racing around everyone in no time."

He chuckles and I smile, shaking my head. Someone calls Jace's name and we look off to the side to see his race engineer waving him over.

"I guess it's that time," he sighs.

Side by side with the boys in front of us talking animatedly, we walk back to the teams garage where we will leave them with the woman Jace introduced me to last week, Anne, for the entirety of the race.

I'm bummed to be missing Cooper's first race experience, but she promised to take as many pictures and videos as her phone would allow so that I got to see it afterwards.

With the promise to meet right back here after the race, she heads off towards the stairs that will lead them to the investors' box above the garage. It's a great spot where they'll be able to watch the race without anyone having to worry about them getting in the way.

"Ready?" Jace asks, breaking away from his engineers.

"Yep," I nod, following him out of the back of the garage and towards the team's clubhouse.

My head is still a flurry of worries as I gather my camera equipment and I'm so lost in my thoughts that I don't realize he's saying something until I look up at him.

"I'm so sorry, what did you say?"

He studies me a moment before stepping closer and gently grabbing my arm. "You okay?"

I sigh, setting down my camera in its slot in my bag and zipping it up. "My mind is just all over the place. I just want him to be safe and have fun. And I'm just worried that maybe I should have stayed home—"

"What? No." I look up at the slight panic in his voice and he takes a deep breath, shifting on his feet. "It's going to be grand, Kinsley. I trust Annie with my life because that's what Beckham is. He is *my life* and I don't hand that over to just anyone. Cooper is in great hands and he's going to have so much fun, I promise. He's good and you are good."

I nod, sighing at the instant relief I feel because of his words.

He ducks his head, catching my eye. "But know that I'm here if you need anything, okay? Big or small, whatever you ask for, it's yours."

I smile, pushing his arm playfully. "Jace—"

He chuckles. "I'm serious. You're not in this alone, Kinsley. We're all here for you and that amazing little boy. You're ours now and we take care of what's ours."

And just like that, he eviscerates the rest of my worries.

I swallow, letting instinct take over, and step into his personal space. Wrapping my arms around his waist, I lean my head on his chest and close my eyes at the sound of his steady heartbeat.

"Thank you," I whisper.

His arms slip around me and I feel him lean his cheek on top of my head. His fingers flex, arms tightening as he blows out a slightly shaky breath.

"Anything for you," he says quietly.

I lean into the hug for a few more heart beats before pulling back and smiling up at him. He watches me with a small tilt of his lips and I freeze when he lifts his hand, tucking a rogue lock of hair behind my ear.

"I'll see you after the race?" he asks nonchalantly. Like he didn't just say the sweetest thing someone has ever said to me, then followed it up with a move I'd only ever read about in the silly little romance books Rose gives me.

"Yeah," I whisper. "I'll see you after the race."

"Make sure you get my good side," he smirks, walking backwards towards where his dressing room is located.

"Yes sir," I salute him, blaming a trick of light at the quick shift in his gaze before he shakes his head and spins, walking down the hallway.

I watch his toned back as he goes, losing sight of him when he turns the corner. Rolling my lips, I reach up and touch the side of my face where I could have sworn I felt his thumb brush before he tucked my hair.

He was just gathering the pieces so it wouldn't be in my eye.

Yeah, that has to be it.

Shaking myself out of my thoughts, I finish gathering my gear and head out to my assigned post. It's a short five minute walk to where I'll get a front row seat at one of the track's shorter straights.

There's a slight platform there and I climb the stairs, but come to a stop with my foot on the top step. I look over the small area and catalog everything.

Chair.

Safety helmet.

Cooler.

Wait. Cooler?

I set my stuff down by my seat and tilt my head at the mystery case. There's a folded piece of paper taped on top and I pluck it off, a smile breaking across my face at the messy scribble.

Some snacky snacks and hydration for the best photographer ever. Now I can go out and win this race knowing the boys and you are taken care of.
—Yours, JC

I laugh, opening the cooler and sifting through the sweet and salty options as well as some different drinks. Shaking my head, I pull out a blue Gatorade and crack it open.

My eyes scan over the note and my fingers trace over his initials as a single thought creeps into my mind.

My nerves never really stood a chance did they?

CHAPTER 31
KINSLEY

THERE's a little foot in my face.

I could have sworn when we laid down, there was a sweet head of curly brown hair laying on the pillow next to mine.

I lean up on my elbow and squint down towards the foot of the bed. Cooper's lying on his stomach, face pressed into the side of my thigh. His arms are splayed out around him, one draping over my legs and the other clutching onto the race car Jace got him last week.

I'm reminded about what woke me up when the fan turns back this way, blasting me with air. I shiver and my eyebrows pinch as I take in the state of what's left of our bedding.

Leaning over the edge, I get a glimpse of the fluffy duvet piled on the floor. The sheet looks like it's been through war, stretched and crushed into the bottom corners of the bed. There's a low glow to the room as light peeks around the edges of the curtains.

I pick up my phone, seeing that it's almost seven in the morning.

My pout over the fact that I could have had a few more minutes before my alarm was due quickly morphs into a muffled giggle as Cooper mumbles something about a cereal party before making a slurping sound.

Pinching my lips together, I reach over and brush the hair back from his eyes. He grumbles, his little face scrunching in annoyance and flips so his head faces away from me.

I shift to my knees and lean over him. "Little monster, time to wake up." He wiggles, worming his body farther down the bed. I chuckle and flop down next to him, poking his cheek. "Come on, sleepy head."

"Mmm," he whines.

Sighing, I roll out of the bed and head for the bathroom, calling over my shoulder dramatically, "I guess there'll be more delicious waffles for me then."

Picking up my toothbrush, I yelp when I look in the mirror and see a disheveled little boy standing in the doorway behind me. My lips twitch as he shuffles into the bathroom and climbs up onto the step stool, grabbing his race car toothbrush and holding it out to me.

I put some toothpaste on the bristles and he sticks it in his mouth, his nose scrunching.

"Ish show spishy," he says around the toothbrush.

I laugh, brushing his hair back as foam spills out of the corners of his mouth. "We'll get you some more of your toothpaste when we get home next week, okay?"

He nods and we finish up in the bathroom before I

help Cooper get dressed in the jeans and Miller Racing T-shirt that I laid out for him last night. He picks out his black hat to wear with it and jumps around excitedly when I hand him the matching one for Beckham.

I'm slipping on my Miller team shirt over my compression long sleeve when there's a knock at the door. "I'll get it," he yells, running across the small room.

"Wait." He doesn't listen as he yanks the door open, but it slams shut when it ricochets off the secondary lock. His head jerks back. "What the?"

There's a familiar muffled chuckle on the other side of the door and I walk up behind Cooper. Sliding the security bar out of the way, I pull open the door and he slips in front of me.

"Becks!"

"Coop!"

"I feel like that's how everyone should greet each other. It's so much more exciting than 'hey, what's up' don't you think?" I laugh and he smiles. "Are you two ready to head out or do you need a few minutes?"

"Let me just throw my hair up real quick and grab my camera bag."

I move back into the room, flipping the lock to keep the door open. As I'm brushing my hair, my ears perk up at Cooper's bright voice. "Look."

Jace gasps and I shake my head with a smile knowing exactly what Cooper is showing him.

"That's my driver number."

"Mummy got me it yesterday. Oh, I also got this for you, Becks. It's so we can match."

"Sweet. Dad, look what Coop got me."

"That's awesome, dude. What do you say?"

"Thanks, Coop. Dad, can we change my shirt so we can match even more?"

My stomach dips at Jace's soft chuckle and I close my eyes, picturing the smirk on his face as he looks down at his son. "Sure thing, bud. We'll stop by our room on the way out."

"Yes," the boys whisper cheer in unison.

I grab my camera bag and Jace looks up as I step into the hallway with them. He glances down at my bag. "Here, let me." Leaning down, he takes the bag from me and my attention catches on the flex of his arm as he slides the strap over his shoulder.

My cheeks heat as my eyes trace the veins of his strong hands and the image of him holding my face, his thumb swiping across my cheeks floods my mind.

I jump slightly when there's a tap on my arm. Looking down, a giggle burst out of me when the hat on Beckham's head flops to the side.

"Hold on." I squat down in front of him and take his hat off, tightening the strap. I fix it back on his head and tap the brim. "There you go, handsome."

"Thank you."

I straighten and the boys take off down the hallway towards the lift. Jace knocks his arm into mine as we follow behind them, nodding towards where they stand taking turns hitting the button. "He likes you."

"You think so?"

He nods as we make our way to the boys. When the doors open, I guide them in and swear I hear him whisper 'he's not the only one' under his breath.

I track him as he joins us and watch his reflection on the doors when they close. The small space fills with the boys' voices as they animatedly talk about what they think breakfast will be today.

His eyes meet mine and my face flames at being caught. But instead of discomfort, there's a softness in his gaze as they dance over my face.

I blink as the doors open and we silently follow after the boys. After changing Beckham's shirt, we head down to the car and load up, making our way through the city to the track.

"Dad, do you think you'll win today?"

"Of course he will," Cooper says matter of factly.

Jace chuckles, glancing in the rear view mirror. "You think so?"

My son nods. "You have your good luck charm, right?"

Jace looks over at me for a beat before focusing back on the road. "I do."

"Then luck's on our side, right, Mum?"

I twist in the seat and smile at him. "Absolutely."

"How fast do you think you'll go, Dad?"

"I don't know? As fast as I can?"

"A bajillion kilometers a minute?" Cooper asks, eyes wide.

"Not that fast, but we can sometimes hit two hundred and fifty kilometers a minute here."

My eyebrows shoot up. "Really?"

He nods. "It's one of the faster paced races of the season, even for a street circuit."

"Wow," Cooper coos.

"Which race is your favorite?" I ask.

"I'm partial to Silverstone since it's my home race, but I love a good turn around Monaco. It's just iconic. I remember watching Ryder's dad race there growing up. We'd be on the edge of our seats the entire time watching him speed through the narrow streets like he was out for an afternoon drive."

"I like that we get to hang out on the boat afterwards," Beckham chirps.

"You guys have a boat?" Cooper asks, jaw dropping.

Beckham nods. "And we do a cannonball contest off the back. I'm the champion. Uncle Ryder and Uncle Lawson are okay, but Dad's terrible."

Jace mocks outrage. "Oi, my balls are spectacular!"

I choke on a laugh and the boys burst into a fit of giggles.

Cooper wheezes, "You said balls," before immediately throwing his head back as a laugh wracks his tiny body.

I shake my head, my eyes sliding to Jace as he pulls through the back gate of the paddock. His jean clad legs are spread as he leans back into the seat with an arm draped over the wheel. There's a small smirk on his lips as he glances between the road and our boys in the back.

As if feeling my stare, he looks over and winks.

294

I dip my head to hide my blush, my lips twitching at his quiet chuckle.

I dare anyone to *not* react this way to that wink.

Seriously, I think he could get grown men to swoon with one look.

Breakfast is filled with sticky fingers, whipped cream tipped noses, and more berries on the ground than what made it into our mouths after a competitive round to see who could catch the most.

Hopped up on sugar, the boys take off on the track with Jace and I chasing after them. As we round the last corner, we slow to a much more relaxed pace behind them.

"Boys, don't go too far," Jace calls after them, breathing heavily.

I laugh under my breath as he shakes his head, glancing at me.

I smile and bump my shoulder into his. "Are you ready for the race?"

He nods. "I think it'll be a good one. There's always lots of action here."

"I kind of like those 'boring' races, though." My eye's meet his and I say quietly, "They're a lot nicer to my heart."

He pauses. "You worried about me while I'm out there, Jones?"

"I'd be lying if I said I didn't get nervous when you're battling it out with another driver."

His eyes dance between mine, his smile growing. "Careful now, or I'll start to think you might like me or something."

I open my mouth but the denial doesn't come and I realize I don't want it too.

For weeks I've felt these flutters of butterflies whenever I'm around him. I've tried to ignore the sparks that skate over my skin whenever he brushes by or the skip of my heart when I feel his eyes on me.

The physical attraction, I could handle, but it's the little things he does and says that I'm in trouble of falling for.

Like how he makes sure I have a bag packed with snacks and hydration at my position on the track for each race so I don't risk my blood sugar dropping.

When he insists on carrying my camera bag—or any bag for that matter—when he's around.

The SOS texts he sends me when he's trapped in a meeting.

How he makes it a point to say good night to Cooper, even if it means over FaceTime.

Our breakfasts and morning walks around the track with the boys these past three weeks since they've started traveling with us.

Little by little, pieces of my guarded heart have fallen away for this man.

And something inside is urging me into the freefall.

Someone calls my name and I glance to the pitwall.

"I got them." Jace nods towards the boys and takes off in a jog.

I meet with the other photographers and we go over everyone's placements one last time before breaking apart. I start walking towards the starting line, pausing when I see Jace squatting down in front of the boys, talking to them.

There's a beat before both of them nod and Beckham moves to the other side of Jace. The boys match his pose, squatting down and placing a hand on the pavement.

I slowly raise up my camera, peering through the lens as Jace dips his head down and closes his eyes with the boys following his movements. The shutter of my camera freezes the moment and I smile down at the preview on my screen.

"What's got you smiling like that?"

I jump at the closeness of his voice, realizing I'd been standing here staring at this picture longer than I thought. Long enough for them to creep up on me.

Jace leans over my shoulder, looking down at the camera's screen and freezes.

"I'm sorry. I shouldn't have—it's just it was such a good moment and I—I'm so—"

"Amazing." His eyes slowly meet mine, a myriad of emotions swirling in their blue depths. "You have and will always be amazing." It comes out as a whisper and my lips part at the feelings behind his words.

Broken.

Yet hopeful.

The boys yell that they're going to be with Lawson in the garage and Jace turns, breaking our simmering connection.

"Listen to your uncle and stick together," he calls out to them.

We hear a duet of 'yes sir' before the shuffle of little feet.

He turns back to me and tilts his head. "Shall we finish our lap?"

I fall in step with him as we take the last few steps to the finish line. "So. Any big plans for the break next week?"

"I'll probably take the spawn to see his grandparents. Other than that, I plan on getting as much sleep as possible before we hop into this next leg." He chuckles, bumping his elbow into mine. "What about you?"

I shrug. "Probably spend every day at the coffee shop, helping Rose as much as I can since we won't be home for a while." I glance at him, this next part coming out cautiously. "You can always stop by if you'd like."

His head whips towards me and I blush, stammering over my words. "I—I just know Cooper's already dreading spending that much time away from Beckham."

He nods. "Oh, of course. I could probably bring him by so they could hang out."

"Yeah? Cooper would really like that."

He smirks. "Maybe I'll stick around as well."

Maybe I'd really like that too.

CHAPTER 32

JACE

SHE DIDN'T DENY IT.

That's all that's been running through my head through the last forty-eight hours.

When I jokingly insinuated that Kinsley might like me, I'd expected her to laugh, to brush it off like she has so many times these past few weeks.

But she didn't.

Her silence neither confirmed nor denied it, and I am taking that as a win.

I've been on cloud nine since then.

Even coming in P6 couldn't bring me down.

What did though was when we went our separate ways yesterday after landing in England for the week long break.

Every time she walks away from me, a piece of my heart goes with her. And she's been collecting those pieces for years now without even realizing it.

Now I have a real shot at being hers again.

And this week's break is ruining that blissful feeling.

"I won't try to take the look personally."

I glance over at Mum. "What look?"

She holds up her phone, before flipping the screen to show a picture of my scowl. I smooth out my features and sigh. "Sorry."

"Where's your head at, my love?"

Where it always is, on—"Kinsley."

She hums. "How are you doing?"

I look down at my lap. "I love her."

"I know you do, sweetheart." She reaches over, placing her hand over mine and squeezing. "And you really can't tell her?"

I shake my head. "I can't—*won't*—risk her well being. The doctors I've spoken to say it could potentially distort whatever she does remember from that time. Right now there's still a chance her memories can come back." I meet her eyes. "I won't be the reason she loses it all."

She nods, sadness lacing her features. "I just want you to be happy."

"I am." I squeeze her hand. "I will be."

"Dad."

"Oi! I didn't know we were in the splash zone." I chuckle when Beckham rushes over flinging water on the two of us.

He winces. "Sorry, Gran."

She laughs and I scoff. "What am I?"

"My dad?"

Since I'm soaked as it is, I wrap my arm around him and

pull him down, ruffling his hair. "He's a comedian, ladies and gentlemen."

Beckham giggles, wiggling out of my hold. "Can we invite Cooper over to swim so he can practice his cannonballs for when we're in Monaco?"

"Who's Cooper?" Mum asks, her eyebrows furrowing.

I clear my throat as Beckham excitedly tells her, "He's my new bestest friend. His mum works with Dad."

"And who's his mum?"

"Miss Kinsley. She's the best, Gran. She doesn't yell at us when we wrestle. Whenever we get to a new hotel, she looks up all the best places for us to try food and one of them is always an ice cream shop that has sugar free options for me. She loves pineapple on her pizza like me too. Oh! She got me this." He points to the superhero themed adhesive patch for his Omnipod.

Mum's eyebrows raise. "Wow. She does sound awesome."

Beckham nods enthusiastically. "And Cooper is so cool. He loves pizza, but not with pineapple, so he and Dad always share and I share with Miss Kinsley. He wants to be a race car driver when he grows up and said we could be on the same team. His favorite color is red, too, just like me!"

He turns to me with pleading eyes. "So can we?"

"I'll think about it. Check back after lunch."

He nods and turns to Mum. "Granny, when are we having lunch?"

She laughs and pats his face with the towel. "I'll start on it soon, okay?"

He takes off towards the pool, cannonballing into the

deep end and splashing water all over Sydney. I catch Mum staring at me but I don't take my gaze away from the pool.

"Jace."

I hum, looking off to the side. Wow, her roses are looking extra rosy this month.

"Jace Collins. Look at me right now."

I slide my eyes over her but quickly look away and she huffs.

"Jace Cooper Collins!" My head whips towards her and I see the questions swirling in her tender gaze. *Why didn't you tell me?*

I drop my head, messing with the label of my water bottle so I don't break down. When Sydney first told me Kinsley's son's name all those weeks ago, I didn't know what to think or how to feel.

Then she told me how Kinsley came up with the name.

It was from a dream.

But it wasn't a dream. It was a memory.

And I know exactly the moment she was in. We were hanging out with everyone in this very spot and Sydney had just dropped Lawson's full name on him when he beat her for the fifth time in Cards Against Humanity.

When I dropped her off that night, she'd asked what my full name was. *Just in case.*

I smirked and told her only if I got to know what hers was too. *You know, just in case.*

Kinsley Hope Jones.

Jace Cooper Collins.

There's a part deep down in my girl that remembers. And I can sometimes see the moments it happens. She'll say or see or hear something and get this far away look, like her brain is trying to connect the dots, but it's never quite there fully.

Like there's a wall the memories can't quite get over.

But Cooper's name?

That one has slipped through the cracks.

"His name is Cooper," Mum whispers.

"His name is Cooper," I confirm.

She watches me for a moment before standing. "I'm going to go prepare lunch."

"Okay," I say, watching her slide open the back door and step into the house.

Wait. That's it?

"You good?" Sydney asks, sitting in the chair next to me, towel drying her hair. She twirls a finger around me. "Your face is doing this weird thing."

"Something's wrong with Mum."

"What?" She sits up, alert.

"She didn't ask any questions."

"What?" Her face twists in confusion.

"Beckham just spilled the beans about Cooper and I was prepared to be hounded with questions because, well, it's Mum." I turn to look at Syd. "But there was nothing. Not a single question."

"What did she say?" She glances to the window where we can see Mum moving around the kitchen.

"She said 'his name is Cooper' and I confirmed it. Then

she got up, said she was going to fix us some lunch, and walked away."

"That is strange."

"When have you ever known Eleanor Collins not to pester her children about something?"

"Never," she snorts. "She once asked me a minimum of fifty questions on why I decided to change my coffee order to include one extra pump of caramel. Because I love caramel, Mother. That's why."

I chuckle, shaking my head and she leans back in her chair. "Honestly, take the blessing in disguise for what it is. A blessing."

Dad walks up with a burrito wrapped Beckham thrown over his shoulder and deposits him in my lap. "Where's your mum?"

"Getting lunch ready." Sydney looks up at him with a raised eyebrow. "She's being weird."

He snorts. "More than usual?"

We all look over as the sliding door opens and Mum struts out holding her purse. "Sorry, my loves. I burnt lunch. Is everyone okay if we just go to eat somewhere?"

We glance at each other before Syd and I roll our heads to look at our father. He shrugs and smiles at Mum. "Of course, sweetheart. Let us get changed and we'll head out."

Sydney stands up, whispering, "I thought we were having sarnies for lunch?"

I hum peering at my mum. "Something's fishy."

Beckham gags. "Fish. Bleh."

I chuckle as I stand with him in my arms. Mum smiles,

tickling his cheek as we walk by and I squint. She looks up at me, full of innocence. "What?"

Innocence I can see right through.

"Funny. That's my question. What are you up to?"

She rolls her eyes and struts off into the house.

"Not dodgy at all, Mother," I yell after her and she waves.

"No idea what you're talking about, Son."

After changing, Sydney, Beckham, and I follow behind our parents in my car. Twenty minutes into the drive, Beckham groans that his stomach is eating itself and I look at Sydney. "Did she say where we're going?"

She shakes her head. "Just said it's a little sandwich place one of the ladies in her knitting club told her about."

I nod as we turn down a street leading out of the city. My eyebrows furrow as we get farther into the countryside. "What friend of hers lives all the way out here?"

"No clue. Maybe she got the address wrong or—" Her words break on a gasp as we pass a sign and she shifts in her chair, looking out the windows. "Oh no."

"What?"

"Oh no. No. No." I turn onto a street and she groans, dragging her hands down her face. "Mother, what have you done," she mumbles.

"What are you going on about over there?"

She sits up and leans over the center console. "Don't freak out. Whatever you do, promise me you won't freak out."

I park and turn off the car. "Why would I—"

"Hey, this is where Aunt Sydney gets those cookies."

I take in the small pink building to the side as we get out.

Beckham runs off towards my parents and Sydney drags me to a stop by my arm.

"Jace—"

"You two coming or what?" Mum calls out.

We meet them by the front of the shop and Dad opens the door. Mum nods for me to go in and Sydney slaps a hand to her forehead.

Tentatively I step through the doorway and scan over the green and white checkered floors, pink walls, crowded bookshelves, and mismatched tables.

A gasp pulls my attention to the counter and I stop in my tracks.

"Kinsley," I whisper.

"Jace?"

Someone shoves at my legs and Beckham slips in behind me. "Coop!"

Cooper's head pops up from where he's sitting at a corner table with paper and color pencils spread out around him. "Becks!"

He jumps down from his chair and runs, the boys meeting in the middle for a hug.

Kinsley smiles at them before she looks up at me. "What are you doing here?"

"Gran burnt lunch, so we decided to go out instead," Beckham answers for me as they walk over to the counter.

She laughs, tilting her head to look around me.

"Uh, Son? Mind moving so we can come in?"

No. I'm good right here.

Sydney puts a hand on my shoulder and moves me to the

side. Our parents step into the shop and Mum waltzes right up to the counter. "You must be Kinsley."

"Yes ma'am."

Mum waves a hand. "Pfft. None of that 'ma'am' stuff, sweetheart. Just call me Eleanor. I'm Jace and Sydney's mum."

Nope. My mum's a sweet soul. I don't know who this woman is.

Kinsley beams. "It's nice to meet you. I hear you're looking for some lunch?"

Mum laughs and orders for her, Dad, Sydney, and Becks before settling in at a table. I haven't moved from my spot just inside the door, but the moment she looks at me, I take a step. Then another. And another. Until all that separates us is the countertop.

"Hi," she whispers.

"Hi."

"What would you like?"

You. Always you.

I clear my throat and lean onto the counter. "What do you recommend?"

"My personal favorite is the turkey, bacon, and avocado wrap with lettuce and apple slices."

"I'll have that then."

She blushes, nodding. "Okay." I pull out my card to pay and she waves me off. "None of that. It's on the house."

I shake my head. "Kinsley—"

"Nope. My house, my rules."

I chuckle and slide my wallet back into my pocket, raising my hands. "Yes, ma'am."

She gives me a few waters to take over to the boys and I make sure they're all good before settling into a chair. I watch her as she disappears into the back before sliding a hard look to my mother.

"You."

She sips on her lemonade. "What?"

Sydney leans on the table. "How did you even know this was where she worked?"

"Sydney, darling. You still live at home."

"Okay, wow. How is that relevant to your explanation?"

"Because you suddenly started bringing home these pink baggies with delicious baked goods almost every day."

She cringes and I glare at her. Recovering, she points her finger at Mum. "But that doesn't explain how you knew this was where I found her."

Mum shrugs. "You're right. I didn't. I took a gamble—" Kinsley walks out of the back with a tray full of our food. "And it just so happened to pay off."

"Here we are," Kinsley says. I shoot out of my chair and help her with the heavy tray. She smiles. "Thank you."

We set everyone's plates down, and take the boys theirs. I ruffle Beckham's hair. "There's a cookie in your future if you eat all of this. I'm talking licked clean."

The boys giggle and Kinsley brushes Cooper's hair off his forehead. "Maybe even two."

They look at each other with wide eyes before bending

over their plates, two boys on a desperate mission for their sweet treats.

I walk with her back to the counter and lean against it. "Are you going to join us for lunch?"

"It's okay. Enjoy the time with your family before you're stuck with me for the next few weeks." She winks and my heart gallops at the thought of it being just the four of us.

"You think I'm stuck with you while we're traveling?"

She shrugs. "I'm sure there's other people you'd rather spend your time with. Don't feel like because the boys want to hang out all the time that you have to be around me just as much."

"Ever thought that maybe I want to be around you?"

She stops wiping down the counter and stares at me. "What?"

I smirk, leaning with my hands directly beside hers. "I said that I want to spend that time with you, Kinsley. Maybe it's me using the fact that Cooper and Beckham are inseparable as an excuse to be around you."

She ducks her head, that beautiful pink hue blooming on her cheeks.

I push away from the counter and walk backwards towards the table. "Grab yourself something to eat and join us."

"Are you going to save me a seat?"

I pull a chair up to the table. "Right next to me."

She laughs, shaking her head. "I'll be right over."

I sit down with a smile and look across the table. Mum

watches me with a victorious smile and winks before digging into her sarnie.

"When did you start liking turkey?" Sydney asks, face twisted in confusion as she looks down at my plate.

She's right. I don't like turkey. Never have.

I look over as Kinsley carries her own plate of food to the table. She sits down and picks up half of the wrap, taking a big bite and softly groaning at the flavors.

But the girl I love does.

CHAPTER 33

KINSLEY

"If I didn't know better, I'd say you got laid." I choke on my spit, coughing uncontrollably as my head whips towards Rose. "But I know you didn't."

"There's no way you know that."

"We've talked every night you've been away. If it hasn't come up now, then it hasn't happened. And, you haven't asked me to watch Cooper once since you've been home."

"We've been home for three days. What, did you think I'd come home and immediately go out on the prowl like I've been away at sea for months?"

"No. That's ridiculous. But you're a beautiful twenty-five-year-old woman and yet my sixty-eight-year-old arse has seen more action in the past month than you have in years."

My face twists in horror and I throw my hands over my ears. "Oh, god!"

"Something I'm sure you haven't screamed since before Cooper was born."

"Rose." I glance over my shoulder to see my son bopping his head along to whatever he's watching on his iPad while he eats. Thank the lord I decided to let him have some screen time while I cleaned up the shop.

"When did you get so dirty?"

"Do you not look at my book when we have a book club? Pink highlighter is for cute moments. Blue for sad. Yellow for happy. And red is for the spice. I've now been through three red highlighters in the last year."

My jaw drops and she laughs. "I'll pull a couple of recommendations for you."

"Please, don't—"

"Nope, we're going to pop that spicy romance book cherry."

She shuffles over to the bookshelves and taps her chin. "Ah, this one is good." She turns to me. "The love interest is a tall dirty blond with blue eyes." She waggles her eyebrows. "Remind you of anyone?"

I snatch the book out of her hand. "I have no idea what you're talking about."

She hums, grabbing a few more off the shelves. "I'll just slip these into your luggage for you." I shake my head as she disappears down the hallway.

"So, what *does* have you floating around here with that smile on your face?" she asks when she walks back into the room, dropping a kiss to Cooper's hair. "Because something's certainly given you a new pep in your step."

I shrug. "I'm just happy. Does there need to be a reason for it?"

"I guess not. But—" Her eyes move over my shoulder. "I have a good feeling about a big part of that reason."

The bell over the door jingles seconds before little feet slap against the floor. I twist and brace in time for Beckham to collide with my legs, wrapping his arms around my waist.

I laugh, and ruffle his hair as he smiles up at me. "Well, hello there."

"Hi. Is Coop here?"

I nod to the back. "He's finishing up his lunch in the back corner. But here—" I lead him over to the counter and grab two cookies from the tray. "One for each of you. It's a new recipe. Report back with what you think."

"Sweet!" He takes off towards the table and I glance up as the bell jingles.

My smile is immediate as I take in the man standing by the door. He raises a hand and waves and I laugh under my breath as he closes the distance.

"Kinsley."

"Hi, Jace."

"Hi, Jace." A voice echoes from my right.

I jump, clutching my chest. "Jesus, I need to put a bell on you."

Rose shrugs, eyeing the man across the counter. "We meet at last."

Jace chuckles. "You must be Rose."

"I am. And you must be the pep."

He looks at me with confusion and I roll my eyes. "Ignore her." I discreetly pinch her side. "She says the craziest things sometimes. Never know what'll come out of her mouth."

"Can't seem to stay away can you?" she asks.

I flash him a smile, breathing out a laugh. "Like that."

"She's right on this one though. I can't stay away."

Rose laughs, tilting her head towards me with a knowing look. "Smart man."

I shake my head at her before turning to Jace. "What are you doing here? Not that I'm not excited to see you or anything. Because I am. Excited that is. Woo! Yay."

Good lord, please make it stop.

I laugh awkwardly and glance at Rose who watches me with a perplexed look. "If that's you flirting, maybe I should pack a couple more of those romances into your luggage."

I scowl. "Don't you have something you need to be doing. You know. Not here?"

She smiles. "I guess I could—"

"Perfect. Do that, please."

She shuffles into the back, the swinging door dancing behind her.

Jace chuckles, leaning on the counter. "We were here to see if you and Cooper had any plans for today?"

The door immediately swings back open as Rose barrels out. "She doesn't!"

"What are y—" My words cut off with a squeak as she presses a finger into my side. I jump away, swatting but she follows until I round to the other side of the counter.

"Please. Take her." She shoves my shoulder and I trip.

Jace catches me and I watch in shock as Rose unties my apron from around my waist before yanking it over my head. My hair flies around me and Jace coughs.

I look back at him over my shoulder and he chuckles, pulling my hair from where it's stuck along his stubbled jaw. He grunts, his hand finding my hip as Rose pushes us towards the exit.

"Jesus. How are you so strong?" I wiggle away from her.

She reaches over, grabbing my bag from the hook and drapes it over my head. "Pilates."

"Do you even do pilates?"

She winks. "Have to if I want to keep doing what you *should* be." She side eyes Jace.

My cheeks heat and I cover my face with my hands.

"Boys," she calls out and they come running, chocolate crumbs decorating the corners of their mouths. She leans down and wipes their faces before kissing their heads and guiding them over to us.

"Go. Shoo. Have fun."

We stumble through the door and she slams it closed behind us. My head jerks back as she locks it. "So. What are we doing today?"

———

"Boys, stay where we can see you please," Jace calls out as they run away, each holding a bag of bread. "And stay away from the water."

"I thought Beckham knew how to swim?"

"Oh he does. I just don't have a towel with me and he is absolutely not getting in my car soaking wet with pond water."

I laugh, following him to a spot on the grassy hill. "That's fair."

We settle on the small blanket he lays out and I tip my head towards the sky, soaking in the rare spot of sunshine. The sound of the boys' squeals draws my attention to the edge of the pond and I watch them throw bread before running away.

My eyes catch on a family off to the side. A little boy with a too big hat beams up at his dad and a little girl leans into her mother's arms, twisting a flower. The two kids point in my direction and the four of them turn, looking towards me with a wave.

I lift my hand to wave back but searing pain pulses in my head and I squeeze my eyes shut.

"Kinsley." Jace's voice is laced with concern. "Are you okay?"

"Yeah. I just—" I rub my head as the pain eases. "I was just looking at that family over there and got a head rush, I think."

I blink and look over to see him glancing between me and the water's edge.

"What?"

"There isn't a family there, Kinsley. I've been watching the area the entire time. It's just the boys."

My head shoots to the side and I lean up on my knees, twisting to look around. When I don't see the family anywhere, I slowly lower back down. "I could have sworn..." My words drift off and I shake my head.

I turn and he watches me with concern rippling off of him. "Are you sure you're okay?"

Something familiar skitters down my spine and I sigh. "Yeah, I just feel like I've been here before. But I could have sworn I haven't."

He swallows and opens his mouth to say something, but his eyes dart to the side and he shoots to his feet. "Beckham Edward Collins! Put that duck down right now!"

I follow his gaze, my jaw dropping. Cooper's mid lift with his own duck and I dart to my feet. "Oh my god, no!"

The boys look at us with victorious smiles. "Can we keep them?" they yell in unison.

Jace steps up next to me. "Down." He points to the ducks and then the ground. "Now."

I huff a laugh when they throw their heads back and groan before letting the ducks go. "The life of a boy mum. Never truly boring is it?"

Jace chuckles as we settle back on the blanket. "Not at all. I drove my mum nuts as a kid. Didn't help that instead of being the disciplinarian, my dad was right there getting into trouble with me."

"Really?"

"Oh, yeah. Most of the things we got in trouble for were his ideas anyway." He shakes his head. "I just hope I'm half the father for Beckham that my dad was for me."

"You're more." He looks over at me and I smile softly. "You really are. Jace, you impress me every day with how you are with him. He is easily one of the happiest, most loved little boys I've ever seen."

He looks over at his son. "I just want him to have the best life."

"All parents do." I bump my knee into his. "But you're actually making that happen."

"So are you, you know."

I shrug. "I'm doing the best I can."

"You're doing amazing."

My cheeks heat at the conviction in his voice.

"I guess it isn't a surprise by now that Cooper's dad isn't around. He left before I gave birth and a few days later, signed away his rights. That's why he has my last name."

"I'm so sorry, Kinsley. You don't have to—"

"It's okay," I say softly. "I'd been working at the shop for a few months when he came in. After a few weeks of innocent flirting, I finally agreed to go on a date with him. Things were going well, and I guess in hindsight it was going a little *too* well."

His jaw ticks and I dip my head as I continue. "I was on my way to tell him about the pregnancy when another girl opened his door. Turns out I wasn't the only one he'd been seeing."

Jace curses under his breath and I shrug. "When I told him about the baby, he said he was nowhere near ready to settle down and I told him that much was obvious."

I laugh nervously and shake my head. "I said that we didn't need to be married for him to be a part of the baby's life. But he said he didn't want that either. I asked him if he was sure and he said yes. He asked me if I was sure I was going to keep it..." I smile and look over at Cooper. "And I said yes."

"You're incredible." I take in the look of awe on his face,

my heart skipping. "Seriously. I don't think I'll ever stop being amazed by you."

A flash of something shines in his eyes but he blinks and it's gone. I duck my head, hiding my blush and fidget with the threads of the blanket.

"Thank you," I whisper.

"For what?"

"For everything. I wouldn't have been able to get through these last few weeks without you."

"I'd do anything for you, Kinsley. For you... and for Cooper."

I blink at the sincerity of his words. The wind dances through my hair and my chest rises on quick breaths as he reaches up, his fingers brushing against my cheek as he tucks a wayward strand behind my ear.

He shifts, leaning to his side and I move closer without thought. His eyes drop to my lips and I suck in a breath at the heat swirling in their blue depths when they meet mine.

His hand cups my jaw and I lean into the touch, eyes fluttering closed at the feel of his warmth. He lays his forehead against mine and rolls it side to side as if he's struggling to hold himself back.

"Kins—"

A scream pierces the air and we spring apart. Jace helps me to my feet as he looks in the direction of where the boys were.

"Dad," Beckham screams, tugging Cooper behind him.

"What—oh my god," I yell when I see multiple geese trailing after them.

The boys reach us and Jace swoops down, tucking each of them under his arms as I quickly grab our things. The blanket falls from my arms and I stop, but he circles behind me.

"Leave it, it's theirs now."

I squeal when the geese close in on us and take off towards the car. I go to open the door but it's locked. "Jace, the doors."

He tilts a hip out to me. "Pocket."

I look at him with wide eyes but he's staring off to the side. Clenching my teeth, I shove my hand in his pocket and twist it around.

"Woah, not the keys."

"Sorry," I cringe.

When I feel the metal hoop, I pull them out with a cry of victory.

"Hurry. Kinsley, sweetheart. Please, hurry." The panic in his voice increases with each word and I look over my shoulder to see the geese abandon the now battered blanket and flap their wings as they take off after us.

"What is their deal?" I shriek, clicking the unlock button.

I throw the door open and Jace tosses the boys inside. "Beckham!"

"What?"

He straightens out of the car, holding a gosling.

I slap a hand over my mouth but the laugh bursts through my fingers.

"Angel, get in the car and lock the doors."

"You think the geese will be able to open them otherwise?" I giggle.

He rolls his shoulders and cracks his neck. "Wish me luck."

I hum as he takes off running towards the advancing geese, holding out the gosling. "Here you go, safe and sound. My boys just wanted to show them the car, that's all! They're just silly little boys and you're some silly little gooses, so you understand, right?"

A goose honks and he shrieks, setting the gosling on the ground before high tailing it back to the car. "Get in. Get in. Get in."

The doors slam as we dive into the car, the quiet interior filling with his quick breaths. He glances in the mirror with furrowed brows. "I thought I said no."

I look in the back and Cooper smiles shyly as Beckham answers, "You said no to the ducks. That wasn't a duck."

Jace's exasperated eyes meet mine and I burst out laughing. His eyes drop to my mouth before slowly meeting mine and he sighs, his head falling back. "Freaking ducks."

CHAPTER 34

JACE

THE BELL above the door jingles when I push it open and greedily inhale the sweet scent of pastries and coffee. I scan the busy room, pausing on the small figure waving excitedly from the back corner.

"Go join Coop. I'll be over in just a sec."

Beckham takes off, weaving through the crowded tables and I move towards the counter. The door to the kitchen opens and Kinsley comes rushing out, tray full of steaming food. She glances at me and her previously exhausted expression breaks into a beaming smile.

She mouths 'one minute' and I nod. Leaning against the counter, I make sure I'm off to the side so that I'm out of everyone's way and watch her glide across the room.

I spot Rose sitting at a table with other ladies, leaning in to whisper before blatantly pointing in my direction. I wink and the women giggle, one of them stopping Kinsley as she passes.

She leans down and her cheeks blush at whatever the older woman is saying. She glances at me and I finger wave. Straightening, she says something to the table of ladies that have them cheering her on as she walks away.

Shaking her head, she greets the new guests and makes her way to me.

"Jace," she hums.

"Kinsley."

Her shoulder brushes my arm as she passes by and I turn, watching her slide behind the counter. She looks over her shoulder while she prepares a drink. "Three days in a row. Careful now, or I'll start to think you might like me or something."

You have no idea.

Clearing my throat, I lean with my forearms on top of the pastry case as I glance to the front door when it opens. "You weren't kidding when you said it was busy."

She turns completely, holding out a latte for me, her eyes glittering in the sunshine. "It's because of you. The post you made on your socials is what did this."

My eyebrows raise in shock. "Seriously?"

"People have been asking for the 'orgasmic' croissant all morning." She quirks a brow at me and I chuckle.

"I wasn't lying. It was the best thing I've ever experienced. I've had dirty, dirty dreams about that croissant." *And about the woman who made it.*

Her eyes flash and she puts a bag on top of the case, leaning in. "You haven't experienced all I have to offer yet."

I lean in, matching her tone. "Is that an invitation, angel?"

323

Her eyes dance between mine and my heart speeds up, my body growing hot as her gaze drops to my lips. My hands flex on the glass as I restrain myself from jumping over this pastry display, threading my fingers into her hair, and slamming my lips on hers, claiming her for all the patrons here to see.

Someone bumps into Kinsley as they pass behind her, breaking us out of our heated stare down and she blinks. "Let me go grab Cooper's things. I'll be right back."

I watch her disappear down the hall until she's out of sight before pushing off the counter and heading towards the boys. I'm halfway there when a hand on my forearm stops me.

Looking down, I smirk. "Rose. Lovely as ever."

"Charmer as always. Jace, I want to introduce you to some of my friends. This is Gwen, Betty, Ada, and Gertie."

I nod towards the four older women. "Ladies, lovely to meet you."

"We've heard so much about you," Betty coos.

I chuckle. "All good things I hope."

Gertie's eye's trail me up and down. "Pictures didn't do you justice, my boy." I huff a laugh as she leans over the side of the table. "What size shoe are you?"

Rose backhands her arm. "You know very well that shoe size has nothing to do with it."

"That was one man and it's not my fault I didn't realize they were clown shoes." She looks back at me and wiggles her eyebrows. "But you're right. This one has BDE in spades."

I glance at each of them. "BDE?"

Betty leans over, smiling from ear to ear. "It means big di—"

"Here you go," Kinsley says loudly, sliding up next to me. She lifts the bag up and I take it, not missing when she glares at the giggling group of ladies.

Sparks ignite when she places her hand on my arm, trying to guide me away from the table. "Let's get you boys out of here before they corrupt you more than they have already."

"I have a feeling he'll be the one doing the corrupting," Rose calls out as we walk away.

Kinsley's cheeks flush as I chuckle and she mockingly glares at me. I smile when we reach the boys' table. "Who's ready to go swimming?"

They both hop around in their chairs, arms held high. "Me!"

Kinsley squats by Cooper's chair and brushes his hair from his forehead. "Be good and listen to Jace and the others today, okay?"

"Yes, Mummy."

"Good boy." She kisses his head as she stands. "We close around six, but it usually calms down before then. I can always come get him—"

"We'll be here at six."

She sighs before popping up on her tiptoes and I freeze when her lips brush my cheek. Pulling back slightly, her eyes dance between mine. "Thank you for this. You're amazing."

You are.

Someone calls her name from the kitchen and she glances

over her shoulder before facing me again. My lips twitch and I jut my chin towards the kitchen. "Go."

She nods, bending to place one last kiss on his head. "Okay. Have fun. I love you."

"Love you, Mummy."

She glances at me with a smile before dashing across the bustling shop and diving into helping the others behind the counter.

I love you.

I turn to the boys and clap. "Ready?"

They nod and I follow them as we make our way to the front with a slight pit stop for Rose to give each of us—there was no way she wasn't including me—a kiss on our cheeks, to which the boys furiously try to wipe at their faces to get rid of her red lipstick.

"Well lookie who it is."

"Uncle Lawson," Cooper cheers as they load into the car.

"Are you ready to have some fun?"

"Is Uncle Ryder coming too?" Beckham asks as he climbs into his seat.

I help buckle him into his seat as Beckham finishes fastening his. "Yep and guess what."

They both look at me with bright curiosity. "What?"

"He's bringing Uncle Nik with him too."

They gasp and Cooper whispers, "It's a boys' day."

I smile, ruffling his hair. "It's a boys' day."

By the time we pull into my parents' driveway, the boys are vibrating in their seats from excitement. Lawson and I have barely opened the doors before they take off running for the house. We follow behind them, pausing at the door when Ryder pulls up.

I squint at the six packs in both his and Nik's hands. "Are those root beers?"

"Blake sent us over with them. Thought the boys would get a kick out of having a 'drink' with the guys."

"Your wife is awesome and way too good for the likes of you."

"Don't I know it," he chuckles.

We make our way to the backyard just as the boys come flying down the stairs in their swimming trunks.

"Oi, Coop. Let's get your vest on."

He shuffles over and I help him snap the floating vest on before he takes off after Beckham. Standing up, I reach down and pull my shirt over my head, throwing it at Ryder when he whistles.

Sneaking up behind my victims, I scoop the boys into my arms and they giggle as I make a run for the pool, jumping into the deep end.

We take turns tossing each of them round in the water until our arms are on the brink of giving out, sighing in relief when they ask if we can take a break to eat a late lunch. The root beer is—no surprise here—a hit and we send photos to the girls.

"Heard from the she-devil recently?" Lawson asks.

I give him a warning glare, glancing at Beckham where he and Cooper sit munching on their peanut butter and jelly sarnie.

"She gets back Saturday. Asked if she could have Becks for the night."

His eyebrows shoot up. "What did you say?"

"She's his mum, Law. What was I supposed to say?"

"How about 'wow, how gracious of you wanting to play mum for a night when you haven't bothered to even pick up the phone and call your son the past month we've been gone.'"

"Or 'how convenient that you're coming back right as we're about to leave again and only have time to spend just the one night with him,'" Nik chimes in.

"Or 'nah, we're good, catch you next time,'" Ryder quips, sipping on his root beer.

Lawson snaps, pointing at him. "That's the winner. Short and sweet."

Sighing, I lean back in my chair and groan, scrubbing a hand down my face. "There's nothing I can do lads. I'm not going to outright keep him from her."

Lawson shakes his head. "I still can't believe you fell for her tricks."

Ryder shrugs. "At least he saw her for who she really was before it was too late."

Nik tilts his head. "I'd say her having his kid goes way beyond that."

The guys hum, all of us glancing over as the boys start cleaning up their trash and disappear into the house. "I'd do it all over again if it meant I'd have him though."

A couple minutes later, there's a tap on my shoulder. "Dad?"

"Yes, Beckham?"

"We've been really good."

I bark out a laugh. "That you have."

"Granny Rose said that when someone's been good, they deserve a reward," Cooper muses and I choke on my spit knowing damn well that lovely, but pleasantly dirty old ninny isn't talking about something as innocent as ice cream.

I nod and they pull their hands in front of them, each holding multiple kid size containers of lemonade flavored Italian Ice. "We brought some for everyone," Cooper cheers.

The boys hand the lads their treats before crowding onto my chair, each of them sitting on one of my legs. Cooper's shoulders do a familiar wiggle as he takes his first bite and I watch with a tilt of my lips.

Gets that from his beautiful mum.

"Dad?"

"What's up?"

"Are you and Miss Kinsley dating?"

I choke on my spoonful of ice.

"Your dad wishes," Lawson murmurs.

"Do you?" Cooper's twists, staring up at me.

I glare at Law and Ryder nudges his arm. "Kids hear everything, don't you know that?"

"Yep," Beckham hums around a spoonful.

My hands are suddenly clammy and good god who turned the sun up a million notches? I give the boys my attention again. "Why are you asking?"

Becks shrugs. "Aunt Sydney says that if two people spend

a lot of time together then they are in love. And you are with Miss Kinsley *a lot.*"

The boys steady themselves on the table when I shift in my seat. "No. We aren't together."

The disappointment on each of their faces mirrors the break in my chest as I grit out the words. Cooper twists his lips, much like his mother when she's thinking about something she probably shouldn't say but does it anyway.

"Yet?" *Yep. Just like that.*

The lads snicker and I send each of them a glare as I shift the boys so they're facing me more. "Why are you two really asking?"

Beckham sucks in a long breath before saying at lightning speed, "I've always wanted a brother. Someone I could go on adventures with like you do. Cooper's my best friend and I thought that maybe if you and Miss Kinsley were together then that would mean we really could be brothers."

I'm stunned silent as he stares up at me. My mind scrambles for something to say and it isn't until Lawson shifts in his seat, catching my eye, that I find the words.

"You know that you two can be brothers even if me and Kinsley aren't together." I nod towards the lads. "How do you think I ended up being stuck with these three nincompoops?"

The boys giggle as the lads all scoff, mumbling how it's really them stuck with me.

Cooper sobers, tilting his head. "Do you not like my mummy?"

Very much the opposite. Kinsley Hope Jones has ingrained

herself in my soul. Hell, she is *my soul. I gave it to her willingly that day eight years ago.*

I'd give it all up for her. For you. For this family.

"I do, Cooper," I whisper. "I do like your mum."

"So then you and Mummy are together." He slurps up the remnants of his treat.

Lawson chuckles. "Not quite how that works, lads."

His little eyebrows furrow. "But if he likes Mummy and she likes him, then that means they are together. Right?"

My ears perk. "You think your mum likes me?"

He nods, licking his spoon. "I heard her talking to Granny Rose when we got home last night." He pauses, looking at me with worry. "Don't tell her I was easy dropping."

I huff a laugh. "Eavesdropping."

The boys lean back against my chest, playing with the rings on my fingers as Cooper sighs. "Then how do we know if you are together?"

"Well, first I'd take her on a date."

His head tilts. "What's a date?"

"It's where we spend time together, usually over dinner."

He hums, glancing at Becks.

"Then it's settled," my son declares, smiling at Cooper.

My eyes dart between them. "What's settled?"

They giggle and I glance at the lads who shrug.

They don't bring it up again over the next few hours and I have half the mind to think it didn't even happen. But the soft chuckles of the lads every now and then when Cooper talks about his mum's favorite food or activity is a good reminder.

We're pulling up outside of the coffee shop at five till six when I pin them in their seats with a curious glare. Their whispered conversation halts and they look at me with wide eyes.

"What are you two little schemers up to?"

"Nothing," they say in unison.

I squint at them, but something catches my attention through the window. My lips part as I watch Kinsley dancing around the shop, her head thrown back as her lips move.

The boys climb out of the car and I follow as they bolt into the shop.

"Oh my gosh!" She startles, turning the volume on the speakers down.

Cooper and Beckham crash into her legs and she laughs. "Did you have fun today, my little monsters?"

They nod and Beck shares a look with his partner in crime.

My eyebrows furrow. "Boys—"

"Will you go on a date with my dad?" Beckham blurts out.

"Like where you spend time together over dinner?" Cooper tacks on.

I stand there frozen as she glances from them to me. "I—"

"He likes you like you like him." Cooper breaks away and grabs my hand, pulling me over. "I asked."

She croaks a disbelieving laugh, her cheeks flaming.

"Your wingmen are a little younger than most, don't you think?"

I shrug. "Gotta do what you gotta do to get the girl."

She hums and I clear my throat, I stuff my suddenly shaking hands into my pockets as my eyes settle on her bright ones. "What do you say? Dinner? Saturday?"

She watches me a moment before she slowly nods. "I'd really like that."

I see the boys high five out of the corner of my eye but I don't look away from her. I can't look away from her because...

Holy shit. I have a date with Kinsley Jones.

CHAPTER 35
KINSLEY

HOLY CRAP. *I have a date with Jace Collins.*

I run shaky fingers through my curls for the tenth time in five minutes, trying to calm my rampant nerves. I look over my favorite floral sundress and beat up white Converse before grabbing my bag. I make my way out to the living room, checking that I have everything.

"Mummy, you look so pretty!" I squat down as Cooper runs over from the sofa. He plays with the ends of my hair. "Like a princess."

I kiss the tip of his nose. "Thank you, my handsome boy."

"Are you ready for tonight?" Rose asks and I stand, brushing Cooper's hair off his forehead.

"As ready as I'll ever be." I smile and look down at my boy. "Are you sure you're okay—" my words break into a laugh when he nods frantically.

Rose wraps her arms around his shoulders, placing a kiss

on top of his head. "We're going to have fun tonight, aren't we my wee matchmaker? Now go get your bag."

My eyebrows furrow as he takes off towards his room. "Why is he getting his bag?"

She waves me off. "You don't have a curfew tonight, my dear. Cooper will stay with me so that someone else can stay with you."

"Rose," I gasp.

"What? I saw that scrap of lace you snuck into your purchase at the shops yesterday." My cheeks flame and she cackles.

Cooper races back into the living room, his Miller Racing bag bouncing on his shoulders and a replica of Jace's car in his hands.

"Be good. Listen to Granny and no more than three sweets, okay?"

"Yes, Mummy."

I bend, kissing his cheek. "I love you."

"Love you more! Tell Mr. Jace I said thank you."

I laugh as they walk down the stairs. "Thank you for what?"

"For making you happy, of course."

I'm struck by his words as they disappear around the corner, my words failing me as I realize what he said is true. Jace Collins makes me unbelievably happy.

And he makes me feel wanted. Something I haven't experienced in a really long time. One I never really thought I'd get to again.

My phone pings and I rush over to it, smiling down at the

screen. Locking up, I skip down the stairs as a giddy nervousness flutters through me.

I look up through the glass door as I round the corner and stumble a step. His lips part as I slowly walk over to the door, unlocking it and pulling it open.

"Jace," I whisper.

"Kinsley."

And just like that, my nerves about tonight fizzle out completely, replaced with a wildfire of excitement and hope.

He holds up a bouquet of daisies and I pinch my lips closed to hold back my school girl squeal. "You remembered."

"I haven't forgotten anything about you, angel."

I bite my lip as I motion to the counter. He follows me into the shop, leaning against the shelf as I put the flowers in a vase and set them on top of the pastry case.

When I turn to face him, he's already watching me and a shot of confidence drives me as I unabashedly take in his brown leather jacket, white shirt, and dark washed jeans.

His cologne envelops me in its warmth as he shifts closer and I blush, ducking my head. Tucking his finger under my chin, he lifts my head back up. He opens his mouth, pausing as his eyes dance over my face.

"God, you're beautiful," he whispers.

My hands drift to his arms as I lean into his touch.

I feel him tense, as if he's holding himself back and a part —bigger than I can comprehend right now—wants to yell at him to stop. To let go and take me under with him.

"Ready?" His soft question breaks through my thoughts and I hum.

Sparks ignite over my skin as he trails his hand over my shoulder and down my arm. The little—and big—girl in me squeals when he interlocks our fingers before leading me out into the cool evening air.

"Oh, pretty," I coo when he opens the door of his blue sports car. I lean against the door, my face inches from his, and smile. "The color is very you."

He laughs under his breath and smiles as I slide into the seat. My eyes never leave him as he rounds the hood and settles behind the wheel.

"Trying to impress me or something?"

"I'm always trying to impress you." He smirks.

I laugh, placing my hand on his arm. "Well, you don't really need to *try*. You do it effortlessly every day anyway."

He watches me for a moment before sliding my hand into his. I suck in a breath when he lifts it to his lips and brushes his lips over my knuckles. I'm frozen in my seat even as he sets my hand back down, but a squeal bursts out of me as the engine roars to life and I giggle.

"Cooper is going to be so jealous."

Jace chuckles, pulling away from the curb and I lean back in my seat, actively trying to keep myself from staring at how he handles the car.

On how his hand flexes on the wheel.

How his jeans hug his thighs just right so I can see the rippling muscle as he accelerates.

I'm definitely not mentally sewing my mouth shut so I don't drool at how the passing streetlights dance across his chiseled jaw, flowing through his golden waves, accentuating his Adam's apple as he—

Dear lord, Rose and her 'cute little' romance books are a terrible influence.

"So, where are we going?" I ask, trying to get my head back from the dark side.

"It's a surprise."

"Can I get a hint?" He quirks a brow and I pout. "That's a no."

He chuckles. "How do you figure that?"

"Because I've seen you give that same look to the boys when they're asking for something completely ridiculous."

He barks out a laugh and I suck in a quiet breath when his hand slides over my thigh. He tenses, eyes flashing to mine and starts to retreat, but I whip my hand out to cover his.

My heart flutters when his fingers pulse under mine and I bite my lip.

Soft music plays over the speakers as we drive towards the city and I lean against the window when he parks the car. I glance over my shoulder at him and he smirks.

"Stay right there."

Without another word, he hops out of the car and rounds the hood. Opening my door, electricity hums the air and up my arm the moment I slip my hand into his.

"This is so cool," I say in awe, taking in the group of food vans and twinkling lights hanging over the open space.

"I was thinking we could order something from each spot?"

"Oh, yes. I like that plan. We could do a couple appetizers and mains. Of course some desserts, right? Then we can compile the best plan of attack so when we come back next time, we'll know exactly what to get and from where."

"I thought you don't share your food?"

I wink. "I'll make an exception for tonight." He stops walking and I look up. "What?"

"Marry me."

My heart stops at the glint of conviction in his voice, but then he smiles and I breathe out a laugh. Shaking my head, I pull him towards the first truck. "Come on, Romeo, let's get through this date first."

We end up ordering three different appetizers, two mains, and two desserts before finding a spot on the grassy area to sit.

Jace lays out a blanket before shedding his jacket and holding it up around my waist so I can get situated without fear of showing the entire park my underwear.

Ones that I definitely did not specifically buy for tonight.

Because this is only our first date... technically.

I smile at him as he drapes it over my lap. "Thank you."

"Be right back." He jogs off towards the lines of food vans and picks up each of our orders.

His arms are full as I help him set everything out between us. He sits down next to me, rubbing his hands together. "Okay. What's first?"

"Oh, wait!" I dig through my bag and pull out my little notebook and pencil with pizza printed all over it. Turning to him, I nod. "Okay, now we can keep track."

He chuckles, handing me the first container. I take a bite and my happy dance shimmers over my body at the burst of flavors. I glance over to see him watching me with a poorly contained smile.

I lift the fork up to his mouth and tilt my head. "What's got you smiling like that?"

He chews, nodding towards me. "Cooper got that from you."

I laugh. "He used to wait to eat so that I would take the first bite. He said he knew it wasn't poisoned if I did my little dance."

"Why was he worried about poison?"

"He was *really* into the whole kings and knights thing at the time."

"So you were his food tester then?"

I pause with the next forkful in the air. "Huh. I guess so."

I look down at what is possibly the most delicious looking bite of our next appetizer and raise it in offering to him. He glances at it before focusing back on me. "How will you know if it's poisoned or not?"

"Guess you'll just have to show me."

He hums and my gaze drops as his lips wrap around the fork, sliding off before his tongue swipes. I blink, watching as he chews, his head tilted, eyes closed.

Looking back at me he smirks before leaning closer and shimmying his shoulders. A laugh bursts out of me when he plucks the fork out of my hand and holds up a bite for me.

"I need a dance partner for this one."

I giggle through my nose as I slip the bite into my mouth,

my eyes closing on a moan at the orgasmic balance of sweet and savory.

When I look at him, he raises his shoulders and I laugh. Slowly I move mine with his and we pick up speed until we're both dancing around in our spots, no doubt drawing attention of those around us.

But we don't care.

Because when we're together, it's just us.

And I like who we are, just the way we are. Goofy dances over amazing food and all.

"Okay. Okay. That was really good. This last one has some big taste buds to fill."

He snorts at my cheesy—makes sense since this next bite better *be* cheesy—joke and hands me the next container. I make a show of selecting my bite before popping it into my mouth.

My head drops back and I fake swoon, rolling myself back up into a sitting position. Pointing to the dish with my fork, I mumble around my bite, "If you ever do anything right in your life, it's eating this. Solid eleven out of five."

"Oh yeah? That's high praise."

"It totally earned it."

He chuckles, taking a bite of his own. "*Ohmygod.*"

"Right?"

"That should be illegal."

"But I'm so glad it isn't."

We polish off the rest of our appetizers and he wipes his hands before grabbing my notepad and pencil. "Okay. Which one was your favorite?"

"Let's say it at the same time."

He laughs under his breath. "Okay."

"One..."

"Two..."

"Three."

"That last one."

"Illegal cheese."

We say together and he bursts out laughing when he realizes what I said.

"It will forever be known as illegal cheese now, I hope you know that. We'll just have to be careful to say the actual name when ordering it next time though. I don't need to go down for accidentally ordering the wrong kind of high."

"I honestly don't even remember the real name of it."

"Don't worry, I got it." He flashes his phone and I quirk a brow.

"Are you taking notes or something?" He blushes and my jaw drops. "Wait, are you really? Can I see?"

"Absolutely not."

"Oh come on. Please?"

"That pout won't work on me," he says.

"It does when Beckham does it."

"He's a little kid, no one can say no to a cute little kid pout."

"Is my pout not cute enough, then?" I ask.

"Your pout is adequately cute, don't worry."

"Great. Can I see the note now?"

I lean in patting my eyes and he sighs, holding out his phone and whispering, "I never could say no to you." I cheer and dance around in my spot. "Code is zero two one four. Note app should already be open."

I unlock his phone with a smile but it slowly drops as I read.

Daisies

Blue

Brownies over cake

Favorite fruit: watermelon

Loves suspense books but hates scary movies

Anything cheesy – cheesy crispers from Holloway's food van*

"These are all of my favorite things," I whisper as I continue to look over the seemingly never ending list.

"There's some things you don't like in there too," he says sheepishly and I look up.

"Why?"

"Because I wanted to make sure everything was perfect."

Our stare doesn't waver as people pass around us, the wind rustling through my hair. I'm frozen under his gaze, trying and failing to figure out how I got so lucky that this man cares enough to do this.

The cheers of a rowdy group breaks through our bubble and Jace clears his throat as I hand him back his phone.

"We should eat the rest of this before it gets too cold."

We each pick up one of the entrées and dig in, switching halfway to sample the other.

"So, is Beckham with Syd tonight?" I ask.

"He's with his mum, actually."

My eyebrows shoot up in surprise. "Oh."

He nods in understanding. "She just got back from some shoot she was doing and wanted a night with him before we left for the next couple weeks."

I twist my lips before blurting out, "You two never married, right?"

He shakes his head. "Nope. Never been married. To her or anyone else."

"How did you two meet then?"

"She's actually the granddaughter of one of the team's investors."

I nod. "Ah, forbidden fruit."

"You could say that." He rubs the back of his neck. "Sorry. Nothing like talking about an ex on the first date."

"No. It's okay."

We decide to save the desserts for later and clean up the rest of our trash. I lay down on the cozy blanket, rubbing my hand over my stomach.

He lays down next to me and I drop my arm to my side. The heat of his hand is so close that my skin prickles. Nibbling on my lip, I inch my hand closer to his.

As if sensing me, his pinky reaches out, brushing against mine before pulling my hand into his. I turn to look at him but freeze when something in the sky catches my eye.

I gasp. "A shooting star. Quick, make a wish." I close my eyes and repeat my wish three times. When I look over at Jace, he's already watching me. "What did you wish for?"

His eyes bounce between mine. "I'll tell you when it happens."

Kiss me.

As if reading my mind, he leans in and I tilt my head. His lips brush over mine softly before he pulls back, his eyes dancing between mine with hesitancy.

I smile and press my lips against his. When I pull back the weariness is gone and he breathes out a sigh of relief. Shifting onto his back, he pulls me into his side and we watch the stars twinkle in the sky.

I listen to the deep vibration of his voice as we talk and smile at the rumble of his laugh. Every so often he twists his head, brushing his lips against my hair as he holds me a little tighter.

We stay like that until the lights shut off and the small park clears. The drive back is filled with the brush of his fingers and soft smiles.

When he walks me to the door, I drag my feet a little.

I don't want this to end.

I lean back against the side of the door.

"I don't think I can say goodnight to you," he whispers, his thumb brushing over the back of my hand where it lays on his chest. "You'll have to do it for me."

"I don't think I can do that," I say quietly, my fingers twisting in his shirt. "I don't think I *want* to do that."

All I feel is the racing of his heart under my palm.

All I see is the relief flooding his face.

And all I hear is his small curse before his lips are one mine.

CHAPTER 36

KINSLEY

THE DOOR SWINGS open and we stumble into the quiet shop, tripping over each other as we try to get inside without breaking our connection.

His arm lifts, slamming the door closed and I hear the faint click of the lock. I slide my hands over his shoulders and down his arms, interlocking our fingers before I all but drag him to the stairs.

A squeak slips out between kisses when my foot misses a step and I go hurtling towards the unforgiving hardwood, but Jace is there. His arm bands around my waist, pulling me tight against his chest.

"I gotcha," he whispers, huskily.

I giggle, looking up into his usually bright eyes now turned dark by lust. Stepping back, I perch on a step higher so we are face to face and wrap my arms around his shoulders.

He smiles as I pull him in for another kiss. It breaks on a

squeal when he slips his hands under my thighs and lifts. I laugh as he takes the stairs practically two at a time before pressing us against my flat's door.

His hand on the back of my head slides back to my jaw and tilts as he swipes his tongue over my lips. My back arches and he groans into the kiss when I roll my hips.

"Keys," he rushes out between soul shattering kisses.

I wave my hand blindly with my bag, but freeze when it clatters to the ground.

"Bag?" he asks breathlessly.

"Bag," I confirm.

He smirks, pulling away from the door with me still in his arms. I cling to him with a laugh when he bends over, swiping up my bag and handing it to me. I fumble with the zipper, thrusting my hand inside and pulling my keys out with a cry of victory.

We crash through the door and he kicks it shut with his foot before my back meets the wood a second later. I arch into him, my fingers threading through his hair and he moans when I tug on the strands slightly.

He pulls back until our eyes meet. "Are you sure?"

The world around us fades as a vision flashes in my mind. It's him... but it's not? The same words echoing as he looks down at me with overwhelming affection.

I blink and the image fades, leaving behind a concerned looking Jace. "Angel? Are you sure about this?"

I nod, flexing my fingers in his thick hair as I lean in a whisper against his lips, "I'm sure." He kisses me and I pull back so he can see the sincerity in my eyes as I say, "I want you."

A breath rushes out of him and he smiles as he lays his forehead against mine. "Sweetheart, I've been yours for far longer than you know."

His lips are back on mine in an instant and I whimper when he thrusts his hips forward. My legs tighten around his waist as his hands snake under the hem of my dress.

"Bedroom," I gasp between kisses.

He pulls us away from the door and carries me down the short hallway, all the while his lips never leave mine. The door ricochets off the wall when he kicks it open and I look over my shoulder.

A giggle bursts out of me. "Wrong door."

"What?" he asks dazedly, tilting his head to look over my shoulder.

"Last time I checked, I don't sleep in the tub," I whisper, kissing his cheek.

I gasp when his hand comes down on my arse and he growls, nipping at my neck.

Spinning on his heel, he pushes the door at the end of the hall open and drops me on the bed. I laugh breathlessly as I bounce against the soft duvet and lean up on my elbows.

I watch as he walks back towards the door, closing it before turning to me. The only light in the room is the lamp on my bedside table and it casts the room in a warm glow.

He leans back against the door and my skin tingles with his stare. Slowly, I slip off the bed and walk over to him until there's no space between us.

His eyes don't stray from mine and I tilt my head back to hold them, my chest brushing his. I reach for the hem of his shirt and he helps me lift it over his head.

I break away from his gaze, taking in his toned chest and defined abs. Leaning in, I place a kiss on his heated skin, reveling in the feel of his heart racing under my lips.

His hand slips over my jaw, tilting my head up and I loop my arms around his neck as our lips crash together. I walk backwards as he guides us to the bed, squealing when we fall back on it. He catches himself with a low chuckle, hovering above me with a smirk

"Hi," I whisper, tracing my finger over his temple.

He leans down, placing a soft kiss against my lips. "Hi."

Pressing up to standing, he drops to his knees and I lean up on my elbows, watching him unlace my shoes before slipping them off and kissing the inside of each ankle.

I frame his face with my hands, dragging his lips to mine as I reach for his belt. Together we slowly strip each other until there's nothing separating us.

I shiver under his touch as we lay back on the bed, him propped over me with an arm on either side of my head. My hands drift up his sides, and over his chest.

He leans down, brushing his lips over mine. The move causes him to shift and his hard—good lord—*long* cock swipes over me, teasing my clit.

I moan into the kiss, nipping at his lip. My fingernails score his back as I run my hands down to his arse. He groans, pulling back slightly when he thrusts forward, rubbing himself against me.

"Shit," he slurs. "I'm not even inside you yet and I'm already on the very edge."

I giggle and reach down between us, wrapping my hand around him. He sucks in a breath, groaning and I smile, pumping up and down his shaft.

My body responds to his, my back arching as his hand runs down my stomach. His fingers brush over my clit and he swallows my moan, his tongue diving between my lips.

I release him, grasping the sheets as he brings me to the brink.

"That's it, sweetheart. Let go for me."

"Jace," I whisper, reaching up and pulling his head down for a deep kiss as wave after wave of pleasure rolls through me.

The room fills with my heavy breaths when he pulls back and I slowly open my eyes to look up at him. He watches me, a myriad of emotions flitting over his face.

"Beautiful," he whispers.

My lips part but nothing comes out.

"What's going through that head of yours, angel?"

I sigh, lifting my hand to brush his hair off his forehead. "Just trying to wrap my brain about why it feels this way with you."

"What way?"

"Right." I push up, brushing my lips against his. "It all feels so right with you."

His cups my jaw, tilting until our eyes meet. "Because this is where we belong."

All I can do is nod because I'll never be able to find the

words to explain how there isn't a part of me that doesn't feel the same way. From the moment I bumped into him in the hallway on my first day, I've felt this pull.

Like this was where I was meant to be. And he was who was meant to be there with me.

He brushes my hair off my forehead and I feel him tense as he traces the small scar decorating my hairline with his thumb. His eyes fill with heartache as his voice cracks on a whisper. "What happened?"

I reach up, soothing my hands over the sides of his face, trying to ease the lines of pain. "The doctors said it was an accident. I had a bad head injury that required them to put me in a medically induced coma for a couple days. When I woke up, I couldn't remember anything from the two years before, let alone whatever happened to me."

He drops his forehead to mine. "I'm so sorry."

"I'm okay," I whisper, pressing a soft kiss to his lips. "I'm here."

He pulls me into another kiss and I wrap my arms around his waist when he pulls me to him, until there's no space between us.

His leg bends until mine hooks over his hip as he thrusts forward. I gasp, dropping my head back against the pillow at the sensation of his shaft running over my already sensitive clit.

He drops down, kissing, nipping, and licking at my neck. My fingers dive into his hair and I use the hold to pull his mouth back to mine.

His head notches at my entrance and I whimper, my hips

rolling. He groans as he slips in an inch before pulling back. My hands slip down his sides and around his lower back, my nails scoring his skin.

"Fuck," he grits into our kiss as he presses forward until he's fully seated and my breath rushes out of me as I adjust to his size. "Are you okay?"

I hum, nodding as I smile at him. "I'm perfect."

"Yeah," he whispers, tucking my hair behind my ear, "You are."

He leans down, taking my mouth with his as he pulls his hips back before sliding into me again. With each roll he brushes my clit just as he hits a spot deep inside me, making me see stars. His hand slips between us and I moan.

"Give me another."

My fingers flex on his back, my head tilting back as I cry out his name. He works me through my release and I open my eyes in a daze.

He's watching me, a look of victory in his gaze. "I'll never get over the sight of you coming with my name on your lips."

My laugh breaks on a moan when my sensitive core clenches around him. He groans, his hips moving faster. Harder.

I arch my back, my nails digging into his skin. The room fills with the sounds of our moans, of slapping skin, and the headboard meeting the wall.

"Jace," I breathe as another climax builds.

"I've got you, sweetheart."

He leans back on his knees, lifting my hips off the bed

and my legs to his shoulders. The new position drives him deeper and I cry out.

"Fuck, you're so tight."

"Deep," I gasp.

"Too much?"

I shake my head, my heavy eyes meeting his heated ones. "More."

He smiles. "You want more, angel?"

I nod, tracing his abs with greedy fingers. "I want it all."

The shift is instant, dominance exploding off of him as a growl vibrates through his chest. "Place your hands on the headboard, sweetheart." I do as I'm told, arching my back on a gasp when he thrusts into me. "You want it all?" he rushes out.

My moan breaks on a shriek when he reaches out, pinching my nipple. My eyes shoot to his and he smooths a thumb over the stinging skin.

"Words, angel."

"Yes," I rush out. "I want all of you, Jace Collins."

He turns his head, his lips brushing my ankle as he says, "You have all of me, Kinsley Jones. Always have."

His hands drop to my waist and he pulls back before slamming into me. My arms lock, bracing against the headboard as I suck in a breath at the sensation. He smiles, repeating the movement and the room fills with a mix of grunts and moans.

"I want one more, sweetheart."

"I can't—"

He slips a hand between my legs, swirling his thumb around my clit and I whimper. "Yes, you can."

My body shakes as ecstasy swirls in my core.

Good lord, he's right.

I reach for him as the first wave crests. "I need you."

He drops my legs from his shoulders, collapsing on top of me and crashing his lips to mine. I cling to him as he moves, crying out when my climax slams against me.

He props himself up on his forearms, thrusting in once, twice. His moan caresses my ear as he comes and I take a mental picture at the sight of his powerful form flooded with ecstasy.

"You were right. I'll never get over the sight of you coming with my name on your lips," I echo his words.

He chuckles under his breath, dropping down and taking my mouth with his. I hum into the kiss as his fingers brush along my jaw.

"Are you okay?"

I nod, kissing his jaw. "I'm perfect."

He leans down and kisses me softly before rolling out of bed and disappearing into the bathroom. He's back a moment later, sliding on his boxer briefs.

I slip his T-shirt on and smile when I catch him staring. "What?"

"Just thinking about how I can get rid of all your clothes without you getting mad at me."

"Why?" I laugh as he slides into bed, pulling me against him.

"Because I love the sight of you in mine so much more."

I giggle as he rolls onto his back, taking me with him. I lay my head on his chest and close my eyes to the steady beat of his heart.

His arm tightens around my waist and I tilt my head, looking up at my favorite shade of blue.

"Thank you," he whispers.

"For what?"

"For finding me."

My head pulses and a vision of him looking down at me flashes in my mind. But instead of him saying the words, it's my broken voice whispering them.

"Kinsley?" I blink, Jace's face etched in worry coming back into focus. "What's wrong?"

I place my hand over his when he cups the side of my face.

"I'm okay. Just a sense of déjà vu is all."

His thumb brushes over my cheek. "You've been having a lot of those lately."

I hum, kissing his chest. His hand drops, fingers tickling my skin through his shirt. "Must be a glitch in the matrix."

He groans, tilting his head towards the ceiling. "Lord, you've sent me the perfect woman!"

I smile, tucking my face into his chest. He rolls us until I'm on my back with him hovering over me. He looks down at me before leaning down and nipping at my lips.

"You're such a goof," I laugh.

"You like me anyway," he hums, settling his full weight on me.

"I do," I whisper, running my fingers through his hair as

my heart races with something that feels a whole lot bigger than just 'like.'

CHAPTER 37

JACE

Jesus, she's beautiful.

Kinsley mumbles something as she snuggles into my chest. Her leg is tucked between mine, her arms curled between us with her palms pressed over my heart.

I reach up, brushing her hair out of her face and trace her temple.

Last night was something straight out of a dream. A dream that once haunted me the years we were apart, but has brought me hope the last few weeks.

I've wanted this for so long, that it still doesn't feel real.

My arms tighten around her and she sighs. I close my eyes and soak in the heat of her body. The feel of her hair tickling my skin. The sound of her steady breathing.

This is really happening, right?

I glance at the clock and sigh. Looking back down at my girl, I lean in and kiss her forehead, whispering against her skin, "Time to wake up, angel."

She growls, cuddling deeper into my arms and I chuckle.

"I know, but I've got to go soon, sweetheart."

Even though I'd rather stay right here with you. Always.

Her eyes flutter open and she hums, a soft tilt to her lips.

"Hi." She blushes, covering her mouth with her hand when I lean in to kiss her.

"What are you doing?"

"I haven't brushed my teeth."

She squeals as I roll us so she's under me. "You think a little morning breath is going to keep me from kissing you?"

She tucks her lips and I reach up, gently grabbing her jaw. Tilting her head, I lean in and kiss her neck. She gaps when I rake my teeth over her pulse point and I take the opportunity to claim her mouth.

Her arms band around my lower back, pulling me down as I press my hips forward. I groan into the kiss when she slips her hand under the band of my boxer briefs.

She hikes her leg up my side, and I slide my hand over her smooth skin. She shifts under me when I drag my fingers over her hardened peak.

"Jace," she breathes.

I slip my hand farther down, a smile tilting my lips at her gasp when I swirl my fingers against her clit. I lean down, licking the column of her delicate neck as I move my fingers lower, teasing her entrance.

"So wet already, sweetheart," I growl, nipping at her ear.

"I slept next to you all night, what do you expect?"

"That makes two of us then." I thrust my hips forward and slam my mouth to hers. "You're soaking my briefs."

"Then take them off," she whispers against my lips.

Her fingers are already pushing them over my hips and I help her, kicking them off to the side as she sits up to yank my shirt over her head.

The morning sunlight streams through the windows, bathing her smooth skin in a warm glow. Her hair fans out around her in a dark halo as she looks up at me with heated eyes.

"God, you're beautiful."

Her hands frame my face as she pulls me down for a searing kiss. "You are."

I laugh under my breath, sealing my mouth over hers. A groan rips through me when she reaches down, wrapping her fist around my shaft and positioning me at her entrance.

I thrust home as I pull her hands above her head, threading our fingers together.

"Fuck, you feel so good. Too good," I grit out.

She nods, her breath tickling my lips. "Don't stop," she gasps.

"Never." I kiss her fiercely, putting the weight of my words behind it. "I'll never stop."

Her legs come up wrapping around my hips and she uses the hold to meet each of my hard thrusts. The headboard bangs against the wall and her moans echo in the air.

"Come for me, angel."

Her hands squeeze mine as the first flutters of her climax ripple around me.

"Oh god. I'm going to—"

"Come," I growl.

She turns her head, biting my shoulder with a scream and I groan as she tightens around me. Letting go of her hands, I grip her hip and she threads her fingers into my hair.

My hips slam into hers as I chase my own release and I slip my hand from her hip to between her thighs. "One more."

"Jace," she moans, her nails digging into my neck.

I grab her hand and place her fingers over her clit. "Get yourself there, sweetheart. I want you to come around my cock one more time."

I lean back on my knees, taking in the sight of her playing with herself. Her head is thrown back, face eased with pleasure as her perfect tits bounce with each of my thrusts.

Her wetness coats my hard cock and a possessive growl vibrates through my chest when I see the slight finger indentations on her hips.

"Lift your hips." She does as she told and I slip a pillow underneath her. We moan at the new angle and she throws her hands into her hair.

"God, if you could see how mesmerizing you look right now. You're taking my cock so well, sweetheart. It's like you were made for me."

She groans and my hips pick up at the feel of her tightening around me. I fall down over her, gripping her jaw in a tight yet gentle hold and speak against her lips. "Who's pussy is this?"

"Yours," she gasps, her eyes lighting at the claim as she digs her fingers into my side.

"That's right, sweetheart. It's mine." I grit the words out as the base of my spine tingles.

Her mouth drops open and her eyes widen. "Jace, I'm—"

"Come with me, angel."

"Jace," her voice cracks as she screams.

"Kinsley," I moan as I thrust deep, body shaking with my release.

My head drops to her shoulder and her fingers dance through my hair. Our heavy breaths fill the quiet room and I turn my head to see her face tilted towards the ceiling.

As if sensing my eyes, she tilts her head catching me with a smile.

"What a way to wake up," she whispers.

I chuckle, kissing her bare shoulder. "I'll make sure to do it every morning I can."

She hums, brushing her lips over mine. "Promise?"

"Promise." I deepen the kiss, but it's cut short when my phone rings.

"You should get that. It could be Becks," she whispers when I make no move to get up.

I sigh and pull out of her, rolling out of the bed. She slides to her feet and kisses my cheek as she shuffles to the bathroom. Lifting my phone to my ear, I immediately regret not checking caller ID to see who it is.

"Where are you?"

"Angie," I curse.

"Why aren't you home?"

"Why are you at my home? I thought I was picking up Becks this afternoon."

"Something came up and I needed to drop him back off with you. But here we are and since you neglected to give him his keys this time, we can't get inside."

Because I didn't want you entering my house without me there, AGAIN.

I sigh, scrubbing my face. Kinsley walks back into the room dressed in a pair of sleep shorts and T-shirt, her hair in a messy bun. I pull her to me, tucking my chin on top of her head.

"I'm on my way." I hang up before she can ruin any more of my morning with Kinsley than she already has.

"Everything okay?" She wraps her arms around my shoulders, her fingers threading through the hair on the back of my neck.

I lean down, kissing her and the tension that grew from only talking with Angie for less than a minute completely dissipates when Kinsley leans into my hold.

"Everything's fine. Just have to head home. Angie's dropping Beckham off early, they're waiting there now."

"Oh, yeah. Of course. Go." She pops up to her toes, kissing my cheek. "I'll go make you a coffee to go and throw in a little something for Becks."

She bounces out of the room and I get dressed before joining her downstairs. I lean against the doorway, watching her sway her hips to the soft melodies playing over the café speakers.

She spins around, using tongs as a microphone and startles when she sees me. I walk over, wrapping my hands around hers and pulling the tongs to my face, mouthing the next lyrics.

She laughs and I pull her into my arms, dancing to the beat as we sing along. I drag her into a dip and she throws her head back laughing when I playfully bite her neck. I hold her to me as we straighten and she pulls my head down to hers, kissing me softly.

"You've got to go," she whispers.

I groan, rolling my forehead against hers. "I do."

She slips out of my arms and skips over to the counter, holding up a bag and cup. "It's the biggest coffee I have. Figured you'd need all the caffeine you could get after last night."

She smiles cheekily and I laugh, taking it from her. "And a few pastries. That cinnamon roll better make it back to Beckham." She squints at me and I roll my eyes with a small tilt of my lips before bending to steal a kiss.

"I promise not to touch his treat."

"I'll know if you do."

I chuckle as she threads her fingers through mine, walking me towards the door. The bell jingles as I step over the threshold, turning to watch her lean against the door jam.

"Thank you for last night. It was..."

"Perfect," I finish for her and she hums. My eyes bounce between hers as a step closer, cupping her jaw. "What's running through that head of yours?"

"How do you know—" I use my thumb to pull her bottom lip out from her teeth. She shakes her head. "I guess I'm just thinking about what this means. About what's next."

"Whatever you want."

Her lips tip up. "What?"

"I don't want you to overthink this. Us. We'll take this at whatever speed you want or need. All of it is up to you. I'll take whatever you're willing to give."

"What if last night was it?"

"Then I'd replay it over and over in my head every chance I got."

She laughs, laying her hand against my chest. "What if I wanted more?"

"Then it's yours. Anything you want is yours."

"Okay," she whispers.

I lean in, brushing my lips over hers. "One day at a time."

"One day at a time," she whispers into the kiss. She presses against my chest with a smile. "Okay, you really need to go. Beckham's waiting for you."

I take a few steps away before running back to her and stealing one last kiss. She pushes me away, covering her giggle with her fingers.

"I'll see you tomorrow, angel."

The drive home flies by as images of last night and this morning replay through my mind. I'm riding a wave of euphoria as I pull onto my street, but I pack it away in the safest part of my heart when I catch a glimpse of the pearly white car in my driveway.

I pull my Porsche 911 into the garage and shut off the engine, taking a moment to gather myself before stepping out of the car.

"Where were you?" Angie stands by the door, her arms crossed.

I ignore her, bending down as my little boy throws himself into my arms. "Dad!"

"Hey, bud. Did you have fun last night?"

He glances over at his mum before pasting on a practiced smile. "Yeah. We ate out at a new restaurant and watched a movie when we got home."

Translation: his mum ignored him while she got drunk with her friends and then he watched a movie in his room when she passed out on the sofa.

My jaw ticks as I force a smile. "Why don't you go inside? Here, Kinsley made me promise not to eat your cinnamon roll."

He pumps his fist in the air. "Score. Thanks Dad."

I step around Angie and open the door for him. He goes to move inside but she stops him with a stiff hand on his shoulder, her bright pink claws—sorry, nails—gleaming in the sunlight.

"No goodbye for your mother, poppet?"

Beckham kisses her cheek when she offers it before mumbling a quick goodbye and disappearing into the house.

I tell him that I'll be right in before I close the door and turn to her. "You had him for one night. One single night. And you still couldn't make him the priority?"

She rolls her eyes. "He had a grand time, Jace."

"He won't say otherwise in front of you, Angie. He doesn't want to hurt your feelings, but I can read between the lines. I know what going to a 'new restaurant' means and I know what happens afterwards."

"You're overreacting. He was fine."

"He should have been *more* than fine."

"What do you want me to say, huh? I'm doing my best. I'm not the cool parent that races cars for a living and get's to bring him with me on the road. He doesn't get excited over sitting at photoshoots or traveling to places where there are no other kids. How am I supposed to compete with the *amazing* Jace Collins?"

"It's not a competition, Angie."

"Says the man who is always winning," she sneers.

"All you have to do is be there for him. Even if you did nothing but lounge out in the living room and watch movies all day, he would say he had the best time of his life because you were there with him. You were spending time *with* him, not just *around* him."

"I was spending time with him."

"Oh yeah? What did he tell you about the past couple weeks?"

She glares. "Oh, don't worry, I got an earful about the grand time he's been having with his new best friend, Cooper, and that mum of his."

I grit my teeth. "And because he was having a good time without you, you decided to act like the child instead and ignore him?"

"You're being ridiculous."

"No, I'm being protective of my son."

"And you think you have to protect him from me?" she sneers.

I stare her down, my jaw ticking. "I won't stand for him being neglected, Angie."

"When are you going to stop holding that against me?"

"He could have died," I explode, my chest heaving. "He could have died."

Something akin to regret flashes in her eyes before she snuffs it out as they trail down my body. "Where were you?"

"That's none of your business."

Her eyes flash up to mine. "If you plan on bringing her around my son, then it is my business."

I bark out a disbelieving laugh. "That's rich. Tell me, how many of your significant others you brought around him without my knowledge?"

She eyes me. "It's her isn't it."

It's not a question.

But I'm not playing her game.

"We leave tomorrow and won't be back for the next few weeks. If you can't come meet us to see him, then the least you could do is pick up the phone and call him this time."

I open the door but stop when she calls out.

"Is it her?"

This time it is a question and my neck prickles because I know what she's asking. Angie knows me and Kinsley's history. She was there, watching from the sidelines as I fell hard and fast for this girl.

She also saw the aftermath. Was part of some of the bad

decisions I made in the dark nights where my pain was too much. Moments that I'll regret forever.

I'm not surprised she's put two and two together. For all she is, Angie is an incredibly smart woman. So when Beckham told her about Cooper and his mum, I'm sure she had an inkling.

And my silence only confirms it.

INSTAGRAM POST

@KINSLEYTHROUGHTHELENS

Carousel of images:

1. Video of Kinsley and Cooper hopping off the plane's steps onto the ground

2. Video of Kinsley, Jace, and the boys running into the ocean

3. Picture of Kinsley, Jace, Lawson, Blake, Ryder, and Sydney at dinner

4. Video of Blake beating Jace at a video game, Cooper and Beckham make fun of him for losing and he chases after them, Lawson trips Jace

5. Picture of Kinsley and Jace watching the sun rise on the hotel room patio

Caption: Party in the USA!

Comments:

@thejacecollins: @kinsleythroughthelens You're more beautiful than any sunrise

@thelawsonmoore: Hey @thejacecollins now there's video evidence that you JUST SUCK THAT BAD

@thejacecollins replied to @thelawsonmoore: Now there's video evidence that you're a big grumpy son of a... I can't curse on this, but you know where I was going

@sassycassie: Our plane can not land fast enough!

@ladyblakeking replied to @sassycassie: Excuse me, 'our'?

@daddyjacefanclub: Here for the romance, stays for the comments

@flirtythirtyandf1: Anyone else go straight to the comments for the debate over this game?

CHAPTER 38

JACE

"When are you getting married?"

The sip of coffee I was taking sprays everywhere as I choke. Kinsley looks at me with panic before glancing at her son. "Cooper."

"What?"

Beckham looks at me with a raised brow. "Are you okay, Dad?"

I cough then nod my head, and Kinsley grimaces. Clearing my throat, I take a sip of water and tilt my head to Cooper. "Why are you asking that?"

He shrugs. "You've already been on a date. Next you'd get married, right?"

I chuckle, shaking my head. "Not quite, little man."

"But why? Don't you love each other?"

My eyes flash up to Kinsley's.

With all that I am.

I open my mouth when her cheeks blush but she smiles

and turns to him. "We've only been together for a week, sweetheart. There's still many, many dates to be had."

His little shoulders drop and he looks between us. "But you'll get married someday, right? And we can be a family?"

"One day," I say automatically, my heart stopping.

Oh look, I guess I'm eating my foot for breakfast.

Cautiously I look over at Kinsley.

Note to self, lock down on the big feelings. For me these thoughts have been brewing for years. For her? Well, we still have separate hotel rooms, so that answers that.

But she hasn't run off yet, so I'm taking that as a good sign. And her next words have me wanting to fall at her feet right then and there.

"Yeah. One day," she whispers.

My lips tip up and she clears her throat, nodding towards the boys. "Today however is race day and we don't want to miss out on our track walk, do we?"

They shake their heads furiously and she smiles. "Then eat up, my little monsters."

After breakfast, we stop by Kinsley and Cooper's room so she can grab her camera gear. I carry it out to the car with her hand in mine while the boys walk in front of us.

The day we came back to work, we talked with HR. She was scared that by being with me, she'd lose her job and I wasn't about to hide her from the world when I'd *finally* had her.

Luckily, we don't have to do anything since she is a photographer and has no direct impact on my role. They sent us off with a 'congratulations' and 'good luck' with telling the world.

It was something I wanted to do the minute we left. I may or may not have looked for the nearest rooftop, but she talked me into letting it all happen naturally.

She did however sit back as I spoke over the intercom to announce it to our friends on the flight here. We were bombarded with cheers and hugs. Sydney even looked between us with tears streaming down her cheeks.

They knew what it meant for me in that moment.

They knew what *she* meant to me.

And they knew I wouldn't take this chance for granted.

I wasn't lying when I said that one day we'd be married. Because I have every intention of making Kinsley my wife, of making Cooper my son, and spending the rest of my life loving them both the way they deserve.

Fans are lined up along the fences as we pull into the back gate and even though they can't see into the car, the boys wave wildly back at them.

We walk hand in hand through the gates, garnering a few looks. I squeeze her hand and she looks up at me. Her shoulders relax when I smile and she leans into my side, cuddling the arm of the hand holding hers.

I press a kiss to her hair as we round the corner, but I stumble back when someone collides with me. I choke on a wild mane of red curls as she wraps herself around me like a koala.

"Sneak attack!"

I bark out a laugh, shaking my head with a smile when she hops down and looks up at me with her bright blue eyes.

"Cassie."

She smiles. "Golden boy." Punching me in the arm, she pops out her hip. "Still can't believe you made me wait to find out with the world about your girl. I thought we were closer than that." She leans in. "We've cried over *Free Willy* together," she not so quietly whispers.

"Hey, that is a heartfelt magical story and I'd be worried if you *didn't* cry." I point at her.

A snort sounds from the side and my eyes dart over Cassie's head to a wide eyed Kinsley barely holding in her laughter. Cassie follows my eyes and gasps before practically tackling her.

"Oh my god, it's so nice to meet you," she screeches.

Kinsley's laugh breaks free with a smile. "It's nice to meet you too. I've heard a lot about you from everyone."

"Yikes. Whatever they've said, I swear it wasn't my idea."

"Correction, it was almost always her idea," Blake chimes as she wraps an arm over her best friend's shoulders. "Have you been training because I swore you didn't used to be that fast?"

Cassie shrugs. "I've been running a lot. I get up every morning at five for a two mile jog."

"Dear god, why?" Sydney pops up next to Kinsley, linking their arms together.

"Because when the zombie apocalypse starts, I need to be faster than all you fuckers."

The girls burst into laughter and I shake my head,

walking over and pulling Kinsley into my side. Blake's the only one not laughing and I don't miss the concerned look she gives Cassie, but it quickly disappears when Ryder slips behind her, wrapping his arms around her waist.

"Aw, aren't you two just ador—ah!" She squeals when a little body collides with her legs. Ryder reaches out, grabbing her arm so she doesn't topple over.

"Beckham," she cheers, wrapping her arms around his shoulders and shaking him from side to side. "How are you doing, little man? Creating havoc like I taught you?"

He nods. "Dad says it's the CCC zone."

She tilts her head. "CCC?"

"Channeling Cassie's Chaos." We all turn to see Nik stride up to the group, his eyes locked on the fiery redhead.

"Nikolai," she whispers.

Beckham tugs on her arm and she rips her eyes away from the brooding team principal, smiling down at my boy. "Miss Cassie, I want you to meet my best friend."

"I thought I was your best friend?" she gasps dramatically.

"You can have more than one best friend," he muses with a giggle.

"You're right. Okay who is this new best friend because I just so happen to have a slot open for one myself?"

He bounces over to Cooper and wraps an arm around his shoulders. "Cooper, this is my Aunt Cassie. She grew up with Aunt Blake here in America."

Cassie laughs under her breath as she squats in front of

Cooper, extending her hand. "It's very nice to meet you, Cooper."

"Hi," he says shyly, shaking her hand.

She hums, tilting her head. "Marvel or DC?"

"Marvel."

"Favorite superhero?"

"Iron Man, but Spider-Man is my other one."

She nods, tapping her chin. "Blue or red?"

"Red." He peeks up at me and I wink.

"Breakfast for dinner?"

"We do that all the time! My mummy makes the best pancakes with smiley faces on them."

Cassie's jaw drops. "Smiley face pancakes are my favorite."

Cooper giggles and I smile as the fun little boy I love starts to break out of his shell.

"Okay. This last one is very important."

Cooper nods.

"Coffee full of sugar or black?"

"Ew! I don't drink coffee, I'm six!" He giggles.

She hums, a playful smirk tilting her lips. "Good answer."

I clap my hands to get everyone's attention. "Okay, we have a walk around the track to get to, you lot are more than welcome to—"

"In the wise words of Shania Twain, let's go girls," Sydney sings, pulling Kinsley with her towards the track. Blake and Cassie each scoop up one of the boys and take off after them, leaving me and the lads standing there.

"This is a recipe for trouble," Lawson grumbles.

I shrug. "I think it's a recipe for an adventure." I backhand his and Nik's chests. "Lord knows you both could use some excitement in your lives."

"Babe!" a voice calls from the side.

We all turn and watch a man approach the girls.

"Shit," Ryder curses under his breath, glancing at Nik.

Lawson and I share a confused look.

"Maybe he's talking to someone else?" I look off to the side. "Like her—" I cringe when a different guy grabs the chick I pointed to from behind. "Never mind. Uh…"

There's two options as to what's about to happen.

One is that this guy is talking to someone completely unrelated to the two available—not *really* available—ladies out here and we will move on with our day. Or…

By the sound of Nik's leather glove squeaking as the seams threaten to break under his unforgiving fist, he's about to walk up to the only woman who's gotten under my dark and guarded best friend.

He thinks he's sly, but I see the way his eyes always seem to linger or how he tunes into our conversations more when her name comes up or the slight tilt in his lips when she's rambling.

I have a feeling it's the latter…

I hold my breath when the guy slips past Sydney, freezing when he wraps his arm around Cassie. Slowly we all slide our weary gazes to Nik.

There's a snapping sound and he clears his throat, his stare unwavering from where it's glued to the tiny redhead. "I've got to go talk with the crew."

He walks off without another word and I glance down at the ink trail his broken pen leaves in his wake. "Uh-oh. Code black."

Lawson rolls his eyes and takes off after the girls. Ryder bumps my shoulder. "At least it's not Sydney, right?"

I glance over at my sister. Her face lights up when she sees Lawson coming and she bends, whispering into my boy's ear. They all smile before taking off and attacking him, each of the boys taking one of his legs as she jumps on his back.

"It's never going to be her. Not with anyone else."

Ryder sighs. "But why did it have to be Cassie? I met the guy earlier, he's a total prick. Comes from some well off Southern family and thinks he shits gold."

"Daddy Ryder doesn't approve?"

He glares at me and shakes his head. "The guy rubs me the wrong way. There's something about him that isn't right. And you should see the way she is when he's around. It's like a less colorful version of the Cassie we know and love."

"What does Blake think?"

He sighs. "She agrees, but Cassie's also her best friend. If she's happy then we're happy for her." He shrugs. "But the minute she isn't, I'll be on a plane myself to help her pack her bags."

"Wait, she's living with him already? I haven't even met this guy yet!"

Ryder's chuckle follows me as I stalk over to the group, inserting myself right next to Cassie and the—oh god, did he bathe in cologne before coming here? I clear my throat to try and hold in my cough at the abrasive scent and smile.

"Hiya, I'm Jace. And you are?"

Kinsley giggles, smiling at me from the side. Cassie snorts but covers it with a cough, covering her mouth with her fingers as her eyes dart to the man at her side. "Sorry. Jace, this is my boyfriend, Richard. Richard, this is Jace. He's Beckham's dad."

"Is that my identifier? 'Beckham's dad?' What happened to 'the handsomest golden boy in the realm?'"

She laughs. "That title belongs to Cooper now, sorry."

I gasp, placing a hand over my heart. "The betrayal. But, I'll let it slide since it's true." Offering my hand to a slightly scowling Richard, I give him a friendly smile. "Dick was it? Nice to meet you."

He shakes my hand, squeezing. "Richard."

"What's that?"

"My name. It's Richard."

"Ah, my bad, mate." I internally smirk when he winces as I tighten my grip before pulling back. "Joining us for the track walk, Rich?"

"No, I have to go talk with some people." He turns to Cassie, speaking low.

I watch her the entire time, cataloging the slight twitch in her fingers as she fumbles with the hem of her jean shorts, the small dip of her shoulders as he literally speaks down to her, and the way she stiffly nods before offering him a kiss on his cheek.

He strides off without a goodbye and Cassie claps her hands, speaking with more excitement in her voice than ever before. "So! Anyone care to make today interesting? Because all my money is on Blake."

"Aww thank you," Blake coos. "I'm always down for a good game."

I shake my head. "Oh, no, no, no. Last time I made a bet with you, I wound up dancing on stage in front of strangers in only red briefs." I lean in. "I had glitter in places no one should have glitter and it took weeks for it all to finally disappear."

Kinsley raises her hand. "I'm sorry, but I'd love a recap on how that happened and possibly if any of you have photo evidence?"

I wrap my arm around her shoulder, leaning in to whisper in her ear. "If you're a good girl, I'll give you a personal performance later."

She laughs, pushing at my chest.

The group chases after the boys, making their deals for the race as we walk behind them. Kinsley leans her chin on my arm, looking up at me as she twists her lips.

I smirk. "Yes, angel?"

"How about we make a little wager of our own? Maybe it'll be a better incentive for you?" She pulls back, a sly smile on her lips.

I nod furiously. "You have my attention."

She laughs. "Okay. How about if you win I'll spend the night on my knees for you."

I groan and she smiles.

It's been a damn pleasure to watch her confidence grow this past week. She no longer hesitates when talking with me, whether it's about the boys or work or something only the two of us know about in the quiet of the night.

Licking my suddenly dry lips, I shuffle closer to her and wrap my arms around her waist. "And what if I don't win?"

She hums, looping her arms over my shoulders. "Then you have to get on yours."

I bark a laugh. "I don't think you understand how this works, sweetheart. I'm not supposed to be rewarded for losing."

She smiles. "My bet, my rules."

I huff a laugh, leaning down for a brief kiss. "Yes ma'am."

Whatever my girl wants, she gets.

And later that night, I spend what feels like hours worshiping her from my knees, never once feeling like I lost a thing.

GROUP MESSAGE

Cassie has added Kinsley to the chat

Cassie has changed the group name to "The Spice Girls"

BLAKE:

I call Sporty Spice.

CASSIE:

As if you would have been any other one? Ha! You kill me.

BLAKE:

Okay, Scary Spice.

SYDNEY:

Wouldn't she be Ginger Spice?

BLAKE:

Oh no.

CASSIE:

Why would I be Ginger?

Is it because I have red hair?

Are you stereotyping me right now?

What? Next you'll say each of my freckles are a mark of the souls I've eaten since I don't have one of my own. Or I can't be out in the sun because I'll burn like a vampire. Or that I'm too feisty for my own good and would gladly take down someone twice my size if they tick off my short temper. Or that my daddy is Satan himself and that's why I have flames for hair.

SYDNEY:

...

Scary Spice it is.

KINSLEY:

Do I also get to pick or...

SYDNEY:

Why not Baby Spice?

BLAKE:

Oh sweet princess angel BABY...

Because that's you.

SYDNEY:

Why?

Because Baby Spice is blonde and I'm blonde? Next you'll say it's because I'm also obsessed with all things cute and fluffy, bonus points if it's all pink.

Who's stereotyping who now?

BLAKE:

Baby's got claws.

gif of kitten meowing with the words "rawr" waving over its head

CASSIE:

They grow up so fast.

SYDNEY:

No one puts Baby in a corner.

CASSIE:

As for you my gorgeous, talented, Kinsley girl...

You are Posh Spice because you ARE our hot HOT mama.

BLAKE:

Yesssss!

SYDNEY:

I am SO here for this.

KINSLEY:

I accept.

But please don't call me Mummy.

CASSIE:

Riiiight.

You get that enough from your boys...

All three of them.

SYDNEY:

Three?

BLAKE:

Wait for it. It'll come to her.

KINSLEY:

gif of an overly blushing girl with wide eyes

SYDNEY:

What?

Oh.

Oh!

No!

Cassiopeia Marie Burrows! That's my brother!

BLAKE:

And there it is.

CASSIE:

gif of kid evil laughing

KINSLEY:

If it makes you feel any better, I swear he doesn't call me that.

CASSIE:

What?! Don't ruin the illusion!

SYDNEY:

Please ruin it.

For her. Not me.

I'm begging.

KINSLEY:

Eh, usually that's me.

BLAKE:

I just spit out my drink all over Ryder.

SYDNEY:

I just threw up all over Lawson.

CASSIE:

Yes Kinsley! Go off!

KINSLEY:

I had to give her something... I'm sorry.

CASSIE:

No she's not and neither am I.

BLAKE:

Be grateful because Cassie wouldn't have stopped until she eventually got something much more scarring.

KINSLEY:

And there's a LOT more.

CASSIE:

This is going to be a BEAUTIFUL friendship.

CHAPTER 39
KINSLEY

"GIRLS' night, girls' night," Sydney cheers, skipping onto the boat with a brooding Lawson following behind her.

"Girls' night, girls' night," Jace mocks and I backhand his chest.

"Quit your pouting."

"I won the race, so I should be the one having fun with my girl, but my sister is stealing her away." He pulls me into his arms, sticking out his bottom lip.

I laugh under my breath and wrap my arms around his shoulders. "We can still have some fun later tonight when I get back."

His pout turns into a smirk and he leans down, brushing his lips against mine. "I'm going to hold you to that, sweetheart," he whispers against my lips.

"I come bearing gifts from our favorite redhead," Blake calls out as she and Ryder walk down the pier.

Ryder sets down the box on the table and we crowd around as Blake rips it open. "She said she wishes she didn't have to miss out on tonight, but at least this way she'll be with us in some small way."

"Oh, very cryptic." Jace drums his fingers together.

Blake peaks into the box and chokes on a laugh, quickly shutting it with wide eyes.

"What?" Ryder leans around his wife, trying to get a look.

"What's in the box?" Jace drawls.

She glares up at them. "Who says this stuff is even for you?"

Jace shrugs. "I'm nosy."

Sighing, Blake opens the box and lifts up a black bodysuit.

"Is that—"

"Jesus Christ—"

"She's insane—"

"She didn't—"

"Oh, she totally did," Sydney squeals through her laughter and dives for the box, pulling out a pink bodysuit before handing me the white one.

I hold it out in front of me, uncontrollable laughter bursting out of all of us as we look at the mini Cassie faces printed on them.

"That is so Cassie," Nik grumbles, but I hear the slight humor in his voice.

He's right. This is *so* Cassie.

Vibrant. Bold. Tenacious. Loving. Funny.

She's 100 percent the girl you'd call to help you hide the dead body... hell, she probably would have been committing the act with you.

I have to admit, I was nervous to meet her at first.

She's everything I wish I could be.

She speaks her mind without worrying about what others think and if you don't like it, then she'll give you a closeup of her middle finger.

She's very much extroverted and isn't afraid to draw attention, especially if that means making new friends wherever she goes. In our short stay in Miami, she got more phone numbers from girls than the table full of blokes next to us at the club.

I can see why her and Jace became best friends. I'm pretty sure if there was a freaky Friday moment between them, we probably wouldn't be able to tell the difference.

The man himself wraps his arms around my waist as he rests his chin on my shoulder. "At least Cassie will be there to make sure my girl doesn't get hit on by any creeps tonight."

"You don't think I can get anyone's number while wearing this?"

His eyes widen. "Please don't try."

I turn in his arms and take his face in my hands. I place a soft kiss on his lips and hum. "There's only one man I want hitting on me."

"Please say it's me."

I pull back, laughing. "Of course."

"Yes," he quietly cheers and leans down, stealing a kiss.

"Oh look!" We turn as Blake reaches into the box, pulling out a note. "I couldn't leave out my favorite boys. I hope they bring as many happy tears to your eyes as they did mine."

She hands off black bags to each of the lads and two smaller ones for the boys. I help them rip open their bags and they both gasp.

"Oh my god, Mummy, look, it's Iron Man!"

"And I got Spider-Man!"

They each hold up their bright red swimming shorts decorated with the superheroes.

"Oh my goodness, that's so cool. Do you want to change into them?"

They nod furiously and Jace snorts. I look up at him and he slams his bag shut. "I'll take them."

He shuffles the boys off without another word and Sydney pokes my side. "What's his deal?"

"Son of a—" Lawson closes his bag with a sigh and stomps off after them.

"Okay, what's going—" Ryder and Nik get up, skulking into the cabin area of the boat. "—on..." Blake trails off as her husband turns back to wink at her.

Sydney pops her hands on her hips, her brows furrowed. "I feel left out of the know and I don't like it."

I shrug, holding up the bodysuit. "Might as well take the opportunity to change."

"You really don't have to—" Blake starts, but Sydney cuts her off with a laugh.

"Oh yes we do. You think Cas will let us ever forget it?

We're wearing these and taking as many pictures in them as possible." She skips off towards the upper deck.

Blake slaps her thighs. "Alrighty then."

We follow the bouncing blonde and change into our new outfits for tonight, falling into fits of laughter every time we look at one another.

Climbing back up to the main deck, we bump into each other as Sydney comes to an abrupt halt. "Jesus, Syd," Blake cries out, clutching onto the railing to keep from falling back down the stairs.

"Oh my god," Sydney whispers.

Blake balances on her tiptoes to look over her shoulder and a laugh barrels out of her. "Oh this is gold," she says as we make our way towards the guys.

Sydney doubles over, clutching onto the bright pink swim shorts with her face on them that an unentertained Lawson is wearing.

"At what point does your skin burst out in hives since an actual color other than black is touching it?" She wipes away a tear, sighing. "God, I love Cassie."

Lawson scowls down at her, but I catch the hint of a smirk as he watches her break out into giggles all over again.

Blake walks over to Ryder and tugs on the band around his trim hips. "This is a good look for you." I swear I hear him growl before he bends down, taking her lips in a fierce kiss that has her laughing.

She breaks away and glances at Nik. "Hey, we're twins." He shifts in his black swim shorts with Cassie's face on them, exactly like Blake's bodysuit. He shakes his head with a faint smirk, adjusting the sleeve of his compression shirt.

"Mummy, Jace has your face on his swimmers." Cooper giggles, running over to me and takes my hand. I look over and Jace strikes a pose.

He throws his arm over my shoulder and winks. "Now everyone will know who I belong to."

I laugh, shaking my head and pointing to my shirt. "Does that mean I belong to Cassie?"

His eyebrows furrow. "What? No." I squeal when he bends and licks the side of my face. "I licked you so you're mine," he growls in my ear and I laugh, pushing him away.

A phone rings and Blake holds up her phone. Cassie's bright smile and freckled face framed wild red curls appear and her eyes widen as she slaps a hand over her mouth.

"Oh my god, it's better than I could have imagined."

"This was brilliant, Cas," Jace calls out, wrapping his arms around my shoulders.

"I still can't believe Lawson is wearing his," she giggles. Her eyes slide over the screen and she squints. "Oh my god, Nikolai. You—"

"Don't," he growls and she squeals.

"Who are you talking to?" A voice cuts through the background and she looks off screen. She waves whoever it is over and a second later her boyfriend, Richard, appears by her side.

"Oh, hey." He squints at the screen. "What the hell are you all wearing?"

Blake flips the camera and shows off each of the guys.

Richard's amused smile hardens when the phone pans to a scowling Nik.

Cassie bounces in her seat, giggling. "Aren't they great?"

Her bright attitude falters when he glances at her. His phone rings in the background and he quickly excuses himself. Her eyes track him off camera a moment before she looks back at the screen with a forced smile. "What about my two favorite little boys?"

The boys get on camera and thank their Aunt Cassie for their new favorite swim shorts and she raves about how great they look in them. She tells us to go have fun tonight and to send her all the pictures before hanging up.

I turn in Jace's arms and his eyes trace over my body. "I really want to tell you how amazing you look, but it just feels incredibly weird to do so when there's hundreds of pictures of one of my best friends looking at me."

I laugh and he leans down. "But you do. Look amazing, that is," he whispers against my lips.

"Ew!" The boys giggle.

Sydney points at us, fake gagging. "Yeah, get a room."

"I would but you decided to steal my girl from me for the night."

I playfully push on his chest and he nips at my lip.

"Well, we should probably get to that before this," she twirls a finger towards us, "escalates." Hopping to her feet, she ruffles the boys' hair and grabs her bag.

"It's only a few hours you leech," she cries, prying Jace's arms from around my waist.

With one last kiss, I step away and slip my bag across my chest. "Have fun!"

Blake, Sydney, and I climb off the boat. "You too, but not too much," Jace calls out, watching us walk down the pier.

"No promises," Sydney yells over her shoulder. She takes mine and Blake's hands before we take off in a jog, giggling all the way to the car. "Girls' night," she cheers as we drive through the streets of Monaco.

———

"Oh, he's cute." Blake bumps Sydney's shoulder as she sips on her rum and Coke.

She pretends to glance in the man's direction before shrugging. "Not my type."

Blake quirks an eyebrow. "What, is he too smiley for you?"

"I like my men smoldering, on the verge of looking like they want to burn the place down."

Blake snorts and shakes her head. Sydney finishes what's left of her drink and shifts towards me. "So, Kinsley."

Here we go.

"How's it going with you and my brother?"

And there it is.

I smile around the straw of my Diet Coke. "Amazing."

"Oh, come on. You've got to give us more than that." Blake laughs.

"But not too much, please. He's still my stinky older

brother, so maybe keep it PG-13, yeah?" Sydney pleads before quickly ordering another drink from a passing waiter.

I set down my drink and nibble on my lip as my mind replays the past month. "It's seriously been incredible. He's incredible."

I laugh when Blake wiggles her eyebrows and Sydney scowls at her.

"It feels like a dream, really. But it also feels right. Like this is exactly where I'm supposed to be and who I'm supposed to be with." I shake my head, smiling. "I don't know if it's ridiculous to say that since we've only been together for a month—"

"It's not ridiculous," Sydney says, grabbing my hand.

"You don't think it's too soon for me to be feeling this way?"

"Absolutely not. You and Jace are soulmates."

I smile at her as my heart flutters at the thought. "How do you know?"

"When you first met him, how did you feel?"

I laugh, thinking about how I ended up on my arse, staring up at him after we collided in the hallway. "Flustered, but oddly at peace? When I looked into his eyes, I felt this weightlessness in my body and mind."

"So you'd say there was sort of this instant connection?"

"Without a doubt." I laugh under my breath, blushing. "I don't know how to explain it, but those first few weeks it was like I was drawn to him. Every time I walked into a room, I knew if he was there because I could feel it, like this string between us. I'd follow that pull and there he'd be at the end of it. Almost like he was waiting for me to find him."

"I think I've read about that in one of Cassie's romantasy books," Blake hums.

"It's honestly what it feels like. Like this is some fantasy."

Sydney squeals. "I'm so happy for you. Obviously I'm happy for my brother, but I'm truly happy for you, Kinsley. You deserve this and so much more."

I lean over in the u-shaped booth we're in and hug her. "Thank you."

She pulls back. "For what?"

"If it wasn't for you, I wouldn't be here. I never would have met Jace or made new friends." I glance at Blake and she smiles. "This is all happening because of you, Sydney."

"It isn't because of me at all, Kinsley. This is all because of you, it's always been you."

It's always been you.

My eyebrows furrow slightly and I open my mouth to ask her what she means when a song comes on and she jumps in her seat. "Oh my god, I love this song!"

She drags me and Blake out onto the dance floor and soon we lose ourselves to the music. The next few hours pass in a blur of drinks, laughter, and flashing lights as we take endless pictures and videos for Cassie.

It's long past midnight when we stumble up the stairs and I pull out my key. Unlocking the front door, we spill into the apartment and follow the sound of the TV to the living room.

"Look," Blake whispers.

I follow to where she's pointing and my heart skips.

Jace is tucked into the corner of the L-shaped sectional, his head back and mouth slightly parted. Beckham is cuddled into his right side and Cooper is practically sprawled out on his chest.

"Gah, I want one," Blake sighs. Me and Sydney whip our heads towards her and she waves us off. "Not anytime soon. I want that championship first."

Sydney sighs. "That's fair, I guess."

She looks at the guys and snickers under her breath as she tiptoes over to a passed out Lawson. She creeps up behind his head and takes out her pink lipstick. Lightly, she runs it over his lips, freezing when he shifts.

Taking out her phone, she snaps a picture of him and then bends down, taking a selfie. Stuffing her phone away, her eyes dance over the softened face of an otherwise hardened man.

My heart cracks when I see her reach up and lightly brush his hair off his forehead as her eyes fill with longing. As if sensing my gaze, she glances up and blinks, her lips tipping into a sad smile.

Standing, she takes a breath and reaches out, shoving his shoulder. "Come on, you can sleep in my bed."

Lawson grunts, peeking up at her. "Trying to get me in your bed, sunshine?"

"Just don't want to have to deal with your whining tomorrow. I know sleeping on the couch can do a lot of harm to your old joints."

He scowls, but stands and follows her down the hallway to her room.

Blake walks over to her snoozing husband and crouches in front of him, speaking softly. I can't help but swoon when his eyes flutter open and he smiles, reaching out to cup her face.

He follows her out of the living room, saying a quiet goodnight to me before they walk across the hall to their own flat.

I walk around the back of the couch and bend over, brushing my lips against Jace's. He stirs, his head tilting to chase me as I pull back. His eyes flutter open and he smiles.

"Hi," I whisper.

"Hi, beautiful. Did you have a good night?"

I hum, nodding. "I missed you, though. How was your night?"

"We missed you more. The boys tied in the cannonball contest and I treated them to victory gelato. Then we came back here, had some dinner while we played games, and watched a film."

"It was good, though?"

"It was amazing." He smiles, looking down at our boys and chuckles. "They're little heaters though. I'm sweating more right now than I did during the race."

"Come on, let's get them to bed."

Together we walk down the hallway, carrying them to Beckham's bedroom. Closing the door to Jace's room, he turns and pulls me in for a passionate kiss.

Pulling back to catch my breath I smile up at him. "What was that for?"

"Just making up for the times I didn't get to kiss you tonight."

I giggle, pressing my lips against his.

He hums. "Now there was something about having some fun with my girl when she got home later."

"Oh yeah?"

He nods, his eyes darkening. "It's later, sweetheart."

I squeal when he picks me up and dives for the bed, losing myself in the feel of his body and the unspoken feelings that burn between us.

CHAPTER 40

JACE

I'm in love with Kinsley Jones.

Do I want to tell her?

Every second of every day.

Have I told her?

No. I have not.

It's not that I'm a coward or worried she doesn't feel the same way.

Okay, I'm a little worried she might not feel the same way.

For me, these feelings have been there for years. I've loved her since the first time I woke up with her in my arms all those years ago. That love didn't disappear when we were apart, it just tucked itself away until we could be together again.

But for her, we've been together for only two months. Then again, we've spent that time being around each other practically 24/7. Hell, we've been opting to share a hotel suite for the past month since she stayed with me at my flat in Monaco.

So is it really too soon?

Asking for a friend.

Because the words are on the verge of bursting out of me.

Literally.

Just last week I bit my tongue so hard I swear I was seconds away from adding a scar right alongside the other one.

And it's getting harder.

Every morning she wakes up in my arms and the moment her eyes flutter open, I have to roll out of bed and rush into the loo so I don't let them slip out when I'm under a sleepy haze.

My sister says I need to man up and tell her. That there's no way Kinsley doesn't feel the same. When I asked her how she knows that, she shrugged and said she could see it in the way she looks at me. *"It's the way Mum always looks at Dad,"* she said.

I'd always wanted a love like my parents. The kind of love that withstood it all. Where the love between you is so powerful that others can't help but stop and marvel in it. A love that inspires romance novels and people daydream of.

The kind of love that knocks you on your arse and changes how you view the world. Because with them everything is brighter, more colorful. The bad days aren't as crushing when they're there to hold you through it and the good ones are something you'll never forget.

It's the kind of love that crosses lifetimes and universes. A love that finds you over and over again because you were always meant to be. Then. Now. Forever.

I thought I had it all those years ago.

Then it was gone.

Now I have my second chance at that love.

And I plan on making this the final beginning to our inevitable forever.

I know I have to tell her.

There's a lot I have to tell her.

And I will.

Just not tonight.

Sydney volunteered to watch the boys so I could take Kinsley out on a date. And she eagerly accepted the extra few quid I slipped her to keep them overnight.

Tonight is for just me and her. It's only our second kid-free date and I want to give Kinsley a night where she can dress up in one of her dresses and not have to worry about anything other than having a good time.

I love our boys with all my heart, but it's always good to take time to be just Jace and Kinsley.

I look up from my phone when the bedroom door opens and Kinsley steps out. Her light blue sundress hugs her chest, the skirt flowing out from her waist, ending just above her knees. Her hair cascades over her shoulders in soft waves, half pinned up in the golden clips I gave her a couple days ago.

"Jesus, sweetheart. You look stunning."

I walk over and cup the side of her face, tilting her head

and kissing her softly. She hums, placing her hands on my chest. "You don't look too shabby yourself, handsome."

I thread our fingers, bringing her knuckles up to my lips. "Are you ready to go?"

She nods and we make our way to my waiting car outside the hotel. I help her settle into the passenger seat before sliding behind the wheel.

I drive with one hand on the wheel, the other on her thigh as she rests hers over it. Every so often I glance over and watch her as she takes in the city outside the window with a soft smile.

When I pull up to the restaurant, I hop out of the car and open her door. As it always does when we touch, my skin tingles when her hand slides into mine.

We're seated right away at a secluded table in the back side of the soft lit patio. I pull out her chair for her before settling in my own across from her.

"I feel like you're so far away," she whispers.

The table between us is maybe two feet long, but I hate any amount of distance when it comes to her anyway. With a glance around the area, I get up and drag my chair to the side.

She giggles as I shuffle things around the table so that my place setting is next to hers. I lean over and with my hand cradling her jaw, pull her to me for a soft kiss. "Better?"

She hums, taking my hand and laying them on the table. "Much."

The waiter comes over and takes our order, smirking at the new seating arrangements. He leaves a moment later and I watch the candlelight dance over Kinsley's face.

"What?" she asks.

"I'm just thinking about how lucky I am."

She smiles. "About as lucky as I am."

We meet in the middle for a tender kiss that's interrupted by our appetizers being delivered. We dig into the bread and dips, Kinsley reaching over to wipe my chin when some escapes out the side of my mouth.

Laughter breaks out next to us and she glances over. I follow her gaze to the family seated at a table on the other side of the patio.

The mum is wiping off the face of her youngest as the dad and two boys laugh when the little girl grabs another fist full of her food, smearing it over the mother's face.

Instead of lashing out, the mum licks her lips and rubs her nose against the toddlers, her shoulders shaking.

"Do you want more kids?" Kinsley asks softly.

Our eyes meet and I tilt my head. "Do you?"

"Yeah. I think maybe one or two."

An image conjures in my mind. A little boy with my blond hair and her golden eyes chases Beck and Coop around the back yard. A little girl breaks away from them, toddling over to me. I pick her up and brush her dirty blonde curls out of her piercing blue eyes.

Turning to my side as Kinsley tucks herself under my arm, I lean down and brush my lips against hers as our little girl giggles and the boys groan.

I blink and the image burns itself into my hopes and dreams.

"One or two sounds perfect." My voice is barely a whisper and she smiles.

Music filters through the small patio area and I glance around as older couples stand. They make their way to a cleared area off to the side and begin to sway to the romantic melodies.

I look over at Kinsley as she watches the couples. Pushing my chair back, I hold out my hand and she looks up with bright eyes. She slips her hand into mine and I guide her to the makeshift dance floor, spinning her before pulling her tight against my chest.

We sway to the music, her hand in mine tucked against my chest. Her other hand plays with the hair at the base of my neck and my thumb brushes her hip.

"Thank you for tonight."

"I should be the one thanking you."

"And why's that?"

"For giving me a chance."

"Jace—"

"I care about you a lot, Kinsley. I have for a while now."

"Me too," she whispers and I shake my head.

"You have no idea how much you mean to me." I lean my forehead against hers. "But I'll spend every day of the rest of my life showing you if you'll let me."

"Jace." She breathes out shakily as she presses up on her toes, sealing her lips over mine.

The kiss starts off slow but it isn't long before her fingers lace through my hair and my hands flex on her hips as we steal each other's every breath.

Her body fits perfectly against mine and I groan when she shifts, her hip brushing against my quickly hardening cock.

Pulling back slightly, her dazed eyes slowly blink open. They dance between mine and her finger slides over my lips. "If we don't stop, I don't think I'll be able to make it through dinner."

As if on cue, I see the waiter drop off our food.

"Okay, sweetheart. Dinner first. Dessert later."

———

The drive back to the hotel is filled with soft brushes of my hand on her thigh and the press of her lips to my knuckles.

I toss my keys to the doorman when we pull up out front of the hotel and practically run through the reception, a giggling Kinsley trailing behind me with her hand in mine.

We jump onto the lift just as the doors are about to close and I silently thank whatever cosmic force out there that allows us to have the small area to ourselves.

Pulling her against me, I tilt her head back with a hold on her jaw and seal my lips over hers in a hungry kiss. She moans into my mouth as I walk her backwards until her back meets the wall of the lift.

Her leg lifts, wrapping around my hip and I drop my hand, running my fingers over the smooth skin. My lips trail down her neck and she drops her head back against the wall, her heavy breaths filling the quiet space.

I slide my hand under the hem of her dress until my

thumb brushes against her center. "Tell me, angel, how long have you been this wet?"

"Since I walked out of the room to see you standing there in your suit."

I pull back and she smirks up at me before using her hold on my hair to pull my face down to hers. She rolls her hips, causing my thumb to press against her and we both groan at the contact.

The lift dings and I glance to the side as the doors open on our floor. Bending, I lift Kinsley over my shoulder and she squeals, laughing as I quickly walk down the hall to our suite.

I'm just getting to our door when a key is held up in my periphery. I chuckle and tap her arse. "Thank you, sweetheart."

Her laugh quickly turns into a moan, when I slip my hand up her skirt and my fingers under her underwear, brushing against her.

The room is dark except for the light coming through the large windows and I head straight for our room across the shared space. Kicking the door closed, I toss her onto the bed and she bounces with a giggle.

I follow her down and brace myself with my hands on either side of her head, taking her lips with mine. Her legs instantly wrap around my waist, her fingers diving into my hair as I press myself against her.

She rips at my shirt and I pull back. Buttons fly all over as I rip it apart and shove it down my arms before slamming my mouth back on hers.

Her fingernails scrape down my back and I growl into the kiss, nipping at her lip. I roll my hips and she gasps, tilting her head back at the friction.

"Jace," she moans.

"I know, sweetheart. Let me take care of you."

I trail my lips down her neck, nipping at her chest through the fabric over her dress as my fingers curl over the hem of her underwear. She lifts her hips and I slide them down her legs, tucking them into my pocket.

I bunch her skirt up on her lips and kiss my way down until I bury myself between her thighs. She moans at the first swipe of my tongue, her fingers finding purchase in my hair and her thighs are over my shoulders.

I bring her to the edge and she whimpers as I plunge a finger inside her tight pussy. "Are you going to come all over my face, angel?"

"Please," she breathes.

"Please what?"

"Let me come."

"Where?" I keep pumping my finger in and out as my thumb rubs over her clit.

Her head lifts and her lust filled eyes meet mine. "Please let me come all over your face."

I growl and seal my mouth over her clit, sucking hard. Her back arches and she screams as I curl my finger, rubbing that perfect spot inside her.

"Come for me."

Her legs shake as she pulses around my hand and I lick

up every bit of her orgasm. Crawling up her body, I slam my lips to hers and she moans as she tastes herself on my tongue.

Her hands fumble with my belt and she pushes my pants and boxers over my hips. I groan when her hand wraps around my cock, thrusting my hips into her hold.

Pushing up, I stand and rid myself of the rest of my clothes before helping her out of her dress. I wrap my arm under her back and shift us up the bed. My fingers run through her hair as she pulls me in for a kiss and I gently pull out her pins, blindly placing them on the night table.

Rolling us so she straddles me, I smirk at her whimper when she rolls her hips, her clit running along my shaft.

"Ride me, angel."

My hands flex on her hips and she presses up, her palms firm against my chest as she rubs against me. Her head is tilted towards the ceiling and I watch, enamored, as she takes what she wants.

Her body flushes as her moans pitch and I groan when I feel the first flutters of her orgasm pulsing against my cock. "Fuck, I'll never get over the sight of you coming."

She laughs as her hips slow and she looks at me with an easy smile. Leaning down, she kisses me and I thread my fingers through her hair.

We fall into the kiss, her body melding to mine. Her hips shift and we still when the head of my cock notches at her entrance.

I slowly push forward and she whimpers, her legs locking behind my lower back. I wrap a hand around her thigh as the other one braces my weight by her head. The room fills with the sounds of her soft moans and my heavy breaths as our bodies meld together.

"Jace," she pleads.

"I know, angel."

"Fuck," she calls out when my hand dips between our bodies, my thumb circling her clit.

"Come on my cock, angel. I want to feel you squeezing me."

She nods, her eyes not straying from mine as I pick up speed and power in my hips. Bending down I seal my lips over hers, our teeth crashing as our lust burns into hunger.

The base of my spine tingles and my hips falter.

"Jace, I'm gonna—"

"Come with me," I growl, slamming into her.

She jolts and her hands fly up to hold the headboard as I pound into her. The first flutters of her orgasm hit and I thrust forward at a maddening speed, chasing her over the edge. Her arms lock around me as she comes and I throw my head back, coming with a roar, her name on my lips.

The room fills with the sounds of our heavy breathing as I slow my hips, guiding us down from euphoria.

Rolling onto my back, I pull her with me so she lays across my chest. She brushes her lips against my skin, her eyes sparkling in the moonlight. I reach out and tuck a strand of hair behind her ear and she turns into my hold, kissing my palm.

I pull her against me and she settles into my side.

Eventually, her breathing evens out and I lay there, my eyes on her angel face, my fingers playing with the ends of her hair, and my heart racing.

I'm not scared to tell her I love her anymore.

But I'm terrified when I tell her *everything else...* that maybe love won't be enough.

THURSDAY PRESS
CONFERENCE TRANSCRIPT
BRITISH GRAND PRIX

Jace **COLLINS**, Lawson **MOORE**, Ryder **KING**

Q: Well, well, well. Look what the cat dragged in. Thank you guys for sitting down with us today.

Jace COLLINS: We wouldn't want to be anywhere else, Ed.

Q: Tell me, how are you guys feeling about this weekend's race?

Ryder KING: I'm feeling pretty good. We're in a good spot this season over at Nightingale. We've got a great car and last season we took P1 here, so I'm hoping to make a repeat of that this weekend.

JC: We'll see about that, won't we? [elbows teammate Lawson MOORE]

Lawson MOORE: [grunts]

JC: That means 'Jace is completely right as he always is and no one should ever question him. He's the best driver out there and will completely annihilate the competition, securing yet another

413

home race win. I will probably come in second and Ryder can have a peek at what the bottom podium tastes like.'

RK: I don't think that's what he was—

LM: It's not.

JC: It was the gist.

Q: Jace, you brought up that this is actually a home race for you three—

JC: That was actually Lawson. I was just—

LM: Let the man speak, Collins.

Q: [chuckles] So would you say Silverstone is special for you three? Isn't there quite a bit of history here for each of you?

RK: There's a lot of memories here, that's for sure. I have a bit of a mixed relationship with this track which given the history isn't surprising. But it will always hold a special place in my heart.

JC: We each got our racing licenses on this track. We raced here when we were nothing but wee lads who thought we were indestructible. We grew up here, I raised my son here. Silverstone isn't just my home race, it's where all of this started for me.

LM: I've always felt at peace on the track, but Silverstone is home. It's definitely my most looked forward to race of the season.

Q: What about this particular track is something you look forward to most?

JC: The high speeds.

RK: High speed.

LM: What they said.

Q: [laughs] I guess that's kind of a unanimous thought then. Okay, then what are some things you'd need to consider if you want to be quick around the track?

414

JC: The speed is definitely where it's at, but it can be tricky with the wind. With it being such a wide open area, we encounter a lot of gusts which are very difficult to master when you're at the kind of speeds we are. I mean you can go from getting rocked by headwinds to tailwinds in the snap of your fingers and that lends to your balance being thrown off and can result in some serious challenges.

RK: The wind is definitely a major factor because sometimes it doesn't even affect you directly. Just last season, I had to dodge the majority of the grid when they would get thrown into my path because of the wind.

JC: What is so funny? [glares at MOORE]

LM: I'm just thinking of that edit of you someone did a couple seasons ago.

RK: Oh! The spinning one?

LM: [snaps fingers] That's it.

Q: The one with the 'you spin me right round baby' song?

JC: Ed, not you too!

RK: That song was stuck in my head for days. Funny enough, Blake actually found that video the other day when she was looking up dash footage. Now she walks around and every time she spins, she sings it.

LM: Syd has it as the ringtone for his contact.

[KING and MOORE chuckle]

JC: The point is, you need to be cautious of the wind going into this race because you never know what will happen. Because if you spin out, apparently no one will ever let you forget about it.

Q: How do you balance that? You all grew up together, practically like family. Does the competitive nature of racing ever get to any of you?

RK: I'd say it's a lot like a family game night, just with higher stakes. Yeah, the competitiveness is there and we all want to be the one on the top podium, but we don't let things hang when we are off the track.

LM: When we first got into racing, we made a rule to always be open with one another, well, to an extent since there were four of us and only two drivers to a team. But if we had a problem with someone, we'd talk it out. If Ryder didn't like that I cut him off in a corner, well get over it, it's a race, but we don't carry that outside of the fences of the tracks. We know this is a professional competitive sport, but out there, it doesn't mean more than a lifetime together.

JC: Like you said, we grew up together. These lads are my brothers. We fight, have disagreements, and no doubt want to punch the other one in the face for something. But that's what families do. At the end of the day, we love and respect each other and like both of them said, we understand that this is a competitive job, but it's just that. A job. We love this job with everything we have, I mean we've dedicated our lives to it, but not even racing will come between me and the lads.

Q: Lawson, you mentioned that there were four of you. I'm assuming you're referring to Nikolai Morozov who used to race alongside all of you since karting. Ryder, he was your teammate for your rookie season. How has it been having him on as team principal and not in the car next to you?

RK: I think I can speak for all of us when I say we miss having him out there. Nik was born to race and it was heartbreaking to see that ripped away from him.

JC: Especially when what happened wasn't his fault.

RK: But having him as my team principal… [shakes head] There's no one else I'd want in that position. He may not be in the car next to me, but he's in my ear all the way telling me everything he could have done better than I did.

[everyone laughs]

Q: With this being a home race, is there anything you three are looking forward to most?

RK: Other than sleeping in our own beds?

JC: The crowd. God, there's nothing like the roar of a home crowd.

Q: Is it pretty rowdy out there?

JC: It was so loud last season that at times I could hear them over the car.

Q: Would you say there are some added pressures to perform for this race?

RK: I'd say there are. [COLLINS and MOORE nod in agreement] Like you pointed out, there are pressures at every race, but a driver's home race is a little more special. To win at home is one of the best feelings.

JC: [groans] We get it, you know the feeling on a deeper level than we do.

RK: And if I have it my way, you'll never experience it again.

JC: Oh those are fighting words.

CHAPTER 41

JACE

"Oh my god, it's Jace Collins," a woman yells.

"Jace, marry me," another one screams.

"Let's go Jace," a guy wearing a Miller Racing hat yells.

"You can park in my garage," another woman yells in a suggestive tone.

Kinsley snorts at that last one and I chuckle when she mocks the fan quietly. She glances over at me and I smirk. "Jealous?"

"No. You already have a garage. Hers is probably dirty anyway."

"I don't know how I feel about you referring to yourself as a garage."

"Yeah, I heard it as soon as I said it."

I pull into a spot and shut off the car. The roaring of the crowds on the other side of the fence is muffled by the windows as I turn to her. "You know you have nothing to worry about, right?"

She sighs. "I know."

"You're it for me, Kinsley. No one has ever and will never compare to you."

She leans over the center console, kissing me gently. "Same goes for you, you know. There's no one else I'd rather be with."

I pull her back in for a desperate kiss, shuttering as her words roll over me. It might not be the three little words I'm struggling to contain, but it's as close to them as we both are getting right now.

We walk hand in hand through the back gates and I weave our way through the crowded paddock lane. We're stepping through the table lined front entrance of the Miller Racing club house when someone calls my name.

Turning, I internally groan when I see the petite blonde storming her way over.

Kinsley squeezes my hand and leans farther into my side. "Play nice."

I guess that groan wasn't as internal as I thought.

We walk back down the stairs, meeting Angie at the bottom. Her eyes flick to Kinsley, and my body tenses at the pure hatred seething in that single glance. Irritation rolls off of her, softening as she slides her eyes to me.

"I just wanted to wish you luck."

My head jerks back, my eyebrows furrowing. "When have you ever—"

She throws her head back laughing, placing her hand on my arm. I shift back, breaking the contact and pull Kinsley closer to my side.

I glance at her and she smiles up at me, but it's not any of the ones I love. This one is closed mouth and her eyes waver with a hint of pain. I squeeze her hand and turn back to Angie.

"If you'll excuse us, my parents should be here any minute with the boys and we need to head out on our walk—"

"You still do that?" Angie giggles.

My jaw ticks.

She always thought my morning track walk the day of the race was a ridiculous superstition. The one day she did everything in her power to make me miss it, I ended up crashing during the race and fracturing my hand. I was out for six weeks after that.

I haven't missed one since.

And I don't plan on breaking that streak today.

"Yes. I do." I step back, pulling Kinsley with me. "Goodbye, Angie."

Kinsley drags her feet, giving Angie a smile reserved for those she truly can't stand but doesn't want them to see otherwise. "If you stick around, the boys should be here any minute with Jace's parents. Then you can say hi to your son. I'm sure he will be surprised and happy to see you waiting here for *him*."

She emphasizes the last word with a pointed stare before she turns and follows me towards the team garage. I pull her into my side, placing a kiss against her temple. "Thank you."

"For what?"

I shake my head, looking down into her golden gaze.

For finding me.

For saving me.

For protecting not only me, but my boy.

For being everything I always knew was missing.

"For being you."

When we make it out to the starting line, I stumble a step. Ryder and Lawson turn with head nods, but it's the silent man standing next to them with his hat low and sunglasses covering what I know are sharp eyes.

Nik's lips tip up when my jaw drops. "Daddy Nik—"

"No—"

"—coming out to walk with us mere mortals?"

I feel the heat of his glare scorching my skin as he growls, "You've been talking with Cassie too much."

"Don't act like you don't like that nickname."

"You are not a toddler and I am not your father."

I imitate Darth Vader's breathing, grunting when Kinsley pinches my side. I pout looking down at her. She mouths for me to stop poking fun at him and I smirk, stealing a quick kiss.

"Never," I whisper against her lips.

Straightening, I clap my hands. "Okay, who's ready for a stroll?"

The conversations revolve around our glory days, when the four of us made this track our home. Kinsley listens with rapt attention as the guys spill all the beans possible about my mistakes, her cheeks turning red with laughter.

Luckily, since I grew up with these fools, I also have enough stories of my own on each to write a whole biography. I think I'll title it 'If You Didn't Want it Talked About, You

Shouldn't Have Done It' or 'How to Embarrass Your Friends in 10 Stories.'

With every step around the track, my heart beats faster. My nerves sizzle. My mind clears. And by the time we make it back to the starting line, the crowd, the teams, my friends, and me... we're ready for lights out at Silverstone.

————

"That's what I'm talking about," I rush out, checking my mirrors.

"Alright, mate. That puts you in P3. You've got Moore ahead of you now," my race engineer says over the radio and I turn my full attention back to the road in front of me.

"How far?"

"Two point four seconds."

"Okay then. Time to get to work."

I accelerate through turn five into the straight, catching a glimpse of Law's back wing as he races around turn six. We're on lap forty-two with ten more to go, and I can taste the first place podium champagne already.

There's only one thing standing between me and winning my home race.

Well, two things really.

Okay, maybe three since I have to take into account the jackrabbit behind me.

Lawson holds steady at second, chasing down Ryder in first. Blake is breathing down my neck after I overtook her and the girl is driving as if this is *her* home race.

Blood thirsty little competitor she is. But we love her all the same.

I close the gap between me and my teammate by lap forty-six. The thing about how sucky this scenario is though? Lawson Moore is one of the best defensive drivers I have ever seen.

But right now I need him to bugger off. Please and thank you.

"Jace, Moore is going to pull to the side on the next straight to give you a clear path."

"Excuse me, what? Why would he do that?"

"You have the better chance at catching King both in this race and with the season points."

"That's bullshit," I yell, slowing down when he slows down.

"I'm so—"

"No. I'm earning this on my own. Tell him to get out of his head and let us just fucking do what we do." I slam on the brake when he gives me the open lane, refusing to pass him. "Drive."

I know when my race engineer has relayed the message when I see Lawson pick up speed, shifting into his defensive mode. It's both freaky and alluring to watch. He matches every move you make, as if you're looking in a mirror, making it near impossible to get around him.

Near being the key word here. *So you're saying there's a chance.*

And here's mine.

I swing out from behind him as we barrel out of turn

eight. I'm quick enough that he can't jump out in front of me to defend, creeping up on his left.

The position I'm in lines me up for the outside of turn nine, and he knows it. But at the last second, I slam on my brakes and twist, squeezing between him and the sidewall on the inside.

His reaction is quick, flinging himself away from me, costing him speed. I accelerate out of the turn, effectively knocking him down into third.

"Well done. King is three seconds ahead."

And a simmering dark prince—as my sister loves to call him—hot on my tail.

We all want this win.

Badly.

I've only won our home race once, which is nowhere near the number I want.

Lawson and Nik each have one as well.

Ryder, the greedy bastard, has five.

And he's well onto his sixth if I don't do *something*.

Pushing my car to its limits, I'm pulling through lap fifty-one when I catch sight of his rear wing. "Gotcha."

That glimpse is all I need to really light the fire under my arse as I take the turns at higher speeds, eat up the straights in record time, and close in on the one man standing between me and my win at home.

"Last lap. Last lap."

"Yep. Thanks."

Like I didn't already know it.

Sweat trickles down my spine. My hands flex on the

wheel. My breathing slows. My heartbeat drowns out the cheering of the crowds and the roar of the engine.

Less than eighteen turns stand between us and the finish line.

No time like the present to show them what I got.

Gritting my teeth I engage DRS and push up next to Ryder. He skillfully blocks me from the inside of the turn as we pull out into the long curve of turn nine.

My race engineer calls out for me but I tune him out as I push my car to the brink. Dodging when I almost run into him on a tight turn, I silently send an apology and breathe out a sigh of relief.

This track holds a lot of memories, good and bad, for Ryder. I'll be damned if I create another bad one today.

There's a limit when you push yourself and your car. A limit that, if you exceed it, you very well may take out the person in the car or cars around you. More than one of us have experienced that at the hands of a rookie or hot shot driver.

I back off, playing it safe and bide what little time I have left to find my opening. There will be no bad memories made today.

My patience pays off because my opening comes in the form of a sliver of space between him and the inside side wall on turn fifteen.

Slipping through it, I hold back my cheers of victory as he stays side by side with me down the short straight. He holds position at my side through turn sixteen, pushing me off the quickest line and gaining ground.

I curse under my breath as we go nose to nose through the last turn and cross under the waving chequered flag. I know before they even announce it that I didn't win.

"P2. That's P2."

Running down the gears, I release the breath I'd been holding through that last series of turns. "Thanks, mate. Thank you everyone. It was a good race."

I pull up into the second place spot and climb out of my car. Ryder stands off to the side waiting for me and claps a hand on my shoulder, bringing our foreheads together. "You've gotten much faster."

I snort. "And you've gotten more slippery. I'll never understand how you can pull that shit out of your arse." He chuckles, pulling me in for a hug and I pat him on his back. "Seriously. Happy for you, bruv."

Pulling back I point at him. "But next year," I motion to where his car sits in the first place spot, "that will be me."

Lawson pulls into the third place spot and climbs out of his car. We meet him over there and pat each other on the heads before taking off towards the teams lining up along the fence.

I spot Sydney, our parents, and the boys down the line and rush over to them with Lawson right behind me.

"Oh, my babies, that was amazing. We are so proud of you," Mum cries as she pulls me and then him into a tear filled hug.

"Not too bad, big brother." Sydney smirks. "Still can't believe you got past this one."

Lawson scowls. "He got lucky."

I snort. "I'm a high performing athlete. That's talent, not luck."

"Dad!" Beckham hops up and down next to Cooper and I bend over the railing, pulling them both into a sweaty hug.

"That was so cool." Cooper pushes up to his toes, whispers, "And you totally almost had Uncle Ryder."

"Hey, I heard that." The man himself pouts from a few steps away.

The boys laugh and someone taps me on my shoulder, pulling my attention.

"Sorry. I have to go do a few things, like accept my trophy and all that—"

"Have you ever been humble in your life?" Sydney cuts me off and I smirk.

"Love you. Boys, listen to Granny and Pops."

"Yes sir," they yell out together as I retreat for the after race interview and cool down.

Ten minutes later, we're walking up onto the stage as our names are called. Standing in front of everyone with Ryder and Lawson on my right, I can't help but feel like there's something missing.

"And accepting the team trophy for Nightingale Racing, Nikolai Morozov," the announcer booms as the crowd explodes into cheers.

Nik walks out onto the stage, stoic as ever. We all glance at each other, smiles growing on our faces—even Lawson and Nik's lips seem to tip up a fraction.

A loud whistle causes all of our heads to turn towards the surrounding audience and I bark out a laugh when I see

Blake, Sydney, and Kinsley all standing above the crowd on a Nightingale branded luggage box.

They cup their hands around their mouths and cheer us on. There's a moment of silence as we all listen to the British anthem before we're instructed to pick up our bottles of champagne. Kinsley lifts her camera as we release the bubbles, spraying each other down before turning our collective celebrations on Nik.

It's not usual that the team principal would be up here to accept the team's trophy, but Nik isn't just any ordinary principal. And this is his home race. We're here to celebrate his win too.

When the champagne slows, we each hold up our trophies with an arm wrapped around one of the other's shoulders. The crowd goes wild as we cheer and I catch Kinsley wiping at her cheeks from behind her camera.

Making our way down back to the track, I use the towel given to each of us and wipe away as much of the sticky liquid as I can. Nik and Ryder break off to head back to their garage and Lawson pats me on the back as we weave through the crowd.

I spot the girls down towards our team garages and smile when Kinsley's eyes lock on me. Her bright smile brings out my own and I wink.

"Jace!" A voice off to the side catches my attention and I slow down, motioning for Lawson to go ahead.

I freeze when I see the petite blonde standing a few feet away and whisper, "Oh my god."

She smiles, tears pooling in her blue eyes. "Hey there, stranger."

"Lily." I huff out a laugh and open my arms as she closes the distance and wraps me in a tight hug. Pulling back I shake my head and squeeze her hand. "What are you doing here?"

"We're visiting Harry's family. We surprised his dad with tickets to the race for his birthday months ago. Thought I'd pop in to see an old friend."

I look around the crowd spotting her husband with his father. I lift my hand and wave. "Let me know if you need anything, okay?"

She hums, watching me closely. "How are you?"

I smile. "Amazing. Everything is absolutely amazing."

"How is she?"

My smile falters slightly and I squeeze her hand once more. "She's Kinsley."

She laughs, nodding. Harry calls out her name and she glances over her shoulder. "I better get back. Go celebrate. Give her a hug for me?"

"I will." I pull her in for another hug and she squeezes tight. "Don't let another eight years go by before I see you again, okay?"

"I promise." She wipes away a rogue tear and smiles, waving goodbye as she walks over to her husband. I watch them disappear into the crowd and silently swear that no matter what, I won't let even eight months go by before we see each other again.

Twisting back towards the garages, I spot Kinsley and

close the distance. Cupping her jaw, I tilt her face up. "Hi, angel."

"Hi," she whispers before pressing up onto her toes for a quick kiss. "Your parents are still in the garage with the boys. They asked if they could have them over for a sleep over tonight."

"God, I love my parents."

She giggles when I pull her into my chest. "I'm taking that as a yes?"

"Hell yes."

I may not have won the race, but I'll celebrate winning this girl every night for the rest of my life.

CHAPTER 42

KINSLEY

WE CRASH through the front door of Jace's house with mouths fused, hands roaming, and moans echoing off the foyer walls.

He kicks the door closed as he slips his hands under my thighs, lifting me. I wrap my arms and legs around him, my fingers slipping into his thick hair.

"Everyone will be here soon," I gasp between kisses.

"They'll want to shower before they come over. We have plenty of time." He captures my mouth with his, silencing any retort I was struggling to even come up with.

He stumbles on the stairs when I roll my hips and I laugh as he wraps an arm protectively around me to keep me from falling.

The door to his bedroom has barely closed before he tosses me on the bed and peels off his shirt. "But just in case. We better make this quick."

I squeal when he pulls me to the edge of the bed by my ankle and falls on top of me, pressing his hard body into mine and sealing our lips together in a hungry kiss.

I push on his chest and sit up, ripping my shirt over my head and unlatching my bra. His eyes drop to my chest and he licks his lips, his chest heaving. I reach out and undo his belt before pulling his jeans and boxer briefs down his toned legs.

Now it's my turn to lick my lips as he stands in front of me bare, his cock hard. He reaches down and wraps his hand around his shaft, pumping. I drop to my knees and slap his hand away, slipping him into my mouth.

The room fills with his deep groan as I swallow around him, running my tongue along the underside of his thick shaft. His hand fists my hair and his hips move in sync with my mouth until he's practically fucking my face.

I moan around him as he uses me, keeping my eyes on his.

Suddenly he pulls out of me. "Fuck, if you keep doing that I'm not going to last. Get your gorgeous arse up on that. I want you face down on your knees for me, angel."

He helps me up off my knees and out of my pants before guiding me onto the bed. I press my chest into the soft down comforter, curving my spine so that my hips flex in the air.

I feel the heat of him as he climbs onto the bed behind me and suck in a breath when the head of his cock brushes my center.

"I can't be gentle right now, sweetheart. We don't have a lot of time and I want to feel you shatter around me at least twice before everyone shows up."

I moan, nodding into the comforter. With one thrust of his strong hips, he's buried deep inside me and I fist the sheets as he finds a punishing rhythm.

"Fuck, fuck, fuck. You feel amazing."

"So do you," I gasp, a high pitched mewl escaping when he bands an arm around my waist and slips his fingers over my clit.

The tantalizing swirl of his fingers mixed with the brutal pounding of his cock have me on the brink of ecstasy within seconds. Bending over my back so his lips are next to my ear, he licks up the column of my neck and whispers, "Come for me."

And I do. Stars burst behind my eyes and electricity shoots through my entire body as I explode in euphoria. He whispers sweet musings as he rocks me down from my high before pulling out and flipping me onto my back.

I wrap my legs around his lower back and pull as he thrusts back into me, wanting him to be as close as possible. Leaning over me onto one forearm by my head, his other hands cups the side of my face, his eyes dancing between my heavy ones.

"What?" I whisper.

He shakes his head, brushing his thumb over my temple. "Just wondering what I did in order for the universe to lead me to you."

My eyes well with tears at the emotional weight in his voice.

Because I know that I feel the same way.

I don't know exactly when it happened, but little by little this man has burrowed his way into my heart. Into my soul.

From the moment I met him, everything has just felt so right. With him, I don't feel unwanted, or uncared for. I don't have to second guess what I say or do in fear that he'll turn his back. Every day he makes me feel special and truly seen. He doesn't treat me as if I'm a burden, but a gift that he treasures.

With him, my dreams are worked for, my words are heard, and my feelings are safe.

With him, I'm home.

I lean up, closing the distance between us and brush my lips over his. Our bodies move as if they've done this for a millennia together.

I suck in a shaky breath as he slowly presses his hips forward, smiling as his body shutters when he's to the hilt. His eyes don't stray from mine as he takes me slowly, tenderly.

I love you.

I want to say it, but he steals the words out of my mouth when he uses his hold on my hip to lift, hitting a new position.

"Jace," I whisper as his hips pick up pace.

"I know, angel."

He does.

I can see it in his unwavering blue gaze.

I can feel it in the racing of his heart under my palm.

It's in the way he holds me.

The way he looks at me as if he's scared to blink and I'll be gone.

I hold onto him, our foreheads pressed together as he takes us to the brink. His hand slides into my hair, tilting my face up so that his mouth can claim mine.

The kiss is slow, filled with our combined wants, needs, and feelings. My stomach tightens as he takes me to the edge and I suck in a breath when his hips move out of sync.

"I'm going to—"

"Come," I breathe. "Come with me."

"Fuck," he groans, pumping into me once, twice, three times.

I throw my head back as pleasure rolls through my body, my nails scoring his back. His hips slow, working us both back down to earth. Falling to the side, he takes me with him and I lean my forehead against his heaving chest.

Our heavy breaths fill the room and I hum as his fingers glide over my back and into my hair, tilting my head back. I gaze up into his cool depths and smile.

"Hi," I whisper.

He chuckles, ducking his head for a soft kiss. "Hi," he whispers against my lips.

"We should probably get up. Everyone will be here—"

The sound of the doorbell echoes through the house and I sigh.

"Soon," I pout.

Stealing a kiss, he rolls out of bed and slips on a pair of jeans, sans underwear. I lean up on my elbow and watch as he gets dressed, taking in the way his muscles ripple with each movement.

"I have half the mind to tell the lot to bugger off," he

growls, leaning over me. I giggle when he peppers my face with kisses before standing. "Take your time, I'll have the lads help me set up everything in the garden."

With one last kiss, he walks out of the bedroom and I listen to his footsteps on the stairs before he opens the front door. The soft murmur of our friends' voices has me smiling as I listen to them joke with one another.

Quickly slipping into a pair of leggings and one of Jace's T-shirts, I pull my hair into a messy bun and skip down the stairs.

"Oh, I know that look." Blake smiles, wiggling her eyebrows.

"Ew, no. Stop that." Sydney fake gags and twirls her finger around me as we walk into the kitchen. "Turn it off. I don't want to think about my brother getting laid."

I choke on a sip of water and Blake throws her head back laughing.

"What's so funny in here?" Ryder asks as the boys walk into the kitchen from the sliding glass door. He steps up behind Blake and wraps his arms around her waist, placing a kiss on her neck.

"The horrors of finding out that your twenty-eight-year-old brother, who has a child, has had sex." Blake snorts, smiling at a scowling Sydney.

"I know he's had sex, obviously."

"How about we don't talk about anyone's sex life?" Jace says, tossing a water to Lawson before standing behind me with a hand on either side of my hips. "Not like I want to hear about my little sister's scandalous adventures either."

Water splashes on the floor and we all look at Lawson. The floor around his feet is soaked and the bottle crinkles under his tight grip.

I glance at Sydney who's staring at him with too many emotions to break down, longing slowly winning out among the others. As if sensing me, she looks over and gives me a tight smile.

"Okay. Who's hungry? I'm starving." I clap, scooting out from Jace's hold and pull the marinating chicken we had prepped for tonight out of the fridge.

"I bet you a—oomf. What the hell, pip?"

I glance at Blake who sends her husband a warning glare and he smirks, nipping at her lips. She laughs, pushing him away by his face and drags a suddenly quiet Sydney out to the gardens with the two men following behind them, carrying platters of snacks.

Jace slides behind me, taking the tray of chicken from my hands with a kiss on my cheek and I follow him with a pitcher of lemonade outside.

The front door opens and Nik strolls through the house, meeting us on the patio.

"Sorry I'm late. I had to stop back at home to change after stopping at the store," he says, setting down a large platter on the table.

"What's that?" Jace eyes the cling film covered dish.

"Stuff for s'mores. Lawson tex—"

"Hell yeah," Sydney cheers as she bounces over to the table. "I love s'mores. Thanks Nik."

He glances over at the silent shadow of a man before

nodding. "No problem," he hums, walking over to snag a water bottle.

Lawson watches as her face lights up when she leans over, stealing a marshmallow. He looks up and meets my stare, and there's a darkness in his eyes that I've only ever seen part for the light Sydney brings when he's looking at her.

With one last glance at her, he stalks off towards the grill, joining Nik and Ryder.

"Do you need anything?" Jace asks, kissing my cheek.

"I'm okay. Thank you though."

He hums, squeezing my waist as he scoots around me. Leaning over, he swipes up a piece of chocolate and Sydney scowls at him. Walking backwards, he takes a dramatic bite and grins.

She sticks her tongue out at him before taking a piece for herself.

"You know, if you eat all the ingredients, there won't be any to make s'mores with later," Blake says, dodging a flying marshmallow that Sydney throws at her.

"Oh look," she says, pulling out a small package from the tray. "Looks like Nik picked you up some zero sugar chocolate too, Kins."

"What?" I take the bag and smile down at the zero sugar Hershey's. I look up across the lawn, catching Lawson's eye. I mouth a 'thank you' and he nods once before turning back to the boys' conversation.

A little while later, we crowd around the table and devour our meals. The boys talk about what happened during the race while us girls discuss some things we'd love to do with the three week break coming up.

After everyone is done eating, I go inside and pull out the surprise cake I'd been working on for this weekend. Stepping out onto the patio, the girls cheer while each of the boys watch with small smiles on their lips.

"Ta-da," I sing, setting it on the table. Jace steps up next to me and pulls me into his side, kissing my temple as we cut into the Silverstone track shaped cake.

When the sun dips below the horizon and the stars come out to play, Jace sets up the firepit. Sydney skips over with the tray of s'mores ingredients and sets it down right next to her seat.

"You're seriously already wanting s'mores? We just had cake," Jace's words end in a disbelieving laugh.

She glares at him. "I'm not making them right this instant, Jace. I just don't want to have to get up later when my stomach calls for them."

"Fair," he muses, plopping down into his chair and pulling me onto his lap.

"I have my own spot—"

"I know. It's right here," he cuts me off, snuggling into my neck.

I laugh under my breath, shaking my head. I catch Sydney shiver and I hold out my blanket for her.

"No, no, I'm okay," she says, waving me off.

"Take it. I'll go get some more from inside in case anyone else wants one." Hopping off of Jace's lap with a quick kiss, I head into the house and check the hallway closet.

I've become rather comfortable here over the past few days. Ever since Jace asked me and Cooper to stay with him during the break, I found myself not wanting to be anywhere else.

His home is cozy, full of love and memories. He told me that it was actually his grandparents' home where he and Sydney would visit often when they were growing up.

I love it here.

The only other place that felt like a home was the small two bedroom apartment above the bakery, but here? From the moment I walked in, I felt like this was where I belonged.

The first few places I check are empty but I remember a night in his study where I cuddled up with the softest blanket I've ever felt as he worked on sponsorship programs at his desk.

Opening the heavy wooden door to the cozy room, I walk over to the small closet and grumble when I notice the blanket is nestled onto the top shelf. Pressing up on my toes, my fingers just brush the edge of the fabric, but not enough to get a hold of it.

Looking over my shoulder, I check that no one is there to see what I'm about to have to do before I place my foot on the bottom shelf. Hoisting myself up, I stretch out and grab onto the blanket with a silent cheer of victory.

A victory that's short lived when the sound of splintering wood echoes in the quiet room.

I let out a small shriek when the shelf I'm standing on collapses under me. I topple to the floor, landing on my arse with the blanket thrown over my head.

Lifting the edge off my face, I cringe at the mess of papers scattered all over the floor. Shifting to my knees, I pick up the shoebox with more papers spilling out of it and move to collect the rest.

I grab a few of them only realizing they're actually photographs when I turn one of them over. And in the blink of an eye, my world stops turning.

CHAPTER 43

KINSLEY

"Angel? You find more—" Jace's words drift off as he steps through the open doorway of the study, finding me clutching onto some of the images scattered across the floor.

"What is this?" I whisper, my gaze slowly drifting from the floor to him.

"Kinsley—"

"What is this?" I yell, holding up the picture of me and him. Except it isn't *us*. The us in the picture can't be more than eighteen and twenty-one.

I look back at the picture, taking in his smooth jaw and longer hair. The image itself is in black and white, reminding me of when I used to take pictures with my older cameras.

As I look at the image of us smiling, I can almost hear the ghost of his laugh. Almost feel the weight of his arm wrapped around my shoulder.

My head pulses, but I push through it and pick up another picture off the floor. This one shows me with a younger Sydney. We're standing in the pit lanes of the very track I was at today.

"Kinsley," Jace whispers brokenly. He falls to his knees in front of me and reaches for my hands. "I can explain."

Slowly I look up into his eyes, tears building as my bottom lip wobbles. "Why do you have pictures of me? Of us? Jace, what is all of this?" I throw my arms out to the mess around us.

He opens and closes his mouth and I raise my eyebrows, waiting for him. To. Say. *Something.* But he doesn't and I shake my head, a tear logged hiccup exploding from my chest.

"Nothing. No words come to mind to explain any of this?"

"I have plenty to say, but I can't," he says quietly, gritting out the last word like he's in pain.

"What do you mean you can't?" Anger laces my words.

"Angel, lis—"

"Do not call me that right now," I growl, shooting to my feet and glaring down at him. "Tell me why you have hundreds of photos of us from what looks to be years ago. How do you have these images of me when I didn't even know you until this year."

He stands hesitantly, his face etched with agony. "It's complicated. The doctors said—"

"The doctors said," I echo. "What doctors? What are you talking about?"

"Remember how you told me about this?" He steps closer to me and I don't stop him as he cradles my face and brushes

443

his thumb over my scar. "Remember how you said there was a period of time taken from you because of it?"

My mind races with where he's trying to lead me with his words, but there's a black fog blocking my path when I attempt to connect the dots. My head pulses painfully and I wince.

I feel the heat of his body as he steps closer seconds before his hands come up to cup the sides of my face. He looks down at me, worry radiating off of him.

"What's wrong? Are you okay?"

"I—headache," I say, my voice void of emotion since they're all too busy battling to see which one will take over.

"What can I do? What do you need?" he asks, his thumbs swiping over my cheeks.

"Please tell me what all of this is. Why do you have pictures of us? What were we to each other? When did we meet? H-how did we meet? Why weren't you there after the accident? Why now? Why are we together now? What—"

"Kinsley," he whispers, breaking me out of my ramblings. "Breathe, sweetheart."

I suck in a shaky breath, following along with him and my once rapidly rising chest steadies. Tears skate down my cheeks and I glance around the room at the images scattered across the floor, showcasing a past I don't remember ever living.

I slowly look up into his eyes and blink, his thumb swiping at my tears. "You knew me."

His face twists in agony. "Yeah," he says on a broken whisper. "I did."

I glance at the door. "They did too, didn't they? Sydney, Lawson, Nik, and Ryder?" I look back at him. "Your parents?"

He sighs and nods his head, and I drop mine to his chest. My mind races as I mentally catalog all the images I saw, trying to piece together anything I might recognize.

The pulsing in my head increases and I sway on my feet, but Jace is there and he wraps his arms around me. He gently guides me over to the small sofa and sits down next to me as his hand rubs lightly over my back.

"Should I call a doctor?" he asks quietly.

"No. No, I'm okay."

We sit in silence for a moment as I stare out among the sea of us. My face crumples when my eyes land on a picture of us cuddled up much like we were ten minutes ago around the fire.

In the image, my forehead rests against his, matching smiles on our faces as one of his hands tucks a strand of my hair behind my ear.

We look happy.

I look happy.

My heart breaks for the carefree girl in the photo. It breaks for the years I spent alone and the one I lost without warning.

A sob leaves me and I slip my hand over my mouth to smother it.

"Sweetheart, talk to me," he whispers, his voice weighed heavy with sorrow.

"What do you want me to say, Jace?" I look at him, my

skin prickling with anxiousness. "Want me to tell you how my first thought was that I was stupid?"

"What?" His body tenses, his eyes frantically rolling over my face. "Kinsley, why would you think that?"

I shoot off the couch holding my arms out as I spin to face him. "Because I thought all of this was real. I thought—"

"Kinsley," he rushes out, moving to stand in front of me. His hands come up on either side of my face. "This is real. *We* are real. It has been from the very beginning."

"Which 'beginning' are you talking about, Jace? The one I know from months ago or the one I don't ever remember us having?"

"Both," his voice cracks, tears glistening in his eyes. "You are the best thing that has ever happened to me. Both now and when you came into my life all those years ago."

"Then why hide all of this? Why not tell me?"

His head dips as his arms drop to his sides. I cross my arms to keep myself from reaching for him as my insides wage war against the need to be in his arms.

Maybe that should have been my first sign. The comfort I felt from the moment he was ever near me or touched me and how I quickly grew to yearn for it.

His glistening eyes meet mine. "Because I couldn't."

"What do you mean you couldn't?"

"When Sydney found you and learned about your memory loss, I talked to multiple doctors who all strongly recommended that I not tell you about the past. It could hurt you, sweetheart. If I told you about the experiences, it could distort what little grasp on the memories you had and you could lose them forever."

He shakes his head, taking the step I so desperately want to and holds my face in his hands as his thumbs swipe at my tear stained cheeks. "And I couldn't lose you again. I couldn't be the reason you got hurt like that. Breaking you would have completely destroyed me."

He swallows and I let go of my already loose hold on my reactions and reach up, wiping away his tears.

"I didn't even know Sydney had found you. I didn't know that she showed you the photographer's job and that you were coming to work for the team. The first time I'd seen you in eight years was in that hallway on your first day. When you looked up at me with golden eyes I'd only seen in my dreams was the first time in a very long time that I felt like everything was finally right."

His voice cracks and he clears his throat. "When I found out about your memory loss and that it could be dangerous to tell you, I figured that if we couldn't have our past, then we could build new memories together."

He looks at me, the first sign of hope flickering over his features. "And we have, haven't we? We've made memories that will last a lifetime."

I nod and he tilts his forehead down to rest against mine. "I'm sorry I didn't tell you, if I could go back, there are so many things I'd do differently."

Even though he isn't saying the actual words, I know he isn't just talking about the past few months. I feel it in the way he touches me and see it in the way he looks at me that he would go back to the very beginning, changing our path so we wouldn't ever be apart.

"But I can't and I'm sorry. Please forgive me and together we can take this one day at a time? Or if the doctors said it was okay, we could even take it one story at a time if you wanted."

"I—"

My words cut off when my eyes catch on a photo in the corner. Walking over, I bend and pick it up. I trace my finger over the image of me and a blonde girl in a fierce hug, our faces lit up with laughter.

"This is her."

"Who?" Jace asks, watching me from across the room.

"The girl I saw you talking to today after the race."

He walks over, looking down at the image in my hand. "Lily." I glance at him and he gives me a sad smile. "She was your best friend."

I look back down at the image and walk over to the sofa, collapsing onto it with a heavy sigh. Setting the picture to the side, I drop my head into my hands.

"Tell me what you need," Jace asks and my heart cracks at the waver in his voice.

"I just—" I look up at him, my chest twisting with my next whispered words. "I think I need a little time."

His jaw ticks, but he nods before he looks at the ground. "Of course."

I glance around the room. "Do you mind if I take some of this—"

"Of course." He drops to his knees immediately and

frantically gathers the pictures, setting them back in the box and placing it on the cushion next to me. "It's yours. All of it."

I nod and stand with the box in my arms. "I'll—"

"I know, sweetheart. Whenever you're ready. I'll be here."

Every part of me shatters as I leave him kneeling on the floor and with every step I take away from him, my heart cracks a little more.

For the boy who lost his love.

For the girl who didn't know what she was missing all those years, yet felt it's absence every single day.

For the future I suddenly feel slipping out of my reach.

CHAPTER 44

JACE

It isn't the light streaming through the curtains I didn't close last night that wakes me.

Or even the quiet murmurs just outside my door that started thirty minutes ago.

I know for a fact they've been here much longer, some arriving before the sun even crested the hills. I heard the distinct creak of the front door open and close three times in the past hour.

Sydney was already here, not wanting to leave me completely alone after everything that happened last night. The others wanted to stay, too, but she convinced them that I just needed some space to digest everything.

Whoever said little sisters are the worst obviously don't have mine.

So that means the rest of my friends are currently downstairs—or right outside my bedroom door—and my time is up.

I didn't sleep at all last night, the echoing of her cries and the thoughts running wild in my head about how this could be the end kept me from falling into the nightmares my dreams surely had in store.

At least when I'm awake, I can control the direction my mind wants to go. *Barely.*

There was absolutely no way I was going to give myself over to my uncontrollable unconsciousness when everything around me felt like it was on fire.

So I laid in bed, staring up at the ceiling all night long as the soundtrack of everything that's happened in the past eight years played on a loop.

I smiled into the darkness when the image of Kinsley— both from before and now—looked at me with the small tilt to her plush lips.

The quiet room filled with a pain filled chuckle when I swear I could hear her laugh.

My heart grew at the ghost of her touch when I shifted to look at her side of the bed.

And tears filled my eyes when I remembered how my whole world walked away, curled in on herself as everything she knew was brought into question.

I never wanted that.

I never wanted her to question this. Us. Even herself.

She was asking me all the questions I wouldn't be able to answer and it gutted me to see the trust I spent every day building, slowly slip away.

If it were up to me, she could take whatever she wanted

from me and I would willingly give it over to her on a silver platter.

But not at the cost of her memories.

I still hold out hope that she will remember one day. That we'll wake up, right here, and she will look up at me from where she rests her head on my chest and I'll be able to see it all reflected in her eyes.

It's that hope that gives me the strength to roll out of bed this morning.

She'll come back.

Even if I have to wait another eight years, I'll be right here whenever she's ready.

I walk over to my bedroom door on quiet feet and pull it open. The not-as-quiet-as-they-think they're-being whispers stop abruptly and the three of them look up at me cautiously.

Sydney glances down my body and jerks back, pinching her eyes closed. "My eyes," she hisses, slapping a hand over her face and the other in front of me as a shield.

I roll my eyes and lift a brow at two of my oldest friends.

"We'll just let you get dressed," Ryder says, shuffling towards the stairs.

Lawson grabs a stumbling Sydney by her shoulders and guides her away, their whispering picking back up the moment they hit the first step.

I go back into my room and pull on a pair of gym shorts and a T-shirt. After brushing my teeth, I stand in front of the bathroom mirror and stare myself down. *She'll come back.*

I repeat the thought over and over until I really believe it.

Blowing out a breath I push off the countertop and run my hands through my disheveled hair.

"Time to face the music," I whisper to the quiet room.

The stairs creak under my weight and when I hit the bottom, I look up to a living room full of my inner circle.

Nik sits in the single armchair off to the side, his forearms resting on his knees. Ryder and Blake are cuddled into a corner of the couch. Lawson is perched on the edge of the ottoman, staring off into the kitchen where I have no doubt my sister is.

I'm proven right when a second later, she comes flying into the room carrying a tray of—

"Are those Mum's buttery biscuits?"

Sydney hums, holding up the tray. "Your favorite. I've been watching her make them my entire life, so I thought I'd give it a try."

I walk over and lift one to my mouth, letting the buttery vanilla flavors coat my mouth as the biscuit dissolves on my tongue.

"These are really good, Syd."

"They're not Mum's though," she shrugs.

I throw my arm over her shoulder and pull her into my side. "I feel better already."

She smiles softly up at me and we walk over to the sofa. She sets the tray on the coffee table before settling in next to me on the cushions.

"How are you feeling, mate?" Ryder asks.

"I've been better," I murmur.

"What exactly happened? We were all around the fire,

then she went into the house, and you followed after her. You were gone for a while before a tear-streaked Kinsley came outside to apologize but said she needed to go. By the time we all got inside, you were locked in your room. Did you have a fight?" Blake asks, her face shadowed with concern.

My chest restricts as I think about last night. About walking into my office to see Kinsley on her knees in the middle of our past laid out around her.

I tell them how I tried to explain it all to her but that the limitations set by her amnesia made it hard. I choked on the words when I recounted her asking for some time to think about everything.

"Did she say how much time?" Sydney asks.

"It doesn't matter. I'll give her however much time she needs."

My sister slides closer, placing her hand on my back and rubbing up across my shoulder blades in comfort. I sigh, dropping my head into my hands.

There's a soft knock on the door, but no one moves to answer it.

"It could be Mum and Dad with the kids," I say quietly.

"I'll get it," Sydney whispers, her hand squeezing my shoulder as she stands from the sofa.

"I'll go with her to keep them distracted," Blake says, before I hear her follow after my sister.

There's a heavy pause after I hear the front door open and before I even hear Sydney say the words, I know who's at the door.

I've always known when she's near.

Can feel it down to my bones.

My very soul.

"Jace," Sydney calls.

I stand up and make my way to the front door, my heart rate increasing with every step. My sister and Blake watch me with hopeful expressions as I step around them and open the door wider.

"Kinsley," I whisper.

She looks up at me with tired eyes, her arms banded tight around the old shoebox. Her hair is piled on top of her head, her clothes disheveled like she just rolled out of bed—she yawns—or never went to sleep, like me.

"Hi. I'm sorry to show up here so early. I know I said I needed time, but—"

"No. No. It's okay. Would you... would you like to come in?"

"Please?"

I heave out a breath and move to the side. I don't look away from her as she steps over the threshold and takes off her shoes, lining them up next to mine on the shoe rack.

Standing back up, she gives me a closed mouth smile and I nod towards the living room. I lead the way down the hallway, cursing when I remember that we aren't alone.

"Oh." She stops abruptly next to me. "Hi."

Everyone waves at her and Sydney stands up offering the tray of biscuits. "Would you like something to eat? Or maybe a drink? I can make you something, whatever you want. Or—"

Lawson cuts her off with a hand on her arm and she plops down next to him on the sofa.

"I'm sorry, we can go somewhere else if you'd like to talk just the two of us," I say quietly to Kinsley.

She glances around the room before meeting my eyes. "It's okay. I... I have a lot of questions and maybe they can also help answer some of them? I mean, they're also a big part of everything that's in here, too, aren't they?"

She shifts the shoebox and I nod. "Yeah, I guess they were."

We shuffle over to the sofa and she sets the shoebox on the coffee table. I breathe out a silent sigh of relief when she sits down next to me before looking around at everyone.

"I'm sorry about disappearing last night," she says.

"No. It's okay. You don't need to explain anything to us." Blake reaches over and places her hand on her knee. "We're here for whatever you need."

"Thank you." She takes a deep breath before blowing it out and staring at the box.

I move on instinct and cover her hands with mine. "We take this at whatever speed you want, okay? Whatever you want to know, we'll tell you, but promise me one thing."

She nods and I squeeze her hands gently. "Please don't push yourself too hard. If at any point this all becomes too much or if you feel like your head is starting to scramble, we stop. We stop and come back when we are sure nothing bad is happening."

She watches me for a moment before she nods, her fingers pulsing under my palm. "I promise," she whispers.

Leaning forward, I take the box off the table and set it in her lap. "Now where would you like to start?"

For what feels like hours, we walk her through those three weeks we were all together. Three weeks, eight years ago, that changed the trajectory of my forever.

We make sure to stick with the facts, leaving feelings—past and present—out of our stories. That was one of the biggest requirements the doctors told me when I first contacted them all these months ago.

"You cannot under any circumstances tell her how she felt. You are not and were not her so you do not have enough of an understanding of how she felt in that moment to tell her present self how she handled things in the past. If you do, this can completely distort whatever she may or may not know of her past self," one of the physicians said.

I told her that before we started diving into our past, but as we get closer and closer to talking about *us*, I'm finding it harder and harder to tell her everything.

"Did I love you?"

My heart stops at the whispered question. I look over at her, but she's already gazing down at a photo of us, her fingers tracing our faces.

She took this photo the morning before she disappeared from my life. We are laying in bed, she's on her side with me behind her, and my arms are wrapped tight around her waist with my head buried in her neck. I smiled down at the pure joy on her face and reach out when she offers the picture to me.

"I'd like to think so, but..." my words trail off when my eyes shift to hers.

"But I never said it," she confirms.

I shake my head. "We may have never said the words out loud, but I'd be lying if I told you I didn't feel them every day I was with you. Especially towards the end."

Tears pool in her eyes and I set the picture down, taking her hands in mine. "I don't know for sure what it is you felt for me, but I can tell you that there isn't any part of me that didn't fall hard for you, Kinsley Jones."

She lets out a watery laugh and dips her head.

"We all did," Sydney says quietly and we look over at her. "You quickly became a best friend to me even though I was just the annoying little sister."

"You were good for him. For all of us," Ryder chimes in and Lawson hums his agreement.

"We were and still are a family," Nik muses and Kinsley smiles softly at him. "We will always be here for one another. So know that if you need anything, you can always call one of us and we will come running. Because that's what family does."

I could see the shift in her with every story told, every question answered. She wasn't going anywhere and after hearing them say that they are here for whatever she needs, she confirms my thoughts by shifting closer to me.

"How are you feeling?" I ask, tucking a strand of her hair behind her ear. "After everything we've talked about. I know there are some questions we couldn't answer, but of what we told you—"

"I'm okay," she whispers. "I feel a lot better. Thank you. All of you. I know there's still a lot of questions out there but now I feel like I can fully understand why you didn't tell me before."

She looks up at me and squeezes my hand. "I wasn't ready before. All of this would probably have scared me and hurt me in the end."

"Which I never want to do. I never want to be the cause of your hurt, angel."

"I know," she says quietly with a smile. "Which is why I think I was never mad or truly upset with you. I was just scared that maybe I wasn't living up to the Kinsley you knew before—"

"Don't. Don't ever think that. I loved you before and I love you even more now. We may not be the kids we are in those photos any more, but I've fallen for you all over again anyway. Harder even."

Her tears flow freely and I cup her face when she lays her hands on my chest. "I love you, too, Jace. And I know you can't tell me how I felt back then but there isn't a part of me that thinks there's any possible way I couldn't have fallen for you."

A breath rushes out of me and I lean in, kissing her softly before leaning our foreheads together.

"Thank you," she says, pulling back to look at everyone. "Thank you for finding me." She shifts, looking directly at my sister. "Thank you for bringing me home."

Sydney breaks out in sobs and stands. Kinsley does the same, meeting her in the middle for a fierce hug. There's a sniffle at my right and I look over to see Ryder pull his teary-eyed wife into his arms.

The girls separate and Sydney goes back to her spot on the sofa, leaning her head on Lawson's shoulder.

Kinsley joins me back on the couch and I lean back as she lays her head on my chest.

"What do we do now?" she asks quietly, her fingers twisting in my shirt.

"We take it one day at a time."

CHAPTER 45

KINSLEY

For years I'd have these dreams that I didn't think were anything other than just that.

Dreams.

But now, as I look down at the few pictures in my hand, I'm left wondering if those weren't dreams at all. What if all these years, piece by piece my mind has been showing me glimpses of my past and I never even knew it?

"You sure you don't want me to come with you?" Jace asks, wrapping his arms around my waist and resting his chin on my shoulder.

"I think I have to do this alone." I lay down the pictures and lean into his hold, soaking up all the comfort I can.

"Okay, sweetheart. But I'm only a phone call away, one ring and I'm there before you reach my voicemail."

I turn my head, pecking a soft kiss to his lips. "Thank you."

He glances over at the clock on the stove and sighs. "You should get going."

I hum, moving to gather my purse. He walks me to the door, pulling on my hand until I face him. "I'm serious, Kinsley. If you're not ready for this, one ring and I'll be there."

"One ring," I echo and he kisses me one last time before I leave.

I make it to the small café we agreed to meet at ten minutes early. Fiddling with the small cup on the table, I try to organize my rampant nerves as I wait.

"Kinsley?" A soft voice draws my attention up to the petite blonde. She gracefully slides into the chair across from me, her smile wavering slightly.

"Lily," I whisper.

She laughs under her breath. "Hi."

"Thank you for meeting me."

"Of course. Thank you for calling."

I tuck my lips, my nerves clamming up my ability to form coherent sentences when everything is threatening to spill out all at once. Luckily I'm given time to collect my wits when the waiter comes over and she places her order.

"The croissant has hazelnut," I murmur.

"What?"

My eyes shoot up to hers. "I... I don't know why I just said that."

Her lip wobbles and she sniffs wiping under her eye as she quickly changes her order to the strawberry cream muffin. The waiter leaves and she watches me with a warm gaze.

"I'm allergic to hazelnuts," she whispers.

My mouth opens when our eyes meet but nothing comes out. Our staring contest is broken when her drink and pastry are dropped off and she quietly thanks the waiter.

I clear my throat and lift the small collection of pictures I brought with me, sliding them across the table. "Do you remember any of this?"

She takes the stack and flips through. I watch as her eyes light with every picture, a laugh slipping out at some. "Oh my gosh. We were just babes." Her finger traces over the photo.

I smile when she flips to the next one, a snort escaping as she breaks into a fit of giggles.

"I remember this. It was the night of your photography showcase. We all went out to get a bite to eat afterwards. You had been complaining about how much your feet were hurting after I had you walking around in those 'death traps I call heels' all night."

She shakes her head and sets down the picture of me and Jace walking down a cobblestone street. "He said it couldn't be that bad, so you dared him to walk back to the car wearing them. And we all know Jace isn't one to turn down a dare."

My lips tip up. "No he is not."

"He couldn't even make it to the corner. Said it was because of your freakishly small shoe size. Kept telling us that if he had heels to fit his feet, there's no doubt he would have been able to walk that distance."

"Sounds like it was a really fun night," I muse.

"It was an amazing night." Her eyes meet mine and she smiles, but it's tinted with sadness. "I can tell you whatever you want to know, Kinsley. At least everything that I know."

"Jace said we were best friends?"

She nods. "We were. We met when you transferred to my school during our leaving cert year. It was sisterhood at first sight."

She laughs and I smile, leaning my chin on my palm, listening as she tells me all about our adventures in the year we'd been inseparable.

I congratulate her when she tells me about her fashion program and how she wound up going on to create her own brand. It is currently small, but she loves every second of what she does.

I tell her about how I got into sport photography and she shakes her head knowingly when I tell her that it was Sydney who'd initially introduced me to it.

"She's always been a bit of a schemer. I'm honestly proud of how long she held out on approaching you."

"Why is that? Jace told me that you and her hired a private investigator to find me years ago. Why didn't either of you come see me when he told you where I was?"

She sighs. "He told us about your amnesia and how the two years before your accident had been erased from your memory. So even if I did come to you, you wouldn't have had any idea who I was."

"But Sydney did, eventually anyway."

"We were heartbroken when you disappeared. We spent years looking for you. And when we finally found you, it was hard to know what to do because of your diagnosis. We read article after article about how to approach someone with amnesia, but everything we saw said that if we did, then we shouldn't try to tell you about the past. It could distort your memories and create these false realities where you think you know something but it wasn't actually true."

"Yeah," I whisper. "Jace mentioned that's what he read too."

"I knew that if I saw you, I wouldn't have been able to act like you weren't the best friend I'd been missing all these years. And you seemed happy. I mean, you had a baby, Kinsley."

I smile, thinking of my little man. "Cooper."

She tilts her head, eyes glistening. "He's beautiful."

"He's really amazing."

"You had a family, a whole new life."

"But I was also apparently missing one, Lily."

"I know." She sucks in a shaky breath. "And I'm so sorry. Please know that. I am so incredibly sorry for everything that happened to you. For not showing up sooner. For being too scared to face you—"

"It's okay." I reach out and place my hand over her shaking one.

With my free hand I wipe under my eyes as a few tears escape. "It's okay. It all happened for a reason. I thought about it over and over the past couple nights. My first thought being, why me? Why did this happen to me? I even wished I could go back in time so that I wasn't at that bus stop."

I shake my head and pull out my phone, flipping the

screen towards her. "But then he called to tell me about all the fun he was having with Jace's parents and Beckham."

She takes my phone, studying the image of Cooper I have as my background while I continue. "Do I wish I could have these memories back? Yes. But I'd be lying if there wasn't a part of me that is grateful for what happened. Because if it didn't, then I wouldn't have my son. We can't go back and change the past, no matter how much any of us wish we can. It's something I've come to terms with these past couple days."

She hands me back my phone and I look down at the pictures. "I'm not saying what happened to me is grand, because it's not. It took a lot away from me—from all of us. But it led me to where I am right now. And right now, I'm happy. I have my son and Rose. I have Jace and Beckham. Sydney and the lads."

I squeeze her hand. "And I have you. Together maybe we can find the answers of the past but I don't want it to hinder the future."

"How are you so okay with all of this?"

I shrug, my lips tipping up as I glance down at a younger Jace. "I have a lot to be thankful for right now. I've got my second chance at a real family. I don't want to waste it this time."

She laughs through her tears, wiping at her face. "Ugh, look at me, I'm a mess."

I hand her a napkin as I wipe my own. "We both are."

She takes a deep breath before slowly blowing it out. "So where do we go from here?"

I smile. "We take it one day at a time."

The cool morning drifts by as we sit outside the little coffee shop, swapping stories about the past, the years we were apart, and our dreams for the future.

She shows me pictures of her wedding and I gush over her dress, blushing when she says that maybe one day she can make me mine.

By the time we've paid our checks, the sun is high in the sky and the breakfast board has switched to lunch. We gather up our bags with the promise to grab lunch one of these days, this time with Sydney too.

I'm stepping out of the patio gate when someone comes barreling around the corner. Cold liquid drenches my front as I stumble back from the collision.

Lily rushes to my side to steady me and I hold my wet shirt off of my chest.

"Do you have any idea how much this costs?" Her high pitched screech draws my attention and I freeze. Blazing ice cold eyes stare back at me and she sneers. "Of fucking course."

"Angie, I'm so sorry. I didn't see you," I say, taking the napkins Lily hands me to dry off.

"Sure you didn't. You just keep finding a way to crash into my life and ruin everything don't you, *angel*."

My body tenses at the disdain in her voice when she says the nickname Jace has only ever called me. How does she know about that nickname? And why did she say that I keep ruining her life?

"What are you talking abo—"

"Save it! God. I thought I was rid of you, but of course that annoying little pixie couldn't let it go. She was always meddling between me and Jace."

Is she talking about Sydney?

"Hi, I'm Lily. You are?"

Angie glares down at her outstretched hand and scoffs. "I don't see how this concerns you."

"Funny. You're talking like you know who I am."

"And you're an annoying gnat that needs to disappear along with your cow of a friend here." Angie's eyes slide to mine. "Again."

"Okay. What is your—where did you get that?" Lily tenses next to me, her stare fixed on Angie's neck.

"What are you talking about?"

"Your necklace. Where did you get it?"

Angie fiddles with the gold chain. "That's none of your—"

Her words break on a scream when Lily steps forward, yanking it off her neck. She quickly flips the pendant over and her shoulders shake on a disbelieving laugh.

"You know. Next time you commit a crime—" She holds up the necklace, glaring at Angie. "—maybe don't take a souvenir."

Angie's eyes widen and I step up to Lily's side. She places the necklace in my palm and I look down at the small circle pendant.

And there it is, almost too worn to truly see, a carved L and K.

I slowly look up at Angie. She's frozen, her eyes bouncing

between me and Lily. Everything around us seems to slow as we stare at one another.

Then she pounces.

She dashes to the side, but Lily reaches out, grabbing her by the hair and yanking her back. Angie screams, turning and swatting blindly at her.

She lands an open palm slap to Lily's cheek, shaking me out of my frozen stupor. I jump forward, grabbing her wrist and she twists.

I stumble back as she steps into my space, pressing her body against mine.

"You couldn't have just stayed gone, could you? He was mine! We may not be together right now, but he was mine!"

"What are you talking about?" I scream out when she drags her nails down the side of my face. My ankle twists on the uneven pavement and she grabs my shoulders.

"I'm talking about you," she sneers. *"Kinsley."*

She uses the hold to push me and I fall into the street, the back of my head slamming into the unforgiving pavement.

Stars burst behind my eyes as her saying my name echoes, melding with distant shouting. I close my eyes as an onslaught of images flash in my mind, voices past and present blurring.

Kinsley!

A damn breaks and everything hits me at once, flooding all my senses. My head pounds as image after image plays as if I'm watching them all on the big screen of the cinema. Everything speeds up until all that's left is a quiet darkness.

Kinsley!

Come on, wake up.

Please!

"Kinsley!"

I suck in a breath and blink open my eyes. Wild blue ones filled with worry stare down at me, a curtain of blonde draping around us.

"Oh my god. Are you okay?"

Lily helps me slowly sit up and I glance around, my heart racing. "Where is she?"

"What are you—"

"Where is she? Where's Angie?" I frantically stand up, looking over the growing crowd.

"I don't know. She must have taken off when I ran over to help you. Kinsley, she pushed you in front of a car." She looks over her shoulder.

I glance over at the worried driver, standing to the side of his running car in the middle of the street. "I remember," I whisper. I shake my head, twisting around to see any sign of her as my chest heaves.

"What?" she whispers as her eyes fill with tears.

"I remember." I spin to look at my best friend. "Everything."

She pauses before throwing her arms around me and I hold her tight as we burst into tears. She pulls back and takes my hands. "You really remember everything?"

I nod, wincing when my head throbs. "I need to get to Jace."

"No, we need to go to the hospital. Kinsley—"

"Please. I'll get checked out after. I just—I need to talk to Jace. Please."

She studies me for a heartbeat before sighing. "Okay. I'll drive."

We rush to her car and I hold on for dear life as she breaks all the traffic laws to get us out of the city. Coming to a screeching halt outside of Jace's cottage, she's barely put the car in park before I have the door flung open.

I race up the steps and swing the door open as I call out his name. Lily runs up behind me, right as he comes running.

"What's wrong?" he asks, glancing between me and Lily.

A sob breaks free and I throw myself at him, wrapping my arms around his neck. His arms band around my waist, holding me to him. Setting me back down on my feet, he cups my face.

"Hi," I whisper through my tears.

"Hi," he whispers back, his eyes dancing over my face. His eyebrows furrow and I suck in a breath when he brushes his thumb over the cut on my cheek from Angie's nail. "What happened to you?"

I shake my head and reach up, threading my fingers through the hair at the back of his head and pull his face to mine. Our lips meet and he hums, relaxing into me. A throat clears and we break apart.

He glances to the side. "Lily?" His eyes bounce between us. "What's going on?"

I place my hands on his chest. "I remember," I whisper.

He freezes, his heart skipping under my palm. "What?"

"I remember."

"You remember," he whispers.

I nod. "I remember *everything*."

CHAPTER 46

JACE

It's been one week since Kinsley got her memories back.

A week of us making up for lost time.

Of finding each other again.

Of relishing on our past while making new memories with each other and our boys.

We've spent days in the rare stretch of sunshine in the UK, chasing ducks in the park, swimming at my parents, and picnicking in the garden. The nights are filled with movie marathons, pillow forts, late night ice cream sundaes, and all the cuddling you could ever ask for.

We've shared stories with them about how we met, laughing about how similar both instances were.

"You couldn't help but crash into my life, could you?" I asked her through a laugh.

"Never been happier for my lack of coordination," she hummed, kissing me softly.

This week has been one straight from my dreams. I have

everything I've ever wanted right here back in my arms. My girl and our boys.

But you have to wake up from your dreams eventually.

And between all the lasting memories we've shared and made, the uglier parts of our reality have started to creep in.

Since the day Kinsley got her memories back, Angie has been in the wind. No one can track her down and no one has heard a single peep from her. Not her work. Not her parents. Not her so-called friends.

Every other day we've been meeting with detectives or taking calls from them. When Kinsley told me she remembered everything, I never expected to hear her say she remembered who it was that pushed her the night of her accident.

And I *never* expected her to say it was Angie.

So far the investigation into Kinsley's accident has been put on hold until they can locate my ex, but I wish there was *something* more I could do.

I've held her in my arms as nightmares from that night haunt her dreams, whispering against her damp skin that I'm right here and I won't let anything happen to her ever again.

I've installed security cameras around the property and installed the app on our phones, giving the people closest to us access to the app. We've given the boys phones with location services turned on so if they aren't with us, we still know where they are at all times.

Every day we wake up thankful to be back in each other's lives, but there is still that lingering fear that it could all be ripped away from us in a blink of an eye.

And last night, I blinked.

Lawson and I were pulled away for a meeting that ended up running into the night at the team headquarters. I was listening to Mitch review the plan for the second half of the season when I picked up a frantic call from Kinsley.

I'll never forget the terror in her voice when the line opened. Her screams that she saw someone standing just outside the fence of our back yard, hiding in the shadows of the untamed bushes.

I practically broke the sound barrier getting back to the house. Flashing lights lit up the dark street and I left my car running in the driveway as I sprinted inside.

Kinsley stood in the kitchen with two police officers and when her eyes met mine, my heart shredded at the relief that flooded her panicked eyes. I held her as she described everything that happened to the police officers and she leaned her head against my chest, breathing me in as I recounted my side.

They told us that since the person that was there was too far into the shadows without any distinguishing factors to identify them, then there wasn't much else they could do. They did, however, promise to have a car come drive by periodically both day and night.

It took hours for Kinsley to fall asleep and just like every night, I held her close and whispered against her forehead that I loved her, I wasn't going anywhere, and I won't let anything harm her or our family ever again.

Now the morning rays peak through our curtains, casting a warm glow over her smooth skin. She's curled into my side, her leg and arm thrown over my waist, head on my chest, and her thick chocolate waves spread out over my arm.

I reach over with my free hand and brush her wild waves back from her face, cupping her jaw. She hums, nuzzling into my touch.

Leaning down, I press my lips to hers. A low chuckle rumbles my chest when she chases after me as I pull away.

Her eyes blink open slowly and she smiles. "Hi."

"Good morning, angel." I steal another kiss.

Propping herself up with her arms crossed over my chest, she leans her chin down and hums. "Morning, handsome. Did you sleep okay?"

"I did." *I didn't sleep at all actually.* "How about you?"

Her small smile wavers. "Yep." *Oh, my pretty little liar.*

She tossed and turned the few hours we were actually in bed—only gaining at most four hours of broken sleep where she kept whimpering and hiding from the nightmares. It took me a while but eventually I realized that her memory from the night of her accident collided with the events of last night.

Before then, her terrors seemed to be getting better. She was staying asleep longer, the crying out and quick breaths were getting farther apart. She was getting better.

But now it's like everything has resurfaced when she's barely had the time to recover.

I cup the side of her face, my thumb tracing her cheek. "I have an idea. Why don't we get out of here for the weekend? We can go anywhere you want."

476

Eyes I've seen slowly dim over the last couple days shift, lighting up with relief. With hope. With love. "Really?"

I nod and she beams, throwing herself on top of me. I laugh as she peppers my face with kisses before my mouth.

"Where shall we go?" she asks breathlessly.

"Wherever you want."

She hums. "The beach?"

I smile, leaning up for a kiss. "Done."

She squeals, hopping up to her knees and dancing. I smile, watching pure happiness take over her for the first time in days. Falling back over me, she kisses me deeply and I moan when she rolls her hips.

"Nope." My head drops back against the pillow with a huff, my hard cock weeping as she hops off of me and the bed, skipping to the bathroom. "No time for that! I have to pack and you have to go wake up the boys!"

Grumbling under my breath, I roll out of bed and walk up behind her at the bathroom vanity. "You'll pay for that little tease later, angel," I murmur in her ear, thrusting my hips forward.

She giggles, smiling around her toothbrush as I hop in the shower. Her eyes heat as they move down my naked body.

I tisk, turning away from her. "Nope, you have to pack and I have to go wake up the boys."

I smile, listening to her mumbling as she packs our toiletries before moving back into the bedroom. After getting ready, I kiss the back of her head as she packs a suitcase and walks down the hallway to the boys' room.

"Time to wake up, little monsters."

I flick on the bedside lamp and sit down on Cooper's bed. I had another bed brought in the moment Kinsley agreed to stay with me over the summer break. It turned into a whole redecorating of Beckham's room because he wanted Cooper to feel like it was his room now too.

"What's going on?" Cooper mumbles, rubbing his eyes.

"How would you two like to spend the weekend with Granny and Grandpa?"

They both immediately perk up, Beckham bouncing over to join us on Cooper's bed.

"Really?"

"When?"

"Are we leaving now?"

"Do we get to have another messy s'getti night?" Cooper asks.

"Oh my gosh, I'm so excited."

"Can we bring our new toys to show them?"

"Will Auntie Sydney be there too?" Beckham inquires.

"I hope we get to go feed the ducks again."

"Okay, okay." I chuckle, raising my hands in surrender from the rapid fire commentary. "You two were both just knocked out cold, how do you already have this much energy?"

They shrug and I shake my head, smiling. "Both of you get ready, and me and your mum will be in shortly to help you pack a bag."

———

"You know, when I said the beach, I would have been fine with the one right down the road." She looks up at the grand foyer, the sound of crashing waves echoing through the quiet reception.

I wrap my arm around her waist and she giggles when I pull her against my chest, sealing my mouth over hers. "I wanted to get away with you. 'Down the road' wasn't nearly far enough."

"But Italy was?"

"Kinsley, I'd go to the ends of the earth for you. A two hour flight to Italy is nothing."

She smiles, pressing up on her toes and kissing me. "I'll never know what it is I did to deserve you, but thank you. You're amazing."

You're everything.

"Do you think the boys are okay?" she asks, her moods sobering slightly.

"They're fine. You should have seen Mum and Dad's faces when they opened the door. They are looking forward to having our little monsters all to themselves."

"Okay," she hums.

There's a whistle behind us and we turn back towards the entrance. Kinsley squeals, running over to the girls as Lawson and Ryder walk over to me.

"Oooh, this is niiice, giiirl," Sydney drawls as she looks around.

Blake snorts, walking over to one of the chairs of a small seating area. "How do you get sparkles in the back of an animal? What is this?" She matches Sydney's drawn out voice.

"She needs to stop sending memes back and forth with the girls. This is getting out of hand. I swear half the things she says is an inside joke with one of them or is a meme that goes right over my head." Ryder sighs, shaking his head at his cackling wife.

"Is that what that is? I've just been smiling and nodding whenever Kinsley does that."

The girls finally make their way over to us and Kinsley tucks herself into my side. After getting checked in, we follow the resort employees to our cluster of suites down by the beach.

We drop our bags in our respective villas before meeting up at one of the many restaurants the resort has and dig into the incredible food Italy has to offer. Kinsley's handy dandy notebook makes an appearance as she writes down the name of each dish we got so she can look up recipes to make back at home.

Home.

I don't think she's realized it but she's been calling my house home more and more over the past week. And every time, my heart stumbles.

Because the place we live may be home to her, but for me, my home is where she and our boys are. Where they laugh and smile. Where they tell stories and make funny faces. Where I get to show each of them the love they deserve.

After dinner we retire to our suites, promising to meet up for breakfast in the morning. Walking out of the shower, I stop in the doorway and watch Kinsley where she stands at the large sliding door out onto our private terrace.

Slowly walking over to her, I wrap my arms around her waist and she leans back against my chest. I lean down, kissing her neck. "Are you happy?"

She turns in my arms, her fingers sliding into my damp hair. "Immensely," she whispers. Tracing a finger down my naked chest, she flattens her palm over my heart. "And it's all because of you."

A breath rushes out of me as she pulls on my towel. It drops to the ground around our feet and I shiver at the cool air on my body.

She leans in, brushing her lips over my chest, slowly trailing her tongue down my abs as she lowers to her knees in front of me.

"What are you doing?" I grit out when she wraps her hand around my already hard cock.

"Showing you how happy I am. Now watch the most beautiful view I've ever seen and let me show you how thankful I am."

I don't take my eyes off of her as she takes me in her mouth, one of my hands bracing against the glass, the other tangling in her still damp hair.

I groan when she pushes me deep, swallowing, and my hips involuntarily press forward. She glances up at me and pulls me out of her mouth with a pop. "I thought I said—"

"You are the most beautiful view I will ever see," I cut her off, my heaving breaths echoing with the sounds of crashing waves.

Her eyes water and she stands, slamming her mouth to mine.

"I love you," she whispers against my lips.

I pull back leaning my forehead against hers as she continues.

"I think—no, I know I fell in love with you eight years ago. I've loved you even when I didn't know I was loving you. And I fell all over for you again years later." Her lip wobbles and my thumb catches a tear rolling down her cheek.

"You found me, even when I didn't know I needed to be found. You brought me back, Jace. I'm here because of you. I'm here for you. Thank you for not giving up on me."

"I love you with everything I have, Kinsley. I loved you when I was just a boy at twenty-one. And I still love you now. I don't think—no, I know," I sigh, repeating her words, "I never stopped loving you. I won't ever stop."

"Please, don't."

I slam my lips down on hers and lift her into my arms. Her robe falls open and I walk us over to the bed, trying not to stumble when she rolls her hips, brushing her wetness over my ready cock.

We fall onto the bed and I prop myself above her, pulling back. "I thought I lost you," I whisper, cupping her face.

She turns her head, kissing my palm. "I'm right here."

"I won't lose you again. I can't lose you again. I won't be able to survive it."

"Jace." She pulls my hand over her chest, her heart beating strong under my palm. "This is yours. I'm yours. I was then. I am now. I will be forever."

"One day—"

"And every day after."

Our lips meet in a moan filled kiss as I slide into her and she hooks her legs over my hips. I lift up and yank the robe from her body, shuffling us farther up on the bed.

My hips move slow but heavy as our bodies move in sync.

Everything in this moment aligns. Me. Her. Us.

The stars shine brighter. The sheets feel smoother. The ocean sings a romantic chorus.

And when she comes, everything shatters until there's only her.

My home. My love. My life force.

I've lived for years with the hope that Kinsley would find her way back to me.

I will live the rest of my life showing her how thankful I am that she did.

Rolling onto my back, I grasp her hips as she braces herself with her palms on my chest. "Ride me. Let me watch the most beautiful view I've ever seen, while you soak in yours."

She glances up, realizing I've positioned us so she can watch the stars dance over the waves and sparkling sand. Her eyes meet mine and she leans over, flattening her chest to mine. Her hair falls, creating a curtain around us as she speaks against my lips. "You are the most beautiful view I've ever seen."

I groan as she lifts herself up before lowering back down. She rides me in slow, smooth, long strokes. My hands run all over her body and her nails dig into my chest as she picks up speed.

I bend my legs and she squeals when I shift, thrusting up into her. Her giggle turns into her moaning my name as I meet her thrust for thrust, hitting just the right spot.

"Oh god. I'm going to—"

"Come for me, angel."

My spine tingles and I slide my hand between us. She gasps, shivering when I swirl my thumb over her sensitive clit. Our movements falter as we chase our joined euphoria.

"Jace!"

"Come," I growl.

Her back arches before she curls over and bites my shoulder, smothering her scream. She flutters around me, sending me right over the edge with her.

We settle onto the rustled sheets, her laying against my chest, my dick still inside her. I brush back her hair when she turns her head, taking her mouth in a soft kiss.

"Still happy?"

She giggles, brushing her lips over mine. "Absolutely. Are you still happy?"

"How about I show you?" I thrust my hips, my cock already hardening.

She smiles, nodding. "Please?"

She doesn't even have to ask. I already planned on showing her just how happy she makes me, every single day. For the rest of my life.

CHAPTER 47

KINSLEY

I look down at the unpacked luggage and groan.

"How hard would you judge me if I said I had no intention of unpacking that today, or maybe even tomorrow?"

Jace chuckles, coming up and wrapping his arms around my waist, resting his chin on my shoulder. "Not at all because I, too, do not want to do that."

"I applaud those people who are able to unpack the moment they get home. But I need that adjustment period between vacation and the real world."

"Where you ignore both the responsibilities of the real world and shove down the urge to be back on vacation?"

"Exactly. To mentally prepare before jumping back into it all."

I feel him nod before his lips brush against my neck. "Makes sense to me."

"Thank god." I spin, looping my arms over his shoulders as his lips meet mine. "Did I thank you for this weekend?"

"Only about a hundred times," he chuckles. "And in more ways than one."

"Well, let's make this one hundred and one." I press my lips to his. "Thank you."

This weekend was *exactly* what I needed. What *we* needed.

Time to get away from all the monsters of our past who have found their way to our present.

For just the two of us to be together.

To find our way back to one another after years apart.

It was the perfect weekend with amazing people.

And it's all because of this man.

"I love you," I whisper, pulling back to look into his blue eyes.

Eyes I've dreamed of for years but never even knew it.

"I love you." He kisses me again and I lean into his touch, only breaking apart when his phone rings.

I walk down the hall to the boys' room while he talks, smiling when I see them trying to figure out where to display all the pictures they made with Jace's parents.

"Hi, my little artists." I fall onto Beckham's bed, propping my head up on my hand.

"Mummy, do you think we could go to see Granny Rose today? Me and Beckham want to give her a present."

"Oh? And what did you get her?"

"We wanted to give her the pink pearl necklace we found at the market. Granny Ellie said the metal it's on is called rose gold. So we thought it would be perfect for Granny Rose."

My heart swells. "I think she would absolutely love that. How about we ask your dad if he's up for a trip to the shop?"

At that moment, Jace walks in and his face is a mask of stone.

I sit up. "Everything okay?"

He glances at the boys, giving them a small smile. "Yep. I just have to head out."

"Aw, so you aren't going to come with us to Granny Rose's?" Beckham pouts.

"I can meet you there after my meeting, okay?" The boys nod. "Go get your shoes on."

The boys scamper out of the room and down the stairs as Jace steps in, pushing the door almost closed before speaking. "That was the detective. They found Angie's car and want me to come in to see if I notice anything out of the ordinary with it."

"Why you?"

His jaw ticks. "Because there was a note left for me on the passenger seat."

I shoot up to my feet. "You can't go."

"Kin—"

"What if it's a trap? What if this is exactly what she wants? To get you alone?"

"She wasn't with her car. They found it abandoned on the side of the road."

I shake my head. "I don't like this. It feels wrong."

"Hey," he whispers, pulling me into his arms. "It's going to be okay. Maybe whatever is in that letter will help me think of where she could be. Then this will all be over."

I lay my head against his chest, breathing in his cologne. His lips brush my temple and he speaks against my skin. "You should get going. I promise I'll meet you and the boys at the shop when I'm done, okay?"

I pull back and nod, pressing my lips to his.

"I love you," he whispers against my lips.

"Today and every day after."

———

The bell above the door jingles as the boys sprint into the coffee shop, beelining for Rose.

"Oh my, this is a surprise," she sings as they envelop her in a group hug.

"We got you something," Beckham says.

Cooper holds out the pearl necklace and she gasps.

"For me? Oh thank you, my loves." She peppers them with kisses. "Why don't you go see if Mary will treat you two to whatever you want out of the pastry case?"

They don't need to be told twice and take off across the shop. I bend, kissing her cheek before taking the seat next to her.

"Hi, sweet girl. How have you been?" Her hand squeezes mine.

"I'm better. I needed that time away."

"Any updates on the case?"

"Jace is actually there right now. They found her car and he went to check it out. Apparently there was a note with his name on it so they want him to see if he notices anything that might give them any indication on where she is."

"That's good then. One step closer, right?"

"Yeah," I whisper. "I just can't help feeling like something isn't ri—"

"Mummy! Can we go to the new park down the road?" Cooper yells out as they run over to us, cutting me off.

"Please?" Beckham knocks his elbow into Cooper's and they both fold their hands under their chins and stick out their bottom lips.

Rose chuckles and I smile. "Sure, let's go."

"I think I'll join you. Walking is good for these old bones."

The cool breeze dances through my hair as we walk down the cobbled sidewalk. The boys run ahead of us when the park comes into view while Rose and I take a seat at a bench facing them as they race around.

I smile as they run up the stairs and over to the slide, seeing who can get down the fastest before doing it all over again.

Glancing over at Rose, I find her eyes are already on me with a soft smile tilting her lips.

"What?"

"You seem happy, my girl."

"I'm incredibly happy."

"And how's your head? No more migraines?"

"Not lately. I think with all the memories flooding back at once, it was too much for me to handle, but now that I've had time to recover it's not nearly as frequent."

"I can't believe you have them back. How does it feel?"

I smile, looking back at the boys as they attempt the monkey bars. "I feel whole again. I didn't realize it but a part of me was missing for all those years. I never thought this is what I'd find when my memories came back, but now that I have them..." My words trail off as I look at her.

"I am and will always be grateful for what you did for me and eventually for us. You showed me the love I'd always craved and never knew I had before it was all taken away. You stepped in and took a damaged girl and helped me become the woman I am today. These memories may have made me feel whole again, but Rose... you're the one who kept me together all those years."

Her chin wobbles and she bats away a stray tear. "I did not plan on crying today, this mascara is *not* waterproof."

"I'm sorry." I laugh, wiping away my own tears. "I just wanted you to know how thankful I am for you. I feel like I don't tell you nearly enough."

"You don't have to tell me, sweetheart. I can feel it. In here." She places a hand over her heart and another over mine.

I sniffle, placing my hand over hers. "I love you, Mum."

"Oh." Her face twists as tears pool in her eyes. "Now you've done it."

I laugh, as she pulls me into a tight hug. "I love you too, my sweet girl."

My phone rings and we pull apart, wiping at our cheeks. "Hi, handsome."

"Where are you?"

I freeze at the panic in his voice. "We're at the new park down the street from the shop."

"Get back to the shop and lock the doors, right now."

I shoot to my feet. "Jace, what's wrong?"

"I'm on my way right now with some officers, just please—"

"Mummy!" Cooper comes running towards us, his knees and arms scraped.

I bend down as I look him over. "Dear lord, what happened, sweetheart?"

I hear Jace calling out to me, asking what's wrong. Cooper sniffles and points to the back corner of the park. "The lady pushed me."

"What lady?" Rose growls, shoving up from the bench.

My heart stops as I look around the park. "Cooper, where's Beckham?"

"The lady—"

My instincts kick in and I yell for him to stay with Rose as I take off around the park. Rounding the backside of the big slide, I skid to a stop, my eyes widening.

I lift the phone to my ear. "She's here."

"Kinsley," Jace yells.

"Hurry."

I shove my phone into my pocket and take off in a sprint, chasing the retreating forms of a petite blonde and struggling little boy.

"Stop," I call out as I push through branches. I can feel them cutting my skin, but I don't slow. My legs burn, heart pounding as I quickly close the distance between us. "Angie, stop!"

Beckham calls out for me, his broken voice driving me to push harder. I break through to the small clearing where there's a waiting beat up car.

Beckham reaches for me and Angie yanks him back, slamming him against the car. I see red when he collapses to the ground, holding his arm against his chest as he cries.

I don't stop running, slamming my body into hers. We collide with the side of the car before falling to the ground. I shuffle to my knees, crawling over to Beckham.

"Becks. Baby, I'm here."

"Mummy," he cries, reaching for me.

"She is not your mother!" Right before our fingers brush, I'm pulled back by my hair. A scream barrels out of me as I'm thrown back.

I look up and freeze, finding the barrel of a gun pointing back at me. "Angie," I whisper.

"You just couldn't stay gone, could you? You had to come and fuck everything up for me, all over again!"

"What are you talking about?" I yell. "Angie, I didn't do anything to you."

"You took him from me."

"I didn't take anyone from you, he was never yours."

She pulls the trigger on a scream and I stop breathing, curling in on myself. A blast explodes next to me and I cry out as debris pelts my arms and face.

"Next time, I won't miss," she grits out, stepping over me and pressing the gun to my head.

"Angie, please. What do you want?"

"I want the life you stole from me."

"I don't know what you're talking about," I cry.

"He was mine. I was having his baby, but it wasn't enough. I thought it would be. I thought that if I could get pregnant that he would stay for me. And he did after Beckham was born. For a little while he was mine again."

She leans down, sneering in my face, "We fucked all the time."

"Angie, ple—"

"Please, Angie. No, Angie. Stop, Angie," she mocks. "Shut up, you stupid whore."

My body shakes as she stands up, throwing her arms around. The gun passes over Beckham as he lies curled up against the car.

"Angie, you're scaring him."

Her eyes dart to her son and her face twists. "He needs to grow up and stop being a little bitch. God, if I knew I was going to have a child as soft as him, I would have switched him out with a different one long ago. Although, his diabetes diagnosis did bring me and Jace close again there for a little while. So, I guess it wasn't all that bad."

I grit my teeth as anger holds together my breaking heart. He shouldn't be hearing any of this. He's a sweet, loving, strong, incredible little boy. I'm going to spend the rest of my life showing him just how wrong this monster is.

I slowly stand and she turns back to me, cackling. "What do you think you're going to do, Kinsley? You've lost. I have the boy and soon I'll have Jace. We will be the little family

I've always known we will be and you will rot six feet in the dirt. Don't worry, I'll bring them every so often to visit you. As a reminder of the mistakes he had to make in order to find his way back to me."

She scoffs as she steps closer. "Really, I should be thanking you. For a while there he was fucking anything that had a skirt. But you coming back into his life cut out a lot of that extra work for me. I was getting really tired of dealing with his trash."

She takes another step, her head tilting. "Now all I have to take care of is you," she tisks. "But don't worry about your son. I can't have any reminder of you for him to cling on to."

My body freezes at the threat. "No—"

"You have no idea what I would do for him," she yells, slamming the butt of the gun into my head.

I crumple to the ground, holding my throbbing temple as blood coats my skin. There's a flurry of crunching footsteps behind me and Angie's eyes dart towards the sound.

They immediately light up and I slowly look over my shoulder, my stomach dropping.

"Jace," I whisper.

His eyes harden when he takes in Beckham's small form. "Angie, what have you done?"

She steps towards him. "What do you mean? I did this for you. Everything I do is for you. Yes, sometimes we don't see eye to eye on things, but we can get past it. We always do, baby."

I take the opportunity to inch my way towards Beckham.

He recoils when I touch him, but when he realizes it's me, he all but throws himself into my arms.

I prop my back up against the car, holding him to my chest as I watch Jace take a step towards Angie with his hands raised.

"You need to put the gun down."

"But I need to take care of her first. Jace, as long as she's around, we can't be fully together. I have to make sure there's nothing standing between us. You'll understand."

"Angie, this doesn't have to happen."

"What do you mean? Yes it does. I thought I took care of her all those years ago, but that'll teach me to leave before making completely sure. I won't mess up like that this time though." She goes to turn towards us. "You'll see. We'll be so much better off without her. We can start over and finally be a family."

I curl around Beckham, waiting for the hit, but it never comes. Jace calls out her name and I peek up, watching as he grabs her wrist. She looks back at him with a surprised expression.

"Okay. We can be a family. You don't need to do this, though. Let's get Beckham, get in the car, and go."

"Really?"

"Yes," his voice cracks and tears pool in my eyes.

"But what about her?"

"Let her see us. Let her go on knowing that she lost. That you won and get to have me all to yourself. Just like you wanted."

My stomach rolls as he steps closer to her, sliding his

hand to cup her face. She smiles at him before glancing at me. "How about we give her a little preview now?"

Before he can answer, she pulls his head down to hers, her mouth attacking his. Her eyes are closed so she misses it, but I don't look away as much as I want to.

His face twists in disgust as he slides his other hand to the small of her back. It trails over her arm and down her wrist. She pulls back asking him what's wrong and he sneers.

"You."

Snatching the gun from her hand, he jumps back as multiple police officers rush out of the surrounding woods. They all scream for her to show them her hands and to get down.

"How could you?" she screams, jumping towards Jace.

An officer catches her and slams her to the ground. Jace hands off the gun and rushes over to us, collapsing to his knees and pulling us into his arms.

"Oh my god," he cries, his hands running over both of us. "You're okay," he chants over and over, looking us over.

"I think he broke his arm. We need to get him to the hospital."

"We're getting you both to the hospital."

"Okay," I whisper as the adrenaline leaves my body and tears fall.

It's a flurry of movement as we make our way back to the park where multiple police cars are waiting as well as an ambulance. Rose and Cooper sit off to the side and as soon as he sees us, he takes off running.

We fall to the ground and Jace pulls us all into his arms as the boys cry. "It's going to be okay. Everything is going to be okay," he whispers.

I look off to the side as they shove Angie into a car. Turning to Jace, he's already watching me and I nod. "One day at a time," I whisper.

He leans over, gently pressing his forehead to mine. "One day at a time."

CHAPTER 48
JACE

I almost lost her. Again.

Two days ago, my world was moments from falling apart. And since then, it's been the worst game of 'what if' going round and round in my mind.

What if I hadn't gotten there in time?

What if she didn't pick up the phone?

What if I didn't leave her?

What if they never went to the park?

What if I'd listened to her and the gut feeling she had that something was wrong?

What if Angie hadn't missed that first shot?

I don't ever want to think about the possibility of that last one. I can't.

I can't picture a future without Kinsley. Without either of my boys.

And two days ago I almost lost them.

After they took Angie away and we gave our initial

statements, we rushed to the hospital. Kinsley walked away with a concussion and a few scrapes and bruises, but she didn't care. Her entire focus was on the little boy who refused to leave the safety of her arms.

The doctors checked her out as she held him plastered to her chest, only moving when they needed to do a couple different tests. But the moment they said it was okay, he was back in her arms.

I held onto Cooper just as tight as we watched his mum and brother get patched up. He was the first to sign Beckham's blue cast for his broken arm.

When we got home, it was to a house filled with covered dishes. Mum and Dad walked out of the spare room, hugging each of us and telling us that they were there to help with whatever we needed.

Kinsley and I washed up the boys together before handing them over to my parents with the promise that we were right down the hall. When I was sure they were okay, I led a barely awake Kinsley up to our room.

She didn't say a word as I helped her out of the scrubs the hospital gave her to change into. She soundlessly followed when I guided her into the warm spray of the shower.

I gently washed away the dirt and dried blood from her body. When we were both clean, she curled against my chest and I whispered to her that everything was going to be okay and that I was there and nothing would happen to her ever again.

She immediately broke down and we stayed in that shower until her eyes had gone dry. I carried her to bed and held her close as my parents took care of the boys. Only to wake up to them snuggled between us.

It's been our new normal the past two days. I go to sleep with Kinsley in my arms, only to wake up with all three of them there instead.

Except this morning.

My hand searches blindly, feeling around the cold sheets. Shooting up in the bed, I look around the dim room. The morning sun is kissing the horizon, early light mingling with the darkness as it slowly chases away the shadows.

I slip out of bed and pull on a pair of sweatpants before padding down the hallway. I poke my head into the boys' room to find it empty, but a clatter and whispers from downstairs catches my attention.

Quietly sneaking down the stairs, I peek across the living room to the open kitchen and see Kinsley standing between our boys on their stools. They're all covered in a white powder, and the island is covered with what looks like baking supplies.

"Daddy is going to love this surprise," Cooper whispers excitedly.

My heart stops along with every other function I need to live.

Daddy.

Kinsley looks down at him. "Did you just call him your daddy?"

Cooper nods sheepishly. "Is that okay?"

"Is that what you want? You want to call him your dad?"

"Yeah. I've wanted him to be my dad for a long time."

I hear her sniffle. "Okay, baby. You know, I think you should ask him."

"Today?"

"I think that might be the best gift you could ever give him."

"You think he'll say yes?"

I want to run down and scoop him into my arms, but I don't move. Not wanting to ruin the moment.

"Of course he will," Beckham chimes in. "He loves you and you're my brother. So he's Dad and," he wraps his flour covered arms around Kinsley, "this is Mum."

She laughs through her tears, leaning down to kiss both of them on their heads. "Okay, let's hurry before Daddy wakes up."

"Can we take it up to him and have breakfast in bed?" Cooper asks and Beckham 'oohs,' saying that's a good idea.

"I think that would be fun, yeah. But we have to hurry."

As quietly as I can, I make my way back up stairs and climb back into bed. I don't want to ruin the surprise.

Almost an hour later, I smile as I listen to soft voices getting louder as bare feet pad across the floor. I quickly shuffle back down in bed and close my eyes, acting as if I'm still asleep.

The door creaks open and seconds later two little bodies catapult onto the bed.

"Happy birthday," they cheer.

I make a show of cracking open my eyes and yawning. Sitting up in bed I wrap my arms around our boys and wrestle them into the mattress. They giggle, pushing back and copying me as I settle with my back against the headboard.

"Who's birthday are we celebrating?"

"Yours silly," Cooper laughs.

"Mine? I don't think so."

"Yeah, you're forty!"

"I am *not* forty," I choke on my laugh as the boys roll over, cackling. "I'm twenty nine!"

"That's almost Grandpa's age."

"It is not."

"Need me to go get your walker?" Kinsley tucks her lips to smother her laugh, her words sending the boys into a fit of hysterical laughing.

"Har-har. A bunch of comedians, the lot of ya."

She sets the tray down on the nightside table and climbs into the bed on my side, snuggling into me. I smile down at her and lean in, kissing her softly.

"What?" she asks when she sees me staring.

I lift my hand, cupping the side of her face and brushing my thumb over her cheek. "I'm happy to see this smile again."

She laughs under her breath, pecking my lips. "We're going to be okay."

I nod, pulling her tighter against me.

It's not that I didn't think I'd ever see her smile or make a joke or hear her laugh again, but they've been hidden since the events at the park.

"One day at a time," I whisper against her forehead, kissing the bruising there.

"Well, *today* is an extra special one." She turns, reaching for the platter of food and sets it down in front of me. "Happy birthday, handsome."

"Happy birthday, Daddy." Beckham hugs my arm and Cooper inches closer.

"You okay over there, Coop?"

He fidgets with the blanket. "I was wondering if I could maybe, if it was something you wanted too... maybe I could call you Dad? Maybe you could be my dad?"

Beckham scoots over and I pull Cooper in for a crushing hug, tears threatening to spill. "I'd love nothing more than to be your dad, Coop."

"Can we eat the cake now?" Beckham asks and we all break out laughing.

"Oh wait!" Kinsley reaches over and picks something up. "There." She smiles, lighting the candle in the biggest slice of cake. "Make a wish."

I look around at my little family and smile. Closing my eyes, I lean forward and blow.

"What did you wish for?" Kinsley asks, taking the candle out before the wax can melt onto the frosting.

"Now you know I can't tell you that."

Because I didn't make one for myself. My wish, the wish I had on this day eight years ago and have wished for every year since...

It's finally come true.

EPILOGUE

JACE

FIVE MONTHS LATER

I MAY NOT HAVE WON this season, but as I watch my best friend walk up to accept his championship trophy, presented by his wife and our other best friend, I know I'm exactly where I'm meant to be.

I look down at the woman clapping at my side and know that I've already won the best thing in this universe.

I glance at our boys, Sydney and Lawson holding each of them steady on their chairs so they can see the stage. Sydney smiles down at them before her eyes slide to Lawson.

There's a sparkle in her gaze, weighed down with longing. She catches me watching and gives me a sad smile before looking back at the stage and cheering.

Lawson looks at her the moment she looks away and I roll my eyes.

I can't wait for the day these two figure it out and quit dancing around each other.

We all sit as Ryder steps in front of the podium, one hand holding his trophy, the other holding onto his wife.

I hand Kinsley my handkerchief and she wipes away a stray tear. She's been crying a lot more recently. But they're all happy tears.

Cute puppy video. Tears.

Sweet parenting video. Tears.

A basket of blooming flowers. Tears.

The boys show her a drawing they've made. Tears.

I tell her I love her before a race. Tears.

The boys have taken it as a challenge to see who can get her to cry more. Something I am definitely not supporting... but I did get ten points when I made her cry after bringing home her favorite takeaway the other night.

She backhands me when I chuckle as she wipes away more tears. Ryder finishes his speech and we all cheer him on as he holds up his trophy.

We're told that dinner will be served shortly and Kinsley shimmies her shoulders in excitement, picking up her diet soda.

Ryder and Blake make their way back to our table, taking their seats across from us.

"Great speech, mate. Where was my thanks?" I smile behind my glass as he scoffs.

"Thank you, Jace. I couldn't have possibly done this without you," he deadpans.

"Aw, shucks. Anything for you, mate."

He shakes his head, but I see the small tilt of his lips when he goes to take a sip of his drink.

There's a tug on my sleeve and I look over to see two scheming faces.

"Yes boys?"

"Can we go look at the dessert table?" Beckham asks innocently.

"Just to look. Pinky swear," Cooper adds, holding out his little hand.

I squint at them. "Hm, I don't know."

A chorus of whispered pleas catches Kinsley's attention.

"What are you two up to?"

"They want to go *look* at the dessert offerings." I raise an eyebrow at her and she smothers a laugh, knowing very well these two will do more than just look.

I give it two minutes before there's crumbs dusting the corners of their mouths.

Kinsley hums, rubbing my arm. "What do you think, sweetheart?"

"Well they have been rather good tonight."

"So good," Beckham chimes.

"The bestest," Cooper agrees.

"I guess it's alright if you promise to bring back something for your mother."

The boys high five before taking turns hugging first me and then Kinsley. I watch them run off just as the waiters start delivering our entrées.

"You know they are going to spoil their dinner now, right?"

I turn, kissing her cheek. "You're only a kid once. Plus, we get a bonus dessert out of it since they're supposed to be bringing out dessert later anyway."

She leans into my side with a dreamy expression. "Jace Collins, you're an evil genius and I love you."

I lean over, brushing my lips over hers. "I love you, too, angel."

As much as Kinsley's been looking forward to the meal, she only pushes around the food on her plate. I help her out, stealing bites of her food when I'm sure no one is looking.

We've been waiting to tell anyone until after the end of the season, but I've been bursting at the seams since the moment we found out.

As if sensing where my mind has gone, Kinsley looks over, taking my hand in hers and giving it a squeeze. I lean over, meeting her for a quick kiss.

The rest of dinner passes with stories from the season, our hopes for the next, and our plans for the future. The boys quickly lose interest, dashing away to play with the few other kids who attended with their parents.

Music starts up and I steal away my girl from where she's been hiding away in the corner with my sister and Blake. She giggles when I spin her, pulling her into my chest as I sway us to the soft melody.

Cameras flash and we glance over. Ryder poses with Blake, her parents, and Nik holding up both the driver and team championship trophies.

I smirk, my gaze sliding back to my girl. Kinsley's already looking up at me with a smile and I lean down as she pushes onto her toes, our lips meeting in a soft kiss.

"That'll be you next year," she whispers against my lips.

"Maybe." I shrug, pulling her closer. "But even if it isn't, I have everything I'll ever want right here."

INSTAGRAM POST

@KINSLEYTHROUGHTHELENS

Single Image: Jace kissing Kinsley's finger with a emerald cut diamond, gold engagement ring

Caption: [Blue Heart Emoji]

Comments:

@shessosydney: Sisters! [two dancing girls emojis]

@herefordaddyjace: So this is what it feels like to be incredibly happy and sad at the same time? Congratulations!

@ladyblakeking: Yessss! Congratulations! [ring emoji] [heart emoji]

@lilybellfashion: I'm so happy for you two! It's been a long time coming [heart emoji]

@jacecollinsfanpage: And the cries of women were heard around the world

@ryderking: I'll start preparing my best man speech

@thelawsonmoore replied to @ryderking: I'll stop you right there

@thelawsonmoore: Also, congratulations

@sassycassie: Get your girl! I'm 100% crying happy tears right now. Congratulations!

ACKNOWLEDGMENTS

We've really made it. BOOK TWO! Holy guacamole.

There's a long list of individuals I need to thank for making *Jump Start* a possibility:

First, I want to thank my editor, Kristen. You are a rockstar and I seriously could not do this whole author thing without you. Thank you for putting up with my out of pocket texts and late night voice memos. You're the true MVP and none of this would be possible without you.

To my alpha reader, Jess. You saved me. You brought me back from the edge and helped me get my chaotic thoughts organized. This book would not have gotten this far without you. You are an amazing and beautiful human being, and I am forever grateful to have been introduced to you.

Speaking of the woman who introduced us... Miss Rebecca Wrights. Thank you for being the friend I never knew I needed but am incredibly thankful for having. You've guided me through so much more than writing and I couldn't have made it through a lot of this without you. Everyone needs a friend like you in their lives, but they can get their own because you're mine.

To my beta readers, thank you for the laughs, the insight, and for keeping me accountable. You're amazing readers and

I still look back at your comments whenever I need to silence the doubts in my head.

Thank you to Ellie at LoveNotes PR for all the hard work on ARC applications and distribution. I can't even fathom how I would have gotten through this step without you or the amazing ARC readers.

I also want to thank my friends and family for the never ending support. I would have never been able to take this step without you.

To the amazing people at Podium Entertainment. Thank you for all the hard work you put into bringing my words to life for all audiobook lovers.

To my husband. Thank you for putting up with my random midnight breakthroughs and for forgiving me every time I paused a movie to talk through an idea with you. I know I can be a lot, what I do can be a lot, but thank you for loving and supporting me anyway. I love you.

Lastly I want to thank you, my amazing readers. Thank you so much for taking the time to read Jace and Kinsley's story. This one was tough, but I'm so very happy with how it turned out and I hope you don't hate me for the wild roller coaster ride it was.

I love being an author. None of this would be possible without any of you, so THANK YOU.

MORE FROM KAYLA JAMES

The Grid Series

Lights Out: Blake + Ryder

Jump Start: Jace + Kinsley

Book #3: Lawson + Sydney (Coming 2025)

Book #4

————

There are so many stories still to come, ranging from small town to life as a rock star to other kinds of sports. No matter the theme, you can always expect to experience that soul-deep kind of love. A love that is authentic with plenty of heart and heat. Where all roads lead to a happily ever after.

ABOUT THE AUTHOR

Kayla James is a romance reader obsessed with happily-ever-after's, swoon worthy moments, epic book boyfriends, and a little —okay, maybe a lot—of spice.

Her author journey starts with her debut series, The Grid. A Formula 1 sports romance series following a group of talented drivers and their leading ladies. You can find them on Kindle Unlimited, in paperback format on Amazon, and in audio format on Audible.

When she's not writing, you can find her with her sketchbook or Kindle, because you can never really stop the creativity.

Made in the USA
Columbia, SC
08 January 2025

49793200R00319